I0764666

Mayhem in the Hamptons

Dr. Cassundra White-Elliott

Mayhem in the Hamptons is a work of fiction and is a creation that stems purely from the writer's imagination. Any resemblance to actual events or persons is purely coincidental.

Published by CLF Publishing, LLC. 3281 Guasti Road, Seventh Floor, Ontario, CA 91761. (760) 669-8149.

ISBN 978-0-9857372-8-3

Printed in the United States of America.

Introduction

Mayhem in the Hamptons was written as the third story in what has now become a trilogy. The trilogy began in 2010 with *The Preacher's Daughter,* with the creation of the main character Tinisha. In 2011, after much insistence from the reader base, *The Preacher's Son* was written with the creation of Tinisha's cousin Romero. Finally, in 2012, *Mayhem in the Hamptons* was birthed.

If you have not read any portion of the trilogy, begin your reading with *The Preacher's Daughter,* follow with *The Preacher's Son,* and end with *Mayhem in the Hamptons.*

The three stories are not connected together- meaning one novel does not begin where the other ends. However, the characters do progress in age and in their careers. Romero, the main character in *The Preacher's Son* is not mentioned in *The Preacher's Daughter,* but Tinisha does appear briefly in *The Preacher's Son.* However, in *Mayhem in the Hamptons,* both main characters, along with the other main characters, come together for their own adventure. Therefore, it is recommended that the three novels be read in the order they were written. However, the choice is certainly yours.

Enjoy the reading!

One

Tinisha

On the west coast, in the overly-populated city of Los Angeles, the weather was warm and inviting. It was calling to all the city inhabitants to take the day off and cruise the shores of Venice or Redondo Beach or even the Santa Monica Pier. While some people were able to take the opportunity to enjoy a day of sun and indulge themselves upon the sandy beaches, others were not as fortunate. Some had professional responsibilities that could not be thwarted.

In her private office suite, Tinisha Salisbury sat at her desk tapping her Cartier pen against the mahogany wood of the desktop. She, like many others, was required to be at work to meet the needs of her clients, should they have any special requests.

Sitting quietly, she could feel the butterflies in her stomach doing a dance as her eyes gazed out the window. She was not looking at anything in particular. Her mind was busy wandering from thought to thought. She briefly reminisced about the notification she had received last week, regarding the performance review she would be given. Today was the day.

As she sat waiting for her turn to meet with the founders of the law firm, Snyder and Beckman, she reflected over the recent years of her life. It had been seven years since Tinisha accepted the invitation to practice law at the firm.

It had also been seven years since she married her best friend Rafael Salisbury, who continues to be her knight in shining armor. Five years ago, she had given birth to their one and only child Jasmine, who was proving to be a handful. As Tinisha thought about her bouncing and energetic five-year-old daughter, she realized Jasmine is definitely a combination of both herself and her husband. She has Tinisha's dark hair and sharp wit, but she has Rafael's sense of humor and charm.

With all of these qualities, Jasmine captivates hearts everywhere she goes.

It was just around the time Tinisha gave birth to Jasmine that she stopped seeing her therapist. She had begun seeing Dr. Lassenger on a regular basis after her encounter with Joel Patterson who abducted her from her then-job at Pink Panties, a club in Hollywood. Tinisha had never missed her standing weekly appointment. Her meetings with Dr. Lassenger kept her sane and gave her balance. However, after she gave birth to Jasmine, her world seemed to return to normal instantaneously. Up to that point, Tinisha had experienced night sweats accompanied by nightmares. No matter what she did, she could not rid herself of the images of Joel's face.

As Tinisha's mind drifted from event to event that had occurred over the last decade of her life, her thoughts were interrupted by a soft tap at her office door. It was Luisa, her clerk. That was the signal that the time had come where she would meet with the head honchos and listen to their evaluation of her performance over the past year. She quickly made her way from her office to the meeting room where she found both Snyder and Beckman standing as she made her entrance. They always presented themselves as the perfect gentlemen.

After the greeting formalities had been exchanged, Tinisha sat in the seat that was offered to her. Her nerves were getting the best of her to the point where she felt as if she was in an unfamiliar place. This could not be further from the truth. Tinisha had graced the meeting room at least once a week throughout her internship as well as throughout the length of her employment at the law firm.

As she gripped the arms of the chair, in an attempt to keep the room from spinning, Tinisha watched as Beckman opened a folder that had her name on the outside. The folder was much like the client folders that were neatly placed in the corner of her desk. The folders on her desk held confidential information on each client's case. She could only imagine what information the folder contained that Beckman was holding.

Without warning, Beckman started his evaluation, and shortly after, Snyder chimed in to offer his corresponding sentiments.

After awhile, Tinisha realized that the room had become quiet, and both men were staring at her. She realized that she had not heard a word that had been spoken in the several minutes that had passed.

In her embarrassment, Tinisha asked, "I'm sorry. What did you say?"

Snyder responded, "We are considering you for partner. Are you interested in the position?"

Tinisha, clearly caught off guard, replied, "Uh, yeah. Um, yes. I would be delighted to be considered for partner. Are you sure?"

At that point, Beckman spoke up. "Mrs. Salisbury, you have done wonderful work since you have been here with us and even before you were a paid employee. We already knew that you had a promising future here at the firm. Your understanding of the law is impeccable, and your case record speaks for itself."

"I must agree," Snyder began, "Your handling of the case with 'The Dooney & Bourke Thief' proves our point."

The two men rose from their seats, signaling that the meeting had come to an end.

As Tinisha rose from her seat, Snyder offered his hand and replied, "We will contact you of our decision within the coming months."

Tinisha simply nodded and smiled as she accepted his hand and shook it and then shook Beckman's. "Enjoy the rest of the day," she said as she exited the room and headed back to her office thinking about the weird case of the 'The Dooney & Bourke Thief.'

Two

Rafael

In another part of the city, at the Hollywood Division of the Los Angeles Police Department, Lieutenant Rafael Salisbury walked into his office, with a cup of steaming hot coffee in one hand and a copy of the Los Angeles Times in the other. The grin that was plastered across his face demonstrated that he was pleased with the article and picture on the front page. The picture of him had been taken when he received a commendation a few days ago.

Once again, he had received public recognition from the mayor for the heroic acts of his team of detectives and his great leadership abilities.

Rafael missed being a part of the physical action, but he was pleased that he could still have a say in the on-going activities of the police detectives. The article reflected how Lt. Salisbury successfully led his team to victory in capturing the crew of bank robbers that had traveled from state to state robbing federal savings and loans. The thieves had made the mistake of planning a heist in his jurisdiction. The crew was very slick, but after making several mistakes, each crew member was arrested and brought to justice.

After getting comfortable in his chair, he reflected upon the days that he had been paired with Derrick Cassidy as a detective, before making sergeant and eventually becoming a lieutenant. Derrick and Raf had developed a very close relationship as they surveyed the streets of Los Angeles together. They never had any conflicts. They worked very much in synch. They were as close as brothers.

After Rafael had been promoted from detective to sergeant, his partnership with Derrick ceased. However, their friendship continued to blossom. The two officers continue to share vacation time with each other's families, which now include their children.

As Raf thought of Derrick, his mind slowly drifted to Tinisha, his wife of seven years. *Today is the day that she will receive her yearly evaluation,* he thought. He knew that she had nothing to worry about. Snyder and Beckman were very fond of Tinisha. He remembered when they had signed off on her internship a month early after her ordeal of being abducted. *It was kind of them to do that,* Raf reminisced. That act, along with their offer of a job, set Tinisha on her path to becoming a great lawyer. She could not have asked for two finer mentors. Their careers were well known throughout the greater Los Angeles area, as well as most of southern California.

I will check in with Tinisha later, Raf thought. First, he had to meet with his team and give them a new assignment. As he made his way to the squad room, where he knew the four detectives were waiting, he felt his cell phone vibrate on his hip. Reaching down to release the phone from its holder, Raf thought the call may be coming from Tinisha with a report of how her evaluation meeting went. To his surprise, he saw the number of his daughter's school on the caller id. *I wonder what the little rascal has gotten herself into now,* Raf wondered as he smiled thinking that she had inherited her rambunctiousness from her mother.

After talking with Jasmine's teacher, to Raf's further surprise, Jas hadn't gotten herself into anything per se. She was just being a little talkative, trying to help the teacher teach the class. Mrs. Allen, Jas' teacher, was calling to see if Rafael would give Jas permission to volunteer to assist with the other students, particularly those who were having a hard time understanding specific concepts.

Although Jasmine was only five years old, she was already in first grade, but she was demonstrating intellectual qualities of a second grader. Raf quickly consented to Jas serving as a volunteer and ended the conversation. Finally arriving to the squad room, after pausing in the hallway to complete the call, he greeted detectives Zach Malone, Ellis Stabler, Olive Benson, and Dennis Morgan.

Ironically, all four detectives were relatively new to the Hollywood Division. Malone and Stabler had been transferred in one month apart and were subsequently paired together. Benson and Morgan had come to the division earlier in the year.

At times, the four detectives worked on a single case together. However, they mostly worked in pairs. Lt. Salisbury was anxious to begin the Burlingstein Warehouse case, and it would require the manpower of all four detectives.

Last night, at two different Burlingstein Warehouses, the evening managers were found murdered in their offices. The cleaning crew, at each location, had arrived to work between 8:30-9:00 pm, approximately a half hour after the store closed.

When each manager's body was discovered, the police were called immediately, via 911.

Two different medical examiners reported the times of death to have occurred between 8-8:15pm according to the state of rigor mortis of the bodies. When the news hit the police station, several questions arose. Lt. Salisbury quickly briefed the four detectives and sent them out two by two to the two separate stores to begin their investigative work.

Three

Romero

On the east coast, the weather was equally as beautiful as it was for Tinisha and Rafael in Los Angeles. However, the temperature in New York City was nearly twenty degrees cooler, but it was beautiful nonetheless. Outside, the birds were flying overhead, and some were chirping in the trees. It was the perfect picture of spring.

Indoors, kneeling at the altar of his father's church located in the center of New York City, Romero leaned over to grab a Kleenex from the box that sat to the right of him. For the last thirty minutes, he had been praying and thanking God for all of his blessings. Reminiscing about how good God had been to him, Romero felt the tears once again fill his eyes and fall down his cheeks.

It had been a little over two years since Romero had finished his ministerial training. He now held the office of Assistant Youth Pastor. Prior to being elevated to the new position, Romero had only observed the youth pastor while learning the function of the youth ministry along with the many requirements of the ministry leaders. More frequently, Romero had been overseeing events rather than just observing Pastor Moore, the youth pastor.

This week, Romero had planned an outing for the youth at the skating rink. With this small-scale event, he would not need the extensive number of volunteers for supervision that the events normally required. The skating rink was one large room, so he could see everyone with a glance. If one of the younger girls needed to go to the restroom, he would send a teenage girl to accompany her. The same was true for the boys. The teenagers, however, could go to the restroom in groups.

Romero had a strict policy that discouraged the kids from wandering off on their own. He knew there were many sadistic individuals roaming upon the earth. If there were any doubt, his cousin Tinisha's ordeal with Joel Patterson proved the reality of the situation. He would do everything in his power to protect the youth while they were in his custody.

Before finally deciding on the outing to the skating rink, Rome had considered taking the youth on a retreat, but this was not the time to plan something that extensive for a group of nearly twenty youth whose range of ages is from 11-20. He could usually count on his assistant to take care of the major details of any event that he wanted to take place, but she is busy planning her wedding. Actually, she is planning *their* wedding. His assistant is his fiancée Yolanda Bardwell. They have been engaged for the past two years, after having dated for three years. So, they have been together for five years total.

At first, the relationship was touch and go because Romero was so busy taking cases to help get his career into full gear. This drove Yolanda absolutely crazy because he was hardly ever available, and it was hard for him to keep some of their scheduled dates. As a detective, he had to move when the action happened. It wasn't that she didn't want him to be successful. Of course she did. She also wanted some of his time.

Rome owns and operates a private investigation service where he serves as the lead investigator. Actually, he had been the only investigator for several years, and currently, he still is.

Of course, he could always call on his two friends Tyrone and Brian to assist him with a case if he needed them. Last year, Rome took Michael, one of the young men from church, under his wing to show him the tricks of the trade. At the same time, he was grooming Michael for ministry. So, from time to time, he has assistance on cases if needed.

After dating Yolanda for a while, Romero learned how to prioritize his life. He no longer allows work to consume all of his time like he did when he was single. Yolanda, after complaining about Romero's lack of time, learned to schedule her time more effectively as well. You could say she took some of her own medicine. She was quite busy herself at the beginning of their relationship. She had been in her last year of college, working to complete her bachelor's degree, so she could begin her career as a social worker. Now that she has graduated and landed a job, she has more time on her hands. Well, she did until she began planning the wedding. Now, time seems so scarce. But at least she has Mariesha Coleman, the famous wedding planner, to assist her.

Mariesha was referred to Yolanda by Yolanda's sister Andrea. Andrea has a couple of friends for whom Mariesha had planned weddings. Also, Andrea has another set of friends, Kim and John, who will be getting married the day after Romero and Yolanda, and Mariesha is planning their wedding as well.

When Yolanda heard that Mariesha is available and that her cost is reasonable, she could not have been happier to have her working on one of the most important events of her life: her wedding to her best friend Romero. She was tickled pink. This was the dream of a life time. She wanted their wedding day to be perfect, and she simply had no idea of where to begin her planning. Of course, she had her mother and her sister to assist her, but with Mariesha by her side, she could not go wrong.

Four

Tinisha

After Tinisha's evaluation meeting, she closed up her office for the day. She was headed to a late lunch and to meet a client afterwards. Normally, she takes lunch at noon, but because her meeting was at one o'clock, she decided to have lunch afterwards. She couldn't imagine eating while the butterflies were doing a jig in her belly.

Now that she was relaxed and had received the news of being considered for partner, she felt like celebrating. She knew that it was highly possible that she would *not* receive the position, especially when there were more seasoned lawyers at the firm. Nevertheless, she felt proud to be considered. During the meeting, Snyder mentioned her case success rate. To date, she has never lost a case. Not many other lawyers can say the same.

As Tinisha guided her car into a parking space at Carrow's, her phone rang. It was her friend Karen. Karen and Tinisha had met in law school and had become friends quickly.

"Hey, Karen," Tinisha answered excitedly.

"Hey, Nisha. Have I caught you at a good time?" Karen asked just as excitedly.

"Oh, this is great. I am just about to have lunch."

"Now? Isn't it a little late?" Karen inquired.

"I just came out of my evaluation meeting with the bosses."

"Oh, right. That was today. How did it go?"

"Actually, it went very well. They are considering me for partner."

"Oh my goodness, Nisha! That's great."

"Yes, it is. That's why I am having a celebratory lunch just for the mere mention of the thought."

"Is your hubby with you?"

"No, I am actually about to call him in a few. Did you get a chance to see the article on the front page of the LA Times about Raf and his team?"

"I didn't, but Raymond called when he got to work and told me all about it. Raf is doing so well as lieutenant. Isn't he?"

"I would say so. I am proud of him. Okay, enough about us. What's going on with you and your family?"

"Raymond and I are looking to take a mini vacation to celebrate our anniversary. That's actually why I am calling. We are leaving in two weeks, but just for the weekend. Can you and Raf keep the kids for the weekend?

"Is that April 28-30?

"Yes."

"We will be out of town ourselves. That's the weekend my cousin Rome is getting married. We have to fly out to the Hamptons. They are getting married on the island."

"Oh, how exciting! Okay, well I will just have to ask my sister to keep the kids. Let me let you go so you can call your hubby. I will talk with you soon."

Before Tinisha could end the call, her second line rang. Her caller id displayed *Hubby*. "Okay. We'll talk soon, " she said to Karen just before clicking over to the other line.

"Hey, babe," she answered with a smile.

"Do you still have a job?" Raf joked.

"Yes. And I can do you one better," Nisha retorted.

"Oh? How's that?"

"Well, I'm being considered for partner."

"Yeah, I'll say that's better!"

"Let's not jump the gun though. They will make a decision later this year."

"You will do fine. I'm sure they already have your name on the letterhead."

All Tinisha could do was laugh. Her heart beamed at her husband's confidence in her. He is always encouraging and supportive.

After saying goodbye to Rafael, Tinisha went inside the restaurant as she breathed in the spring air. It was a relief to get out of the office. She tried to make it a point to have an escape once a day if possible. Sometimes, she dined with other lawyers and occasionally with Raf, but today, she enjoyed a quiet meal alone. She used her time to allow her mind and body a moment to relax. She had a meeting with a client in an hour. That would be her last stop before going to pick up Jasmine at five o'clock from the after-school care program.

After consuming her meal, Tinisha placed the folder that contained her lunch check on the table with her credit card inside, and she waited patiently for her waiter to return to pick it up. Soon after the waiter retrieved the folder, he returned it to her. To Tinisha's surprise, her credit card was not inside the folder. After bringing it to the waiter's attention, she was told that the card had been returned to her. The discussion about the card went on for five minutes. Finally, Tinisha asked to speak to the manager on duty.

After waiting for what seemed like the longest six minutes of her life, Tinisha watched as a young woman in her mid-twenties approached her table. By the way she was dressed, Tinisha knew she was the manager. As the manager drew closer to the table, a smile suddenly covered her face. Tinisha was steaming inside, and she couldn't figure out what the manager could possibly find pleasing about this situation.

"Good afternoon, Mrs. Salisbury," the manager began as she extended a firm hand. "I am Cynthia Rosales, the manager. I understand that we are experiencing a problem with your credit card."

"Yes, that is correct. After I paid the bill, my card was not returned to me."

"Is it possible that you placed it in your purse?"

"Before we go any further with questions, I suggest you and your waiter go back and look around for my card because I do not have it. It is not in my purse or anywhere in my possession. I have a very important meeting, and I need to leave soon."

"If you like, we can attempt to locate your card, if it is here, and call you to pick it up."

Tinisha noticed how Cynthia was choosing her words carefully. "That plan does not work for me. I would not like to leave without my card. So, if you don't mind, please take another look around."

Seeing the look on Tinisha's face, the manager turned quickly and headed back toward the cash register where the waiter was standing. In less than a minute, the manager and waiter returned together. The waiter produced Tinisha's card and an apology. Cynthia, with a very sheepish look on her face, also offered an apology. Tinisha simply nodded her head and stood to leave.

"It's an honor to have you dining with us, Mrs. Salisbury. I have followed your career in the courtroom over the last several years, especially the work you did on the terrorist case. I hope this incident will not prevent you from dining with us again."

When Tinisha did not respond, Cynthia continued, "Please say hello to your husband Lieutenant Salisbury and give him our congratulations on his latest case." Tinisha could see that Cynthia was trying to make amends for the waiter's actions, so she decided to put her lawyer stance away and be cordial. "I will give him the message," she said with a smile as she headed out the door.

As Tinisha walked through the rows of cars in the parking lot, she reflected back over the manager's words regarding Rafael's latest case and her own latest case. Just the other day, an elderly gentleman had made similar comments about her and her husband. *It seems as though we are making a name for ourselves,* Tinisha thought as a smiled automatically appeared on her face and a burst of warmth filled her heart.

[illegible]

Five

Rafael

When Rafael arrived home, he found his two favorite ladies making dinner. Both Tinisha and Jasmine loved the time they shared. Tinisha found cooking dinner together a great time of bonding between herself and her daughter. For Jasmine, spending time with her mother was the best part of her day. It didn't matter to her what they were doing.

They were laughing so hard at the joke Jasmine had just told that they did not hear Raf enter the house or the kitchen. When he saw that they were heavily engaged in their conversation and did not notice his presence, he sneaked up behind Nisha and placed a bouquet of flowers in front of her face. When Nisha and Jasmine screamed with delight, Raf produced another bouquet for Jas. When Raf saw the smiles that covered their faces and felt the warm "Thank you" kisses that covered his face as a response, his heart beamed with love. He knew that he was the center of their world just as they were the center of his.

"What smells so good?" Raf asked, as he admired his wife who is five feet two inches tall, with pretty brown skin, beautiful brown eyes, and silky black hair.

"Oh, a little bit of this and a little bit of that!" Tinisha answered coyly, attempting to keep the exact items of the dinner somewhat of a surprise, even though she knew he could smell it.

"Yeah, a little bit of this and a little bit of that," Jasmine chimed in.

Raf and Nisha looked at each other and laughed. They were constantly discussing how they must be careful about what they say in front of their daughter because she repeats nearly everything she hears. She is definitely a quick learner, but she can be a smart aleck as well, saying things inappropriate for a five year old. Teaching her the difference and how to be respectful was a priority for her parents.

That night, the Salisbury family enjoyed a seafood feast that consisted of Dungeness crab, Shrimp Scampi, raw and fried oysters, steamed mussels, along with boiled seasoned potatoes and corn on the cob. Afterwards, Tinisha took Jasmine upstairs to help with her homework and get her ready for bed. Meanwhile, Rafael went into the den and made himself comfortable in his Lazy Boy recliner as he turned on the evening news. He was just in time to catch a news bulletin.

Good evening. This is Khalil Flemister reporting live for Channel 7 from Kaiser Foundation Hospital in Hollywood. We just received word that Captain Kurt Ramsey of the Los Angeles Police Department, Hollywood Division was rushed in after suffering a massive heart attack. We are sad to report that Captain Ramsey was reported DOA when the ambulance approached the emergency room doors.

Captain Ramsey served as captain for the last ten years of his thirty-six year career as a peace officer. He will be sorely missed. At age 58, he will be remembered as a fallen hero for years to come.

As he listened to the news, Rafael rose from his comfortable seat and stood in the middle of the floor, not believing his ears. He had just sat down with the captain for lunch yesterday. Captain Ramsey had shared his plans of taking a well-needed vacation with all of his grandchildren in the coming summer, just a couple of months away.

As the tragic news of the captain's death began to sink in, Rafael ran upstairs, taking two steps at a time. Finding Tinisha in the bathroom brushing her teeth, Raf stood behind her with tears falling down his face. When Tinisha noticed his presence behind her, she looked up and immediately saw that he was disturbed. She turned and placed her arms around him and said softly, "What is it?" She didn't know what to expect. *Had the telephone rang*, she wondered. *What could have happened in the last twenty minutes that I had been upstairs putting our daughter to bed?* As the thoughts ran through her mind, she waited patiently for her husband to catch his breath and share the news with her.

Rafael released himself from his wife's arms, walked over to the bed, and sat down. With his head in his hands, he shared the news of Captain Ramsey's death. Tinisha's heart began to beat again as she sighed a sigh of relief. She was relieved that it was not a family member although she was saddened at the same time to hear of the captain's death. Although she didn't know the captain very well, she had been in his company several times since she met and married Raf and had accompanied him to police functions. Captain Ramsey was a very respectful man and very cordial to everyone. She knew that his family would miss him greatly along with the past and present officers.

As the couple prepared for bed, they both wondered which lieutenant would become the acting captain until another captain was officially appointed. Although this was a natural thought to have as a result of the events that had just occurred, neither of them dared to speak their thoughts aloud. In light of the recent events, they did not want to appear insensitive. Yet, they could not help but wonder what impact this event would have on Raf's future, if any at all.

Six

Romero

Two months before the wedding, Romero allowed himself to take on one more new case. After accepting this last case, he vowed to Yolanda that he would not take on any more new cases until after the honeymoon once the cases in his present caseload were solved.

It was now two weeks before the wedding, and Romero had closed the final case. Sitting in his office as he did daily from eight to five, unless he was in the field, he wondered what he would do with himself for the next two weeks. Being a private investigator was his passion. The cases always sent a surge of adrenaline through his body.

Ninety-five percent of Rome's cases came from new clients. However, eighty percent of those new clients were referrals. Occasionally, he had repeat customers. It did not matter to him how or why the clients came to his private investigation agency. He just cared that they did come and that they kept coming. To ensure the clients returned or made referrals, he treated each case with top priority. Each client's case was handled with special care.

As Rome remembered the details of the last case, he realized that the free time he had on his hands actually could not have been more perfect. Two weeks gave Romero enough time to finish his obligations for the wedding. It was his responsibility to secure the venue, the flight over to the island, and his tuxedo. He was also responsible for the other men in the wedding party getting their tuxedos. Lastly, he was required to pick up the rings from the jeweler. Yolanda and Mariesha, the wedding planner, would take care of all the other details: from the wedding itself, the wedding cake, the rehearsal and rehearsal dinner, the bridal party, the flowers, to all the other fine details.

So far, Romero had only taken care of the venue and the flight. These items were crossed off the list four months ago at Yolanda's constant insistence. Instead of booking a flight with one of the local airlines, Rome decided to reserve a private jet to take him, Yolanda, their families, and Mariesha to the Hamptons. Reserving the private jet removed the concern for missing or lost luggage, and it allowed for privacy and comfort. And, having the jet also allowed Rome and Yolanda to travel on their preferred time schedule.

They decided to fly over a day before the wedding day to make sure all was in order and to have the required wedding rehearsal. Mariesha did not believe in having a wedding without a proper rehearsal. And, the entire wedding party had to participate.

Later in the week, Rome and the guys would be fitted for their tuxedoes, and he would pick up the rings.

Just as Rome was about to pick up the phone to call his father and then his brother to remind them of the tuxedo fitting, the door to his office was flung open. Frankly, it startled Rome. His first thought was that it was an irate potential client who desperately needed his services. Okay, maybe that was wishful thinking on his part. He looked up from his desk just in time to see Yolanda turning the corner heading towards him.

"Where's the fire, babe?" Rome asked, as he replaced the office phone back into its cradle.

"I guess you could say it's in the moving process."

"What do you mean?"

"I have been packing for the last week, and I am wondering how I am going to fit everything into your condo. I know we talked about letting my townhouse go, but will you be throwing anything out to make room for my things?" Yolanda whined with her best impression of a spoiled brat mixed with a helpless dame.

"Why don't you have a yard sale?"

"Excuse me? What do you mean a yard sale?" she screamed, immediately ditching the helpless dame routine.

"Babe, I'm just kidding. Calm down and have a seat."

"This is a serious problem, Rome. Why are you smiling? Obviously, you are not taking me seriously."

"Actually, I have been thinking about the same thing since I noticed that you are a pack rat, but I believe I have a solution."

"A pack rat? Oh really? Please share your solution. I can't wait to hear more about this yard sale you think I should have."

Ignoring Yolanda's sarcasm, Rome responded, "I thought it would be a great idea if we went house shopping. That way we could have enough room for both of our things." After a slight pause, he continued, "What do you think?"

"Are you serious? Can we afford it?"

"Let's do this- I will call the real estate agent that I have been talking to and have him show us some houses. Then, we can talk money."

Not hearing any objection from Lan, Rome picked up the phone. As Rome dialed the agent's number that he had stored in his cell phone, Yolanda ran around to his side of the desk and hugged his neck tightly while placing little kisses on his forehead, as she sat on his lap. She was giggling with excitement and nearly turned Rome's chair over with both of them in it.

Hours later, after driving around with Raheem, the real estate agent, the couple was famished. They had viewed house after house after house.

Transferring into Rome's Range Rover from Raheem's car, Rome and Yolanda headed to Denny's for a bite to eat. Once they were seated and had ordered their drinks and meals, they spread the various brochures across the table and discussed each house and the amenities offered as they ate. Although they were exhausted, the excitement of embarking upon their first financial adventure together, their first major purchase, sent their adrenaline soaring. The excitement that they were experiencing would last for a long time.

Occasionally, they would glance up at each other and smile while reaching across the table and touching hands. The act of house shopping seemed to seal the realization of their impending wedding. Although they had been working on the details of the wedding for over six months, each day, the reality of their lives coming together as one was more and more real.

As the couple of lovebirds drove from the restaurant, they discussed what they really want in a home. They both want children in the future, so they agreed it would be best to buy a home with plenty of room for children. This means they need at least two extra bedrooms. They both also want a place where they can lounge in the evenings in a comfortable place where they can watch a game or a good movie on a big screen.

The only thing they did not agree on was having an island in the kitchen. Yolanda wants one, while Rome does not. Rome conceded to Lan's wishes because she will be the one doing the majority of the cooking.

After discussing the types of rooms they want to have, they discussed décor. By that time, they had reached Rome's condo and were having a latté while leaning back on the sofa.

Before long, it was the wee hours of the morning, and the two had fallen asleep on the opposite ends of the couch with their feet touching.

Two Weeks Later

Seven

When the private jet landed at a private Hampton airport, there were two white stretch Hummer limousines waiting for Romero, Yolanda, and the others. After the thirty-minute drive, they were all gathered at the front desk of the Hampton Hotel & Suites to check in. The hotel's décor was perfect for setting the ambiance for the impending wedding. Everyone must have been having the same thoughts because although all were silent, each had a face plastered with a smile, while examining the ceiling, the paintings, and the Italian tile floor.

Although the flight on the private jet was short, each one was looking forward to relaxing before the rehearsal and dinner that would take place that evening.

When Rome arrived in his suite, which one day later would be the honeymoon suite, he noticed a red light blinking on the hotel's telephone. He had stayed overnight in enough hotels to know that the light meant he had a message. He wondered if it was the hotel's standard welcome message. After placing his luggage in the closet and promptly removing his tuxedo from the garment bag and hanging it up, he lay across the bed and reached for the phone.

To his surprise, the message was from Tinisha. She and her family: Rafael, Jasmine, her mother, who is his Aunt Delores and her father, who is his Uncle Earl had made it safely to the island. Her message said she is anxious to see him, and she left her room number. Before the phone settled back into its cradle completely, Rome was walking out the room, heading for the elevator. He too wanted to see his favorite cousin. The last time he had seen her and her family was nearly five years ago at his father's fiftieth birthday celebration. Tinisha and her family had flown into New York for the special occasion.

After spending about an hour with his cousins in their hotel room, Rome retreated back to his room for a short nap. He had about two hours before he was due downstairs in the wedding chapel. He did not know how long the rehearsal would take or how long the family would be at the restaurant having dinner afterwards, so he wanted to get a little rest.

On another floor of the hotel, Yolanda was in the room that she was sharing with her older sister Andrea. She was pacing back and forth across the floor as she filled Andrea in on the houses that she and Rome had gone to see. After their initial home search excursion with Raheem, they had gone out two more times before they found a house that suited them perfectly.

They went through a rapid-approval process and had begun the escrow process just two days before they left for the island. The entire escrow process would take thirty to forty-five days. Meanwhile, they would live in Romero's condo, but they would not move Yolanda's furniture until they moved into their new home.

Yolanda was on cloud nine, but she was experiencing pre-wedding jitters. Andrea was trying to keep her calm, but she was not having much luck. As Yolanda rambled on, Andrea sent their mother a secret SOS text. A few minutes later, Margaret was knocking at their door. "How are my girls doing?" she asked softly, not letting on that Andrea had summoned her. Before answering, Yolanda shot a suspicious look at her sister. However, Andrea's face did not display her guilt. Instead, she displayed her best innocent face while avoiding her sister's gaze.

"We're doing great, Mom. I was just telling Andy about the new house. What brings you by?"

"I just wanted to check on you. You seemed a little quiet in the limo. Are you okay?"

Upon hearing her mother's question, Yolanda burst into tears. Margaret and Andrea exchanged nervous glances. Neither one of them knew what to make of Yolanda's reaction. Both walked over to her and put their arms around her. After about three minutes, Andy asked, "Are you having second thoughts, Lan?"

Immediately, Yolanda's crying turned to laughter. Again, the other two ladies exchanged nervous glances. "Of course not, silly," Yolanda responded. "Rome is the best man I could ever want or need. He is so perfect for me. I believe I am perfect for him too."

"Okay, so what is going on here?" Margaret asked with a serious tone.

"I don't know. I guess I am so excited and nervous all at the same time. I just want everything to be perfect."

"Oh, the ceremony will be lovely. Mariesha will make sure of that," Andrea answered as she thought about the wedding planner. Mariesha has a take-charge demeanor, no-nonsense attitude, and a "command for respect" persona. These personality traits had made her famous, along with her attention to detail and air of professionalism. With Mariesha's outer beauty, one would quickly assume that she was a runway model. She is five feet nine inches tall, has a slender but shapely build, and long sandy brown hair. Her movements are very graceful, unless she is upset.

“Not just the wedding. I’m referring to our entire life together. I just want everything to go well for us,” Yolanda continued.

"Oh, all will go well. There is no need to worry," her mother assured her as she rubbed the back of her daughter's neck being careful not to touch Lan’s recently pinned hair, while wiping a tear away from her own eye.

Before their flight, Yolanda met with her hair stylist to get her wedding hairdo. She loved her stylist's creativity. She just hoped she would be able to keep all the curls and pins in place as she slept throughout the night because she would not be able to replicate the curl pattern.

Noticing her mother’s sudden emotional change, Yolanda averted her attention from herself to her mother. “Mom, what’s wrong?”

“It’s nothing, dear. I am just so happy that I could be here to witness this day with you,” she said as both eyes began to well up with tears. Out of the corner of her eye, she could see Andy shaking her head with an adamant look on her face.

"Of course you are here with me. Where else would you be?" Lan asked naively.

"Nowhere else, darling. Nowhere."

In the middle of her stomach, Lan felt there was something her mother wasn't telling her, but she allowed her attention to shift back from her mother to herself and the wedding rehearsal that would take place shortly. Although this was a joyous occasion, she could not help but to feel a little nervous.

Upstairs, Rome did not have that problem. He was fast asleep, getting much-needed rest. That is, until the best man knocked on the door to escort him downstairs for the rehearsal that would begin promptly at five o'clock.

When Rome opened the door and saw his older brother Lemuel standing there, all he could do was smile. He and Lemuel had their moments of disagreement when they were growing up, and even some as adults, but after their father's health scare five years ago, they came to terms with their differences. Now, they couldn't be any closer.

Lemuel was proud to stand with his younger brother as he made a life-long commitment to his bride, and Romero was proud to have his older brother's support.

When the brothers arrived at the chapel, nearly everyone else was there, and Mariesha had one eye on her wristwatch, the other on the door and one hand one her hip. The expression on her face said she would not be happy if they did not start on time.

As Yolanda sat quietly watching the members of the wedding party gather around the chapel doors, she observed Mariesha. There seemed to be a different air about her than there was last week when the two had met to go over the final wedding details.

Mariesha appeared to walk differently, and she even sounded a little differently. *I know she was getting over a cold,* Yolanda thought. *Maybe she is feeling better and is back to her old self. I think she was hoarse last week. Her voice sounds different now.*

"It's probably just my imagination," she said aloud without realizing it.

"What's your imagination?" Romero said as he walked over to where Lan was sitting.

Feeling embarrassed because she had not realized that she had spoken out loud, Lan said, "Oh nothing," and rose from her seat. Interrupting the couple's conversation, Mariesha began the rehearsal. "Okay, let's get started."

As Lan walked into the chapel, her mother, who had witnessed the brief exchange between her soon-to-be son-in-law and her daughter, wondered if there wasn't something else going on with Lan besides what she stated upstairs in her room a few moments before. She certainly wasn't acting like the daughter she knew. But she thought back to the time when she had her own wedding, the day she married Lonnie, Yolanda and Andrea's father.

She remembered being nervous and crying uncontrollably. Her mother had to calm her by having her drink chamomile tea.

Calmly walking over to her daughter, as not to alarm the others, Margaret sat on the pew next to Yolanda and asked if she wanted her to find some tea somewhere in the hotel. Yolanda quietly nodded, and Margaret slipped out of the rehearsal. As she went her way to locate a cup of hot tea, she couldn't help to think about the secret she was holding in.

Eight

Two grueling hours later, the wedding party, along with some of the other wedding guests, was seated in one of the hotel's restaurants. Three long tables were joined together to accommodate all of them. They were exhausted, to say the least. Mariesha had really given them the wedding rehearsal of their lives. After going through the process seven times of what would take place the next day, no one was bound to forget their places or when to move down the aisle.

They were aware of where the flowers would be placed, how far the runner would be extended, how far to walk behind each other, etcetera. The excitement was definitely building and nerves as well.

To keep the atmosphere light around the dinner table, the wedding party took turns teasing each other about the blunders they had made during practice. They even laughed as they remembered how Tinisha had sauntered down the aisle when she was pretending to be Yolanda. Some even took shots at Mariesha, who joined them for dinner as part of the pre-wedding festivities.

After everyone ordered appetizers to share, Mariesha began to share one of her wedding party horror stories. In the middle of her tale, she suddenly became quiet as her face went pale. Everyone turned to see what had caught her attention as her last words hung in the air.

Standing near the restaurant entrance, a man stood looking around as if he was looking for someone specific. Eventually, his gaze met Mariesha's. Before Mariesha could get out of her seat, the man was standing near their table. Mariesha walked over to him as she asked in a squeaky voice, "What are you doing here?"

"I could ask you the same thing," the man replied. "I need to speak to you."

"Please excuse me everyone. I apologize for the interruption," Mariesha said as she reluctantly followed the man outside into the hallway.

After Mariesha left, no one knew what to say, so Rafael broke the silence. "Who was that?" The question was directed to Yolanda. Yolanda responded by shrugging her shoulders. "Beats me. I've never seen him before."

Not a minute later, the appetizers were delivered, and the group returned to their hearty conversation as they enjoyed the warm snacks. By the time the main course was delivered, Mariesha had not returned to the table. Her plate sat on the table, and her food began to get cold.

Pastor Oglebee, Tinisha's father, looked at his nephew and asked, "Rome, don't you think you should check on her?"

"I think you should," Pastor Turner, Romero's father, chimed in.

Having heard from the two senior pastors in the family, Romero rose to walk toward the restaurant entrance where Mariesha had exited. Just as he reached the other side of the table, Mariesha walked back into the restaurant. She still had a worried look on her face.

"Are you okay?" Romero asked as Mariesha approached.

"Oh, I'm fine. I won't be able to stay for dinner though. Could you please ask the waiter to have my food delivered to my room and placed on my room tab?"

"Certainly. Are you sure you are okay?"

"Yes, I'm just a bit tired. I'm going to head to my room and rest up for tomorrow. I need to be downstairs early to meet the florist." With a weak smile, she lifted her hand and waved to everyone. "Have a good night everyone. I will see you in the morning."

Everyone responded accordingly, resumed eating their meals and the sharing of light banter. Eventually, they retired to their own rooms.

The wedding was scheduled for eleven the next morning, and they all wanted to be well rested, so they could look their best and enjoy all that the festivities had to offer. After all, it wasn't everyday that they spent time in the infamous Hamptons.

Nine

At eleven am on Saturday morning, the medium-sized chapel at the Hampton Inn & Suites was filled to capacity. The chapel was beautifully decorated with Yolanda's choice colors: canary yellow and silver. Tiny yellow twinkling lights covered the sides of the pews as well as the ceiling. The altar was beautifully adorned with spring lilies that had been sprinkled with silver glitter. At various spots around the chapel, white artificial doves appeared to be suspended in air. They gently swung from side to side as if keeping beat with the instrumental tunes that played softly in the background. The décor added just the right hint of romanticism.

Upstairs, in a private dressing room that was large enough for the entire wedding party, the bride and her court were finally prepared to make their way downstairs to the chapel. The plan was for Yolanda to arrive at the chapel at 11:15. This would allow Romero time to arrive ahead of her to take his place at the altar beside his father who would perform the ceremony.

The sign that it was time for the ceremony to begin was Yolanda's mother appearing at the chapel door.

Upon Margaret's appearance, an usher took her arm and escorted her to her seat on the front pew on the bride's side. Next, Romero's mother was escorted in by Lemuel. He took her to her seat on the front pew on the groom's side. Then, he took his place by the groom.

Once both mothers were seated, the organist began to play softly. This was the cue for the wedding party to enter the chapel. As the double doors opened, a hush fell over the crowd. The matron of honor and the maid of honor followed by the three groomsmen and three bridesmaids sauntered down the aisle in tune with the music. Afterwards, the two flower girls, Lemuel's daughter and Jasmine, tossed flowers upon the runner as they made their way to the altar along with the ring bearer who led their short processional.

As Yolanda stood at the double doors of the chapel desperately blinking back tears as she held her father's arm tightly, the guests rose to their feet. Yolanda waited for the organist to begin playing her chosen wedding song, so she could begin her entrance. To her surprise, Andrea, who was the matron of honor, moved from her place at the altar two steps higher onto the stage. She slowly raised a microphone to her lips and began to sing.

The tears that Yolanda had been attempting to hold back fell freely from her eyes now as she watched her sister sing. For a moment, she forgot she was supposed to be walking in. Her father gently pulled her forward. As Yolanda slowly made her way to the altar, the guests looked in awe at how beautiful she was. She had opted for a traditional wedding gown rather than a modern one. Her dress was full with a long flowing train. Her elegantly curled hair was neatly coifed and topped with a tiara suitable for the queen of England or the princess of Whales. To say that she was stunning would be an understatement.

When Yolanda reached the altar, Rome noticed how her faced glistened, and he immediately knew that she had been crying. At the sight of her, a single tear fell from his eye. *This is the moment that will change our lives forever*, he thought as his eyes met hers.

Forty-five minutes later, Mr. and Mrs. Turner exited the chapel followed by the wedding party and their guests. There were photographers on each side snapping as many pictures as they could in an effort to not miss a single moment.

After all the wedding pictures were taken, the bride and groom joined the guests at the reception. Just as they were about to be seated at the beautifully decorated head table, after having spoken to their guests, Andrea walked into the room with her cell phone in her hand and a puzzled look on her face.

Yolanda knew right away that something was awry. She had been able to read her older sister's looks since she was a young child. Because Andrea was holding her phone, Lan assumed Andy had called home to check on her husband and her children. "Is everything okay with the kids?"

"Huh? Oh, yeah. The kids are fine."

"Is it Michael?"

"No, Mike's fine. It's Mariesha," Andy answered quickly to stop Lan's questioning.

"What's Mariesha? What do you mean?"

"I received three messages from Kim saying John had a car accident and is in ICU. The wedding will be postponed, so

Mariesha doesn't need to fly back for the wedding rehearsal that was scheduled for tonight."

"Why didn't Kim just call Mariesha instead of calling you?"

"That's just it. She called her cell and the hotel to try to reach her on the room phone. There was no answer at either number. When was the last time you saw her?"

"I haven't seen her, but I know she had to leave to catch a flight at two this afternoon for Kim and John's wedding rehearsal."

"You haven't seen her all day?"

"Uh no. Babe, have you seen her?" Lan asked Rome.

"No," Rome answered between bites of London Broil.

"Don't you two think we should look for her?" Andrea questioned.

All Rome and Yolanda could do was stare at each other for several seconds. Neither of them had seen Mariesha all morning. Rome had assumed she was with Lan or downstairs in the chapel. Lan had assumed she was downstairs. Just as Lan was about to answer her sister's question, Tinisha walked over to see what the problem was. After a bit more discussion and calling the front desk to see if Mariesha had checked out, they learned that when the florist had arrived at nine that morning to deliver the lilies, Mariesha was scheduled to meet him at the chapel. However, Mariesha was not there.

In an attempt to assist the florist, the catering department had tried calling Mariesha's room and her cell phone on several occasions since then. But the calls were to no avail.

After hearing the story, Tinisha and Rafael thought it would be best to go to Mariesha's room. This is the one thing the catering department had failed to do. In the elevator, Tinisha and Raf marveled over the wedding as they both silently wondered what was going on.

"When we renew our vows, I want a wedding like that," Tinisha stated.

"Oh, are we making plans?" Raf questioned.

Before Tinisha could answer, the elevator door opened. Her mind quickly began to focus on the business at hand: finding Mariesha.

When they approached the end of the hallway where Mariesha's room was located, Raf noticed the room door ajar. Nisha cautioned him about going in. The scene they saw made Raf grab his cell phone and dial 911, while Nisha turned and ran back downstairs. She bypassed the elevator, snatched off her high heels, and took the stairs six flights down to the reception room. At the rate she was going, she would have slipped down the steps due to her stocking-covered feet. Luckily, the stairs were carpeted.

When she entered the reception room, she immediately walked over to Rome and Lan. Trying to catch her breath, she whispered, "Come with me!"

Ten

Once Tinisha, Romero, and Yolanda were in the elevator, Tinisha quickly answered the questioning looks on Rome's and Lan's faces she had been avoiding. When they reached Mariesha's room, hotel security had already arrived and was inside the room. They had asked Raf to remain outside. He was pacing back and forth in the hallway with one arm behind his back and one hand on his chin. This was his usual movement when he was deep in thought.

Rome and Yolanda were anxious to see what was going on inside Mariesha's room. As they moved as close to her hotel room as the security would allow them, Yolanda saw drops of blood on the key card that was just inside the door and a bloody hand print on the door. She gasped and quickly covered her mouth. She wondered if the blood was Mariesha's and what had happened to her. Tears began to fall from her eyes as she grabbed Rome's hand. Unable to do anything else, Rome and Yolanda moved to a corner of the hallway and began to pray.

A few minutes later, four detectives from the East Hampton Town Police Department arrived. As members of the New York Police Department, two of them knew Romero because of his close relationship with the department. When Romero's cases involved criminals who were attempting to evade the law, he passed the information on to the NYPD. This interaction caused him to become a constant figure within the department.

When Detectives Arroyo and Finster saw him, they immediately headed in his direction. After Rome explained the situation about Mariesha, the two detectives along with Rome, Lan, Nisha and Raf went into one of the hotel meeting rooms. With all the excitement, Rome and Lan had momentarily forgotten about their guests at the reception, until Detective Finster noticed Lan's wedding dress and Rome's tuxedo.

"Man, don't tell me this is your wedding day," he said half asking and half making a reply.

"How did you guess?" Rome replied with a little sarcasm and visible irritation. Yolanda immediately placed her hand on the small of her husband's back to calm him. She could tell that he was not in the mood for joking.

Ignoring Rome's irritability, Finster said, "There was a little buzz about your wedding throughout the precinct, but as you can see we are on duty, so we couldn't make it. But we're here now," he finished- trying to add a little humor to what was potentially a disastrous situation.

Once they were all settled into the meeting room, Detective Arroyo wanted to begin asking questions to put the pieces of the puzzle together. However, before asking questions about the apparent disappearance of the wedding planner, the detectives found it necessary to obtain everyone's identity. When they learned that they had a reputable lawyer and police lieutenant in their midst, they seemed even more at ease as they prepared to ask their probing questions.

"When was the last time any of you saw Ms. Coleman?" Rafael took the initiative to answer first. "My wife and I saw her last in Rosalito's when someone came and interrupted our dinner."

"Rosalito's here in the hotel?"

"Yes, the entire wedding party and our families went to eat there after the wedding rehearsal," Tinisha chimed in.

"Okay, tell me more about this person who interrupted dinner."

"He was a black male, between mid-thirties to late forties. He had a bald head and was approximately 5'10"," Rome replied.

"Does everyone agree with the physical description?" Detective Arroyo asked. The other three nodded.

"Tell me exactly what happened when the man showed up."

"We were sitting around the dinner table. Mariesha was telling us a story, but all of a sudden she stopped talking. That's when I noticed a man standing near the entrance of the restaurant. It was obvious that he was looking for someone. Finally, he started walking over toward our table, but Mariesha met him a few feet away. I don't know what was said, but it didn't look to be too pleasant."

"Then what happened?"

"She excused herself and left."

"Was that the last time any of you saw her?"

"No. Nearly twenty minutes later, she walked back into the restaurant and asked us to have her dinner sent to her room. I asked if she was okay, and she assured us that she was fine. She looked more embarrassed than anything," Rome answered.

"Did you or your wife see her later that evening?" directing the question to Romero.

"I didn't," Rome said as he looked over to Lan.

"Neither did I. I went to my room after dinner and got ready for bed," Yolanda answered.

"Did Mariesha call out a name as she walked over to meet the guy, or did she happen to introduce him to the group?" All four shook their heads 'no.'

"What was he wearing?"

"A button down plaid shirt. It was burgundy with blue stripes," Nisha replied.

"What about pants and shoes?"

"I think he had on dark jeans," Lan answered.

"Blue or black?'

"I'm not sure."

"And his shoes?" Everyone just shrugged indicating they did not know.

"Okay. Were there any distinguishing marks, such as birthmarks or tattoos?"

For a moment all were quiet as they tried to refresh their memories of the night before. Finally, Raf spoke up. "I don't remember any marks, but I do remember something that struck me as out of place or maybe a better term is outdated. He had a piece of hair hanging over his shirt collar."

"I thought you said he was bald?"

"Yes, but he had a piece of hair at the back of his head in the very center at the bottom. You remember the style that guys wore in the '80s?"

"Oh yes. I know what you mean. Okay, what was Ms. Coleman wearing?"

"She had on a black dress and black Patton leather red-bottom pumps," Tinisha volunteered.

"Anything else? Anything that stood out?"

"A red belt and a red flower in her hair," Yolanda added.

"Was the flower real or artificial?"

"Artificial," Tinisha and Yolanda answered simultaneously.

After the brief interview, Detective Finster attempted to reassure the two couples. "There is evidence of foul play; however, there isn't a lot of blood for us to be alarmed to believe that your friend, or anyone else, has been fatally harmed. We found her room key on the floor just inside the door. What appears to be all of her belongings were still inside: her purse, toiletries, and clothing. The perpetrator probably interrupted her as she entered her room. They probably struggled, one or both of them probably got cut and that's how the blood got on the floor and door. Samples of the blood are being sent to the lab with her identification, prints, and hair samples. We should be able to use her DNA to see if there is a match with the blood."

"Was there a weapon of some sort?" Tinisha asked the detectives.

"Nothing has been uncovered at this point," Arroyo answered.

After leaving Romero and the others, the two detectives set out to find out who was responsible for taking Mariesha's food to her room. Maybe the person saw something. However, this line of thinking did not go anywhere because Mariesha never answered her phone when the restaurant called, so her food was never delivered.

After talking to the two detectives, the two couples returned to the reception to find the guests in a somber mood. They had no idea why the bride and groom rushed out without a word. Rome decided it best to give the guests as few details as possible because they were now in the midst of an investigation.

Eleven

After all the hugs, kisses, and well wishes had been given and all gifts opened and admired, some of the wedding party and guests retreated to their suites while others left for the airport to return home. The evening was still young, and Raf, Nisha, Rome, and Lan were anxious to discuss Mariesha's case. Rome and Lan changed into their beige and cream after-wedding attire that Lan had purchased and perfectly matched. Then, they went to Raf and Nisha's room. Meanwhile, Rome's only sister Carmen and Andrea moved all of Lan's belongings to the honeymoon suite.

Fifteen minutes later, the two couples were seated in a private lounge away from earshot of anyone passing by. Before the case was discussed, Tinisha looked at her cousin and his new wife and took one of each of their hands into her own.

"I am so sorry this happened on your wedding day, cousins. I really wanted this day to be perfect for both of you."

"Well, as we all know, life happens as it will and asks no one for permission," Lan responded. "But, as far as the wedding goes, I wouldn't change anything: the atmosphere, the location, the decorations, the wedding party, the guests, and especially the groom!"

With that, they all nodded in response as they laughed. "My sentiments exactly," Rome responded as he gently kissed his wife's lips.

"So, you guys are off in the morning, right?" Raf asked.

"Yes, we will be on our way to Honolulu," Rome answered with a little hesitation. Both Lan and Nisha noticed his slight pause. They knew it was burning within him to assist the NYPD, and if it were not for the honeymoon, he would do just that. Either it was because investigating was in his blood or he felt partially responsible because Mariesha was there with them, and if she had not been, maybe she would not be missing. Lan shot Rome a questioning look. He did not respond. Instead, he squeezed her hand to reassure her that all was well.

It took everything within her to not question him. The bottom line was she didn't need to. She knew him all too well. She knew he would not cancel or postpone the honeymoon without just cause.

Out of nowhere, the faint sound of a phone could be heard ringing. It was Rome's cell phone that he had tucked away in his pants' pocket.

"Romero Turner, private investigator. How can I assist you?" Rome answered instinctively.

"Romero, this is Detective Arroyo. Are you still in the hotel?"

"Yes, my wife and I will be here until about ten tomorrow morning. Why do you ask?"

"It seems as if we have come up with a few more questions. I hate to interrupt your wedding night, but it is absolutely imperative that we try to get as many questions answered about your friend while you are still available."

"Okay. What questions do you have?"

"First, are the Salisburys still here?"

"Yes, we are all together now."

"Can the four of you meet me back in the room we were in earlier?"

"How soon?"

"Now, if you can."

"We are on our way," Rome responded as he quickly hung up the phone as he rose from his seat. "NYPD needs us back in the meeting room. They have more questions."

Raf beat the two ladies responding. "Did they say what is going on?"

"No. Just more questions."

"Well, they must have found more evidence," Tinisha interjected.

"Yeah, well we will find out in a minute," Rome said as they stepped into the elevator, two by two.

Inside the elevator was a lively elderly couple who appeared to be on their way to dinner. The four young adults offered greetings. After looking back and forth amongst the four younger persons' faces, the man finally returned the greeting and posed a question. "Aren't you the young couple that was pronounced married today?" he asked speaking directly into Rome's face.

"Yes, sir," Rome answered while taking a step back right onto Raf's toe.

"Watch the Stacy Adams, little cousin," Raf said to Rome half jokingly.

"Sorry, man."

"And is this your wife, young man?" the older gentleman asked Rafael, noticing the rings on each of their fingers.

"Yes, sir. She is my bride of seven years," he answered with his chest slightly puffed up.

"Can I give you two young couples a bit of marital advice? My wife and I have been married for over thirty years."

"Sure," Lan and Nisha said nearly in synch.

"Never let the sun go down on your wrath," the man continued.

"Ephesians 4:26," Romero and Nisha said simultaneously.

At their response, the man smiled. "Believers are you?" he asked already knowing the answer.

"Yes, sir," all four responded, one after the other.

"As long as you continue to walk with the Lord, you will make it. Remember, a three-stranded chord is not easily broken."

As the man uttered the last word, the elevator, which seemed to be moving ever so slowly, suddenly arrived at the floor of the meeting room. Each of the four said their thanks to the man and departed the elevator anxious to speak to the detectives.

As the two couples entered the meeting room, Detectives Finster and Arroyo had their notepads on the table and were comparing notes. When they noticed Rome and the others' presence, they immediately stopped talking.

"Come on in and have a seat," Detective Finster directed as he pointed to four chairs that were directly across from him and Arroyo. After the four had each taken a seat, Detective Arroyo took the initiative to ask the first question.

"Can anyone give us any information about the young man that was traveling with Ms. Coleman?" As he waited for the answer, he had his pen ready to write all that would be said. The same was true for his partner.

"What young man?" Rome queried.

"There were three sets of boy's clothing hanging in the closet of Ms. Coleman's room, so we assumed there was a boy with her." As seemed to be the pattern of the day, the couples looked confusedly back and forth amongst each other.

"There wasn't a young man with Mariesha," Rome began. "The only man we saw was the one in the restaurant that we told you about."

"Are you sure?" Detective Finister asked.

"We are positive. She flew in the private jet with us yesterday. She was alone," Yolanda shrieked wondering where this line of questioning was going. Noting her irritation, Finster wondered if he should say anything else. It was obvious from their responses they did not know anything about the boy.

After a brief awkward silence, Tinisha asked, as she placed her hand on Yolanda's arm to calm her, "Do you think the clothes could belong to the man we saw last night? What size are they? Can we see them?"

The detectives, still not sure how to respond, communicated silently with each other, using only eye contact. Finally, Finster answered, "I guess it can't hurt. Follow us."

Twelve

As the six people moved from the conference room to Mariesha's room, the two detectives led the way. Raf walked at the rear of the group, so he could get a good reading of the two detectives. He wanted to know how dedicated they were to solving Mariesha's apparent disappearance.

Looking from one to the other, Raf noticed Detective Finster was the taller of the two. He stood approximately 6'3" tall. He wore his hair cut low, similar to someone who is in the armed forces. His shoulders were squared, and his uniform was neatly pressed as if he had not sat down all day. Not a wrinkle could be seen anywhere from the collar of his shirt to the hem in his pants. He was awkwardly slender, looking as though he may miss a meal or two each day. Although he was slender, he did not look completely undernourished because his skin had a very healthy glow and was very taut. Older women everywhere were probably envious of his skin.

Detective Arroyo, on the other hand, was a bit shorter with a height of 5'11." His hair, like his partner's, was neatly cut and combed. Unlike Finster's, Arroyo's hair had a touch of gray at the temples. Raf, however, could not tell if the gray was premature or if Arroyo was actually older than he appeared. His uniform was also neat, but not nearly as neat as Finster's. Arroyo's clothing looked like it had been worn once before without having a trip to the cleaners in between.

After taking in the detectives' physical appearance, Raf listened intently to their conversation. Except for a few jokes with Romero about his role as a new husband, all words spoken were professional and about the case at hand. Raf noticed everyone was at ease with the two detectives as if they trusted them implicitly.

Just as the group reached Mariesha's room, Yolanda's phone rang. While the others entered, she remained in the hallway to speak to her sister who was obviously calling for an update.

"Hey, Andy," Yolanda said into the phone.

"Hey, sis. Any news about Mariesha?'

"Well, there was a question about a boy's clothing in her room."

"Maybe they belong to the guy from the restaurant," Andrea suggested.

"From what the detective said the clothes belong to a boy not a man. But we are at her room now to take a look. So, let me call you back."

After her brief conversation with her sister, Lan joined the others inside Mariesha's room. Detective Arroyo was holding a backpack in his hand, and Rome was looking at it.

"Yes, she had it with her on the plane. I thought it looked out of place with her girlie luggage, but I figured it was one of those things that she had had for a while and liked to keep with her," Rome responded.

Detective Arroyo then reached inside the backpack and pulled out a plastic baggie with toiletries inside. With his gloved hand, he extracted the toothbrush and placed it into a specimen bag. "We will run the DNA from the toothbrush to see if the boy is any relation to the victim. Also, we should be able to lift his prints from this baggie," he said as he emptied the remaining contents into the backpack and place the baggie into a separate specimen bag.

Rome and Lan continued to discuss the issue of the child's backpack with Arroyo. Meanwhile, Finster, Tinisha, and Rafael where standing at the closet examining the lingerie that was hanging. It wasn't the traditional lingerie with lace, silk, or satin. Instead, the three different outfits were made of leather. Two had chains hanging and the third had a studded neck, similar to a dog collar. Sitting on the top shelf of the closet by the extra pillow and blanket was a long leather whip.

After answering all the detectives' questions, the two couples had a list of questions of their own, none of which would be answered immediately. In a more confused state than they were earlier in the afternoon, the couples retired to their quarters for the night.

Thirteen

The Honeymoon

After an eventful wedding day and romantically peaceful wedding night, Romero and Yolanda Turner were excited to embark upon their new life together. Their first adventure was their honeymoon, which would be spent in Honolulu. The honeymoon package was a gift from both sets of parents who had collaborated to give their children a wonderful send off.

Seated in the first-class cabin aboard a Boeing 757 jet, the couple sat quietly with their hands interlocked with one another as they prepared for takeoff. Both had smiles on their faces and joy unspeakable in their hearts. Both knew that getting married was one of the best choices they had made in their twenty-six years of living.

Once the plane was in the air, Romero broke the silence. "Babe, I have some good news for you."

"Really? What is it?" Yolanda asked excitedly finding it hard to stop admiring her three-karat princess-cut diamond wedding ring that was encased by a one and half karat wrap that was designed with baguettes.

"I spoke with Raheem this morning. He said escrow is coming along well, and we may even get an early closing."

At her husband's words, Lan's attention quickly shifted from the ring to Rome. "Oh, honey. That's great news. Wouldn't it be cool to move in when we get back?"

"Yeah, that would be cool, but let's not get our hopes up."

"Yeah, you're right. By the way, I have a surprise for you too."

"Oh yeah? What's that?" Romero asked trying to sound cool and not too anxious. Yolanda did not answer right away. Instead, she summoned the flight attendant and whispered something in his ear. After sauntering down the aisle, disappearing for a moment and returning, he produced a long clear box. At first, Romero thought it was a single rose. He didn't really care for flowers, but coming from his bride, he thought it was a nice gesture. But when Yolanda moved the box into his line of sight, he saw that the container held a dozen chocolate-covered strawberries from Cornerstone Confections. The Cake Dr. herself had made them personally as an extra wedding treat. The strawberries had been meant for the wedding night, but Romero had decided to have chocolate mousse in their suite, so Yolanda tucked the strawberries away for the flight.

"Oh wow," Romero responded at the sight of the mouth-watering treats. His eyes were as big as a kid's in a candy store. Not waiting for an invitation, Rome promptly opened the container, pulled out one of the dark red juicy treats and lifted it to his mouth. Just as Yolanda thought he would sink his perfect white teeth into it, he moved the strawberry to her mouth, so she could have the first bite.

How romantic, she thought as she sank her teeth in for a taste.

After they had finished off the last strawberry, both leaned their heads back on the soft leather seats to take a short nap. They weren't really tired, but they knew there was a long flight ahead.

As Rome sat still waiting for sleep to come, his eyes kept wandering back and forth to the phone that was on the back of the seat in front of him. He had to restrain himself from picking it up and calling one of the detectives to fill him in on any possible developments in Mariesha's case, for he knew that was not the best way to begin his honeymoon or his marriage.

After sitting quietly for ten minutes, Rome realized he was a little too agitated to sleep. He reached under the seat in front of him and retrieved his briefcase. At his movement, Yolanda turned towards him to see what he was doing.

"You aren't about to work are you?" she inquired.

"Of course not. I'm on my honeymoon," Rome beamed displaying his pearly whites.

"So what are you up to?" she asked eyeing his briefcase.

"I thought I would do a little reading. Tinisha brought us a couple of books. She swears they are awesome. She gave *The Preacher's Son* for me and *The Preacher's Daughter* for you. They are both written by Cassundra White-Elliott. Supposedly, she is an excellent author. I will be the judge of that." He handed Yolanda her book, and he leaned back, opened his novel, and began reading the first page.

Before long, after they had become engulfed in their novels, only pausing to eat lunch, the twelve-hour flight came to an end.

Traveling from the airport to the resort where the newlyweds would be spending the next five days and nights, Rome and Lan were able to take in the breath-taking view of Hawaii. Neither of them had been there before, so they were filled with anticipation of the adventure that lay ahead.

After spending the first day together strolling up and down the beach on which the resort was situated, Rome decided it was time to try something neither of them had ever done: scuba diving. They both wanted this honeymoon to be a series of firsts.

So, on day two, a few hours after a breakfast of various types of fruit; hearty omelets filled with mushrooms, tomatoes, bacon, green onions, cheese, and black olives; Belgian waffles; and freshly cooked ham sliced just right, the couple lined up with the other tourists and a few locals to get their scuba diving gear.

Fourteen

Back in New York

A search warrant request for Mariesha's home was sent to Judge Warner early Monday morning and was approved and sent back to the Hampton NYPD precinct late that afternoon. Based on the suspicion of foul play included in the details of the missing person's report, Judge Warner approved the warrant without hesitation.

Early Tuesday morning, Detective Arroyo and Detective Finster rang the doorbell at Mariesha's home. While waiting to see if anyone would answer, the detectives surveyed the outside of the house. The house appeared to be approximately 50-60 years old; however, it had been painted a pale yellow with a white trim within the last couple of years. On one side of the house was an older Mercedes Benz that was covered by a car cover that was so badly weather beaten that it exposed parts of the vehicle. From the leaves that had gathered around the tires, anyone could tell that the car had not been moved for some time.

"That doesn't look like a car a thirty-something single woman would drive," Arroyo stated.

"This doesn't look like a home she would have chosen for herself either," Finster said.

"Maybe she lives with her parents," Arroyo speculated.

After waiting for another three minutes and not receiving an answer at the door, the detectives let themselves into Mariesha's residence. They looked for signs of foul play for nearly thirty minutes, surveying both the top and bottom floors of the two-story house. They did not find anything remotely suspicious.

"Another dead end," Finster murmured as he lifted his hand to open the front door, preparing to leave the same way they had entered.

Just as he turned the knob releasing its connection, the telephone rang. After three rings, the detectives heard a click. Immediately, they looked at each other, but neither said a word. Standing perfectly still, they waited to hear exactly where the noise had come from. Arroyo pointed toward the kitchen after another 'click' sounded.

Moving quickly toward the kitchen with guns drawn, the detectives realized the clicks were coming from an old answering machine that sat in the corner of the counter. They waited for a message to be left by the caller. However, the caller opted not to leave a message.

"Now, I'm really started to feel like I'm in a blast from the past," Finster said as he moved closer to the machine.

"I know what you mean, but let's have a listen to Ms. Coleman's messages."

After pressing the play button and listening to several messages that were either requesting Mariesha's services or thanking her for a job well done, the following message played:

Mariesha, this is Stanley Walberg. As I stated during the brief conversation we had at my wedding reception, my wife and I did not appreciate your behavior at the wedding, nor the attitude you displayed toward us or our guests. Prior to the wedding, I thought we had an excellent working relationship. We are still expecting a full refund of your fees as we requested. We expect to hear from you soon, as we have not received our money back yet. My wife and I can be reached at (212) 555-1212.

Finster rewound the message, and both detectives jotted down the caller's name and telephone number. Continuing to review Mariesha's messages, they came across another message that heightened their curiosity about the missing woman.

Ree, I just got a call from Dr. Segorian. He said you were to begin your therapy a few days ago, but you did not show up at the facility to check yourself in for your two-week stay. I'm calling to check on you to see what's going on. (Pause) Now I know. Expect to see me soon. I don't know where you are, but you shouldn't be too hard to find. Oh, by the way, I'm sure you saw my number on the caller id on your cell phone. It would be nice if you would call back. Either way- I will see you soon!

Arroyo shot Finster a questioning look. "What do you make of that?" he queried.

"Go back to the beginning of the message and check the date the message was left," Finster directed. Arroyo followed the instructions and pressed the rewind button. The message was left the morning before Mariesha's disappearance.

After listening to the remaining messages, Arroyo recorded Stan's and the second caller's messages into his cell phone. As the detectives returned to their unmarked squad car, they hoped these messages would give them a lead into the case.

Just as Finster was about to pull away from the curb, he realized they had not thought to speak to Mariesha's neighbors to see if any strange activity had occurred over the last week or so. This method of inquiry was taught in Detective 101. How could they have overlooked this opportunity to possibly obtain much-needed information? As Finster placed the gear shift back into park, an elderly woman stepped out onto her porch as she glared at their car. Arroyo saw her first. "She must have read your mind."

"Yeah, I guess you did too," Finster laughed.

When the two detectives began to cross the street, the elderly woman smiled a bright welcoming smile. At first, they thought the smile was for them. However, after closer examination, they realized she was smiling at a young man who was sitting in a car in her driveway.

"Excuse me, ma'am," Finster yelled out as they neared the sidewalk.

"Yes?" the woman answered with a smile that was equally as warm as the one she had given the young man in the car.

"Ma'am, I am Detective Finster, and this is Detective Arroyo. Can we speak with you for a moment?"

"What about young man?" the lady responded. Her cheerful look turned to one of concern.

"Do you live here, ma'am?" Arroyo began. He wanted to make sure the woman was a resident and not a guest.

"Yes, my husband and I bought this house nearly fifty years ago when we first got married. He has since passed on, so now it's just me and Buster. I'm Mrs. Margaret Bloomsdale," she said as she extended her hand to one detective and then to the other.

"Nice to meet you, Mrs. Bloomsdale. We would like to ask you a few questions about your neighbor across the street Ms. Mariesha Coleman," Arroyo said as he shook her slightly cold, frail hand.

"Oh," Mrs. Bloomsdale responded looking visibly shaken.

"Is everything okay, Mrs. Bloomsdale?" Arroyo prodded.

"Have you seen your neighbor lately or any suspicious activity?" Finster asked without waiting for her to answer

Arroyo's question. He was anxious to find out any information that may lead to finding Mariesha.

"Well, I guess you could say there is suspicious activity going on over there all the time. Especially during the last twenty years after Mr. and Mrs. Coleman passed away and left Mariesha and her brother alone to be orphans, so to speak."

"Can you share with us what you mean by suspicious activity?"

"Sure, but not now. My grandson has come to pick me up. So, I must be going. You can come back another day, and we can sit and talk." As she prepared to descend the stairs of the porch, her grandson walked around the car to open her door for her and help her get inside the vehicle.

"Would it be okay if we spoke with Buster? Maybe he knows something. Is he home?"

"Oh yes. He's always home. You can ask him all the questions you like. I'm positive he won't answer though," she said with a chuckle as she sat in the front passenger seat of the car. The young man burst into laughter also.

"Why is that, ma'am?" Finster asked as he glanced over to Arroyo who too had a confused look on his face.

"Buster is my dog," she replied as she and her grandson pulled out of the driveway and drove away.

"Funny," Finster replied sarcastically, half to himself and half to his partner.

The pair of detectives knocked on a few doors of the neighboring homes and spoke to some of the neighbors. However, no one was able to provide any clues about what had caused Mariesha's disappearance. Many of them said Mariesha kept to herself, and they only spoke to her when she was either coming home or leaving.

"We need to get in contact with Mariesha's doctor to see if he can tell us why she needed to have therapy treatment," Finster stated as he guided the car onto the nearest freeway onramp.

"That information may prove helpful, but the information will be considered confidential. You know, doctor/patient confidentiality. Furthermore, I think the caller who said she would see him soon is the person we need to talk to. What if he is the one who went to the hotel and took her away?"

"Yes, and he could also have taken her to her doctor to get the therapy treatment. That could be where she is now."

"If that were the case, why would her things have been left behind at the hotel?"

"That's a good question along with the so many others that have been left unanswered."

The rest of the drive was taken in silence. Both detectives were undoubtedly thinking about the case and the bits of information they received that day.

Fifteen

The Honeymoon Continues

At the bottom of the ocean, Romero and Yolanda were enjoying the beautiful ocean floor. Both of their eyes were large with wonderment as they watched an array of fish swim by. They continuously pointed to items in amazement as they shared in the excitement.

Suddenly, Lan grabbed Rome's arm as she attempted to scream in horror. He saw the look of terror on her face and looked in the direction of where she was pointing. She was wiggling and kicking her leg, trying to free it from the grasp that had caught hold to it. Romero was on the case; he moved down the span of her leg to see what the problem was. He quickly grabbed the captor and moved back into Yolanda's view to show her what the culprit was. It was a piece of seaweed that had become wrapped around her leg.

As Yolanda calmed down, Rome couldn't help but laugh. Yolanda used her thumb to point upwards. This was the signal they had been taught to use when they wanted to go up. Romero, still chuckling, with his mouth gear intact, followed his wife upwards, so they could get back into the boat and head back to shore.

Once they had made it safely into the boat, Rome attempted to give Lan a hug, but she brushed him away. She was not at all happy that he was taking pleasure in the incident.

"Awe, babe. Are you mad at me because the seaweed monster attacked you?"

"It's not funny, Rome. That scared me half to death."

"I know, honey. It could have bitten your ankle or sucked the blood from your leg."

"Okay, I know it seems silly now, but I didn't know what it was at first," she said having to laugh a little herself.

After the newlyweds had returned to shore, showered and changed clothes in the comfort of their honeymoon suite, they sat in the living room to decide their next adventure before dinner.

"I would love to go horseback riding along the trail," Yolanda suggested. Before Rome could answer, he noticed he had missed a call from Tinisha. He quickly showed the display to Lan before dialing his cousin's phone number. He wondered if she was calling to see how the honeymoon was coming along or if she had news about Mariesha's case. She, Rafael, and Jasmine had stayed in New York for an extended vacation while Jas was on Spring Break. They had promised to keep close contact with Detectives Arroyo and Finster.

Romero was so anxious to hear what his cousin had to say that he was unable to sit still in his chair. As he listened to the phone ring, he stood up, walked to the window, and began to watch the waves ride up onto the shore. The view was breathtaking.

"Hey, Lan. Come take a picture of this view." Just as Yolanda rose to get her camera, Tinisha answered her phone.

"Hey, Cousin. How is the honeymoon coming along?" she asked full of energy.

"We are having a blast. We are eating everything we lay our eyes on. We have gone scuba diving, and we are getting ready to go horseback riding."

When Yolanda heard Romero mention scuba diving, she hit him playfully on the arm as a warning to not mention the seaweed scare to Tinisha. Romero laughed and nodded to let his wife know that he understood her warning.

"Sounds like fun, if that's your thing. Whose idea was that?"

"It was my idea to go scuba diving, but it was Lan's idea to go horseback riding. Enough about us. What's going on back home? You guys are still in New York with my parents right?"

"Yes, we are still in New York, but we are at Carmen's now. She wanted to hang out and do a little shopping. Plus, my parents are still here too. They are staying at your parents' house. We didn't want to overcrowd them. But, we did leave Jas with her grandparents and her great aunt and great uncle."

"Oh great. So, that gives you and Raf a little break. Sorry to cut to the chase, but have you spoken to the detectives about Mariesha's case?"

"I didn't speak to them personally. Raf did. They haven't found her yet, but they may have a couple of leads. They went to her home and listened to a couple of interesting messages on her answering machine. One was from an unhappy client who was demanding a refund due to her bad attitude at his wedding reception, and the other was from an unknown man who sounds to be someone who is familiar with her. From what I understand, they taped the messages so someone close to her can listen to the tape to see if the voice can be recognized."

"Is that all?" Rome asked in disappointment.

"That's all so far," Tinisha answered.

"Okay, well we will check back in a few days. I am going to go and take my beautiful wife horseback riding while the day is young. Then, we are going to find a luau for dinner. I'll take some pictures of the pig and send them to your phone."

"No thank you. I can do without," Tinisha laughed at her silly cousin.

"Not even if it has a bright red apple in its mouth?"

"Not even."

With that, the two cousins disconnected their phones, ending the phone call.

As Yolanda and her husband made their way to the horse trail, Romero shared the brief information Tinisha had shared with him.

"Andrea may know someone who knows Mariesha well," Lan offered.

"Why don't you give her a call?"

"I'll call her later after our ride. She's still at work. By the time we get back, she should be home."

Sixteen

Just pulling into her driveway, after having picked up her children from school, Andrea's cell phone began to ring. After checking the caller id, she quickly answered the phone. "Hey, sis. I didn't expect to hear from you so soon. What's going on?"

"Well, the police may have a lead in Mariesha's case, but they are asking if there is someone who may know her well. There was a message left on her answering machine that is causing some questions."

"Okay. Was it a man or a woman who left the message?"

"A man."

"If I am not mistaken, she has an older brother. Let me call Kim and ask her a few questions. I will call you back. Before I go, how is the honeymoon coming along? I hope you guys aren't spending all of your time focusing on Mariesha." Realizing how cold her statement sounded, she added, "Let the police handle it."

"We are having an excellent time. We haven't stopped to discuss the case in any great detail since we got off the airplane. A couple of hours ago, Nisha called to give us an update, so we just want to follow up. We know this is our honeymoon, but we want to make sure Mariesha is okay. Prayerfully, she will be found soon. We are on our way to dinner right now. I will check in with you later to see if Kim knows anything. By the way, how is John? Is he still in ICU?"

"He is in a regular room now, but his collar bone is broken along with some ribs and one of his legs. He is awake, but he will need a few weeks of recovery in the hospital before he can go home. He had some internal injuries as well."

"Wow! Can you believe this happened just before the wedding? Do you think this is an omen, you know a sign that they should not be getting married?"

"I don't know about that. The thought never entered my mind. Kim and John get along so well. I believe they were made for each other."

"Oh, okay. It was just a thought. I will call you later, sis."

"Okay, bye."

As Yolanda thought about Kim and John, she remembered a pair of friends of hers who were married a few years ago. Everyone warned them not to get married because of all the problems they had when they were dating. The man was the jealous type, and the woman had personal insecurities. They were always checking on each other to see if something shady was going on. They never seemed to trust each other. They would argue over the smallest issues, and the guy was constantly berating the woman. But, they insisted on getting married and having a child. Two and a half years later, they divorced and fought over who would have full custody of the child.

About a year after the divorce, they tried to get back together and had a second baby in the interim. They never did remarry. Today, the mother lives alone with the daughter, and the father lives alone with the son. The siblings hardly ever see each other because the parents still do not get along well.

After witnessing such a catastrophe, Romero and Yolanda vowed to not rush into marriage. They wanted an opportunity to get to know each other well and their various tendencies. After waiting two years after Rome proposed, they believe they have built a solid foundation for a marriage. They also understand that marriages are not built overnight, but they take constant commitment.

Each of them had excellent role models. Rome's parents have been married for thirty-five years, and Yolanda's parents have been married nearly thirty years.

Seventeen

Sitting in the precinct early Thursday morning, Arroyo and Finster reviewed their notes and planned to visit Margaret Bloomsdale. They wanted to find out what type of suspicious activity goes on at Mariesha's house.

"Didn't Mrs. Bloomsdale say Mariesha has a brother?"

"Yes, she did. Why?"

"Do you think he could have left the message about the doctor? Think about it, who else would have that information?"

"That makes good sense, but it could have also been a boyfriend with whom she trusted her problem."

"Yes, that could be the case, but we don't have any leads in that direction."

"True. But we don't have any leads about her brother either. We don't even know his name."

"No we don't, but because Mrs. Bloomsdale lives across the street from them, she is sure to know. Shall we pay her a visit?"

"She did say it was okay for us to come back."

The two detectives, full of anticipation of gaining ground on closing the case, headed toward their squad car. It has been six days since Mariesha's disappearance, and she had not returned to the hotel to collect her belongings. So, once the crime lab gathered all the evidence they believed would be beneficial in solving the case, NYPD removed all Mariesha's belongings and permitted the hotel to clean the room.

Upon arriving at Mrs. Bloomsdale's home, the detectives were disappointed to learn they had made a trip for nothing. Mrs. Bloomsdale was not home and was not expected back for at least another week the detectives were told by another neighbor who happened to be pulling into his driveway while the detectives were ringing her doorbell.

"When her grandson picks her up, she usually stays with her daughter's family for at least a week," he had said.

After hearing that news, the detectives felt as though they were rats running around a difficult maze. They could smell the stench of foul play, but the odor was not strong enough to lead them in the right direction.

Just as Finster pulled the unmarked car from the curb, Arroyo's cell phone rang. After quickly checking the caller id, he said, "It's Debbie." Debbie is the crime lab assistant. Her primary responsibility, other than preparing evidence for testing, is to contact police personnel and lawyers to give them the results for any tests run for their cases.

"What do you have for me, Deb?" Arroyo asked, still hopeful for a lead in what had become an almost hopeless case. As he awaited her response, he quickly put the phone on speaker so Finster could listen in.

"I have the results for the blood droppings that were on the key card and room door collected in the Coleman case. The DNA from the blood does not match the hair sample we took from the hair brush or samples from the toothbrush. But, the keycard had two sets of fingerprints on it."

"I'm assuming one set belongs to the victim," Arroyo interjected. "Right, and the other prints, according to AIFIS, belongs to a Kerry Coleman. Once we saw that the last names are the same, we ran the DNA against each other to check the alleles to see if there is a genetic match between the victim and Kerry Coleman, so we could rule out other possible relationships such as husband and wife."

"What did you find?" Arroyo asked anxiously in an attempt to hurry the information along.

"I'm getting to that," Debbie retorted, not pleased at the detective's shortness with her. "Kerry Coleman and Ms. Coleman are siblings." Finster and Arroyo shot each other a quick look and nodded.

"I appreciate the information, Deb. I have a question for you."

"Yeah, go ahead."

"Did the results come back yet on the second toothbrush or the prints from the baggie?"

"Not yet, but soon. If not tonight, I will have them for you first thing tomorrow."

"Okay thanks," Arroyo said before disconnecting the call.

"Well what do you know?" Finster said.

"What are you getting at?" Arroyo asked.

"Obviously, it was her brother who came and interrupted dinner and took her away."

"Hold on; we still don't have an answer for the boy's clothing. The person she could have been struggling with could have been the younger male."

"Mrs. Bloomsdale didn't say anything about a third sibling. She said the parents died and left two children: Mariesha and her older brother. Therefore, the blood was from her older brother who we now know is Kerry Coleman."

"Yeah, I see your point. But if Kerry and Mariesha struggled and he had something to do with her disappearance, who is the younger male and where is he?"

Arroyo did not have an answer for his partner's question. He just sat quietly and stared out the window as he thought of a logical explanation.

Eighteen

In Hawaii, Thursday evening

A soft breeze could be felt coming through the windows, and the sound of laughter could be heard from all the people who were enjoying their vacation on the white sandy beaches. Everything was so calm and peaceful as the moon lit the sky, providing just the right amount of light for a late-night excursion. Hawaii was definitely the island paradise that held up to its reputation.

Inside, cuddling on the couch in the living room of their honeymoon suite, Romero and Yolanda were half watching a movie on cable that neither of them had had a chance to see when it was in theatres. Their bellies were well filled with roasted pork and all the trimmings the locals had prepared for them at the luau.

Besides the faint sounds of voices that came from the beach below, the only voices that could be heard for the last thirty minutes or so were those from the actors in the movie.

Rousing Lan from her light sleep, Romero asked while running his hand through the loose curls in his wife's hair, "How are you enjoying your honeymoon so far, beautiful?"

"It's been absolutely wonderful," she responded. "How has it been for you, honey?"

"I couldn't ask for anything more. I could never have imagined how this time would be with you or how the island would really look. It has definitely surpassed all my expectations. Just having this time alone with you is a dream come true."

"When we reconnected after high school, when I saw you at the restaurant, did you ever think we would go this far?"

"Let me put it this way. I always knew there was something special about you, but I can't say I thought it would lead to marriage at the beginning of our relationship. But as time went on, I knew in my heart that I wanted to spend the rest of my life with you. Not to sound too cliché, but there is a magnetic pull between us that cannot be broken."

"That is so sweet, honey. I hope you know you mean the world to me. I know what you mean about that magnetic pull. I don't think I could break free from you if I wanted to," Yolanda responded as she laid her head on his chest and looked up at him. She admired her husband. He had great mental and physical strength, was very charming, and was deeply sincere. All of these qualities always had a great pull on her emotions and made her desire for him unquenchable.

He felt the same about her. When he looked upon her beautiful face, he felt something flutter within his heart, especially when he had not seen her for a few days. Now, he would have the absolute pleasure of seeing her everyday and touching her in ways that he was never able to touch her before.

As the two lay quietly on the couch, holding each other and trying to make sense of the movie after having missed bits and pieces, Rome suggested they take a walk along the sandy shore. Lan demonstrated her consent by slowly moving toward the bedroom to find something suitable to wear in the evening air. As she was changing from her lounge wear to a short sundress and low-heeled sling-back sandals, her cell phone rang.

Without looking at her caller id, she knew it was Andrea. "I forgot to call Andy back," she yelled out to Rome who was waiting patiently on the couch for her to change.

"I bet that's her now," he responded.

Not taking the time to answer Romero, Lan answered her sister's call.

As the lovebirds walked along the shore, Lan filled Rome in on the small amount of information that Kim was able to give Andrea. Mariesha does have an older brother who practically raised her after their parents died in an airplane crash when she was a little girl. Her brother is nearly ten years older than she is, and he was given custody of her because their grandparents lived in a different state and were quite elderly. Both their mother and father were only children, so there were no aunts or uncles to take them in.

Kim did not know how to contact Mariesha's brother, but at least she was able to provide his name: Kerry Coleman.

"Do you mind if I call Rafael and give him this information, so he can contact Detectives Arroyo and Finster in the morning?" Romero asked his wife.

"Of course not. I don't know how far they can get with his name, but I am sure every bit of information that we get will move us closer to finding out what is going on."

"You would be surprised how far a name can take you."

After speaking to his cousin's husband and relaying the information, Rome learned the two detectives had already learned from Mariesha's neighbor about her brother. However, the neighbor did not give them his name. When Rafael had spoken to the detectives earlier that morning, they were preparing to go to visit the neighbor to try to get more information.

Unfortunately, he had not had an opportunity to get in contact with them afterwards because he spent the day with his wife, daughter and in-laws. He assured Rome, however, that he would get in contact with the detectives soon.

Nineteen

New York

On Friday morning, Rafael made it a point to call Detective Finster to let him know the name of Mariesha's brother. Before Raf could reveal what he considered crucial information that could cause a break in the case, Detective Finster filled Raf in on all that was learned the day before. After completing the call with Rafael, Finster moved to his next step: obtaining a phone number or address for the brother. When he and Arroyo had gone through Mariesha's home, they saw no evidence that he still lived with her.

After locating Kerry's address, Arroyo and Finster decided to drop in for a surprise visit. Not knowing what to expect and the reasons for the apparent controversy between the siblings, back up was requested. Immediately, eight additional squad cars were dispatched to Mr. Coleman's home.

Meanwhile, the Salisburys headed to the airport to catch a flight back to California. As Rafael, Tinisha and Jasmine made themselves comfortable in their seats as the pilot prepared for take-off, Raf's cell phone rang. Noticing an incoming call from the 213 area code, Raf answered, "Lieutenant Salisbury."

"Lieutenant Salisbury, how are you?" a voice asked.

"I'm doing well. To whom am I speaking?"

"Lieutenant Salisbury, this is Mayor Villaraigosa."

"Yes sir. How are you?"

"I'm doing just fine. I understand you and your family are on vacation, so I will make this brief. Due to the untimely death of Captain Ramsey a few weeks ago, we must install an interim captain. We can no longer delay the inevitable."

"I understand, sir," Raf responded when the mayor took a pause.

"Lieutenant Salisbury, it would be an extreme honor if you would serve as interim captain. Can we count on you officer?"

Hearing the instructions on the plane's speakers to cease all cell phone use, Raf immediately said, "Yes, sir. You can count on me. I will report for duty right after we land at LAX later today."

"I'll see you then. I will make it a point to stop by the station. Thank you."

"It's my pleasure, sir." Before Raf could share the news with Tinisha, Jasmine asked, "Who was that, Daddy?"

"That was the Los Angeles mayor offering Daddy a promotion. Right, honey?" Tinisha asked with a smile.

"What's a promotion?" Jasmine wanted to know. The trip home for the Salisburys was like a game of 'question and answer' until Jasmine fell asleep.

Twenty

At the Honolulu Airport

Once again aboard a 757 Boeing Jet, the newlyweds had concluded their honeymoon and were returning home. After the twelve-hour flight, it would be nightfall when the couple landed. Both were looking forward to their first night together at home. Also, they were anxious to get updates on Mariesha's disappearance and the escrow of their new home.

In New York, Detectives Arroyo and Finster, along with the additional set of officers who would provide any needed support, were standing outside Kerry Coleman's front door. With guns drawn, Finster rang the doorbell. Almost immediately, the front door swung open. To Mr. Coleman's surprise, a total of fifteen uniformed and plain-closed officers surrounded his home. Startled, Mr. Coleman stepped back inside just as quickly as he had stepped out. In the process, he dropped his cell phone that had been up to his ear. He was obviously on a call with someone.

To prevent him from closing the door, one of the uniformed police officers placed his foot inside the door well.

"What's the problem?" Kerry exclaimed with his hands extended upwards.

"Are you Mr. Coleman?" Finster questioned.

"Yes, I am."

"Mr. Kerry Coleman?" Finster asked for clarity.

"Yes! Yes! What is going on?" Kerry nearly begged.

Noticing the bandage on Kerry's arm and the small amount of blood that had seeped through, Finster proceeded with his line of questioning. "What happened to your arm?"

"I was cut," Kerry quickly responded.

"Mr. Coleman, we are here regarding the disappearance of Mariesha Coleman. Can you tell us how you know her?"

"Mariesha is my sister. What do you mean disappearance?"

"Ms. Coleman was last seen at the Hampton Inn & Suites last Friday night in Rosalito's just after someone who matches your description interrupted dinner." As Finster answered Kerry's questions, he showed him the police sketch that was drawn based on the physical description that Rafael and Tinisha had provided along with a warrant to search the premises. Finster then motioned for the uniformed officers and other detectives to go inside the residence to do a search for Mariesha.

Realizing his privacy was about to be seriously invaded, Kerry, with his hands on the sides of his head, said, "There is a mistake. Mariesha is not missing. She is with Dr. Segorian."

"How do we know that you are telling us the truth? From the scene in her hotel room, there was a struggle and the evidence proves you were involved." At Finster's words, Kerry suddenly remembered he had dropped his cell phone. Before bending down to get it, he pointed to it and asked if it was okay to retrieve it from its place on the porch. Arroyo reached down, picked it up, noticed the call was still live, and handed the phone to Kerry.

"Dr. Segorian," Kerry began saying into the phone, "there is an officer here who needs to ask you a question." Kerry handed the phone to Finster and said, "Ask him if Mariesha is there." Finster spoke briefly with Dr. Segorian and confirmed her brother's statement. Mariesha was currently with him, but he would not say how long she had been there or the reason why.

Finster quickly called the officers out of the home and released them. He and Arroyo took Kerry inside to get a full explanation of what was going on. However, they did fully intend to make a personal visit to Dr. Segorian's clinic to see Mariesha for themselves and ensure her safe condition.

After spending nearly an hour with Kerry, Detectives Arroyo and Finster left his home with Dr. Segorian's address and a full account of the last twenty years of Kerry and Mariesha's life.

When Mariesha was thirteen years old and Kerry was twenty-three, their parents were killed in a tragic airplane crash. Kerry was awarded custody of his younger sister. She was to remain in his care until she became eighteen years old.

One night while Kerry was working, Jeremy one of Kerry's friends stopped by their house. Because Mariesha knew Jeremy, she let him come inside. He told her Kerry knew he was coming by and he was to meet him when he came home. Mariesha had an early day at school the next morning, so she decided to turn in early and left Jeremy in the living room watching television.

After having been in bed for about thirty minutes, Mariesha heard someone coming into her bedroom. She couldn't see the person's face due to the darkness in the room, but as the person drew closer, she knew from his smell that the person was her brother's friend whom she had let into the house just moments before. She asked him what he wanted, and the only word he said was "You."

When Kerry returned home from work, he checked on his sister as he did every night, whether or not he went to work. To his astonishment, his sister was not in the condition that he had left her. He found her huddled in a corner, in a pool of blood. She had been brutally raped and beaten. She was only fourteen years old.

He immediately called 911. The police arrived and took her statement. The ambulance arrived and took her to the emergency room.

Before arriving at the hospital, Kerry searched the local pubs for Jeremy until he found him. He was on a desperate search to avenge the harm committed upon his sister. When he found his so-called friend, he beat him until he was unrecognizable and near death.

Immediately afterwards, Kerry went to the hospital to check on Mariesha. Shortly after his arrival, the police showed up and arrested Kerry for assault. His friend was also arrested for rape of a minor and assault. His friend was later sentenced to jail, but Kerry was given leniency by the judge.

As time went on, Mariesha, who had been withdrawn and sullen, seemed to become more jovial, but she was never quite the same as she had been before her ordeal. She had always been a carefree, light-hearted child, even after her parents' deaths, which had a tremendous impact on her life. Her tight-knit family of four suddenly became a parent-less family of two. However, Mariesha had managed to cope as she emotionally clung to her brother who then played the role of mother, father, and big brother to her. She had continued to do well in school and in her extracurricular activities. After she was violated, she became a different person. But that's putting it mildly.

Eventually, even though Mariesha had graduated from high school, had begun college, and was technically an adult, Kerry thought it best to have his sister begin to see a therapist. At first, Mariesha convinced Kerry that is was just his imagination and that she was fine. She tried to convince him further by passing her classes with good grades and attempting to have a social life.

At one time, she even began dating a very sociable and well-educated young man from their church named Frederick. As Frederick and Mariesha grew closer, or so Fred thought, Fred tried to kiss Mariesha while out on a date at a movie theatre. Instead of Mariesha responding in kind, she quickly raised her hand and slapped Fred, leaving a bruise on his left cheek. There was no denying what she had done; the evidence spoke for itself.

After this incident, Mariesha agreed to therapy. Over the next five years, Mariesha was seen by at least six different therapists. For one reason or another, she did not get along with the therapists or either the therapists refused to attempt to engage with her any further. This was very frustrating to Kerry, but Mariesha was very nonchalant about it all.

Finally, after seeing Dr. Segorian once a month for two years, she was diagnosed with Multiple Personality Disorder. Shortly afterward, Dr. Segorian had recommended psychotherapy, so the four personalities could be merged into one.

One of the personalities was a scared ten-year-old girl named Ree-Ree who would come forth when a frightening situation presented itself. It could be something very simple, but Mariesha would feel as if her life was in danger. For example, if Mariesha was riding in a car and the driver swerved to avoid an object or another car, Mariesha would covered her eyes and peeked through her fingers. This childlike behavior was a clear sign that Ree-Ree had surfaced. Also, her voice took on a childlike tone.

The second personality was Candi, a tough sex kitten who enjoyed S&M. The description speaks for itself. In order to be in control and to prevent being controlled, Candi would choose the men she wanted to date rather than allowing them to choose her. She never wanted to be in the role of a victim by being used to fulfill someone's fantasy who did not have genuine emotions for her. The truth of the matter was she never allowed anyone to get close enough for her to find out.

The third personality was not clearly identified as male or female, and the fourth was a thirteen-year-old boy. After Mariesha was raped, she spent a lot of time thinking if she was a boy, Jeremy would not have been interested in her. Thus, the fourth personality was created.

The fourteen-year-old boy and the sex kitten were the most dominate personalities. That was why Mariesha had the weird lingerie and the boy's clothes and backpack amongst her belongings. These were items she kept with her during most of her travels. That is also why Yolanda noticed changes in her voice and personality from time to time. And, that is why some of her clients complained about her while others praised her talents. When her alters took over, she would cease being the professional wedding planner and she would become someone completely different, who cared about nothing and no one.

When Dr. Segorian had recommended the two-week psychotherapy, Mariesha consented after her brother's constant nagging and insistence. However, when the time came, she completely ignored her commitment to her healing. So, Kerry located her in the Hamptons and forced her to go with him. He took her to Dr. Segorian and signed her in. This was pre-consented by Mareisha herself when she initially had agreed to the therapy.

Prior to leaving Mr. Coleman, Finster once again inquired about Mr. Coleman's arm. Kerry informed the detectives that Candi has surfaced during his encounter with his sister. Candi has a strong personality and can, at times, be violent. In an attempt to resist her brother's threats of taking her from the hotel, Candi pulled Kerry's pocket knife from its holster on Kerry's belt and began swinging it violently. Kerry was cut in the process as he tried to defend himself and keep from harming his sister at the same time.

Twenty-One

When Rome and his bride landed at the airport back in New York, they both turned on their cell phones to check their messages. After listening to his messages, Rome learned there was a break in Mariesha's case: She was safe with her therapist. He was invited to stop by the Hampton Station of the NYPD to get further details. Also, Kerry Coleman's phone number was left on his voicemail in case he wanted to obtain first-hand information about Mariesha.

When Yolanda checked her voicemail, she had an urgent message from her sister Andrea. Earlier that day, Margaret, their mother, had been rushed to the emergency room at Coler-Goldwater Memorial Hospital. Upon hearing her sister's message, Lan began to hyperventilate. She had a sickening feeling in the pit of her stomach. "Oh my God!" she gasped.

"What is it?" Rome asked.

"It's my mom. We need to get over to Memorial right away."

Rome found his wife a place to sit as she called Andrea to find out what was going on with their mother. Rome quickly collected their luggage and returned to get Yolanda, so they could catch the shuttle to the parking garage. They had left their car in the long-term parking before going to the private airport to catch the jet to the island.

When Rome returned to Lan, he asked, "What did she say?"

"She only said to hurry up and get there," Lan answered between sobs.

The drive to the hospital was pretty quiet, except for the few minutes when Rome shared the information about Mariesha's whereabouts. Arriving at the hospital, Rome pulled the Rover up to the emergency room doors. Lan jumped out before waiting for the vehicle to come to a complete stop. Andrea was waiting outside. With hands interlocked, the sisters rushed into the emergency room doors.

"Mom has Cancer, Lan," Andy began.

"What?" Lan asked in bewilderment.

"Listen, she has Lung Cancer, and it has really begun to spread."

"How long have you known, Andy?" Lan asked while looking her sister straight in her eyes. At that point, the two sisters were standing outside their mother's door. Andrea knew that was not the time to explain or protest about not having told Yolanda sooner. She quickly answered her sister's question. "Two months."

"I assume because of the wedding Dad, Mom, and you decided not to tell me."

"Yes, we thought it best."

"Okay, I'm going in." When Yolanda resisted arguing with her sister about how unfair it was to keep her in the dark, Andrea didn't know whether to follow her sister into the room and expect a balling out later or what.

Inside, Lan, bypassing her father and the on-duty nurse, went directly to her mother's side and took her hand. Seeing her mother with an oxygen mask on and various tubes protruding from her arms caused Lan's heart to be gripped with fear. She had never seen her mother in any other condition than in good health. To say the least, she was terrified of the possibilities of what may happen next. She slowly looked up to search for her father's eyes to see if they held a look of peace, despair or desperation.

From a child, she could usually read concern on her father's face. Today though, his look was one of uncertainty. Without realizing she was speaking, she suddenly spoke. "What are the doctors saying? What is her prognosis?" As her questions seemed to hang in the air, tears began to stream down Yolanda's face. After about a minute of silence and looking from her father to the nurse and back again, the nurse answered, "Dr. Jones will be in shortly to answer any questions you have."

While Lan and her father waited, they held hands and prayed. Meanwhile, Andrea entered the room, and Romero entered shortly after. Approximately ten minutes later, Dr. Jones came in. He filled Yolanda and Romero in on Margaret's condition and provided the details of the treatment she would undergo once she was stabilized. The doctor's report was very hopeful as the treatment success rate was encouragingly high.

After Margaret's oxygen mask was removed and she was stabilized, Yolanda and Rome left for home. Feeling much better about her mother's condition, Yolanda thought it best to get her husband home although she was certain that he would not have minded staying at the hospital as long as needed.

Twenty-Two

Los Angeles

Late Friday afternoon, after taking his wife and daughter home and putting on a tailored dark blue suit, Lt. Salisbury went directly to the precinct. He was excited to be home again and amongst his fellow officers. Upon stepping only one foot inside the front door, Rafael began to hear sounds of clapping and cheers. Without asking, he knew the applause was for him. His heart beamed with pride even though he knew his 'promotion' was temporary. With a large grin spread across his face, he welcomed the congratulations, the hugs, and the smiles that all the employees offered him. He definitely felt the warmth and love of his work family.

Raf eventually made his way to his desk, gathered his materials, and walked to the debriefing room. He was anxious to speak to Detectives Malone, Stabler, Benson, and Morgan in person about any developments that were made in the Burlingstein Case.

The four detectives sat with somber looks on their faces. They knew Lt./Captain Salisbury would not be happy with the report they were about to render. They had not only *not* solved the case and brought the criminals to justice, but there had also been new developments. Last week, there had been another string of murders at four Burlingstein locations. At 10pm last Tuesday, two other Burlingstein locations had been 'hit'. A store manager at each store had been murdered. At 9:45pm the following Friday, two additional Burlingstein locations had been 'hit'. Although all four detectives deeply desired to have case closers and prevent more senseless deaths, they had received no viable clues as to who was committing the crimes. The only thing that was apparent was there was a crew of murderers. This was obvious because the murders were being committed at the same time at two different locations. Therefore, there were at least two killers, one operating at each location. At this point, the only thing the four detectives could do was further investigate.

Twenty-Three

New York

On Saturday morning, Romero dropped Yolanda at the hospital and took a drive to Dr. Segorian's clinic to see Mariesha. He was meeting Detectives Arroyo and Finster there who had come over to the mainland to check things out and close the case. It was Dr. Segorian's policy that patients had no visitors during the duration of their therapy treatment. Due to the special circumstances, Dr. Segorian permitted Romero and the officers five minutes with Mariesha, but he stayed in the room the entire time.

Rome verified her identity for the officers, and they asked her a few routine questions about her being there of her own free will. Once the detectives were satisfied, they considered the Coleman case closed and departed the facility. Rome said his goodbyes to Mariesha, and she responded in kind although she was very solemn and appeared to be medicated.

Rome was happy to know that Mariesha was receiving the help she needed for her emotional and psychological well being although his heart was a little heavy from knowing what she had endured and the damaging effects of it.

When Rome returned to the hospital, Margaret's condition had improved enough for her to be moved from ICU. Her chemo treatments were scheduled to begin Monday.

For now, all was as well as could be expected.

Epilogue

(After some time had passed)

Tinisha

A few months later, a meeting was held by Snyder and Beckman with all lawyers, staff, and interns. During the meeting, two partners were announced. Oliver Donaldson was announced as a full partner, and Tinisha Salisbury was announced as the new junior partner.

Margaret

After completing two six-week stints of chemotherapy, Margaret had experienced hair loss along with considerable weight loss. However, the growth of the cancer cells had been extinguished, and her prognosis was looking good.

Rafael

Rafael enjoyed his experience as interim captain. He saw a lot and learned a lot. However, as time passed, it was essential to the operation of the LAPD Hollywood Division that a permanent captain be installed. Lieutenant Robert Swanson earned the promotion.

Romero & Yolanda

Raheem decided to stop in on the newlywed couple to deliver the key to their new home. Lan was in the kitchen at the condo when she heard the doorbell ring. As she walked towards the door, Rome, who had also heard the doorbell, was descending the stairs. Consequently, they both arrived at the door at the same time. Not having seen each other for the last hour, they laughed and briefly kissed as they saw on another. Yolanda yielded as her husband answered the door. When Lan heard Raheem's voice, she came around from behind the door. Dangling from Raheem's hand was a pair of keys.

Rome and Lan automatically knew what that meant. After Rome retrieved the keys from Raheems fingertips, he and Lan hugged each other in the spirit of pure joy. The escrow on their home had closed!

Mariesha

After Mariesha's two-week psychotherapy treatment, Dr. Segorian noticed vast improvements. However, he felt only two of the four personalities had merged. The two dominant personalities, Candi, the sex kitten, and Marty, the fourteen-year-old boy, could still be seen from time to time. Psychotherapy had different levels. Dr. Segorian was sure that he had prescribed the therapy that would rectify two mild personalities and two controlling ones.

However, after witnessing the results during Mariesha's therapy sessions that occurred once a week for the next couple of months, Dr. Segorian decided it would be best to schedule another two-week therapy treatment.

Mariesha readily agreed as she had noticed a change in herself. She liked the way she felt. She didn't experience memory lapse as often, and she felt balanced in her spirit.

After the second psychotherapy treatment session, Dr. Segorian was secure that all personalities had merged well together. Mariesha was developing well into a no-nonsense, fun-individual. Also, she began to interact better with Kerry, as she had unknowingly held him responsible for what had happened to her nearly twenty years ago. Once he understood all that had transpired with his sister, he was able to be more understanding and nurturing as he continued to play the role of mother, father, and brother.

The
Preacher's
Daughter
Dr. Cassundra White-Elliott

The Preacher's Daughter is a work of fiction and is a creation that stems purely from the writer's imagination. Any resemblance to actual events or persons is purely coincidental.

Published by CLF Publishing, LLC

ISBN 978-1-4507-1078-7

Printed in the United States of America.

Dedications

This book is dedicated in the memory of my mother
Gloria "Punkin" Harrison.
(March 26, 1952-March 7, 2010)

I also dedicate this book to all who have ever tried to find their way and to those who may still be searching.
Be encouraged. You will get there!

Saturday

The weather was nice and pleasantly warm for mid-August when Tinisha finally arose in the late afternoon. She thought it would be best to stay home this weekend and get some much-needed rest and relaxation. If she had a change of heart, there were a million things that she could do rather than staying inside the house. She could go shopping with her girlfriends, go visit her mom, invite her dad to lunch, or go relax at the spa. The list of possibilities was endless.

But her week had been very full and eventful- to say the least. On Monday and Tuesday, ten new clients were added to the law firm's client list that Tinisha had been clerking at for the last couple of years. After meeting with each new client and gathering the necessary information for the initial consultation, she made a file for each one. This caused her to stay an extra two hours at the office both days.

Dealing with new clients and hearing about their cases usually proved to be exciting. However, this time many of the clients came in with chips on their shoulders and seemed to want to take their troubles out on Tinisha and the other clerks at the firm. Tinisha did all that she could to treat the clients nicely, even though she had to excuse herself to the ladies' room a few times to calm her nerves. She wondered if this is what she would have to endure when she became a lawyer or if she would have a clerk like herself to take the heat.

Patsy Macintyre, one of the new clients, had come to the law firm because she was being sued for sideswiping a vehicle on the highway. She was angry because her car was hit by an eighteen wheeler, and as she tried to avoid the impact of the eighteen-wheeler, she swerved to the left and sideswiped a Jeep Cherokee. Even though she walked away without a bruise or scratch, her Range Rover was not as lucky. The passenger door needed to be replaced, along with other body repair. She was very perturbed by the entire event, and it showed in every stroke of the pen she made to the application. Patsy's biggest hurt was that the Range Rover was an anniversary gift from her husband, and she had only had it for two days.

Then on Wednesday night, Tinisha ended up having to work overtime on her night job at the club, because one of the other girls did not show up. She didn't enjoy working at the club, but it helped with the bills. Actually, it more than helped with the bills. It paid the bills and then some. She decided working was a better route than running up a lot more student loans. She had taken out her fair share when she earned her undergrad degree.

That night, she didn't get home until three am. That means she was only able to get four hours of sleep before she had to get up and start her day all over again.

Every morning by eight, Tinisha arrives at the law firm. She is completing her internship for law school. When she first started her internship, she was only able to go to the firm a couple of days a week, but now she is required to go five days so that she can acquire the necessary hours to complete the last part of her program.

On Thursday night, Tinisha's boss asked her to work late again at the club. She had to refuse. It wasn't that she couldn't use the money. Oh, quite the contrary. She had her eye on a sexy little number down at Nordstrom's that she wanted to add to her wardrobe. The fact is she has been feeling worn out lately. She is only twenty-six, and according to her parents, she should be full of energy. Putting in hours at the firm in the mornings, attending classes in the afternoons and on some evenings, and working at night is enough to wear anyone out. Not to mention Sundays.

Every Sunday, I have to be at church or I will hear Daddy's mouth, Tinisha thought. It's not that I don't love the Lord or enjoy going to church. Believe me, I do. Worshipping God is a big part of my life. Sometimes I just need a break. Don't misunderstand me. I don't need a break from God, but from Sunday service and church work. Sometimes, I need an extra day to sleep in from a busy week before I begin the next week. Oh, that reminds me; I have to get some things together for the Youth Department.

Speaking of the youth department, Daddy used to ask me over and over again for about a year to take over as the Youth Department leader. The last youth leader we had ended up going to prison for child molestation, after he was found with kiddy porn in his possession. So, I can understand Dad's apprehension about placing someone as a leader over our children. My suggestion was for him to run a background check on any potential volunteers, but his suggestion was for me to be the leader and then he would not need to run a background check.

Having this discussion with Daddy wasn't easy, but this is one of the few times that I managed to stand up to my dad and not give in to his persistent demands. Lately, he hasn't been asking me to head the Youth Department because he knows I have a full-time load with all the law classes and the internship. Don't get me wrong; my dad is my number one supporter, along with my mom. He just really wants me to be more active in the church. I think because he never had a son, he sees me as the one who will take over his legacy. But that's his dream, not mine.

Well, I guess I will turn on the news. I don't remember watching the news all this week. I'm sure it will be business as usual. You know the nightly display of all the depressing things that are going on in the world today. Oh, I am just in time to see a breaking news story.

> *An unidentified woman's body was found today in a dumpster behind a Hollywood club called "Pink Panties." The police have stated that her body was in the dumpster for 2-3 days before she was discovered. The police have not released any photos and will not do so until the woman has been identified and the next of kin has been notified. We will keep you updated on any new developments in this startling event. If anyone has any information, please call the Los Angeles Police Department toll free at 877-555-0010.*

That poor girl! I don't know what goes through people's minds. I wonder whose bad side she got on or if this was a random act of violence. You know a case of being in the wrong place at the wrong time.

Just as I thought, nothing but a bunch of depressing news. Maybe I will just take a nap. When I wake up, I will make myself a bite to eat.

Thirty minutes later, just as Tinisha found herself falling comfortably into a deep sleep, the phone jarred her awake. "I wonder who is calling," she said softly to herself as she reached for the phone.

"Hello?" she answered wearily.

"Hey, Nisha! I hope I didn't wake you. I know you had a long week."

"Oh, hey babe," Tinisha responded groggily. "I was just getting into my nap; I just laid down a little while ago. I thought you had to work tonight."

"Actually, I am at work. Um, I need to ask you a question."

"It must be pretty important because you hardly ever call while you are at work. What is it?"

"It's about one of the ladies that works with you."

"Okay. Which one?"

"The real dark one with the blonde hair and blue fingernails."

"Rafael, are you trying to set her up with one of your cop buddies? What did I tell you about that?" Tinisha yelled, getting a little perturbed.

"No, no! Tinisha, just calm down. It's nothing like that."

"Okay, well what is it? Stop stalling."

"Give me a minute. This isn't easy to say, especially over the phone."

"Oh my goodness, Rafael! Is something wrong with her?"

"When was the last time you saw her?"

"Um, on Sunday. She came to our church.
She was supposed to be at work on Tuesday night but she didn't show up all week from what I heard. And I
don't think she called in either. Why are you asking?"

"Did you hear about the woman that was found in the dumpster behind the club down the street from where you work?"

"Yeah, I just heard it on the news."

"I think it's her, but she didn't have any I.D. on her or a purse. We don't have any leads nor do we know who to contact. Right now, she is just a Jane Doe."

"So what do you need me to do?"

"I was wondering if you could come down to the coroner's office."

"What? Oh my goodness. I don't want to see a dead body!"

"Ok, Tinisha. Calm down. I just thought….."

After catching her breath, Tinisha said, "Okay, I know Rafael. I didn't mean to overreact. Give me ten minutes to throw on a sweat suit. I will be right there."

Tinisha had a no-nonsense personality. She was not the type to joke around non-sensibly. She knew how to have fun, but fun had its place. When it was time to handle business, all joking and playing around was placed on the back burner. The far back burner. The one that was hard to see. In all seriousness, she had the characteristics of an excellent lawyer. She would do well in establishing her cases and presenting them in court.

Sunday

I can't believe that I actually heard the alarm this morning. When I got home from the coroner's office last night, I couldn't move another muscle. I didn't stop to eat. I didn't shower. I didn't wrap my hair. I just fell into bed. I probably fell asleep before my head was deep into the pillow. Even though I fell asleep right away, I only slept on and off. I couldn't get the image of Robin's face out of my mind. I was praying that it wasn't her all the way to the coroner's
office. Rafael met me there. But even with him there,
I was still nervous.

The process of identifying her body didn't take long. I walked into the cold room and followed the coroner over to the wall of drawers and waited for him to open the one that held her body. As he pulled the sheet back, I held my breath and closed my eyes. Then I heard Rafael ask me to look. Slowly, I opened my eyes and right away I knew it was Robin. Tears immediately sprang from my eyes as a million questions flooded my mind. Of all the questions that I had, I really wanted to know who could have done this and why.

I know Robin was a little eccentric, with her platinum blonde hair and her long midnight blue fingernails, but she had a promising future. She was a pre-med student at UCLA and was looking forward to beginning med school next term. She was planning to enter the world of medicine, following in the footsteps of her father, mother, and older brother. Who was going to call her family? I must have asked that question aloud because I heard Rafael say that he or one of the other detectives would be assigned to notify the next of kin.

While slowly driving home, down a virtually empty interstate, I kept blinking back tears while thinking *I'm glad she gave her life to Christ; I'm glad she gave her life to Christ; I'm glad she gave her life to Christ.*

Sitting in church this morning, the same thought went through my mind as I found myself staring at the seat Robin sat in just last week. I was remembering her tell me how she wanted to join our church and the choir. She asked me, "Do you think your dad will let me sing in the choir?" I laughed and said, "Girl, just because my dad is the pastor doesn't mean that he makes all those decisions. Talk to the minister of music Samuel Rockford. And if you really are any good, he may let you sing on one of his cds that he will be releasing soon."

I was remembering how we laughed, when the sound of my father's voice jarred me from my daydream.

"Tinisha, did you bring the banners for the Youth Department Revolution?"

"Yes, Daddy. They are in the trunk of my car. I was just on my way to get them so the ushers can hang them up."

"Okay, sweetheart. After church today, I am going to have a brief meeting with the finance committee, so I will be a little late going to see your mother. Do you want to wait for me or meet me there?"

"I will meet you there. I had a long week, so I probably won't stay at the convalescent home too long."

Pastor Oglebee, who is commonly referred to as Pastor O, is a mild-mannered gentleman of fifty-two. He is twice his daughter's age. He stands 5'10", a little over half a foot taller than his wife who is 5'2". He isn't as lean as he used to be five years ago, but he is yet very handsome and still in good physical condition. His gentle and warm smile is welcomed weekly by the members and the visitors alike. They love to see his pearly white teeth that sit in two perfect rows. He still has a full head of hair that he keeps cut low. He does not wear flashy suits with loud colors, like some of the members. All of his suits are tailored by Mario von Gutten and are either a dark shade or a light shade with none falling in between.

I must say that service was awesome today. The choir ushered in the presence of the Holy Spirit, and I must have sung and shouted myself hoarse. Dad preached a powerful message on "Being Rooted in the Faith." I believe the spirits of the people were uplifted. We are living in trying times, and there is trouble on every hand. People are losing their jobs and even people's careers are not as secure as the world would have them believe. Job losses equal no income, and that leads to loss of homes and even perpetuates homelessness.

Not only are there economic problems, but due to the unexpectedness of these types of events, people are taking their own lives and even those of their loved ones. The only thing that we can do when we have done all that is within our limited human power is to stand on the word of God. I have heard my father preach that message year after year after year after year. I believe that the word of God is true. I also believe that I must do my part in securing my destiny. Some people may not agree with my choices, like working at the club or even working hard to become a lawyer rather than a minister like my father desires. But you know what? They are just that- my choices. I am the one who has to live with myself and the choices that I have made.

After leaving church, Tinisha immediately headed over to the convalescent home to visit her mother, as she had done every Sunday for the past four months. Engrossed in her own thoughts, Tinisha drove on autopilot most of the way there.

I am glad that the convalescent home is in between church and home, Tinisha thought. I am even more tired now than when I awoke this morning. I must have exerted all of the little energy that I had during the morning worship service. After I stop by and visit mom for a little while, I am going directly home. I really, really, really need to get some rest. Rafael wants to take me to dinner after his shift. I think I may ask him to pick up something on his way over instead. Red Lobster's shrimp pasta and award-winning biscuits sound good. And maybe a little shrimp scampi on the side to top everything off.

Ok, let me focus on Mom for now. I am going to take her Sunday dinner. Sometimes I take her homemade food, but today the old Colonel, Mr. KFC himself, will have to do.

After pulling into the parking lot, Tinisha slowly pulled out her makeup bag and touched up her makeup. She didn't want it to be so obvious that she was worn out from this week's activities and the finding of Robin's body. She did not want her mother to worry about her. She wanted her mom to focus on getting well so that she could go home soon. After applying her makeup, Tinisha took a couple sips of her energy drink before stepping out of the car.

Walking into the convalescent home gave Tinisha an eerie feeling. It wasn't that the place wasn't well kept. It just wasn't home. It was a beautiful facility with gold light fixtures and walnut trim around the windows and doorways. Each room was decorated differently from the others, giving it a special touch. Each room was wallpapered or had border around the walls that matched the furniture and the carpet. The beautiful décor made the guests feel as though they were vacationing in a five-star resort rather than simply at a place to receive medical care.

As soon as she laid her eyes on her mother, her spirits were immediately uplifted. She was glad she had come even in her state of fatigue. She loved being in the company of her mother.

"Hi, mom. Aren't you looking beautiful today?"

"Oh sweetheart, how nice of you to come."

"Mom, you know Daddy and I come to visit you every Sunday. I am sorry that I didn't make it on Thursday. I had to work late Wednesday night, and I was really tired. But I brought you the new Rotisserie chicken from KFC. It's actually pretty good."

"Well, girlfriend spread it out. You don't need to wait for an invitation," her mom replied with laughter in her voice.

"It's good to see that you still have your sense of humor, Mom."

"Oh yeah. Some things never change. While I eat, fill me in on what's been going on since I saw you last Sunday."

Delores Ann Oglebee was born Delores Ann Turner. She is a high-spirited and fun-loving lady. She loves to keep people on their toes and smiling. She always has a clever joke to tell and demonstrates a good sense of humor. Tinisha cannot remember a time when she witnessed her mom being angry. Delores' philosophy is "Love thy neighbor as thy love thyself."

Delores has a petite frame and still has most of the curves of her mid-adult life although she has graciously turned fifty, making her two years younger than her husband. She maintains her figure by engaging in a cardiovascular workout three times a week. As a retired third-grade teacher, she has a lot of free time on her hands. Many people mistake Delores for a younger woman because of her physique and her long hair. Many women her age have cut their girlish locks, but not Delores. She says as long as she can style it and it does not become too thin, she will let it flow around her shoulders.

After spending an hour with her mom, Tinisha once again began to feel the pressures of the past week on her body. She decided that she really needed to get some rest before she jumped into another long week. After leaving her mom, she thought about how she avoided telling her about Robin. She knew if she gave any information, her mom would undoubtedly have questions and her mind would be fast at work.

Mom has always been an amateur detective, always managing to put the pieces of any puzzle together, Tinisha thought. I wasn't ready for her to know the intimate details of my job. As a matter of fact, I am not sure I ever want her to know. And I definitely didn't want to give her a reason to worry about me.

After pondering her purposeful evasiveness, she thought about what her mother said about some things never changing. The same can be said about some people, Tinisha surmised.

At church, we have had some of the same members since I was a little girl, Tinisha thought as she turned down her street. And some of them have been acting the same way for over twenty years. Take Deacon Steinbeck for example. He is one of our few deacons who have been around since my dad organized the church twenty-three years ago. Deacon Steinbeck is faithful to the church, and I know he supports my dad's ministry no matter what. It would take the entire Raider football team to tear him away and then some. Even though Deacon Steinbeck has been faithful to our church, I can't say the same for his roving eyes and hands. He has a habit of planting wet kisses on all the ladies' cheeks. And believe me, he is no respecter of persons. It doesn't matter if you are short or tall, skinny or fat. If you are female, expect to get a kiss and a hug. And I don't mean one of those innocent church hugs. He will squeeze you so tight you will wonder if he is your long lost grandfather. Other than the unholy kisses and the bear hugs, I guess Deacon Steinbeck is not so bad. He's a lonely old man looking for love. In all the wrong places!

Then we have Sister Lola, better known to some as Loose Lips Lola. She can't hold water even if it is frozen into a solid block of ice. That's just another way of saying if you tell her a secret, one way or another she is going to let it slip. Let me explain. When Bro and Sis Walden were having their first baby, somehow Sis Lola found out that Bro Walden was not the proud daddy of his wife's baby. Before long the entire church found out. But what she didn't know was that Bro Walden had suffered a terrible accident while enlisted in the armed forces, and he was unable to father children. So, other measures had to be taken for his wife to bear children. This was a private and personal matter that was meant to be only between husband and wife. But with Lola's help, the story was twisted and turned. The damage of Sis Lola's rumors had tried to be corrected but what was done was done, and the couple ended up leaving the church.

These are a couple of the tasteless events involving members at our church, but we also have members that we would be sorry to see go. Take Brother Neal for example. Bro. Neal has only been with us for a few years, but since the time he set foot in the church doors, he has been faithful to everything he set his hands to. He takes care of all the building maintenance and the lawn care. He also oversees the men's ministry. Occasionally, when one of Dad's armor bearers is unavailable, Bro. Neal will step in without question. He is truly a blessing to the ministry and to the work of the Lord.

Then there is Sis. Brenda. She, like Bro. Neal, is a faithful member of our church. Whenever, a ministry leader needs a helping hand, Sis. Brenda is there to help out, even if she isn't part of that particular ministry. She definitely has the gift of helps. She works without complaining and without trying to find fault with someone. She loves the Lord and His people, and it is shown by her every act of kindness.

Spending a quiet evening with Tinisha last night was great. I know she was extremely exhausted because she fell asleep on the couch right after she finished her shrimp pasta. She has been working really hard lately, but I know that all of her hard work will pay off soon. Her internship is almost over, and she will be taking the bar exam in a couple of months.

This is just another hurdle that she has to cross. In the past three years that we have been dating, I have seen Tinisha take on numerous tasks. I am proud to say that she has brought them all to completion. I have never witnessed anyone, other than my mother, who has had so much tenacity and is self driven. She and Nisha would have gotten along well. Tinisha really makes me proud to know her. Not only is she determined, but she is kind-hearted. She helps me with the things that I have going on in my life. I can even talk shop with her. Sometimes, when I am trying to put the pieces of a case together and things just don't fit, I talk them over with Nisha, and she always seems to shed light on things, by showing me another angle that I may have missed. I guess that's the brilliant lawyer mind that she has.

Overall, I believe we complement each other well. We are both career minded. We both love the Lord, and we both want to have a family someday. And we never get tired of listening to each other's war stories from work. Neither of us is in a hurry to rush things in our lives. We are simply taking one day at a time, regardless of what our parents and church members say. They think we have been dating much too long, but timing is everything. And who knows, maybe the time is drawing near for me to drop down on one knee. Time will tell.

Not only do Tinisha's brain and kind spirit have me mesmerized, her beauty makes my heart skip a beat. She stands almost a foot shorter than I at a mere 5'2" tall, has pretty brown skin, beautiful brown eyes, and shiny black silky hair that cascades over her shoulders. She looks like a little China doll. To say that her presence is stunning is an understatement.

Well today is the first day of a new week, so I am off once again to the world of law enforcement. I wonder if Detectives Smith and Erickson have any new leads on the woman whose body was found in the dumpster. I mean Robin. No disrespect intended. I am just not accustomed to referring to victims by name. I do know that when the detectives went to inform her parents of their daughter's death, Mr. and Mrs. Mulberry really took it hard and were very confused as to why their daughter would be a victim of foul play. They immediately came down and made a positive identification of her body. When they saw how she was dressed, they were even more confused. Like Tinisha, Robin had not divulged the details of her job to her parents. They couldn't understand why their pre-med daughter who had a 4.0 grade point average and who had always been considered as a "good girl" was dressed in stilettos, a mini-skirt, fish net stockings, and a sheer blouse that left nothing to the imagination. What were even more horrifying were the bruises that covered her face and upper body.

After Smith and Erickson questioned Robin's parents to see if they could provide any information that could be a possible lead to the perpetrator, Dr. and Dr. Mulberry made a request of their own. They requested that a rape kit be performed, hoping that the evidence would lead to the killer's capture and sentence. With their medical background, they could tell by the ligature marks on their daughter's neck that her air supply had been severely restricted and that the most likely cause of death was strangulation.

After going over the details of the case in his mind, Rafael pulled in the precinct parking lot and immediately entered the squad room.

"Good morning, Captain."

"Hey there, Detective Salisbury. When Detective Cassidy comes in, I need to see both of you in my office. Oh, here he is now. Come on in, Detectives."

"What's going on, Captain?"

"Why don't you two take a seat? We are still trying to gather evidence and connect the dots on the Mulberry case."

"What do you want us to do, Captain? Do you have any leads that you want us to follow?"

"Yes, but not on the Mulberry case. We found another body early this morning. There was an anonymous call that came in just after four this morning. The caller stated that a body was behind a club here on Hollywood Blvd. I sent a squad car over, and two detectives found a body just like the caller described. We haven't been able to make a positive I.D. yet. So, I need you guys to get right on it," Captain Monahan urged.

"Okay, will do, Captain," the detectives replied in unison as they rose from their seats.

* * * * * *

Tinisha

Thank goodness it was a mellow morning at the law firm. I don't think I could have managed another hectic morning. I didn't get as much rest as I had planned this weekend, so I am still very exhausted. At least I have a long break before my shift tonight. Rafael called and told me about the other woman's body that was found this morning. I didn't recognize her from his description. But from what she was wearing, she sounds like one of the girls that work in one of the strings of Hollywood clubs or after-hours bars.

Rafael and I are both worried that there is a maniac on the loose. Not only that, but there are still no clues that lead to Robin's killer. I was wondering if someone had a personal vendetta against her. Now with this second body, I don't know what to think. Rafael said he will pick me up from work every night. I have mixed feelings about that. On one hand, it would make me feel safe and secure to have my own personal bodyguard, especially one of LAPD's finest. At the same time, I would probably feel bad because I know that Rafael has to get up early for work every morning, and I tend to work late at night. I don't want to cut into his sleep. Besides, there is always the chance that he may get called in earlier and get less sleep. I don't want to be an extra cause of his lack of rest. He needs to be alert, so that he can perform effectively. With everything that has been going on lately, he hasn't had much rest himself. He has been working almost around the clock since Robin's body was found.

I am so confused. I don't know what to do. I can't tell my father. He would freak out, lose his cool, and then read me the first, second, and third degrees. I am not ready for that kind of drama in my life.

I guess Raf and I will figure out something, but for now I need to get ready for Karen's visit. She should be here any minute. I called her after I viewed Robin's body and again after the second body was found. Karen and I attend law school together. We met there about two and a half years ago. Six months later, we began to have lunch on a regular basis after our ethics class.

One day at lunch, I confided in Karen and told
her that I was having a hard time finding a decent job that paid decent money that did not require me to work forty hours a week. I remember her saying, "Well, I don't know about a decent job, but I do know about *a* job that will pay decent money for about twenty hours a week." After she filled me in on the details, I must say it wouldn't have been my first, second, or third choice for a job, but at that point in my life, I needed a job. I couldn't continue to rely on my parents for financial support. Karen helped me to get the job. She told me what to say and what to do. If it had not been for her, I would not have landed the job. Now, though, I can't help but to wonder what I got myself into, especially with the latest events.

When I told Karen about Robin and the other girl, she freaked out. But she would not tell me why. She said she would explain when she got here. I wonder if that's her car I hear pulling up outside.

After a few minutes passed and Tinisha did not hear a knock at her door, she assumed the car she heard was not Karen's. Then, all of a sudden, as she listened for another car to pull up, someone knocked on the door. Tinisha was startled and found herself breathing hard from fear. *God has not given me the spirit of fear. God has not given me the spirit of fear. God has not given me the spirit of fear*, she kept repeating to herself as she gathered enough nerve to answer the door. To her relief, it was Karen.

Karen Frederick is five years Tinisha's senior. While finishing her bachelor's degree, Karen had become pregnant with Brandon, her only child. After learning that she was pregnant, she moved her wedding date up and married her boyfriend of four years Raymond Arnold. Because of her pregnancy, Karen postponed beginning law school for a few years. This contributes to her being in a few of the law classes with Tinisha. When Karen began working at the club, Raymond had just gone back to medical school after a year hiatus. Both of them had placed their careers on hold to start their family. Karen's income from the club is a great addition to the family income and assists with the household expenses. But she and her husband both knew that this job was a temporary solution to obtain finances. Soon, Raymond would be Dr. Arnold and Karen would be Karen Frederick-Arnold, Esquire.

"Hey, Karen. Come on in. I was just putting on some Chamomile tea, so we can calm our nerves. As a matter of fact, I think I will have a cup now. What about you?"

"Uh, sure. That will be fine. Tinisha, have you spoken to anyone else at work about what's been going on?"

"No. Only you. I don't really talk to anyone outside of work besides you. I speak to the other girls when I am at work, but that is about it."

"Yeah, same here. I am really concerned about Robin and that other girl being killed. There have been a couple of men coming by the club and harassing some of the ladies."

"Hold on, Karen. What do you mean by harassing?"

"Well, you know how some of the clients want special favors or lap dances?"

"Yeah sure."

"Well, some of them have been getting drunk and being a little rough."

"I know that happens from time to time, but isn't that what the bouncers are for? To bounce them out of there if they get unruly?"

"Yes, but it doesn't stop the men from coming back another night and doing it again."

"Okay, but what does a few drunk and disorderly men have to do with Robin and the other girl getting killed?"

"I'm not sure, but one of the men was not only drunk, but he threatened me. He said, 'I'm trying to be nice about it, but I will get what I want one way or another.' That really shook me up. I told Carmine about it, and he said he would have the bouncers stay closer to us and keep a tighter rein on what's going on."

"Do you remember if you saw any of the guys that were harassing the girls on the last night Robin worked?"

"I can't be sure. I remember you telling me that her body was in the dumpster for two or three days, so I don't know if I was even at work on her last night."

"Do you think you could describe what the guy looks like? Maybe you could describe him to a sketch artist down at the station. Do you want to talk to Rafael about it?"

"Yeah, I would rather talk to him first before I go to the station."

"Okay, let me give him a call. He should be off work now."

* * * * * *

Rafael

"No, Detectives, she is not one of my girls," replied Carmine, the owner of the club where Tinisha works, when Detectives Salisbury and Cassidy showed him the picture of the second dead girl. "You may want to check with some of the other clubs down the street."

"Okay thanks, Carmine. We will be in touch if we have any other questions. Remember, if you think of anything else about the last night Robin worked, please call us. No detail is too small or unimportant; it just may give us a break in the case," Detective Cassidy responded.

"Oh, Detectives, wait a minute. Let me take another look at the picture." After studying the picture for a minute, Carmine replied, "Do you see the receipt book in her apron pocket?"

"Uh vaguely," Detective Salisbury answered, as he squinted at the picture. "What about it?"

"If you look closely, you will see a pink flamingo in the corner. They use those over at the Pink Flamingo. It's a club two blocks over on the corner of Sunset Blvd. and Western Ave. The owner's name is Jack Malloy."

"Thanks, Carmine. You have been a great help!"

After our brief meeting with Carmine, Detective Cassidy and I headed over to the Pink Flamingo. Jack Malloy, the owner, was not in, but the manager Caesar Ramirez was very helpful. He took one look at the picture and identified the woman right away. Her name was Sylvianna Frazier, but everyone called her "Dimples." She was twenty-one years old and had only been working at the club for two weeks. Caesar said she had complained about a few of the customers harassing her. But there was one guy in particular that seemed to be the worst. "I didn't really take her complaint seriously. I figured because she was new she had not become used to the club scene yet. Plus, the guys always get excited when new ladies come to work here. I guess I should have paid closer attention."

"Can you describe any of the guys who may have been harassing Dimples?" I asked him.

"Honestly, the other girls who were also making complaints recently might do a better job at giving a description."

"Okay, when can we talk to them, Caesar?"

"They will be here at eight o'clock this evening."

"We will come back then."

After dropping Cassidy back at the station, I immediately called Nisha. She had called me as Cassidy and I were on our way

to the Pink Flamingo. I knew she was calling for more than just to say hello. I know the situation with the girls being killed must be really spooking her. By the time I called her back, she was asleep, taking a nap before her shift tonight. Her message said that she said Karen wanted to talk to me about the Mulberry case, but Karen had already gone home by the time I called back. I will stop by the club tonight to follow Tinisha home after I stop
by the Pink Flamingo.

"Looks like I'm in for another long night," Detective Rafael Salisbury said aloud, half to himself and half to the empty seat next to him in the squad car.

Like Tinisha, Raf was feeling a little on edge about this whole serial killer bit. He had never been directly involved with a case like this before, and he could have done without it now. But he knew that it would make a difference in his career in the long run. The problem with serial killers was that they were clever. That is until they got careless and got caught.

From Raf's research, serial killers did not usually get careless. They usually got caught when they were ready for their name to be publicized. Raf thought about Charles Manson and Ted Bundy. Both of these serial killers had killed numerous times before they were caught. And when they were caught, they became famous. That was their ultimate goal.

Saturday

It has been a week since Robin's body was found and five days since the police were notified about Dimples' body. Rafael has been dropping me off and picking me up every night that I had to work. I would like to say that I feel safer because he has been with me every night. But the truth is, I still feel so uneasy about everything that is going on. Three other girls have been found dead, bringing the total to five. What's even worse is the police don't seem to be any
closer to catching the perp.

From what Rafael has told me, it seems to be the acts of one person because all the bodies have been found in similar condition. Each body was found close to where the girl worked. Each girl worked late at night at an after-hours bar, club, or gentlemen's club. They have all had signs of reticule hemorrhaging and ligature marks. All had been sexually abused and had facial and upper body bruising. The coroner's reports state that most of the bruising was done post mortem. The coroner also believed that the sexual assaults were also committed post mortem, which would make the perpetrator a necrophiliac. This crime alone is a felony with a prison term of eight years.

Rafael also mentioned that the perp uses a couple of signature marks that the police department is withholding from the public. He thought it would be best to withhold that info from me as well so that there won't be any unintentional leaks that might prevent the capture of the felon. The perp has been labeled as a serial killer even though he had only been known to have killed twice.

To gain more evidence to catch the killer, witnesses have been questioned. The police thought they may have been able to give some insight to who the killer is. First, when Rafael and his partner went back to the Pink Flamingo last week, there were two witnesses who had also had run ins with the same customers Dimples had run ins with. They both gave descriptions to the sketch artist.

After Karen finally got a chance to talk to Rafael, he convinced her to go down to the station and give her statement. While she was there, she also gave a description to the sketch artist. Amazingly, her description also matched that of the other two girls.

Then there was a fourth witness: Chris, a sixteen-year old boy who attends the local high school, Hollywood High. He was riding his bike to football practice on Thursday morning. He made his regular morning stop at the 7-Eleven across the street from his school to get a Honey Bun and an Arizona Fruit Punch. As usual, he left his bike on the side of the store. After purchasing his morning snack, Chris proceeded to place it into his backpack when he heard a soft moan coming from the back of the store.

At first, Chris thought it was a stray cat, as cats are not strangers to the streets of Hollywood. Chris, as curious as he is, decided to investigate. As he rounded the corner of the convenience store, he saw a foot sticking out from under a cardboard sheet. Even with fear gripping his heart, Chris grabbed an old tree branch that was lying on the ground and used it to push the cardboard away from the body that he assumed was attached to the exposed foot. As he did so, he heard another faint moan. With the help of the tree branch, the cardboard shifted but only slightly. By this time, Chris' curiosity overcame his fear, and like a crime scene investigator from the popular TV show CSI, Chris slowly pushed the cardboard off the body, using the branch as a guide. Having seen enough episodes of Law & Order, CSI, and NCIS, Chris knew that he should not disturb any evidence.

The evidence that lay before Chris' eyes was frightening. There in front of him was the most horrific scene he had ever witnessed in his sixteen years of life. There lay "The Hollywood Serial Killer's" sixth victim. Chris immediately jumped back, ran to where he had laid his backpack and quickly grabbed his phone. As fast as his fingers would move, he dialed 911.

After the paramedics and Detectives Salisbury and Cassidy arrived to the scene, they noticed that the victim was still breathing although she was barely conscious. The detectives were hoping that she would be the break in the case that they needed because she was the only victim found alive. Detective Cassidy rode with the victim to the hospital but was unable to question her because the paramedic had placed an oxygen mask on her to assist in her breathing. Detective Cassidy said a silent prayer, hoping that she would pull through so he could question her. However, his hopes were soon shattered because the victim died before she reached the hospital. Meanwhile, Detective Salisbury took Chris down to the station for questioning.

With everything that is going on, I really want to take some time off work, but the money is really good and next semester is approaching rapidly. With school expenses in addition to my regular bills, I can't afford to take any time off. Well, I will have one less expense after this week. I have been assisting Dad with Mom's convalescent bill. But she will be returning home a week from today, on next Saturday morning. When I get off Friday night, I will go home, shower, and take a short nap. I want to get to the convalescent home early, so I can spend some time getting her settled in at home. Dad won't be able to pick her up because he will be the keynote speaker at a men's conference, out of town.

Now that I think of it, I may need to go by Dad and Mom's house to do a little cleaning before I take Mom home. Dad has been living the bachelor life while Mom was at the convalescent home recovering from a triple bypass. Dad is not a messy person, but I am sure the house could use a little spring cleaning. You know, a woman's touch. I am sure Mom will greatly appreciate coming home to a clean house. I just have to figure out what time I am going to do it and when.

I am at the stage in my internship where I am required to go to court and sit in on different cases with the lawyers. Now I get to see all the data that I research being used live and up close. I am actually excited about this next step.

I would say that this is definitely a good reason to go shopping for a new power suit. So, off to Macy's I go. I know that we have all the fancy stores here in Hollywood and even in the not-so-far Beverly Hills, but Macy's is my all time favorite. Plus, I am on a Macy's budget. I am not yet at the Versace or St. John level.

Now, what is a new suit without a new pair of shoes or a fresh hairstyle? I guess I had better give Lamar Jones at *Loved Ones* a call. That man knows that he can style my hair without even blinking twice. He is definitely the stylist of all stylists. I always look like a million bucks when I leave there, and I always get a lot of compliments.

Sunday

On Sunday, Tinisha went through her regular routine of attending Sunday morning service and visiting with her mother at Friendly Faces Convalescent Home. Each week, Tinisha chooses a different person to be her guest at church. It may be a friend, a co-worker, a neighbor, or even a stranger. This week she chose Karen although Karen had visited the church many times before. Karen was a regular member of another church, but she enjoyed fellowshipping and worshipping at Rock of Salvation with Pastor and First Lady Oglebee. Pastor Oglebee always gave an awesome word that always gave her something to ponder and study.

This week was no different. Pastor Oglebee preached about how important it is to use godly wisdom when making decisions. He said a wise person never makes a decision in haste or without considering all the facts and weighing the options. He used the parable of the ten virgins as his foundational text found in Matthew 25:1-13. In this story, five of the virgins were prepared when the bridegroom arrived. They had their lamps properly trimmed with oil and the other five virgins did not. The five virgins with untrimmed lamps failed to make the proper preparations for the impending event: the bridegroom's arrival. They had not fully thought out their options, and as a result they were denied being in the company of the bridegroom. They knew that the bridegroom was soon to come; however, they did not take the proper steps to prepare for his arrival. They packed hurriedly and neglected to bring the necessary essentials. Their ill preparation caused them to miss out on the opportunity of a lifetime.

While Pastor Oglebee gave the benediction, Karen thought long and hard about the message. It reminded her of the choices she needed to make in her own life. She had been pondering whether or not she should quit her job because of the serial killer that is on the loose, but she did not want to act irresponsibly because she did not have another job lined up. She knew in her mind that it was best to wait, but in her heart she felt that something horrible was about to happen.

After church, just as she was about to invite Tinisha out for a quick bite to eat before Tinisha went to visit her mom, she heard a loud voice behind her. "Hey isn't your name Luscious?" the voice asked as she felt a hand on her shoulder. "Uh, you must be mistaken," Karen answered nervously as she kept walking without turning around to meet her accuser.

"No, I'm pretty sure I would know that body anywhere, even when it is fully clothed." As Karen finally turned around, she came face to face with a burly middle-aged man. Right away she recognized him from the club. He was a regular there. When he saw her face, he exclaimed, "I knew it was you, Luscious! What's going on?"

When Tinisha heard what was going on, she immediately stepped in, attempting to diffuse the situation. People had already begun to stop and stare. Very calmly, Tinisha said, "Hey brother, how are you this lovely Sunday afternoon?" The man looked a little confused, as if he did not know how to answer her simple question. He looked from Tinisha to Karen and back again to

Tinisha. Not receiving an answer, Tinisha continued, "This is really not the time or place. We will see you later. Have a good day." Before the man could figure out what was going on, the two friends disappeared into the crowd.

Once they were settled in Karen's car, both were completely silent. Neither knew what to say. This was a moment they had both dreaded but knew was possible.

After Karen and Tinisha sat and had a bite to eat, they parted ways. During their brief lunch, neither of them said a word about the encounter. They barely spoke a word about anything else either. Karen went home to ponder her next move while preparing for work that evening. Tinisha drove to Friendly Faces to visit her mother. During her visit, she and her mother discussed the details of her mother's return home. Pastor O would stop by Thursday, before his evening flight, to take all the heavy items home. It would leave her mother without a personal television for a couple of days, but it was the best plan.

As they sat and reminisced about how Sundays used to be, her mother also filled her in on the events of the last couple of days. The nurses who had always been so friendly and so caring somehow managed to spill hot water on her mom's leg scalding her knee cap. Upon hearing this, Tinisha was glad that her mom's stay at Friendly Faces was coming to an end.

Later, as Tinisha made the twenty-minute drive home, she wondered what else could go wrong that day.

At four o'clock, after settling in after a nice hot shower, Tinisha decided to turn on the news to see if there were any new developments in the Hollywood Serial Killer Case. She had to rely on the television for an update because she had not had a detailed conversation about the case with Rafael since Friday night. She was actually expecting him to drive up within the next thirty minutes, but she wanted to be prepared for anything that he may have to tell her.

A few hours later, Tinisha jumped up abruptly when the phone rang, tearing her from her sleep. Very incoherently, she reached for her cell phone. Rafael was on the other end.

"T, where are you?"

"I'm at home. Why? What's wrong? Where are you?"

"I just left the club. I am coming right over. Don't open the door for anyone. I will use my key."

Tinisha, trying to clear the haze from her eyes, suddenly thought of Karen. She knew that Karen had to work that night. She wondered what was going on. *Why had Rafael had that sound in his voice? Why hadn't he come earlier as planned? Oh no!* She thought. *Not another body. Please, God, no!*

When Rafael came through the door, he immediately went over to Tinisha and hugged her tightly. This really frightened Tinisha. "Raf, what's wrong? What happened?"

"T, sit down. We received another 911 call tonight. Someone got into the dressing room at your job and wrote a message on one of the mirrors. It said, 'You are next!' It was written in lipstick."

"Oh my God! Was anyone hurt? What about Karen? Where is Karen?"

"Calm down, sweetheart. An officer escorted each of the ladies to her home. She's okay. As a matter of fact, she took all of her belongings from her locker. She said she's not going back. I think you should do the same."

Monday

After all of yesterday's drama, today's events helped clear my mind, at least temporarily. Today was my first day in court, and I must say it was awesome! I had on my power suit, and I was ready to take on the world. And I did, right in my chair next to the lawyer who was in charge of the cases. In all seriousness, it was an honor to be invited to sit inside the court room where I could begin to gain the needed experience of how the law works outside of the law books, up close and personal. I witnessed a total of five cases. Each was in a different stage within its trial. Some were in the jury selection stage, others were presenting evidence, and still others were having closing arguments presented. Each case was fascinating.

One case really caught my attention. In this case, the plaintiff, a member of the well-known Carrington family, had accused the defendant, the housekeeper of ten years Greta Molina, of stealing a family heirloom. The family had charges brought against Greta based on evidence gained with the use of a private investigator. The evidence was enough for the judge to issue a search warrant.

However, after the police detectives searched the Molina house, they did not find the missing jewelry in question. But to everyone's surprise, another piece of Mrs. Carrington's jewelry was found lying on top of Greta's dresser. This evidence assisted in the charges being brought again Greta.

Greta, on the other hand, had some information of her own that she had been withholding. When she took the witness stand, she recalled the night Mr. and Mrs. Carrington went to a fundraiser. When the prosecutor asked Greta why she remembered this night and how this tied into the charges that were being brought against her, she responded, "Mrs. Carrington was wearing the broach that night." When the Carringtons returned home that evening, they had guests with them. Mrs. Carrington immediately went upstairs to change into something more comfortable. After she joined her husband and their guests downstairs, Greta saw the Carrington's youngest son go into his parents' bedroom. That is not something that Billy usually did, so Greta found it to be unusual and a little suspicious.

About a week later, when Greta was cleaning Billy's room, she found a receipt from a pawn shop. But again, she did not say anything until now when she found herself accused of the very act she knew someone else was guilty of. Greta's lawyer did some investigating also and found the pawn shop from where the receipt came. The clerk described someone matching Billy's description that brought in an emerald heirloom. The heirloom was still in the pawn shop where it was retrieved by the police department.

Greta was found not guilty, but two relationships were destroyed: the one between Greta and the Carrington family and the one between Billy and his parents. Although I felt saddened about this aspect of the case, I am happy that justice prevailed. The Carrington jewelry that Greta had at her home had a broken clasp, and Greta had taken it to be repaired. And she had the receipt to prove it.

Another case that was equally as interesting but not as sad was one involving an inmate named Hector. Hector had been incarcerated for five years after he committed his second offense. On Sept. 16, 2009, he had just completed his sentence and had been transported to the processing center, from where he would be released. While Hector was in his holding cell, he noticed that two women were in the neighboring holding cell. They had been transferred to the processing center from the women's prison. As Hector peered between the bar screen that served as a small window, he noticed that the two women were caressing each other. Hector could not believe his eyes. The sight of women after not having had any contact with any for five years was enough to excite Hector, but seeing these two engaging in intimate behavior was more than Hector could handle.

After watching the two women for awhile, Hector became aroused and decided to expose himself to the women. After Hector got the women's attention through the screen, he pulled his pants down and began to massage his genitals right in the women's view. The women were immediately repulsed and began to call for the guard. Once the female guard responded and heard the women's complaint, a male guard went into Hector's cell. Just as the women had claimed, Hector had his pants around his ankles and was still standing in the chair that he had used to elevate himself so that his groin area could be viewed through the screen window.

The guard yelled at Hector telling him to get down from the chair. Hector continued with his activities as if though no one had spoken to him. When the guard approached Hector to remove him from the chair, Hector became belligerent. It took two officers to finally get Hector out of the chair and handcuffed. However, the handcuffs were not placed on Hector before he served one of the guards a black eye. The charges brought before the court were assault on a peace officer and lewd conduct.

The public defender who fought Hector's case tried to discredit the police officers who brought the charges against Hector. His tactics were to no avail because his claims of former incidents of police brutality were quickly dismissed because he failed to provide proper evidence. The district attorney, in contrast, was able to present a solid case against the defendant because she had witnesses testify, and she presented DNA evidence. In the midst of Hector's activities, he secreted semen in his cell and the evidence spoke for itself. This evidence alone without the charge of violence was enough to convict Hector of strike three. This offense served as Hector's third offense. On the day he was due to be set free from his temporary prison home, he committed yet another crime that granted him the sentence of life in prison because of his three strikes.

I felt like I was on an emotional roller coaster as I listened to the five cases. Some were sad stories and others were even sadder. By the time I reached the end of my work day, I was emotionally drained. To make matters worse, when I returned home, I turned on the news, only to hear that another woman's body was found earlier this morning.

* * * * * * *

On the other side of town, Rafael's day had been just as full and eventful as Tinisha's. Rushing to arrive at the station on time, he had walked into the squad room just in time to catch the captain's morning instructions.

"Good morning, Detectives. I hope everyone was able to get ample rest last night because it looks like we are going to have a long day ahead of us. As you all know another body was found last night and another one this morning. That brings our count to seven. We believe that all the deaths were the handy work of the Hollywood Serial Killer. It is time to bring this to a close."

"We are with you, Captain," blurted out Detective Erickson.

"Good. That's what I want to hear. Look on the assignment board to find your duties for today. I am expecting a full report from each team tonight. If your partner can't be here, make sure you are here to give the report."

Detective Salisbury and Detective Cassidy were assigned to follow up on the body that was found earlier that morning. Their first stop was to the medical examiner's office to learn the details of the last woman's death. This would tell them without a doubt whether or not this was the job of the serial killer, a copycat or just a random similarity.

On the drive downtown, Rafael could not help but to think about Tinisha. He really wanted her to quit working at the club. He was willing to give her all the financial support that she needed, but he knew she would not hear of it. Tinisha was far too independent for that.

With everything that has been going on, he couldn't imagine how she was able to focus at the law firm and in court. The more he thought about it that was just like Tinisha. She was resilient. She always managed to persevere in times of adversity. He just didn't want her to blow her opportunity at a prosperous future in law by being too tired or stressed to be attentive. Every night for the last two weeks, he had made Tinisha a cup of herbal tea to help her sleep. Then as he lay quietly beside her, he listened to her breathe softly as she slept a peaceful sleep. Every now and then she would twitch or moan. He knew this meant that she was dreaming an unpleasant dream. However, she never awoke.

Keeping watch over Tinisha as she slept caused Rafael to be tired most days. He had even started taking a nap right after his shift before time to take Tinisha to the club. Taking the captain's warning into consideration, Detective Salisbury knew that getting a nap today was out of the question. Maybe he and Tinisha would have an early night tonight because it was her night off. Time would tell. "At least I can hope," Rafael whispered.

"What's that?" Detective Derrick Cassidy asked.

"Oh just thinking aloud, man. It's nothing."

"You must have been thinking about Tinisha. How is all of this affecting her?"

"I know she's freaked out, but she is strong. She is hanging in there," Rafael answered with a smile. He realized that he was actually proud of her.

Derrick is the only one on the squad that knows that Tinisha works at Club Royale. Rafael and Derrick have been partners for five years, and they had grown as close as brothers. Derrick and his wife Melissa have even vacationed with Rafael and Tinisha on occasion. Once a month, the four of them try to get together for dinner.

When the detectives arrived at the medical examiner's office, the examiner was printing his report. When he saw the detectives approaching his desk, he immediately printed two more copies, one for each of them. Having been in the business for nearly thirty years, he knew exactly what they wanted to know and what they were looking for.

"Good morning, Detectives."

"Good morning, Doc," each detective replied in kind.

"What do you have for us Ferguson?" Cassidy queried.

"First off, the victim's cause of death was strangulation which is consistent with the six other victims. There are signs of vaginal tearing which is also consistent."

"Doc, are the ligature marks in the same pattern?"

"Yes, and I think I finally figured out what the killer used to restrict the victims' air supply."

Over the last few weeks, since the killings began, Harry Ferguson, the medical examiner, had removed a rope-like substance from each victim's wounds, either from their neck or wrists. He was finally able to detect the materials that the rope fiber was made from. Then, he was able to narrow down which stores stocked that particular type of rope. He provided the list to the two detectives.

Making a visit to each hardware store that sold the rope was next on the detectives' list of stops. At each store, the detectives spoke to each clerk that was currently on duty and showed them the sketch of the annoying customer that had frequented the clubs where the dead girls worked. However, this turned into a dead end. None of the clerks recognized the man in the sketch as the one who purchased the rope. And, of the five stores that sold the rope, only Haskins Depot had sold any within the last month. The store clerk that made the sale remembered the man vividly because he bought ten separate ropes at one time.

"Do you think you could describe the customer to a police sketch artist?" Detective Salisbury asked.

"I could sure try. I do remember the scar he had on his left jaw. Looks like he had been cut by a jagged piece of broken glass or a knife with deep ridges," retorted Bernard the clerk.

In the interest of time and the captain's desire to wrap this up case, Detective Cassidy immediately phoned the station to have a sketch artist come down to Haskins Depot right away.

When Bernard felt comfortable with the sketch the artist had drawn, after taking nearly an hour to determine if the features were just right, the artist returned to the station to make copies and hand them out to the entire department. Everyone was to commit this new image to mind, erasing the sketches the department had been provided by the girls at the clubs. Their sketches had only led to dead ends. Maybe this sketch would prove to be more fruitful.

After stopping by the station to give their report, Derrick went home to his wife Melissa, and Rafael went home to gather his belongings for a night at Tinisha's house. He said a silent prayer that it would be a calm night. Tinisha would fill him in on her day, and he would return the favor. They would have a bite to eat, and then they would get some rest. That was the plan.

Hours later, the plan was off to an excellent start. Raf and Nisha decided that pizza and an antipasto salad would serve as a quick dinner. Neither was in the mood for much food preparation. With full bellies, they stretched out on the couch and turned to the sci-fi channel. Usually, they loved to watch the crime shows, especially Law & Order. They liked to critique the details of each case on the show. Raf reviewed the aspects that involved the police officers while Tinisha critiqued the actions of the lawyers and district attorney. But they really did not want to be reminded of the ongoing case with the Hollywood Serial Killer. Before long, they were fast asleep.

At a quarter to two in the morning, Rafael's cell phone rang. It was Derrick informing him of victim number eight.

Detectives Smith and Erickson were called to where the woman had been dumped alive. After arriving to the location and detecting a pulse, she was immediately rushed to the closest hospital. After much investigation by the police and a missing person's report filed by her roommate forty-eight hours after she had gone missing, the victim was identified as Sharon Morgan.

Like Robin and many of the other "club" girls, Sharon had a promising future. Her passion was computer technology. She was a whiz on the computer. She could not only program them, but she had just recently learned to assemble the hardware. To begin earning money in her chosen profession, she had set up a few contracts to load programs onto computers for a few private schools in her neighborhood. Prior to that, she had assisted a local pastor who had recently built a new educational/technology center on a portion of the twenty-seven acres of land that his church stood on. Sharon built a network for the forty computers that were placed in the center.

Although Sharon had a pulse when she was admitted to the hospital, she was placed on life support due to low brain activity.

The police were standing by waiting for her to gain consciousness so they could question her. They desperately needed a lead on the killer. All other paths had led them nowhere.

While they waited, they went to go talk to her employer to see if they could get any leads on the killer by finding out what happened on her last night of work. Sharon worked at the Pink Flamingo with Dimples.

When Detectives Smith and Erickson arrived at the club, all of their questions led to a dead end. None of the girls or the bouncers had seen any suspicious activity nor had they heard Sharon complain about anything recently.

From the little the detectives gathered, one minute Sharon was there and the next minute she wasn't. No one thought anything of it because she finished her shift and took her belongings like she did at the end of every shift.

Tuesday

Even though I tried to put everything out of my mind as we watched Alfred Hitchcock's 1963 movie "The Birds" last night on the sci-fi channel, I kept thinking about what Rafael said about the ropes and the guy at the hardware store. As soon as he said the person who bought the ropes had a scar on his face, it reminded me of someone, only I couldn't place my finger on it. I don't think it was one of the customers at the club. Who knows? I can't remember right now.

Maybe it will come to me later.

Right now, I have to get a move on. It is another big day in court. Today, I will spend the day shadowing Matthew Devareaux. Matthew has been a lawyer at the firm for twelve years, and he is up for associate partner. This is an exciting time in his career, and I know there is much that I can glean from him.

In the first case that we heard, sentencing was about to be handed down from the judge, but Matthew asked for permission to be granted for the defendant to present his allocution. Matthew explained to me that he usually suggests that defendants take advantage of the Fifth Amendment that gives them the right to remain silent as to not self-incriminate. However, in this case, Matthew thought the defendant had unique circumstances and that he should speak on his own behalf because he could best tell his story.

The defendant was tried for placing C-4 inside of his neighbor's dog and blowing the dog up. His defense was that he had to take matters into his own hands because the dog had attacked him on several occasions and the owner failed to do anything about it. The defendant had even called the authorities. They came out and made a report, but to his knowledge, they never spoke to his neighbor. When the dog attacked his six-year-old son and tore two fingers from his left hand that was more than the defendant could take.

After the jury heard the case presented, the defendant was found guilty, but he only had to pay a fine. At the same time, he filed a suit against his neighbor. He won his case, and he had enough money to pay his fine and to pay for the surgery his son had already had to have his fingers reattached.

After hearing the verdict read, the judge dismissed the court. We had an extended lunch hour today, so I called Karen to come over to the court house to go have a bite with me. Over lunch, I filled her in on the new developments in the Hollywood Serial Killer case.

"You know, Karen. There is one thing I can't put my finger on. And it is really starting to bug me."

"What is it, T?"

"Well, Raf said the guy who bought the rope had an ugly scar on his face that looked like it didn't heal right. When he said it, I had a feeling that I knew who it was. But it's like a thought that keeps evading me."

"What do you mean a scar? Like a birth mark or a cut?"

"I guess like a cut because the clerk said it looked as if though he had been cut by glass or a jagged knife."

"Do you think we could go down to the police station to take a look at the sketch?"

"Sure, I will be pretty busy here at the court all week, but if you don't have anything planned maybe you can go by there and take a look."

"Actually my schedule is a little tight because I just started my internship at Berkenstein and Fitzgerald, but I will see if I can get by there one evening on my way home. Not having to go to the club at night frees up some time for me in the evening to spend with my hubbie and my son."

"Congratulations on moving to the final stage of your program. You must be excited."

"You know, Tinisha, I am. I finally feel like I am accomplishing something."

"What are you doing for money, Karen? I know things must be getting tight with you and your husband still in school."

"No actually, I had saved up quite a bit of money from all the Girls' Night Out events and bachelorette parties we had a few months ago."

"Great. That's good to hear. Well, sweetheart, I am going to go back into the courtroom. It is good to see that you are doing okay. Let's get together soon."

"Okay, T. I will talk to you soon. Tell Rafael I said hello."

When court reconvened, we moved on to the next case. This one involved a lady who was being sued for being the driver in a hit-and-run case. A woman who was visiting California from Kenya for a teacher's convention was about to cross the street after having purchased food at a grocery store. When she stepped off the curb, a van came at high speed and hit her. The female driver did not stop. She left the lady there in the street to die from internal bleeding. However, as the driver continued down the street, the police had the street blocked off because a high-rise apartment building was on fire and fire trucks lined the street blocking all thru traffic. When the police noticed the van moving out of control when the driver attempted to make a u-turn, officers immediately approached the van and removed the driver.

Meanwhile, a crowd had begun to gather around the African lady's body. A couple of teenage boys ran down towards the van when they saw that it had been pulled over by police officers. After they arrived down the street, the boys were nearly out of breath. The officers that approached them listened to their story about the hit and run. At that point, the lady driver was arrested. Today, she had her day in court. Of course, she lost her case. The evidence was stacked against her.

After court, I stopped by Mom and Dad's to do a little cleaning. To my surprise, the place was spotless. On the counter, I found a receipt for Molly Maid cleaning service. I guess Dad and I had the same idea about the place being clean for Mom's arrival. "Well, maybe I can go grocery shopping. Let's see what's in the fridge. Ah, it's fully stocked. I see Dad is ready for his wife to come home. Wow, look at him. I am impressed. And I must be going crazy because I am standing in an empty house, with my head in the refrigerator, talking to myself."

Tinisha left her parents' house with a smile on her face. All the preparations that her dad had made would save her time and energy. She almost skipped back to her car. The cleanliness of her parents' home made her realize that she needed to wash her car. On the way home, she stopped by the car wash and then the local grocery store to pick up something for dinner.

Maybe I will cook tonight, she thought. Rafael and I deserve a home-cooked meal. I am not scheduled to go into the club until

Friday night, so that gives me more time to relax and take care of home and Rafael.

Wednesday

Today is Hump Day, and both Tinisha and Rafael enjoyed their day immensely. Tinisha began her day in court just as she did the first two days of the week. Today, she shadowed Lindsay Bertroff. Lindsay is a relatively new lawyer of three years. Looking at her face would make a person think that she recently started her career because she looks to be only twenty-five years old. However, Lindsay is actually thirty years old, but she has the knowledge of a fifty-year-old veteran lawyer.

The cases Tinisha was able to witness first hand sent tingles through her skin, telling her that she had definitely chosen the right profession. All the various aspects of law simply set her soul on fire. She knew that she was reaching for her destiny as she pursued her law degree. She could hardly wait until she was able to practice law herself and have her first case. The court was her platform, and she couldn't wait to take center stage.

* * * * * *

Rafael enjoyed his day relaxing at home, after spending two hours in the squad room first thing that morning. While at work, he, along with Derrick, Detective Smith and Detective Erickson, went over the details of the victims. Another body had been found late last night bringing the total to nine. They finalized the display board that held the victims' pictures, names, locations of the bodies, times of death, and workplaces. They reviewed the information to establish the killer's pattern of choosing his next victim. They assumed he would have another victim because ten ropes were purchased, but only nine had been used so far.

They assumed that the killer only used each rope once. They didn't actually have the ropes because each was removed from the victim's body. The detectives assumed the rope had only been used once because it had been cut to use for the victim's hands, feet, and neck.

To prevent any more victims, officers would patrol the area where the bodies had been found. Hopefully, this would lead them to the killer, or at least prevent another crime if the killer noticed the cops' presence.

After reviewing the details of the case, the captain released the four detectives for the day. They were expected to be part of the patrol team, so they were given their schedules before they departed.

While relaxing at home, Rafael decided to do a little cleaning. He had neglected his duties because he had been spending so much time at Tinisha's home. He would be with her again tonight because they were going to mid-week bible study. But in the meanwhile, he would make his two-bedroom condo look like someone lived in it.

The second bedroom served as Rafael's office. On the largest wall, he had another bulletin board like the one in the squad room with all the victims' information on it. When he entered the room, he stopped and took a long hard look at it, wondering who the message on the mirror at the club was for. Was it meant for Karen, Tinisha, or one of the other ladies? He was happy that Karen quit. Tonight, he was going to bring up the subject of quitting to Tinisha.

* * * * * *

After Tinisha arrived home at one o'clock in the afternoon, after being released from court at noon, she took a nice long, soothing bath. As the oil beads ran over her body and the bath salts soothed her aching shoulders, she let her mind wander. She fantasized about her future as a lawyer, being married to Rafael, being a mother of one or two children and living a very comfortable life. As she lavished in the wonderful thoughts, her body began to relax and a smile covered her face. Her daydream abruptly came to an end when her cell phone rang.

Gently lifting herself from the tub, she had to move quickly into her bedroom to retrieve her phone from her purse on the bed. By the time she reached her phone, she had missed the call. The call was from her father. Tinisha immediately pushed the button that had her dad's number programmed in her list of speed dials. When she heard her dad's voice on the other end, she smiled a girlish smile.

"Pastor Oglebee."

"Hey, Dad. It's me. You just called?"

"Hey, darling. Yes, I just called. Sorry to cut right to the chase, but I need you to take over bible study tonight. Bishop Johannsen is in the hospital and it is not looking too good."

"What's wrong with him?"

"He was in his church office today and his secretary heard a loud thump. She ran into his office and found him on the floor behind his desk. The doctor said he suffered a heart attack. He is in intensive care being prepared for a triple bypass. I am headed over there right now. Will you be okay tonight?"

"Yes, Dad. Don't worry about it. You always taught me to be ready at all times. I'm just glad it's Wednesday and not Sunday."

"Oh, you could handle it, Sweet Pea! You can stand in my pulpit anytime."

"Thanks, Dad. Will you give me a call later and give me and update?"

"I sure will, Tinisha. Talk to you soon."

* * * * * *

Later that night, as the members poured into the sanctuary at Rock of Salvation, Tinisha found herself holding her breath. She realized that she was actually nervous about standing in front of the congregation, even though she had done it countless times before. She thought she had made herself clear when she told the butterflies in her stomach to be still. I guess they have a mind of their own, she thought.

After the scripture had been read and the praise songs had been sang, Tinisha approached the podium.

"Good evening everyone," Tinisha greeted the congregation.

"Good evening, Sis Tinisha," they responded.

"I will be standing in for my dad, Pastor Oglebee tonight. Let's get started with our lesson. Tonight, we will be studying the Beatitudes in the book of Matthew."

After service, Tinisha mingled with the members. Many of them gave her compliments on how she rightly divided the word of truth, and others told her how much they missed her being involved in church services. Just as she was reaching for her coat, so she could meet Rafael in the foyer, she overheard several of the members talking.

"I don't know why pastors always feel like their kids have to be in charge when they aren't here. Other people with more experience can run the church," one person said.

"Yeah, that is true. It makes you feel like they don't trust anyone else," responded another.

"What difference does it make who he leaves in charge? It only matters if the person is rooted and grounded in the word," replied a third person.

"I agree with you. Tinisha brought a good lesson, and we should really focus on what she said," stated another.

"Good night, women of God," Tinisha said as she walked by with a smile on her face.

"Uh, good night," they replied in embarrassment knowing that the chances that she overheard were high.

* * * * * *

After returning to Tinisha's home, Rafael thought about how he could delicately approach the topic of Tinisha quitting her job at Club Royale. As he pondered and pondered, Tinisha noticed how he kept attempting to drink coffee from an empty mug. As she laughed to herself, she asked, "So, Mr. Salisbury, what seems to be troubling you?"

"What makes you think something is wrong?"

"You have been drinking air coffee for the last ten minutes."

"Oh, I hadn't noticed that the cup was empty."

"That's what I mean. What's on your mind?"

"Actually, I have two questions for you."

"Okay," Tinisha responded. "I'm listening."

"First, how were you able to simply smile and bid the women a good night after you overheard their conversation about you and your father?"

"Well, it has always been my philosophy that when people talk about me it means one of two things. One, I have done something awful or two, I have done something well. I prefer to believe the latter and move on."

"It really takes a strong person to possess that viewpoint, Tinisha. Have you always been that way?"

"I would love to say that I have always had that attitude, but that is so far from the truth. I believe as one matures in Christ, he/she develops a positive attitude. The women would love for me to get out of character. That would just give them something else to talk about. I won't give them the satisfaction."

"Yeah, I understand what you are saying."

"Good. What is your other question?"

"With everything going on with the unsolved Serial Killer murders, I want you to quit your job or at least take an extended leave of absence."

"Rafael, that wasn't a question. Besides there isn't a human resources department at my job where I can waltz in and request leave. I either work or quit."

"Quitting sounds like an awesome choice to me."

"Oh really? And exactly who is going to cover my expenses here or should I look for the next available cardboard box?"

"Come on, Tinisha. You know I wouldn't allow you to become homeless."

"Okay, so let me hear your plan, and I am praying that it does not include me moving back in with Pastor and First Lady Oglebee."

"Would that really be a bad idea?" Rafael teased.

"So your plan is for me to go back home to Mom and Dad?" Tinisha questioned.

"No, seriously. That's not my plan at all. Okay, here goes. Just hear me out. I will pay all your expenses for the next month. We should be able to catch the serial killer by then."

"And what happens if after a month the killer is caught but I can't get my job back or find another one? What then?"

"Tinisha, I will take care of you. Don't worry about it."

"I am not your responsibility, Rafael."

"Actually, you are. You are my lady. Aren't you, Nisha?"

"Yes, I am."

"Okay then. It's settled."

After their brief conversation, Rafael breathed a sigh of relief. He was extremely worried about Tinisha. Being around the club had proved to be dangerous, and he didn't want any harm to come to Tinisha. Now he could stop worrying about her being there two or three times a week.

Thursday

"Good morning. This is Pastor Oglebee. How may I help you?"

"Good morning, Pastor. This is Elder Williams. I am just calling to compliment your daughter on a job well done last night. I really enjoyed her teaching. I have studied the Beatitudes myself on more than one occasion. But the way Sister Tinisha presented it on last night shed light on a few things. Pastor Oglebee, you have a gifted teacher on your hands."

Throughout the morning and afternoon, Pastor Oglebee received several calls of this nature. Each call left his heart feeling warm, and there was even an occasional tear in his eye. After each call, he lifted his hands and praised and thanked God for his daughter.

After getting in from the hospital last night, Pastor Oglebee had packed his suitcase for his trip to Arkansas. He was looking forward to spending some time away, even though his wife was returning home in a couple of days. He missed her being home with him, and he would miss her arrival. But he needed a change of scenery from being at his church six days a week. He loved what he did, but he had not had a vacation in almost a year. He would have loved for his wife to travel with him as she often did, but she was still under strict doctor's orders.

As Pastor O thought about his trip, he was anticipating the fellowship he would have with his brethren, including pastors and bishops from all over the continental U.S., as well as from overseas. They always had a wonderful time when they came together. They would sit around and swap stories all night about how their congregations were doing and what new adventures they would be delving into.

In the last two weeks, Pastor Oglebee had been in the planning stage of a new adventure of his own. He was looking to erect a new structure on the ten acres of land the church had acquired five years ago. This building would be the church's fellowship hall and dining area. The church was in need of a new facility after the kitchen fire last summer. Also, Pastor Oglebee wanted somewhere he could feed the homeless comfortably.

At present, he was using tents that had to be put up every Sunday morning and taken down every Sunday afternoon. Although California is known as the Sunshine state, one can never truly know what to expect of the weather. Having a fellowship hall would eliminate the concern of inclement weather in the fall and winter months. Also, the fellowship hall could be used for seminars and banquets that the church sponsored.

As Pastor Oglebee sat in his office, he took one last look around to make sure he had taken care of the necessary responsibilities before he departed for his trip. As he sat there, his mind drifted to Tinisha. For some reason, an eerie feeling came over him. As the chill ran down his spine, he remembered that he had the same feeling a few days ago when he had thought of her.

He knew that something wasn't right, but he did not know what it was. So he immediately began
to pray.

After praying, Pastor Oglebee grabbed his hat and jacket and headed towards his car. He was on his way to see his sweetheart of nearly thirty years. They had a dinner date tonight. Sure, they weren't going to a fancy restaurant to sit in a cozy booth that was perfectly lit with the soft glow of candlelight. No, they would have to settle for the comfort of his wife's room at Friendly Faces Convalescent Home. But, to add a touch of romance, Pastor Oglebee had his secretary call a caterer to bring a delicious seafood dinner to the convalescent home for him and his wife to enjoy.

This romantic dinner would serve as a celebratory dinner of sorts. After all, she was making her departure from Friendly Faces in two days and returning to the comfort of their home. Because Pastor Oglebee could not be there upon her return, he thought it would be best to celebrate in advance.

After pulling into the parking lot of the convalescent home, Pastor Oglebee said a prayer concerning his wife's safety. He prayed that she had not had any other incident where she had been hurt. Plus, he didn't want anything to spoil their evening together.

The convalescent home had been highly recommended by several of the members of Rock of Salvation. Delores' stay had been rather pleasant, with the exception of last week when she was burned by the hot water. He didn't want any repeat incidents.

When he walked into his wife's room, their eyes met. Pastor Oglebee smiled to himself. "Earl, why are you wearing that silly grin," Delores queried. Before answering, Pastor Olgebee thought about how he and his wife had shared that same look for nearly three decades. He had not grown tired of it. "Oh, I'm just looking at my beautiful honeylump," he answered. "Awe, Earl! Flattery will get you everywhere!"

As the evening wore on, Earl suddenly remembered that his plane was leaving in a few hours and he still had to stop by the house to drop off his wife's television. In an effort to not be late, he quickly hugged Delores and kissed her gently. "I'll see you Sunday night, Gorgeous," he whispered in her ear before he slipped out the door. "Looking forward to it, Handsome. Be safe, and give them heaven," Delores said as she watched her husband's back disappear down the hallway.

* * * * * *

In a private room in the Intensive Care Unit of Cedar Sinai Hospital where Sharon's body lay perfectly still, her family and her roommate wiped the tears from their eyes as they said their goodbyes. Her parents had decided to pull the plug when they received the doctor's report. There was no hope for a full recovery. If she awoke, she would only live in a vegetative state. Sharon's parents knew that she would not want to live that way, and they wanted to honor her unspoken wishes.

Sharon, undoubtedly, would be sorely missed. She had been a wonderful daughter, sister, and friend. Her parents could not help but wonder why their daughter was taken from them before she could leave her mark on the world. Who knows, she could have been the next Bill Gates. The thoughts her parents had were similar to those Dr. and Dr. Mulberry had about their daughter Robin, who could have been the next top heart surgeon like Dr. Daniel Hale Williams. Now, no one would ever know.

* * * * * *

The news of Sharon's death reached the police station quickly. This placed a damper on the squad because they were hoping for their big break in the case. This was the second victim that was found alive but died before she could be questioned.

Friday

Today is my final day in court for this week. After another full week in court next week, my internship will be complete. Then, I will be ready to schedule my bar exam. I can hardly believe that I have made it to this point. Next week, I will have the same schedule that I had this week. I will shadow the same lawyers. Today, I am accompanying Reginald Jefferson, a veteran lawyer of twenty-three years. His technique of questioning witnesses is second to none. Watching him is like watching a Perry Mason movie. I don't think the witnesses knew what question was coming next. They fell prey to him like a deer caught in the headlights of an oncoming car.

The most interesting case of the day was one involving a syphilis-infected woman who had committed several murders. However, the woman was not the one who was on trial. Instead, Meticulous Life Insurance Company was being sued for negligence. The woman had applied for life insurance and her application was denied after the phlebotomist drew her blood and tested it. When the insurance company learned of her condition, it had a legal responsibility to notify the health department. However, the insurance company neglected to do so.

A few months later, because of the advanced stage of syphilis, the woman had begun to hallucinate. Her hallucinations caused her to kill several people because she believed she heard a voice telling her to do so. Jefferson argued that if the insurance company had notified the health department, the health department would have in turn contacted the woman. She may have been given medication to prevent the hallucinations. With medication, the murders would not likely have occurred. The jury agreed with Jefferson and he won the case. The woman, however, was sent to a mental facility. Her husband received $1.3 million in damages due to the insurance company's neglect.

After a full day in court, Tinisha went home to shower and nap before going to the club. She had an appointment with Carmine during her break later that night. During their meeting, she planned to tell him that she would no longer be working at the club. Tonight would be her last night. She hated to leave him in a lurch. She knew that she would be the third girl that he lost in a two-week period. But, like Rafael said she had to think about her own safety.

* * * * * *

After Rafael's shift, he drove directly to Tinisha's. He was extremely exhausted, but he was excited at the same time. Tonight was Tinisha's last night at the club. After tonight, they both would be able to get more rest. Tinisha had one more week of her internship, and he was looking forward to closing the Serial Killer case. Afterwards, they could begin to plan their future. As he pulled up, he smiled a tired smile to himself as his heart beat with joy.

* * * * * *

At a quarter to nine that night, as Rafael drove Tinisha to the club, he decided it would be best to ensure that she had not changed her mind about tonight being her last night.

"Tinisha, is the plan still on?"

"What plan, Rafael?" Tinisha asked calmly, sounding uninterested.

"Come on, Nisha. Don't be coy."

"I'm not sure what you mean, Rafael."

"Are you still planning on meeting with Carmine tonight? You did call him, didn't you?"

"Oh, was I supposed to call him?"

"Tinisha!"

Laughing uncontrollably, Tinisha responded, "Okay, okay! Yes, I am going to meet with him tonight. The plan is already in motion."

"This is no time to play, Tinisha."

"Oh, Rafael. Calm down. Do you think I am going to chicken out? With you paying my bills, I am set. I am just giving him the courtesy of one more night."

"I wish you didn't have to go in tonight, but I understand. Just make sure ole smooth-talking Carmine doesn't change your mind."

"Don't worry, Raf. I can handle Carmine."

"That's my girl."

After Raf dropped Nisha at the club, he drove back to Tinisha's apartment. He needed to take a nap and since her home was the closest to the club, he figured he would nap there until Tinisha's shift ended at two am.

Rafael was unable to fall asleep immediately, so he found a bite to eat and settled down in front of the television. Tinisha's living room was decorated very comfortably. She had a soft suede sectional that had two lazy-boy recliners built in at each end. They loved to relax there, especially on game days. As Rafael surfed through the channels on the 56" flat screen television, he finally found a movie to watch. Eventually though, Rafael dozed off.

* * * * * *

Tinisha watched as her watch clicked midnight; it was time for her break and her meeting with Carmine. Gathering her thoughts, she walked to the back of the club to Carmine's office. She found Carmine sitting behind his desk talking on the telephone. When he noticed her presence, he waved her in. Waiting for him to finish his call, Tinisha sat quietly in the chair that sat on the opposite side of Carmine's desk.

The few times Tinisha had been in Carmine's office, she hadn't noticed how dark and gloomy it was. It was no different from the rest of the club atmosphere.

"So, what gives me the pleasure of your visit?"
Carmen inquired.

"Well Carmine, you know that a lot of crazy things have been happening around the clubs in this area and to tell you the truth, I have been feeling very uneasy. I can't continue to work here while the serial killer is on the loose."

"I figured that is what this meeting was all about. First Karen and now you. I can't say that I blame you. If I were in your position, I would probably make the same choice."

"Thanks for understanding, Carmine," Tinisha said relieved that he didn't take it too hard. She stood and extended her hand. Carmine stood and grabbed hold to Tinisha's hand and shook it vigorously. "We'll be here whenever you are ready to come back," he said as Tinisha left his office to go back to the bar to complete her last shift at Club Royale.

* * * * * *

A few hours later, Raf's nap was interrupted by the ringing of his cell phone. His first thought as he reached for his phone was that he had overslept and was late to pick up Tinisha. However, when he answered the call, he noticed it was only one am. He still had an hour before he was due back at the club.

"Detective Salisbury," Rafael said when he answered his phone.

"Hey Raf. It's Derrick. I just got a call that there is another body."

"Where?"

"Near the corner of Milton and Burbank."

"Is there a club over there?"

"Not that I know of. I am in route. How long before you can get there?"

"Give me fifteen minutes."

"Ok, see you there."

Detective Salisbury and Detective Cassidy arrived to the location at the same time. As they exited their vehicles, they approached the dumpster behind the convenience store. After putting on rubber gloves, both detectives slowly removed the trash that covered the leg that protruded from one corner of the trash can. The leg was covered with blood. As the trash was removed from the body, Rafael could see that the victim was dressed in similar clothing as the nine previous victims. When Derrick removed the bag that was covering the victim's face, he jumped back and let out a shout.

"What's the problem?" Rafael shouted back.

"Uh, uh, there's no head," Derrick responded visibly shaken.

"What do you mean?" Rafael asked in disbelief.

"Man, she doesn't have a head."

Rafael immediately pulled out his flashlight and shined it upon the victim. Until that point, they had relied upon the light that was in the corner behind the dumpster. This allowed them to use both hands in order to free the victim from her temporary grave. As Rafael shined his light, a million thoughts and questions ran through his mind. As he moved the light above the victim's shoulders, he realized that Derrick was right- the woman's head was missing. What he found even stranger was that there wasn't any blood coming from her neck. As he cautiously leaned in further, he noticed a piece of metal protruding from where the spinal cord attaches the head to the neck. All of a sudden, Rafael reached into the dumpster, grabbed the piece of metal, and yanked the woman upwards as if to propel her from the trashcan.

Derrick was livid with unbelief. "What are you doing? You are going to destroy evidence."

"Not exactly," Rafael responded in a huff.

"What do you mean?"

"There is no evidence. It's a mannequin!"

"What?!?"

"Derrick, who called you about this victim?"

"The call came from the station."

"Call and find out who called the station with the tip. Hey, what time is it?"

"It's about 2:05."

"Oh no Nisha! I'm late to get Nisha! I'll call you later."

Saturday

Rafael drove frantically for fifteen minutes until he reached the club. As he drove, he dialed Tinisha's cell phone number several times. But try as he might, he could not reach her. This worried him and fear began to grip his heart. He tried to reason with himself by thinking Tinisha was still inside the club and could not hear her phone because of the music.

As soon as Rafael pulled up to the club, he scanned the parking lot as he quickly ran to the front entrance. By this time, it was 2:20 am. He was officially twenty minutes late. Walking quickly through the club towards the ladies' dressing room, he questioned each lady that worked there about Tinisha. No one had seen her for the last thirty minutes or so.

When Rafael reached the dressing room, sweat was dripping down his forehead and running down the middle of his back and knots were developing in his stomach. He barged into the dressing room without bothering to knock. The two women who were inside nearly jumped out of their skin. Neither one said anything to him. They both just stood there with their mouths open.

With his revolver drawn, Rafael asked, "Where is Tinisha?"

"I haven't seen her. I just got in," one said in a panicky voice.

"I saw her leaving through the back door," the other said in a half whisper.

"Was she with anyone?" Rafael asked.

"Um, I'm not sure. I just saw the back of her head."

"Ok thanks," Rafael responded as he headed for the back door. As he reached the door, he noticed that there was not a bouncer standing there. Usually there is a bouncer at the front and back exits as well as throughout the club. When Rafael exited the club, he immediately began to look around for Tinisha and signs of foul play. His heart beat heavily in his chest. He remembered the message that was written on the mirror in the dressing room. Then, all the dead women's bodies flashed through his mind.

He reached into his pocket with his free hand to grab his cell phone. He dialed Tinisha's number. Suddenly, he heard a phone ringing faintly in the distance. He pushed the button on his phone to end the call and the ringing stopped. He dialed Tinisha again as he walked over to where the ringing was coming from. Again, the ringing started. This time Rafael kept the call going as he walked closer to the sound of the ringing. It was coming from the dumpster that was about twenty feet from the club door. Afraid of what he might see inside the dumpster, Rafael whispered a quick prayer as he put both his gun and phone away.

Looking into the dumpster, Rafael spotted Tinisha's bag that always held her change of clothes when she went to work. Retrieving the bag, Rafael found Tinisha's cell phone in the side pocket. He immediately grabbed his own cell phone and called Derrick for back up.

"Hey man, get over here to Club Royale. Tinisha is missing. I found her bag in the dumpster."

"Oh wow. Raf, do you see any sign of her?"

"Not yet."

"Ok, don't touch anything. I will be right there."

After Rafael ended the call with Detective Cassidy, he called the station and requested backup for himself and his partner. While he waited, he rushed back to his car and put on a pair of rubber gloves and took out his yellow police tape. In his opinion, this was a crime scene.

Detective Cassidy and other members of the squad arrived, and everyone began to tear the dumpster apart looking for clues of Tinisha's whereabouts. The club was shut down, and everyone who was present was questioned. Hours later, no clues about Tinisha were uncovered. Rafael had even driven over to her apartment hoping she may have turned up there. No luck. At that point, the squad knew that whoever had called in anonymously about the body in the dumpster behind the convenience store had deliberately planted the mannequin to keep Rafael away from the club. That means that Tinisha wasn't a random victim. She had been a target all along. And the perp knew that Rafael would be coming to pick her up after her shift.

Later that morning at Friendly Faces, Delores Olgebee had been waiting for nearly an hour for her daughter to pick her up. Delores had tried calling Tinisha, but she did not reach her. This is not at all like Nisha, Delores thought. "Maybe, I'd better call Rafael," she whispered to herself as she looked through her phonebook for his number. After finding Raf's number, Delores dialed and waited for an answer.

Rafael had not long fallen asleep after getting back to Tinisha's after having scoured the city looking for Tinisha. As he reached for his phone, Raf wondered if Nisha would be on the other end.

"Hello? This is Detective Salisbury."

"Good morning, Rafael. This is Mrs. Oglebee. How are you?"

"Oh, hello Mrs. Oglebee," Rafael responded completely caught off guard. He had totally forgotten that Tinisha was scheduled to pick her mother up from the convalescent home that morning. He didn't know what to say to her. He didn't want her to go into cardiac arrest.

"Is everything alright, Raf? You sound kind of strange. I'm looking for Tinisha. Have you spoken to her this morning?"

"Uh no, Mrs. Oglebee. I haven't. I know she was supposed to pick you up this morning. I will be right there to get you."

"You don't need to do that, Raf. I'm sure she will be right here. I know she's been really tired lately."

"It's no problem at all, Mrs. Oglebee. I will be right there."

After splashing some water on his face and quickly drinking a cup of lukewarm coffee, Rafael headed down the street to Friendly Faces Convalescent Home. He had no idea of how to break the news to Tinisha's mom. He didn't know how strong her heart was and if she could handle the news. How do I tell a mother that her only child is missing? Raf wondered. At that moment, he wished Pastor Oglebee was there so he could break the news of Tinisha's disappearance to him and then Pastor O could break the news to his wife. But that was only wishful thinking because he knew that Pastor Oglebee was out of town. So, he had to be the bearer of bad news.

After pulling into the parking lot at Friendly Faces, Rafael moved slowly toward the door. He dreaded facing his soon-to-be mother-in-law. *Mother-in-law* he said to himself. Hopefully, all will work out well and Mrs. Oglebee would indeed be his mother-in-law.

Sunday

Yesterday was extremely difficult for Rafael. Trying to explain Tinisha's disappearance and some of the minor details of the case to Delores Oglebee was difficult. Delores wanted to know why Tinisha had not mentioned anything to her about the serial killer, why Rafael had managed to not see the mannequin scheme as a ploy, and what the killer wanted with Tinisha. Rafael found himself at a loss for words because the department was in the midst of an ongoing investigation, and he did not want to ruin the chances of catching the psychopath who had killed nine women and who had apparently taken Tinisha. At the same time, however, he wanted to put Delores' mind at ease. At this point in time, that was virtually impossible. All he could tell her was that he and the LAPD would do all they could to recover Tinisha alive.

After leaving the Olgebee residence, Tinisha's cell phone rang. Rafael had put it in his jacket pocket the night before. He didn't really know why he held on to it, but he felt closer to Tinisha by having it with him. He looked at the caller id and saw that it was Karen calling. He dared not answer. He could not bear to tell Karen about Tinisha's disappearance. He would contact her later, he promised himself.

After a difficult day yesterday, today may prove to be a better day for Rafael, especially after the news he received when he walked into the station this morning.

"Hey, Raf. Good to see you this morning. I know yesterday was a nightmare, but we may have a lead," Derrick said with a serious look.

"Oh yeah?" Rafael responded, trying not to sound too hopeful. "Catch me up on the latest findings while I pour myself a cup of java."

"We dropped Tinisha's bag off at the crime lab,
and the technicians were able to get a few fingerprints off the leather straps. It turns out that the prints are from four different people."

"Okay, whose names are on the list?"

"Well, yours and Tinisha's are on the list. Then there are two other names: Karen Frederick and Joel Patterson. Any idea who these people are and why they would have a need to handle her bag?"

"Karen is a good friend of Tinisha's from law school. She helped Tinisha get the job at the club. She was also one of the women who came down to give a description to the sketch artist."

"Is that the same Karen that hangs out with Tinisha and Melissa from time to time?"

"Yes."

"Okay, what about this guy Joel? Do you know who he is?"

"No, I have no idea."

"Well, I'm on my way to get the full report from the lab."

"Okay, I'll ride with you."

After the detectives received the full report that revealed Joel Patterson's criminal record and current address, they immediately headed to his place of
residence in full pursuit.

When the detectives arrived at Joel's home,
Detective Cassidy went to the front door, while Detective Salisbury went around to the back door. After getting no answer at the front door, Derrick used his shoulder walkie-talkie to notify Rafael to come back around to the front because he was going in.

"Derrick, as much as I want to, we can't. We need to get a warrant."

"Not if we have probable cause. Come back to the front."

Rafael was so anxious to see what Derrick found that he ran around the house to the front. He also knew that if there was any hope of finding Tinisha alive, they would have to find her soon.

"Look. There are about ten drops of blood that start from the carport and lead inside," Derrick said as he pointed emphatically at the ground. "Someone may be hurt and need our assistance," he continued.

"Okay, go in. You lead and I will follow," Rafael said in a low voice.

After the two detectives had entered Joel's home and had searched the entire premises, all they found was a bathroom sink splattered with blood. Detective Cassidy immediately phoned the crime lab so someone could come to get a sample to identify the person who was bleeding. After not finding any evidence of Tinisha having been inside, Rafael felt his heart drop into his stomach. He had that sinking feeling again that he had when he sped away from the mannequin in the dumpster two days ago.

Suddenly, as Raf and Derrick made their way back to the squad car, Raf's cell phone began to ring. He did not recognize the number that appeared on his caller id, but he felt compelled to answer anyway. He secretly hoped that is was not Mrs. Oglebee because he did not have any good news to tell her.

"Detective Salisbury," Rafael answered.

"Rafael," a strained voice whispered on the other end.

"Tinisha!" Raf yelled.

"Yeah, it's me. Come get me," she sobbed.

"Okay, tell me where you are," Raf said as he tried to remain calm as he was taught in the academy nearly ten years ago.

"I'm at the Super 8 Motel."

"Which one?"

"I don't know."

"Are you in one of the rooms?"

"Yes, but I don't know which one."

Thinking quickly, Raf said, "Try to look on the phone for the address, Tinisha."

Before calling Rafael, Tinisha had tugged at the phone until it fell on the floor. Her hands and feet were bound, but luckily her hands were bound in front of her body rather than behind. This enabled her to dial the phone. Now she had to turn it over onto its base so she could read it.

"Oh, okay. I found it. It's 3250….."

"Tinisha?"

Rafael called out for Tinisha several times, but she did not respond. The phone line was still open though. Derrick was standing beside Rafael listening to the entire conversation. He asked if the line was still live. Rafael nodded. Derrick immediately called the precinct and had a technician detect the location of the call that came into Raf's phone. Next, he had someone else try to find a Super 8 Motel with a 3250 address.

While they waited for a response from the precinct, Raf walked in circles as he held his cell phone tightly. Ever so often he would call out Tinisha's name, hoping she would hear him. Also, he listened intently to see if anyone else was present in the room with her.

After about ten minutes of pacing in front of Joel's home, Derrick's cell phone rang. He was given the address of where the call to Raf's phone originated. Raf jumped into the passenger side of the squad car still clutching his phone, and Derrick took the wheel. As Derrick drove, he called for an All-Points Bulletin to be placed on Joel Patterson and for backup to meet them at the motel. He told the desk sergeant to have the back up team to proceed with caution.

As Detectives Cassidy and Salisbury drove to the Super 8 Motel, Tinisha lay on the cold floor of the dark room. As the tears seeped from her eyes, deep within the recesses of her mind she prayed as she had done throughout this entire ordeal, especially when the perpetrator lay on top of her and violated her. She prayed and prayed until she slipped away.

At that moment, only two blocks away anyone standing along the street could see the lights on the police cars flashing, but they could hear no sound. With Joel's picture in hand, Rafael was ready to jump out and run to the motel's office to ask the clerk if he had seen anyone matching Joel's description because they had no idea which room the call came from.

As Tinisha lay on the floor with her body racked with chills, a key turned in the door. As Raf and Derrick pulled into the parking lot, they noticed that another squad car had arrived before them, and two cops stood with their service revolvers drawn pointing at a man as he attempted to enter one of the rooms. The man slowly raised his hands and let the key fall to the ground. The officers approached him and placed the handcuffs on him just as Raf and

Derrick reached them. As they turned him over, they recognized him from his mug shot and the long scar that went down the length of the left side of his face. It was Joel Patterson.

Rafael immediately rushed past the men, grabbed the key from the ground, and entered the room. With the help of the light coming through the door, Rafael saw a pair of feet protruding from the other side of the bed and he recognized the nail polish. The feet were bound with yellow rope. As he went to leap over the bed to grab Tinisha, Derrick reached out to stop him for fear that Raf would contaminate the crime scene, but his husbandly instincts caused him to draw his hand back. He knew that if it was his wife in Tinisha's positon, he would dash to her side also.

As Derrick watched his partner check for Tinisha's pulse, he used his shoulder walkie-talkie to request an ambulance. With tears in his eyes, Raf nodded at Derrick letting him know that he had indeed found a pulse. It was faint, but it was a pulse nonetheless.

As he waited for the paramedics to arrive, Raf wrapped Tinisha in a clean sheet that one of the housekeepers brought at his request. While he waited, he cradled her in his arms and thanked God. He had never held onto her the way he held her now. "Stay with me, Nisha," Raf whispered repeatedly in her ear.

Once the ambulance arrived, Raf rode to the hospital with Tinisha. Once settle inside, he searched through his phone to find the number Delores Oglebee had called from yesterday morning. Once he found it, he called to give her the news. She immediately began to cry. She told him she would meet him at the hospital shortly.

* * * * * *

At the Los Angeles International airport, a 757 Boeing jet had recently landed and the passengers had made their way through the exit doors of the plane. Pastor Oglebee hurriedly found the door that led outside for passenger pickup. He immediately spotted

Deacon Riley who had come to pick him up. After arriving at his home, he found his wife already seated in the passenger side of their Mercedes S500 waiting to be driven to the hospital to see their only child.

In one hand, she held a handkerchief that she used to wipe her eyes. In the other hand, she held onto one of Tinisha's dolls that she had when she was a little girl. Delores had found it in Tinisha's old bedroom. Delores was happy that she would soon replace the doll for her daughter.

Monday

At noon on Monday, Tinisha lay in the hospital bed in a comatose state. Every few hours she would appear to be gaining full consciousness, but she would immediately fall back under.

Pastor Oglebee had visited with her that morning with his wife, but he left the hospital to go to the church. He had not been there since he left town on Thursday. He told his wife that he wanted to check on things around the office. The truth is he wanted to spend some time alone praying in the house of the Lord. As he prayed, he found himself weeping as he thanked God for sparing his daughter's life.

When Delores had called him in Arkansas on Saturday morning, he immediately cancelled the rest of his trip and caught the first available flight Sunday morning. He had prayed continuously during the initial flight and also on the connecting flight that his baby girl would be found alive. He was not aware that his prayer had been answered until he had landed at LAX and retrieved the voicemail his wife had left for him.

When he found out that Tinisha had been raped, he felt his heart break again. He had counseled many rape victims and some never got over the trauma of that experience. He knew that his daughter was strong, but he didn't know if she could handle this. To his knowledge, Tinisha had never had any traumatic experiences in her life.

* * * * * *

Now that Tinisha was safe, Rafael took it upon himself to find out why Joel Patterson chose Tinisha and the other nine women to be his victims. From Joel's rap sheet, Raf learned that Joel had been recently released from federal prison for possession of child pornography. He was released only thirty days ago. What confused Raf most was why a man who was supposedly interested in children went around raping and killing women. That baffled him. This was an irregular pattern to say the least. Now it was time to put his detective skills to work.

After getting the court transcripts of Joel's trial, Raf discovered that Joel's jail sentence was only twenty-four months because no witnesses had come forward at the trial. The only incriminating evidence the police found was an abundance of child porn on his home computer.

While Raf was gathering physical data to get a better idea of Joel's motives, Derrick had an opportunity to question Joel. Because Joel was caught red handed, he did not withhold any information from the police. The first thing he said was, "I did it to clear my name."

"What do you mean?" Detective Cassidy queried.

"I was arrested for child molestation and wrongly convicted for child pornography. I love kids. I would never hurt or violate them," Joel explained.

"Yeah, that's what all the perverts say."

"No. You don't understand," Joel continued.

"Okay, well help me understand your claim of innocence," Detective Cassidy said half-heartedly not believing in Joel's innocence.

After listening to Joel for approximately thirty minutes, Derrick finally understood what happened over two years ago when Joel was sentenced.

Three years ago, Joel had become a new member at Rock of Salvation Church. After expressing an interest in working with the youth department, he was permitted to work alongside the youth leader, Beverly Hutton. Making many notable and beneficial changes within the children's department, Joel was promoted to youth leader after Bev moved out of town and left the church.

About a year later, a young child complained that Joel was being "nasty." The complaint was made to Tinisha who subsequently met with the child and her parents. The parents described in detail what their child had told them. According to the little girl, Joel had brushed his hand across her one of her breasts. At the time of the incident, the little girl had complained. Joel apologized and told her it was an accident. The child obviously did not believe him and reported him to Tinisha as she learned to do in her sixth-grade health class.

Once Tinisha received the information and had met with the parents who believed this to be a serious allegation, Tinisha was obligated to contact the authorities. Once the authorities were contacted, a full investigation ensued.

During the investigation, child pornography was found on Joel's home computer which he contends he shared with his roommate. What he couldn't explain was why the pictures were located under his profile rather than his roommate's. Joel said his roommate must have gotten his password somehow.

After being convicted, sentenced, and released, Joel found it impossible to get a job with a felony conviction on his record. At that point, he began to develop his plan to get revenge on Tinisha. "It was all her fault for listening to that lying kid," Joel complained. He included the other girls so no one would automatically suspect him. He wanted to make Tinisha pay for ruining his life.

So much for a new start, Detective Cassidy thought. Joel was headed back to prison. This time he would either get the death penalty or life without parole for the nine murders he committed and the one count of attempted murder on Tinisha.

After visiting Tinisha again at the end of his day, Rafael remembered to call Karen. She had called again late Sunday night, and Rafael knew she was beginning to worry. On his way home, he took out
Tinisha's Blackberry and dialed Karen's number.

"Girl, where have you been? I have been worried sick," Karen yelled into the phone without saying hello.

"Uh, Karen, this is Rafael."

"Rafael, oh I'm sorry. What's going on? Where is Tinisha?"

"Well, Karen, she's in the hospital right now."

"Hospital? Why?" Karen became alarmed.

Rafael took his time to explain everything to Karen and assured her that Tinisha was okay and that the Hollywood Serial Killer had been captured.

As Karen breathed a sigh of relief and wiped the tears that had immediately sprang from her eyes, she laid her head on her pillow and whispered a prayer for Tinisha. Before long, Karen fell into a peaceful sleep, something she had not had for quite some time.

Hours later, Raymond noticed the evenness of his wife's breathing, and he thanked God for peace. She had not yet told him about the serial killer's capture, but he had seen it on the evening news. He breathed a sigh of relief. Now maybe our life will return to normal, he thought. Dealing with a frantic and nervous wife on a day-to-day basis was not easy. A few moments later, Raymond fell asleep with one arm wrapped around his wife.

Tuesday

At the law offices of Snyder & Beckman, the partners had been wondering where Tinisha was on Monday and again today when she did not show at the office. This was highly irregular for Tinisha. She was usually the first clerk there and the last to leave. If she had a problem coming in or being on time, she always called. This week had been set aside for Tinisha to complete her internship hours in the courtroom by shadowing lawyers as she had done last week.

At ten that morning, Rafael left Tinisha sitting up in her hospital bed. The doctor said she would make a full recovery. Before Raf left, he and Nisha had briefly discussed her internship and how it would be prolonged due to her current circumstances. It saddened Tinisha that she would be required to stay off her feet for at least two weeks according to her physician. She needed time to heal from the bruising she received from the rough treatment Joel gave her. She had planned to study for the bar over the next month and take the exam in early October. Now she would have to redo her calendar and create a new schedule.

After leaving Tinisha, Rafael went directly to Snyder & Beckman. Using Tinisha's phone, he called ahead to notify them of his impending arrival to be sure they would be available to meet with him.

Upon reaching the law firm, Raf was immediately escorted into the partners' shared meeting room. Without giving too many details of the ongoing investigation, Raf explained why Tinisha had not shown up at the firm yesterday or today for her scheduled court outings. He told them Tinisha would have contacted them herself but her condition prevented her from doing so. He then inquired as to whether or not Tinisha would be able to finish her internship after she recuperated and is released from her doctor's care. Snyder and Beckman asked Rafael to give them a few minutes to discuss Tinisha's internship amongst themselves.

On that note, they departed through one of the side doors that led to Snyder's office. Upon their return to the conference room, they informed Rafael that they would sign off on Tinisha's internship because she had already put in more than her required share of hours.

"What about her second week in court?" Rafael asked as he was a little uncertain of what was going on.

"The court hours are just a formality. We like to give our soon-to-be's an opportunity to experience the courtroom up close and personal," responded Beckman.

"So, you are saying that you will sign off on her internship and she is done as of this moment?"

"Yes, that is exactly what we are saying. Ms. Oglebee has done a superb job during the time she has been here with us, and we believe she is ready to prepare for the bar exam," Snyder added.

"Great. I will pass the news on to her. She will be ecstatic."

"We just ask one thing of her," Snyder continued.

"Uh, what is that?" Raf hesitated, feeling apprehensive again.

"We just ask that she please call us or stop by when she is feeling better. Please give her our regards."

After assuring the two gentlemen that Tinisha would be in contact, Raphael left with a little pep in his gait. With all that Tinisha was dealing with, this was a bit of news that she would love to hear.

When Raf returned to the hospital, he took Derrick along with him. He called Tinisha's room to make sure both her mother and father were present. He wanted Derrick to explain to all of them at the same time why Joel had attacked Tinisha and to ensure them that he would not be permitted a second chance to attack her again.

After having nearly a two-hour discussion about Joel Patterson, Tinisha stated that she was ready to put it all behind her and move on. This was also the advice of her therapist.

* * * * * *

After everyone had left to go have dinner, Tinisha finally had a moment to herself to begin to reflect over everything that had transpired from the time she got off work to the time she awoke in a hospital bed.

I can't believe this happened to me, Tinisha thought. How could I have been so stupid to go outside for air? The club atmosphere was unbearable that night. I just wanted to be free from it. But how did Joel know that I would be in the back of the club? He must have been inside the entire night watching me. I wonder why I didn't spot him. Well, obviously that was part of his plan.

These were the thoughts that ran through Tinisha's mind over and over again. I have to stop this, she reasoned with herself.

Thinking about it over and over again won't change what happened, she reasoned with herself again. I just need to let my body heal and regulate my mind. I can do this, she told herself.

A few hours later everyone returned. Just as they settled into their seats, Karen walked into the room. When Tinisha and Karen's eyes met, they both began to cry. "Let's give them some privacy," Delores suggested. After everyone had vacated the room, Tinisha went back over the gory details of her kidnapping. She knew that Joel had not intended it to be a kidnapping. She knew he fully intended to kill her. After all, she was his primary target. That thought gave her chills that ran down her spine.

* * * * * *

Tinisha's day ended with her mom giving her a sponge bath and rubbing anointed oil on her wounds. Tinisha recalled that just the other day she was the one tending to her mother in the convalescent home. How the tables had turned. The truth also finally came out about her job at the club, but the main concern her parents had was her safety. Everything else was secondary.

* * * * * *

As Raf prepared for bed, he realized he had completely forgotten to share the good news with Tinisha about the completion of her internship. It will keep until tomorrow, he thought has he nestled his head into the pillow. He missed the warmth of Tinisha's body lying next to him. Soon, he thought. Soon, she will be back safe at home.

(Three Weeks Later)

For the last three weeks, Tinisha has been following the doctor's orders to the strictest letter of the law, and she has been keeping all of her psychiatric appointments. Before she left the hospital three weeks ago, she had her blood drawn because she and her doctor were concerned about the possibility of her having contracted sexual transmitted diseases or HIV from Joel. From Tinisha's recollection, he had not used protection when he violated her.

Just last week, she went in for her two-week check-up. Her blood tests had all come back negative. As the doctor read the results of the tests, tears flowed from Tinisha's eyes. She silently thanked and praised God.

However, her doctor had another concern.

"Tinisha, are you on birth control?"

"No. Why do you ask?"

"I was wondering about the possibility of you being pregnant."

"Oh no! My boyfriend and I have not been sexually active for nearly six months. We have decided to uphold our Christian values and abstain until our wedding night. Why do you ask?"

"No, I didn't mean prior to the attack. I meant as a result of the attack."

"Oh, my God!" Tinisha shrieked, "That would be awful. I hadn't thought of that."

"Well, let's not jump the gun. Let's run both urine and blood analysis. I will call you in a week with the results."

Waiting for the results of the pregnancy test for the last week had Tinisha on edge. At ten o'clock that morning, Tinisha's cell phone rang. Her heart dropped when she saw Dr. Nevel's number on the caller id. Holding her breath, she slowly answered the phone.

"Hello?"

"Tinisha?"

"Yes, Dr. Nevel. It's me."

"I'm sorry, Tinisha, but your pregnancy test came back positive."

"Oh no!" Tinisha yelled as she began to sob. Her sobs turned to deep wailing as she let the phone fall from her hand and hit the floor. On the other end, Dr. Nevel placed her phone back on the receiver. She knew that Tinisha didn't have anything to say at that moment. Her heart went out to her. She had seen this several times before. Each woman dealt with it differently.

Thirty minutes later, still in a state of shock, Tinisha picked up her phone and dialed her mother. "Mom, can you come over right away? I need you."

After receiving her daughter's phone call and request for her presence, Delores Oglebee re-combed her hair and slipped on her shoes. Her husband wasn't there to drive her, but she wasn't concerned. She had already begun driving herself a week ago, plus she had the feeling that Tinisha needed to see her alone.

When Delores arrived at Tinisha's apartment, she took her time going up the stairs. Even though she did cardiovascular therapy three times a week when she was in the convalescent home, stairs were not a part of her daily routine, except for the ones in her home which she was accustomed to. They still caused her to become winded if she went too fast. When she reached out her hand to knock on Tinisha's door, the door opened and before she knew it, Tinisha was in her arms sobbing deeply.

"Whatever it is, dear, we will deal with it," Delores said attempting to comfort her daughter. After several minutes of consoling her daughter, Tinisha told her mother about the pregnancy test results. Suddenly, Delores fully understood Tinisha's hysteria.

"What do I do, Mom? What do I do?" Tinisha wailed.

"I think the best thing is to get your father and Rafael over here and have a family meeting."

Tinisha nodded her head in agreement.

* * * * * *

Later that evening, Rafael received a text asking him to come to Tinisha's directly after his shift. Pastor Oglebee would come as soon as bible study was over. Delores stayed with Tinisha to keep her calm.

* * * * * *

At nine that night, all four sat in Tinisha's living room. Pastor Oglebee could tell that his daughter was deeply troubled, so he began to pray. He asked that God would be with them and guide them. After her dad's prayer, Tinisha felt calm, and she explained the situation to them. Needless to say, both men felt a stab in his heart. Pastor Oglebee felt sickened once again by the remembrance that someone violated his daughter and to top it off, he had left his mark. Rafael felt torn in a million pieces because the love of his life was hurting deeply and he could not prevent it or stop it.

The four of them discussed Tinisha's pregnancy for what seemed like hours. The final decision was for Tinisha to carry the baby to term and then the baby would be placed for adoption. Although Tinisha did not know how she could carry the baby of a man who tortured her, she knew that she could not have an abortion. That one fact made their decision final.

Thursday

In the wee hours of the morning, Rafael and Tinisha were still up after her parents left at eleven o'clock the night before. They were discussing Tinisha's day in court. Today was the day she would face her attacker. The date had been moved up on the judge's calendar because the judge wanted to have a speedy trial and pronounce sentencing, thereby giving closure to the victims' families, ensuring them that justice had been served.

At twelve noon after not getting much sleep, Tinisha and her family, along with the four detectives on the case, sat in the courtroom. Each was ready to testify if called. The case against Joel Patterson was air tight, not to mention that he was prepared to enter a guilty plea. As a result, the prosecution did not believe that Tinisha would need to testify.

The hours seemed to drag on and on as everyone in the courtroom listened to the gory details of each victim. When the time came to discuss the last victim, Tinisha didn't know if she could relive the horror all over again, not that she didn't already do that each day. She politely excused herself as she walked out of the courtroom with her head held high.

On the other side of the courtroom door was Karen. She had taken the afternoon off from her internship at the law firm to be there for her friend. Although Karen and Tinisha had only met two years ago, they had grown extremely close. They had found that they had a lot in common.

By the end of the day, all the evidence had been presented for the judge's review. This proved to be record time, as most cases drag on over a period of several weeks or months. Because Joel Patterson pleaded guilty, a trial was just a formality to present the evidence before the judge so that a ruling could be made. The judge had decided he would enter his ruling the next morning at nine am.

Walking out of court, Pastor Oglebee suggested lunch, but no one had much of an appetite. Tinisha just wanted to go home. She wanted to be alone. So much had happened over the last forty-eight hours, and she really needed more time to process it. She had to mentally prepare for the changes her body would go through over the next eight months or so. She also had to plan out the rest of her life. Snyder and Beckman had graciously signed off on her internship, so she was now ready to study for the bar.

But was she really ready? Could she focus? How would she get the horrible images out of her mind? How could she erase Joel Patterson's face? Would she ever forget his smell?

Friday

At nine o'clock in the morning, all televisions were turned to the Channel 7 news. The judge's verdict for the Hollywood Serial Killer case would be aired live. Tinisha at home in her apartment, Rafael and Derrick at the station along with the rest of the squad, the Oglebee's at home, the Drs. Mulberry from the staff room at the hospital, Dr. Nevel in her office, Karen at the law firm, and all the victims' families at their respective locations all waited on the edge of their seats.

Judge Dominguez walked into the court room looking very dapper in his judicial robe. He slowly lowered himself into his chair and picked up the folder that was already on his bench. He slowly opened the folder and removed the contents.

As everyone held his/her breath, a stillness seemed to fall over the entire city. Judge Dominguez began to read, "In the case of the State of California against Joel Patterson on nine counts of murder in the first degree and sexual assault, he has been found guilty. In the case of the State of California against Joel Patterson on one count of attempted murder and sexual assault, he has been found guilty. The penalty for his crimes is death. Joel Patterson is being awarded the death penalty as consistent with California state law."

Everyone throughout the town rejoiced and tears fell from the family of the victims' eyes as they felt justice had indeed been served.

Monday

After taking the weekend to come to terms with the plans of how my life is going to be over the next eight months, I decided I need to take charge of my life again. I just feel so vulnerable right now. But I must keep going. I can't let this be a halting or stopping point for me. I must not be defeated by a sick bastard who has no control over his life. I am more than a conqueror! I have the victory! Today, I am getting up, and I am getting out of this apartment.

Where shall I go, Tinisha asked herself. I don't have a job or an internship, so what do I do, she wondered. Suddenly, she remembered that she had not thanked Snyder and Beckman. "I'll go to the law firm," Tinisha said aloud.

Everyone at the firm had been so kind and thoughtful. They had sent sympathy cards and baskets full of fruit and nuts. One basket was filled with assorted teas that helped Tinish to relax.

As Tinisha prepared for her departure, she carefully chose an outfit that made her look powerful and alive. She definitely did not want to send the message that she was a miserably depressed victim. To assist in her desired look, Tinisha carefully applied her makeup. When she looked in the mirror after she was completely dressed and had curled her hair, she was pleasantly pleased with the outcome. Just changing her outer appearance made her feel better inside. "I think I should do this every day even when I don't have anywhere to go. I don't need a special reason to look nice. Self respect is reason enough," she said to herself as she walked out the door.

* * * * * *

At the station, the detectives were relieved to have closed the Hollywood Serial Killer case. At several points throughout the investigation, they thought they had good leads, but they all somehow fell through. This was quite disappointing for the detectives. But in the end, they felt excited and victorious. They did, however, feel bad for their fellow officer Rafael Salisbury who had a personal stake in the perpetrator's conviction.

As Rafael and Derrick were riding down the street to investigate a new adventure, a string of robberies, Rafael decided to get Derrick's opinion on a plan he had recently devised.

"I was thinking," Raf started slowly.

"Yeah? About what?" Derrick asked.

"About Tinisha and this whole episode with this Patterson dude."

"Okay. What about it? Is she doing any better?"

"Sure. She's doing better. She doesn't seem to cry as much. I think a change of scenery will do her some good and take her mind off everything."

"That sounds like a good idea, but I don't really think it's realistic to believe that she won't think about it. She will carry the trauma of the rape with her wherever she goes. My sister didn't seem to recover for nearly a year. I still think she has some aftereffects from it."

"Yeah, I know what you mean. But I was thinking about taking some vacation time and taking her on a trip. I think getting away will do her a lot of good."

"What do you have in mind?"

"I was thinking about somewhere up the coast like Santa Barbara. T really likes the water. The scenic and calming environment may help her study for the bar with more ease."

"Has she already scheduled her exam?"

"Yes, it's set for the week before Thanksgiving."

"That's a little over a month away."

"Yeah, I figured we would leave in a week and stay for a couple of weeks."

"Have you talked it over with Nisha yet?"

"Not yet. I'm planning on doing that tonight over dinner. I did speak with her parents about it though. They think it's a good idea."

"You know I have a friend who owns some property up that way. I will give him a call and see what he can do. I will let you know what happens. It looks like we have made it to our destination. Let's go see if the owners have the list of missing items ready for us."

"Is this the one whose housekeeper was here but claims she didn't see or hear anything?"

"Yeah, this is the one."

* * * * * *

Well, here I am at the firm, Tinisha said to herself as she sat in her car wondering if she was ready to face all the sympathy stares.

"Girl, you can do this," she reassured herself aloud as she slowly opened the car door.

A few minutes later, Tinisha was stepping out of the elevator onto the floor that she had become very familiar with. As she approached the front desk, Beatrice the receptionist jumped up from her seat, ran around the counter and hugged Tinisha as tears streamed down her rosy cheeks. Her tears brought tears to Tinisha's eyes.

Beatrice, whom everyone calls Bea, has been with the firm for twenty-seven years. She has been with Snyder and Beckman from day one. She has seen lawyers and interns come and go. She is like a mother hen over everyone. She is loved and respected by all. After Bea had her share of hugs, she walked into the main room of the firm that held the paralegals and the interns that worked alongside them.

As they walked in, Bea cleared her throat loudly and introduced Tinisha. It wasn't as if though Tinisha was a stranger. Everyone in the office knew her. She had been there nearly two and a half years. Bea just had an over exaggerated personality. She liked to do things in a grandiose manner.

Hearing all the commotion from their offices, the lawyers and partners, including Snyder and Beckman opened their doors and stepped into the main room. All of their faces lit up like lights on an over lit Christmas tree. By their expressions, Tinisha's presence was warmly received. This immediately brought warmth to Tinisha's heart, and she knew she had made the right decision going there.

Having said hello to everyone, Tinisha made her way into Synder's office with Beckman following behind. She took her time and graciously thanked them for all that they had done for her. They returned the sentiments.

"When you have passed the bar exam, we would like for you to come see us," Beckman added.

"Yes, we are sure you would be a wonderful addition to our firm," Snyder concurred.

"Wow, really?" Tinisha responded in disbelief.

"Oh yes. We know natural-born skills when we see them."

"Oh, thank you. My exam is scheduled for mid- November. I will call you before the holidays."

"We are looking forward to it. You take care of yourself."

"I will," Tinisha answered as she walked out the door with a smile on her face. She was happy that she decided to come today. This was the best news she had heard in a long time, other than the judge's verdict on Friday.

* * * * *

On the other side of town, Raphael smiled to himself after hanging up the phone with Derrick. He was on his way home to shower and prepare for his dinner date with his girl. He had some good news of his own.

Saturday

Today was the big day! On Monday night, Raf had presented the idea to Tinisha of going on a vacation up the coast to Santa Barbara. Before he could finish giving her the details of the plan, she consented. He could see the change in her mood already. She said it was the perfect plan because she needed to have a change of scenery, so she could focus on studying for the Multi-State Bar Exam, the MBE.

To prepare for the trip, Tinisha went to Barnes & Noble and Border bookstores to look for study materials. She even looked online at Amazon.com. She placed a rush order so the materials would arrive on time. With the study guides and practice tests now in her possession, she carefully placed them into her briefcase. She smiled as she could feel her lawyership in her grasp. Tinisha was not concerned about taking the bar exam. Studying was just a formality. She had put in long hours of study as she took her law courses, and she had put her knowledge to use as she completed her internship. After spending that one week in court, she felt more ready than ever.

After Tinisha had calmed down from Raf's initial suggestion of the trip, Tinisha had listened to the rest of his proposal. A friend of Derrick's owned a house that is usually rented out to the local college students, many who attend University of California, Santa Barbara. However, the house had just been renovated. Since it was October, school was already in session and no one was looking to move. So the house was currently vacant.

Derrick inquired with his friend about the house to see if he would be interested in renting to one of Derrick's fellow officer. After talking to his friend a little longer, Derrick shared a little of Tinisha's ordeal and his friend volunteered to allow them to vacation in his Santa Barbara home free of charge. He wanted to help anyway he could.

At eleven am, Tinisha had her bags packed, so she placed them by the door. When Raf arrived, he almost tripped over them as he entered. "Nisha! Girl, we are only going for two weeks. What is all of this?"

"I'm not sure about the weather this time of year. Fall is right around the corner," Nisha said giggling.

"It looks as if though everything you own is in these suitcases."

"Oh, Raf. Stop complaining. You sound like someone's husband."

"Yeah, yours."

"Not yet, good looking. Not yet," Tinisha responded playfully.

Once the car was loaded, Raf and Nisha began their journey up the coast. It would be an hour and a half drive.

A little over halfway, they decided to stop and have a bite to eat for lunch. Getting off the 101 freeway in Ventura, they pulled into the parking lot of Mimi's Café. Mimi's is a chain of restaurants that serves a variety of foods. Both Tinisha and Rafael opted for the grilled salmon, fresh steamed string beans, and a side of loaded potatoes. Rafael was curious to know if any of those foods would make Tinisha feel ill because of the pregnancy, but he dare not ask. He didn't want to change her mood. He had decided he would not bring it up unless she did. So far, she had not.

Once Raf and Nisha arrived at their destination, at the Potter's home, they both stood outside the car in awe of the beauty of the house. It was mid-blue in color with an eggshell trim. Not masculine, nor feminine. Each window had an eggshell colored awning on top. The landscape was gorgeous. There were a multitude of rosebushes of a variety of colors in the middle of the yard circling a six-foot tall fountain. In the middle of the fountain was an angel who was holding a harp. Leading to the front porch were pebble stones that served as a walkway. On the extra large porch was a pair of white wicker chairs and a little table set between them. On the table sat a large pitcher of lemonade and two empty glasses next to it.

When Raf and Nisha spotted the lemonade, they quickly glanced at each other. It was as if though someone was waiting for them. Before they could utter a word, the front door opened and Mr. and Mrs. Potter stepped out. "Welcome to our home," Mrs. Potter greeted them. "Hello, I'm Rafael Salisbury and this is Tinisha Oglebee. We are friends of Derrick Cassidy."

"Yes, we were expecting you," Mr. Potter responded. "We are glad to see that you made it safely. We just wanted to be here to show you around the place, and then we will be on our way."

Later that evening, after having had a moment to relax, Rafael and Tinisha walked across the street to enjoy the ocean breeze as they took a walk along the pathway in Shoreline Park.

Sunday

Tinisha woke up bright and early with the smell of bacon and pancakes filling her nostrils. Normally, this would have been a welcoming smell, but today it just did not sit right with her. Moments later, she found herself in the bathroom bent over the toilet. Throwing up when she woke up in the morning was painful because there wasn't any food in her stomach to expel. Her body was basically going through the motions.

"Oh no," Rafael thought has he heard the commotion going on the restroom.

Just as he was about to empty the food into the trashcan, Tinisha rounded the corner into the kitchen.

"Hey there. What is that I smell?"

"I can get rid of it if it is bothering you."

"Oh no! I want to eat. I'm hungry."

"But I thought I heard you throwing up," Rafael answered sounding confused.

"You did, but I am ready to move on. I guess my nose is very sensitive, but my belly is saying, 'Bring it on.'"

After eating their fair share of blueberry pancakes, sausage patties, bacon, scrambled eggs, and fresh cut fruit, they were ready to enjoy the morning sun. Tinisha found a slightly worn blanket in one of the hall closets that she thought would be perfect to place on the grass. She placed her briefcase on her shoulder, Rafael grabbed the morning newspaper, and they headed across the street to the park. They found a nice tree to relax under.

Tinisha quickly delved into her study materials, and Rafael read the news items that made the front page of the local Santa Barbara newspaper. However, what interested him more was the string of robberies that were occurring in his own home town. He would miss out on the action of finding the burglar who had violated so many homes.

There had been a string of burglaries that began to occur right before the serial killer was captured. Because no one had become seriously injured in the burglaries, the cases weren't given the highest priority. With the murders behind them, the detectives were now able to focus on who was most likely to have committed these crimes.

After spending some time at the park, Tinisha and Rafael decided to head over to Stearn's Wharf to do a little bike riding. Although they both have their own bikes at home, neither of them thought to bring them along. That may be due to neither of them having bike racks on their cars. Luckily, there was a bike rental booth across from the beach.

Rafael was a little concerned about whether or not Tinisha should be riding in her condition. He wasn't sure if he should say something or not.

"Uh, babe?" he started.

"Yes?" Tinisha answered, lifting her head and seeing the concerned look on his face.

"Do you think you will be okay riding?"

Tinisha wasn't sure why he was asking. She didn't know if it was because of the baby or because of her own physical condition. "Sure, I should be fine." Then all of a sudden, she burst out into great laughter. Raf didn't know what to make of it. "What's so funny, Nisha?" he inquired.

"I'm just wondering if this is how you're going to be when we have children. Every time I make a move, you seem to get tense."

"Yeah, I guess you are right. I guess I am being a little over protective."

"Yeah, well in case you didn't know this let me let you in on a big secret," Tinisha said leaning into Rafael.

"What is that?" Raf answered in all seriousness.

"Women have been having babies since Eve and I don't think that many have died as a result." After her statement, Tinisha pushed down hard on the pedal and before Raf knew it, she was gone down the street. She was laughing as she pedaled away with her hair blowing in the afternoon breeze.

Rafael couldn't do anything but laugh himself as he went riding after her. Catching up to her a minute later, he passed by her as he gently slapped his hand across her buttocks.

As Raf rounded the next corner, he spotted a small flower shop. He quickly jumped from the bicycle, pulled out his wallet and grabbed the first colorful bouquet that he saw. Back on his bike before Tinisha caught up, he waited as she came his way.

When she saw his face, the first thing she saw was his silly grin, reeking of suspicion. "What are you doing?" she asked.

"What do you mean, my lady?"

"Raf, you know you can't keep a secret. I am bound to find out anyway."

"Oh you are no fun," Raf pouted as he pulled the bouquet of flowers from behind his back.

"Oh Raf. They are beautiful," Tinisha said as she grinned from ear to ear. It seemed as if it had been so long since she received flowers for no reason. As though reading her mind, Raf promised, "I know I haven't given you flowers in a long time, but I will get better."

Tuesday

I am ready for a new adventure, Tinisha thought to herself. Raf and I are going to visit one of the historic missions today. That will be a nice drive to another part of Santa Barbara. Afterwards, we will get a bite to eat and maybe catch a movie. I guess I am a month or so into the pregnancy, and I am really beginning to feel like it. The morning sickness has not decreased. It is downright habitual. It comes like clockwork. If I don't stuff something into my mouth upon waking up, I begin to feel nauseous and soon find myself in the most unflattering position in front of the toilet.

After a quick bite to eat, Raf and Nisha headed toward Mission Santa Barbara. When they arrived, they noticed that the mission had been well preserved since its establishment in 1786. The mission was still active as it served as a tourist location and a fully-operated Catholic parish. It was nice to look through the pictures of the centuries of history that the mission held. The other guests that were there seemed to enjoy the history as well.

After walking through the mission and the various rooms, Tinisha felt a little weak. Rafael suggested that they head back to their home-away-from-home. Tinisha refused. In her mind, she didn't want to spoil the vacation for Raf, so she was determined to keep going.

"Why don't we take in a movie?" Nisha suggested.

Noting her determination to keep going, Raf responded, "Okay. That sounds good." He knew that at least for the next two hours she would be off her feet.

Not only was she off her feet, but she fell asleep during the movie. Rafael did not bother her. She needs her rest, he thought. He remembered all the nights he had stayed with her after she had come back home from the kidnapping. He remembered how she tossed and turned and cried in her sleep. She was sleeping much more peacefully these days, and he dared not disturb her.

* * * * * *

After the movie ended, Tinisha was ready for lunch. This time they opted for a quiet lunch at the house. They had gone to the grocery store the day before and picked up slices of roast beef and all the trimmings to make nice roast beef sandwiches. After lunch, Tinisha was out again. Raf smiled at her as he pulled the cover over her. This is exactly what she needed, he thought.

As Tinisha slept, Raf took the opportunity to call Derrick and see what was going on with the burglaries. As he waited for the phone to ring, he knew that Derrick would not pass on the opportunity to make a smart comment about him learning to relax and take a vacation without calling to check on things. When Derrick answered the phone, Raf beat him to it.

"Before you even start in on me about learning to relax, just give me the 411 on what has been going on at the station."

"First things first. How is the house?"

"Man, it is even better than you described. I can't thank you enough. We are having a wonderful time here."

"Don't worry about it. You can repay me by naming your first kid after me." Derrick paused. He didn't mean to be insensitive. "I'm sorry, Raf. I wasn't thinking."

"No worries, man. It's okay. I know you didn't mean any harm."

"So, how is that going anyway?"

"We are just taking it one day at a time. She seems to be doing okay. You know every morning and every night we pray. That is really helping her to stay sane. I don't know how she does it. Nisha is really strong."

"Yeah, I guess so. I was talking to Melissa about it, and she said there is no way that she would go through with the pregnancy. She doesn't agree with abortion either, but she says this case is an exception to the rule."

"All I can say is we all have to live with the choices we make, and Tinisha knows what she can live with and what she can't. None of us have a right to make that choice for her."

"I agree with you wholeheartedly. Okay, let me fill you in on the case."

"I am all ears."

In a nutshell, the string of burglaries had been committed by a group of young boys who lived in a foster home. The boys had been mistreated by their foster parents for some time and decided to break into people's homes and take money and other things they could sell to get money. They had taken it into their own hands to get money to get the things they needed like clothes and shoes because their foster parents weren't supplying them with the basic necessities, except for food, and they were too young to get jobs.

When questioned if they had spoken to a social worker about their living conditions, they said that they had on numerous occasions but to no avail.

They were scheduled to appear before the judge in the next few weeks. It was speculated that they may be placed into a juvenile detention facility or on probation or both. The foster parents, on the other hand, would be placed under supervision and the money that they received monthly for the four boys was suspended.

Rafael was glad to hear about the outcome of the case, but he was sorry to hear about the mistreatment of the boys and the situation it placed them in. How does one judge the acts that one does to survive, he wondered.

Friday

Bright and early in the morning before Tinisha awoke, Raf went for a jog in the park. He loved the smell of the fresh morning air and the sounds of the birds chirping. As he ran, he passed by other joggers who obviously shared in his enjoyment. Some were mothers who ran behind strollers that had three wheels, one large one in the front and two behind. These strollers were built for occasions such as these. Other joggers were dog owners who were taking care of two tasks at once: walking the dog and getting their own personal exercise.

When he returned, he found Tinisha with her head buried in her study guide. This is the position she had been in for the last two days. She was making great progress and was looking forward to her bar exam with great anticipation.

Noticing his entrance, she lifted her head and pushed back the strands of hair that had fallen loose from her ponytail. "Hey there, good looking," she greeted him with a sly smile as she removed her reading glasses.

"Hey yourself," he responded. "How's it going?"

"You know, the more I study, the more I feel ready to take the test. Each day, I get more and more excited, especially with the invitation of calling Snyder and Beckman after I pass the bar."

"I know how you feel. Moving into a position that you have wanted for so long is very refreshing and definitely something to look forward to."

After his comment, Tinisha got the feeling that Rafael wasn't only speaking about her anymore. She began to survey his face a little closer. She noticed the haze in his eyes that told her that he was a million miles away. When he noticed her examining him, he had to laugh. "I thought I was the detective in the family."

"You are, but a good lawyer always looks for unspoken clues that are hidden in the expressions of one's face. So tell me. What is going on?"

"Well, there may be some talk about me making sergeant."

Tinisha jumped up from the chaise that sat right by the windowsill in the master bedroom and put her arms lovingly around Rafael's neck. "When were you going to tell me?"

"The captain just called me a minute ago before I came back in. It's not official. There are some formalities that need to take place."

"Oh sure formalities. You have this in the bag, and you know it, Raf," Tinisha said teasingly.

Raf just smiled as he walked toward the shower.

* * * * * *

Back in Hollywood, the Oglebees were having date night, which they had been doing every Friday night for as long as they could remember. Dressed in an all black form-fitting dress, Delores stunned her husband with her graceful presence. To her amazement, her husband had decided to give her eyes a treat too. He wore a two piece navy blue suit with a cream colored shirt. What she liked best was that he was not wearing a tie. She liked to see him looking relaxed, very smooth and debonair. This gave her goose bumps.

As they went out for their evening on the town, they were able to relax and enjoy themselves because they knew their daughter was in the capable hands of one of LAPD's finest, Mr. Rafael Salisbury.

Tonight, they decided to dine at Benny Hanna's. They loved the cuisine, the service was stellar, and the ambiance was perfect for lovers.

The Oglebees chose a booth in the corner of the restaurant that was lit by a small candle on the table and a soft bulb overhead. As they waited for their waiter to come, they held hands and talked.

Saturday

Feeling in the mood to prepare dinner, Tinisha and Rafael went to one of the local markets to get the necessary ingredients for Tinisha to make her famous spaghetti. When they returned from the store, Rafael set the atmosphere by taking out a pair of long stemmed wine glasses from the cupboard that seemed to be placed there just for their use. In his glass, Rafael poured red wine. In Tinisha's glass, he poured red grape juice. After having a toast, Tinisha put on an apron and switched into her cooking mode.

After preparing the spicy Italian sausage, sautéing the bell peppers and onions, and browning the ground beef, Tinisha prepared the base of the sauce. When it tasted to her satisfaction, she was ready to mix everything together and add all the special seasonings that gave it a delectable flavor. No one who had ever tasted Tinisha's spaghetti could resist it; Rafael included.

As Raf tried to enjoy the Laker/King game as he sipped from his second glass of wine, he was continuously distracted by the aroma that drifted from the kitchen to the living room where he sat in a lazy boy recliner. The temptation finally got the best of him, so he slowly made his way into the kitchen like a thief in the night, after he saw Tinisha go to the restroom.

Trying very hard to be quiet, Raf slowly lifted the lid from the pot that held the sauce that had been simmering for what felt like hours to Rafael. After dipping the cooking spoon into the sauce, blowing it to prevent scorching his tongue, and sliding it into his mouth, he felt Tinisha standing behind him before he could swallow. Very sheepishly, he turned around and smiled a grin full of spaghetti sauce.

"I caught you red-handed, or should I say red- toothed?" Tinisha smiled as she took the spoon out of Raf's hand.

"I couldn't resist. Is it ready yet? I'm starving."

"Yes, I will make your plate. I believe I saw some serving trays in the pantry. I will bring it to you, so you can finish enjoying the game. By the way, who's winning?"

"Unfortunately, the Kings are up right now."

Rafael was a die-hard Laker fan. He couldn't stand to miss a game, even though he often times did. That was the life of a police officer. Crime schedules their time, not basketball games.

After having a complete dinner of Caesar salad, spaghetti, and garlic bread, the lovebirds went for a walk. As Tinisha gazed up at the evening stars, her mind drifted, and Rafael felt her squeezing his hand. He knew that something had captured her attention. She seemed like a million miles away.

"Anything you want to share," Rafael asked in a soft voice. He silently hoped that whatever Tinisha was thinking about was pleasant. He desperately wanted to protect her from all hurt, but he knew that was impossible. Every time he noticed her thinking or being quiet, it gave him a start. He didn't know if she was thinking about Joel or the baby or what.

"I was just thinking about my grandmother. I miss her so much. I just wish she was here right now. I could really use one of her hugs," Tinisha said as an unexpected tear fell from her eye. As she felt the moistness on her cheek, she was amazed at how one thought of her grandmother made her all choked up. Sometimes she did not think that she would ever fully get over not having her grandmother around to share things with.

Rafael knew how Tinisha felt about her maternal grandmother. He was there when she passed away last year. Even though it hurt Tinisha greatly, she handled the death of her grandmother very well. They had been extremely close, and they had spent a lot of time together.

Rafael continued to hold Tinisha's hand as they walked along the pathway through the park. Everything was very peaceful, and it was nice seeing all the families together enjoying an evening in the park. One family was having a barbeque. There must have been at least thirty or forty people at that gathering. Another group was having a birthday party for a little boy who appeared to have been turning a year old. He was having the time of his life. There was even a group of senior citizens hanging out and playing cards. Everyone seemed to be having and enjoyable time; Tinisha and Rafael were no exception.

After watching the stars and seeing each group leave one by one, Tinisha and Raf began to make their way back to the house. The breeze from the ocean had come closer inland, and they were getting a little cold.

Back inside, they turned on the electric fireplace and sat together on the couch with a bowl of popcorn to catch a late night movie. Eventually, Tinisha dozed off, and Rafael picked her up and carried her to the bedroom. I wonder how much longer I will be able to do this, Raf wondered has he thought about Tinisha gaining weight from the pregnancy.

We have only been here for just over a week, but Rafael has run out of clean clothes. And he asked me why I had a lot of suitcases. This is why! So, I wouldn't have to worry about running out of clothes. Luckily, we are staying at this house instead of a hotel. If we were in a hotel, I would have to find a laundry mat somewhere. I'll just throw some of his outfits in the washer, and he should be set for the rest of our vacation.

Now where did Mrs. Potter say the washing machine and dryer are, she wondered to herself. I know she told me, but I was so enthralled with the décor of their beautiful home that I did not hear everything she said. Well, I guess I will go on a scavenger hunt until I find them. Hum, I wonder where this door leads.

* * * * * *

Across the street, Rafael was doing his two-mile run, as he was accustomed to doing every morning back home in LA. He usually used this time to clear his head, but today it seemed really cluttered. One thing that he kept thinking really hard about was his and Tinisha's future together. They had planned to get married after she finished law school and landed a job somewhere and after he focused on making it up the ranks to sergeant. But the more he thought about it he didn't know why those things were so important that they had to come first. After Tinisha's disappearance, Raf had begun to see a lot of things differently.

He knew that it was time for him to take a step in a direction that would solidify their future. The more he thought about it, he didn't really want to pay rent and utilities on two places. He didn't mind doing it if he had to, but the truth is he just wanted Tinisha with him. He wanted to come home to her every night. He wanted to wake up with her every morning. He wanted them to have a family like all the people they had seen in the park last night. He wanted to build a future with her.

The more he thought about it, the more he knew that he had to put a plan into action. First, he needed to get the blessing of her father. He knew that he was in good standing with Pastor Oglebee, but he wanted to be respectful as his parents raised him to be. Therefore, he would go to her father and ask for his daughter's hand in marriage. He would do it when they returned from their vacation, he promised himself. No more prolonging the inevitable.

Thinking of his parents, he was saddened by the thought that they were not alive to witness this soon-to-be happy occasion in his life. They had been killed in a train accident that occurred nearly ten years ago when he had recently entered the academy. After raising their only two children, his parents had decided to take a long vacation. Their son was in the police academy and their daughter had just enrolled at UCLA. So, they decided to take some time for themselves and go on a much-needed vacation.

They were taking a coast-to-coast tour from California to New York. In some cities, they would rent a car and drive to the next city or state. In other places, they would ride the Amtrak train. After spending a few weeks to get to New York, they were on their way back home. In Cincinnati, Ohio, they boarded a train that ended up derailing, taking their lives along with seventy other passengers. He and his sister's only comfort was that they went together. They knew that neither of their parents would have wanted to live without the other. They had been married twenty-two years. They were still young. There life was cut short in the prime of their lives.

Thinking about his future plans, Raf smiled to himself, taking comfort that his only sibling, Yvette would be there to celebrate with him. Two years his junior, Yvette had started her family two years ago. She and her husband Donald have a set of fraternal twins, Yasmin and Donald, Jr. The babies are only a year old and as cute as can be. Raf didn't get a chance to see them much because they had moved to Rancho Cucamonga, in the Inland Empire, about six months ago. But he would do better about seeing them. He didn't want his niece and nephew growing up and not knowing their only maternal uncle.

On the way back to the house, continuing his jog nd still thinking about his plan, Rafael thought about Tinisha's ring. They had gone to look at wedding rings at the jewelry store a few times, so he knew that the princess cut diamond was her favorite. He also knew that when he chose a diamond for her that it should be one that she could see with her naked eye and not have to use a magnifying glass for assistance. He had to laugh at Tinisha. She was pretty specific about what she wanted and how she wanted it.

When Rafael entered the house, he had fully expected to smell breakfast cooking, but he didn't smell anything coming from the kitchen nor did he hear a sound coming from any of the rooms. Where is Nisha, he wondered. After calling her name several times, he stepped back outside to see if his car was still parked in the carport on the other side of the house. Maybe she went to the store, he thought.

After seeing the car still parked in the carport, Raf became concerned. "Where could she have gone?" he asked himself aloud as he felt a knot beginning to grow in his stomach. This is the same feeling he had when he had shown up at the club and Tinisha was gone.

After walking back and forth through the house about four times, Raf finally noticed a door open towards the back of the house. "I wonder where this goes," he said. As he peered through the door, he noticed how dark it was inside.

"Nisha?" Raf called out.

"I'm down here, Raf. Be careful."

"Where is the light?"

"I don't know but one of the steps is loose. Be careful."

"Okay. Are you alright?"

"No, I think I may have broken my leg. It hurts really badly."

"Okay, hang on. I think I remember seeing a flashlight in the drawer."

"Okay, hurry!" The pain in Tinisha's leg was excruciating. She had never had a broken bone before, so she didn't know if it was actually broken, but she knew that something was definitely wrong with it.

After finding the flashlight, Raf made his way down the steps into the basement. At the bottom of the steps lay Tinisha. He looked back up to see how far the broken step was. It was near the top. Tinisha had fallen quite a long way.

"Can you move?"

"No, that's why I am still on the floor."

"Oh, right. Sorry. How long have you been here?"

"I think about twenty or thirty minutes."

Raf attempted to help Tinisha up, but she began to scream so loud that it scared him. "Call an ambulance, Raf."

Raf ran back up the stairs to try to find a phone book. Flipping frantically through the pages, he stopped almost at once. What am I thinking, he asked himself. He quickly grabbed his cell phone and dialed 911.

About twenty minutes later, the paramedics had Tinisha in the back of the ambulance and were on the way to the nearest hospital. Raf followed in his car, so he could drive them back to the rental house. On the five-mile ride to the hospital, the pain was so great that Tinisha passed out before the paramedics could administer any pain medicine.

Once Tinisha was safely out of the ambulance and safely in the emergency room, the nurse asked Rafael if Tinisha is allergic to any pain medicine. He told her that she isn't but she is pregnant so she can't have any. At that point, the nurse immediately began to attach an ultrasound machine to check on the baby.

"How far along is she?" the nurse asked.

"Six weeks," Raf answered.

"When was the last time she saw a doctor?"

"About a week ago."

"And everything was normal?"

"Yes, why are you asking these questions?"

"I am not detecting a heart beat or any movement from her uterus."

"What does that mean?" Raf asked confused.

"We are going to have to do a pelvic exam to check the baby. Please step outside."

Raf's heart pounded as he once again reached for his cell phone to call Delores Oglebee. At least it isn't as bad as last time, he thought as he dialed the number. That thought was only a little reassuring. He still wasn't looking forward to making the call.

Wednesday

When the doctor prepared to conduct the pelvic exam to check the baby's condition yesterday, he noticed that Tinisha was bleeding from her vagina as he and the nurse removed her pants. After the pelvic exam and another look at the ultrasound, it was determined that the baby had no heartbeat. Tinisha had miscarried as a result of the fall.

Once she heard the news, she didn't know how she felt about that. She felt confused all over again. She didn't know if she should rejoice because she didn't have to carry the baby of her rapist or abandon it by giving it up for adoption. She also didn't know if she should feel sad for the unborn baby that she lost. She just felt numb.

Rafael wasn't any better; he just paced the floor. There were a million questions going through his head. He felt like this was his fault again because he wasn't there to protect her. He knew this was unreasonable because neither of them knew that danger awaited Tinisha in the basement. She was merely trying to wash clothes. Nevertheless, Raf felt bad. At the same time though, he felt relieved. He had not agreed with Tinisha's decision to have the baby in the first place, but he respected what she was going to do, and he was determined to stand by her. He was relieved that things had not turned out the way they had originally thought that they would.

* * * * * *

At the Oglebee residence, Delores picked up the phone and dialed Raf's cell phone number. Her husband sat across from her at the dining room table.

After briefly speaking to Raf, she asked to speak to her daughter. Tinisha pulled herself up in the bed and reached for the phone. She shared the news with her mother. She had been too exhausted last night to call again after Raf had spoken to them earlier.

"Well, the Lord works in mysterious ways, Nisha," her mom said softly into the phone. "We can't dwell over the lost. We have to look ahead to the future."

"I know, Mom. You are right."

"You can close this chapter, sweetheart. You have the rest of your life to look forward to. By the way, did you talk to the doctor and ask if everything is alright inside your uterus?"

"Well, they had to do a D&C to make sure that nothing was left inside."

"Yes, but did you ask him if there was any permanent damage?"

"Oh, yeah. He said everything looks fine, and I should have no problem having a baby after my body heals, not that that is something that I am looking to do right away."

"Praise the Lord. That's all I wanted to know. I just want to make sure that you are okay."

After Delores and Nisha spoke for a few moments more, Pastor Oglebee extended his hand towards his wife. This was his way of notifying her that she had done her fair share of talking and that he wanted to speak to his daughter. Delores politely handed the phone over to her husband. When Earl got the phone in his hands, he immediately began to pray. “Tinisha, bow your head,” she heard her dad say. When she heard his voice, she obeyed.

“Father, in the name of Jesus. I thank you now, Lord for sparing my daughter’s life again. I thank you God for keeping her close to your bosom. Father, I know the soul of her unborn baby is with you Lord God….”

As Tinisha listened to her father pray, the numbness left her body and the tears fell freely from her eyes. After Pastor Oglebee finished praying with his daughter, Tinisha handed the phone back to Raf.

Just as Tinisha finished talking to her dad, the nurse came in with her discharge papers and a pair of crutches. It turns out that Tinisha had not broken her leg, but it was badly sprained.

After getting back to the vacation house, Raf and Tinisha decided they were ready to go back home. They had enjoyed their vacation, but it had come to an abrupt end. As Tinisha sat on the sofa in the living room, she gave directives, and Rafael gathered all of their belongings, including his clothes that lay in a heap at the bottom of the basement stairs.

* * * * * *

An hour later, Raf pulled into his garage. He decided to take Tinisha to his condo so she would not have to go up and down the stairs putting undue pressure on her body and ankle. He did not want anything to prevent her from having a successful recovery.

(Two weeks later)

Two weeks later after Tinisha had been released from the hospital and had been letting her body recuperate from the miscarriage and her ankle from the sprain, she was ready to take the bar exam. While off her feet, she studied and studied, until she couldn't study anymore. Her mother had spent time quizzing her during the day, and Rafael and Karen quizzed her at night. Her big test day is tomorrow, one week before Thanksgiving. She had to be at the test location at eight am. After having not been nervous about the test, Tinisha was beginning to feel the butterflies congregate in her stomach.

To make matters worse, everyone was calling to send her well wishes, blessings, and good luck on her test. She felt like the whole world was counting on her to pass the test. How did everyone know about it, she wondered.

To take her mind off the test for a moment, she and her mom decided to prepare for the Thanksgiving holiday. They discussed the menu trying to decide what they would have for the appetizers, the main dinner and dessert. They wanted to make everything extra special because Yvette, Donald, and the twins would be joining them. Tinisha thought it would also be nice to invite Karen, her husband Raymond, their son Brandon, and Derrick and Melissa. They had all been so sweet and had helped out all they could with everything that Tinisha had been dealing with. She felt like they were all one big happy family.

When the menu had been discussed and decided upon, the list included deviled eggs, steamed oysters, clam dip, and chips and salsa for the appetizers; fried turkey, baked honey-glazed ham, beef roast, greens, mashed potatoes and gravy, macaroni and cheese, a green salad, and cornbread dressing for the main course; lemon cake, peach cobbler, and sweet potato pie for dessert. Tinisha almost felt full from just discussing all the tasty entrees.

* * * * * *

At the police station, Raf and Derrick were finishing their day. "Derrick, do you think you and Melissa will make it to Thanksgiving dinner at Nisha's parents' home?"

"Of course. We are looking forward to it. After my parents retired back home to Mississippi, Thanksgiving hasn't been quite the same. So we are looking forward to being with our adopted family."

"I'm glad to hear that you think of us as family. We feel the same way about you guys. Remind me. What is the deal with your wife's family?"

"About five years ago, the truth came out about an affair that her dad had. It just broke the family apart."

"I can see it splitting up the mother and father and even the kids being mad at their dad, but why isn't Melissa talking to her mom?"

"You know, I could never figure that part out, and Melissa doesn't seem too inclined to tell me. So I stopped asking. I figure when she wants to talk about it she will."

"Well, whatever it is she needs to forgive and move on."

"Uh oh, am I talking to Minister Rafael?"

"You know the word says we are all ministers."

"Well, you sound like one more and more every day."

"I will take that as a compliment," Raf said as he got in his car and waved goodbye as he headed out the parking lot.

Thursday

Well, today is my big day, Tinisha thought as she dressed in a pair of wool slacks and a pull-over sweater. She carefully combed her hair into a French roll leaving a few strands of loose hair to fall around her almond-shaped face. Afterwards, she applied her make-up.

"Are you just about ready?" her mother asked from the kitchen as she finished washing out her tea cup.

"I'll be right there, Mom," Tinisha answered from her bedroom.

"Is there anything you are required to take with you?"

"Yes, my driver's license and my registration ticket. Both are in my purse," Tinisha answered as she grabbed her keys and walked towards the front door. Walking by the kitchen, she noticed that her mother had washed the breakfast dishes. "Mom, you didn't need to clean up. I would have done it when I came home."

Delores had come by early that morning to accompany Tinisha to her test appointment. She had decided that Tinisha needed a good start to her day, so she had prepared breakfast. She made Tinisha's favorite omelet with two eggs, bits of sausage and bacon, cheese, onions, and mushrooms. To top the breakfast off were English muffins and strawberry preserves.

"It was my pleasure to do it, honey! I just wanted to keep busy while you showered and dressed. Besides, you know I don't like a dirty kitchen."

"Yes, I know, Mom," Tinisha laughed as they walked down the stairs. "You know, Mom, you are being envied today," Tinisha continued.

"Oh, really? And why is that?" Delores queried.

"There were a few people who wanted to be in the position you are in today going with me to the take the bar exam. Raf wanted to come, but he just took vacation, so I know he needed to be on his beat. Karen wanted to come, but she really needs to complete her internship hours. Dad wanted to come, but I know he had his weekly bishops and pastors' meeting. Even Melissa volunteered to come."

"But you chose me. Now isn't that a privilege," Delores marveled.

"Of course it is. You get to escort the soon-to-be esquire of the family," Tinisha said half jokingly.

"Yes, and it is an honor to do so!" Delores responded looking at her daughter lovingly as they drove down the street. Delores was extremely proud of her daughter. Words could not explain the joy that Tinisha's life brought to her own. Yes, there had been some trying times and sorrowful moments of late, but before that raising Tinisha and watching her grow into adulthood had been a true blessing. Delores and Tinisha had always been close.

Delores did have to wonder why Tinisha had chosen to work at a club. Even with Tinisha's daredevil streak, it was really unexpected of her. She was relieved to hear that Tinisha did not perform any special sexual favors for the male customers. She did occasionally do some dancing, not strip dancing, but her primary job at the club had been as a server.

After giving Tinisha's job choice much thought,
Delores figured that Tinisha had taken her life and all its responsibilities into her own hands. She paid her way through law school without the use of student loans, and she paid all her other expenses, not to mention the help she gave her father for her mother's convalescent bill. Overall, Delores was very proud of Tinisha, and she let her know every chance she had.

Once they reached the test site, Tinisha took a deep breath and exhaled. "You will do fine," her mother assured her.

"I love your confidence in me, Mom," Tinisha answered.

"Oh sorry to burst your bubble, but my confidence is in the ability that God gave you. He has given you a brilliant mind. You just remember that, and you pray your way through this test. You will do just fine," her mother beamed. "I'll be right here working on my crossword puzzle. Then I'll go next door for a little snack. I know you will be a while. Don't worry about me."

As Tinisha walked into the building, she pulled out her cell phone and dialed Raf. When he answered, she said, "Well babe, this is it. I'm going in!" Raf laughed. He liked the way Tinisha made everything sound like an adventure. "Best wishes to you, babe. Call me when you are done."

As Raf closed his cell phone, he whispered a prayer for her. Like Delores, he was proud of Tinisha's progress with her career goal.

After six hours and answering the last of the two hundred questions on the test, Tinisha breathed another sigh. This time it was a sigh of relief. She had passed over another hurdle. Now all she had to do was wait for the test results to be mailed to her.

Sunday

As the congregation filled the pews early Sunday morning, Tinisha made her way to her appointed seat with Rafael by her side. After the opening prayer, scripture, and song, Pastor O gave a special welcome to his daughter and told her that the church had been praying for her and her well being. Everyone stood up, clapped and cheered. Some even walked over and embraced her.

All the love brought tears to Tinisha's eyes. She had not realized how much she missed the love and fellowship of fellow believers. Then even more unexpectedly, Pastor O asked Tinisha if she wanted to have a word. Surprising herself, she walked up to the podium, took the microphone and began sharing her testimony and praising God as the tears continued to fall down her eyes. They were tears of pure joy.

Throughout her years of growing up, Tinisha had learned to expose the enemy. Keeping secrets leads to depression, bitterness, anger, sickness and disease. Tinisha had personally declared that she would not receive any more attacks from the enemy. She declared her authority in her savior. As she returned to her seat, the congregation cheered again.

When Tinisha had awakened that morning, she was apprehensive about going to the service. It had been a couple of months since she had gone. She missed hearing her father preaching the word, but she didn't want to be the victim of ridicule. Now that she had come, she was happy that she did. Her experience was not as she had expected.

Wednesday

The evening before Thanksgiving Day, Tinisha packed a suitcase, turned off all the lights, and headed for the front door. She was on her way for a night away from home. She was going to a place that was very familiar and comfortable. It was a space she could still call her own. Tonight, she would spend the night in her old bedroom at her parents' home.

After Tinisha and her mother made the menu for Thanksgiving, it was decided that to take the proper time to prepare for thirteen people, Tinisha would need to spend ample time at her parents' home assisting her mother. Before going to the Oglebee household, Tinisha prepared the honey-baked ham and the greens. On her way, she stopped by and picked up the fried turkey from one of the local barbeque diners. Every year, the diner offered a special on turkeys to the residents of the local community. The customers could get their turkey smoked, deep fried, or traditional. They even offered turducken, a dish consisting of a partially de-boned turkey stuffed with a de-boned duck, which itself is stuffed with a small de-boned chicken.

When Tinisha arrived at her parents' home, before she could step onto the driveway, her dad was helping her out of the car.

"Hey there, sugar plum," Pastor O greeted his daughter with a warm smile and a tender hug.

"Hey Dad," Tinisha replied as she felt her heart jump. She knew how much everything that had happened had hurt her father. She was determined to let him know that she was doing well. She did not want him to be unnecessarily concerned.

As she made several trips into the house to bring everything in with the help of her father, Tinisha enjoyed the smell of the sweet aromas that filled the air. She reminisced about all the holidays they had spent in this home. The smells of the different foods brought back precious memories. When Tinisha had finally unloaded the car, she searched for her mother.

Not seeing Delores downstairs anywhere, Tinisha headed up the stairs to her parents' bedroom. As she rounded the corner, she and her mother bumped into each other. The two women immediately began to laugh and hug each other. From their actions and the smiles that plastered their faces, you would not believe they had just seen each other on Sunday, three days ago.

By midnight, the two women were fully exhausted. They had laughed and reminisced about old times as they chopped celery and onions for the dressing. In between chopping, cutting, slicing and dicing, they added the two table extenders so that ten adults, one child, and two toddlers in highchairs could fit around the table. By the time all the food had been cooked, fresh linen had been placed on the table along with the dinnerware. Taking a final look at the table and being pleased, Tinisha and her mom went upstairs to their respective rooms.

"Good night, Mom," Tinisha called out without turning her head.

"Good night, sweetheart. See you in the morning," Delores answered.

"Okay, but not too early," Tinisha yawned. Delores nodded in agreement.

Thanksgiving Day

By two o'clock in the afternoon, all the guests had gathered and had made themselves comfortable. Brandon and the twins had found a place to play; Tinisha, Karen, Melissa, Yvette, and Delores were in the kitchen; and Earl, Rafael, Derrick, Raymond, and Donald were in the living room watching a football game. The house was merry with conversation and the aroma of the food filled each room.

The spirit of Thanksgiving was in full effect. An hour later, everyone gather around the dining room table and held hands as Earl Oglebee led grace. Once they were seated and everyone had served him/herself, Melissa asked if it would be okay if each person shared one thing he/she was grateful for. Everyone was in agreement; one by one each person shared.

"I'll begin," Raf volunteered, "I am thankful that my sweetheart is safe and doing well. I don't know what I would do without her." Everyone included Tinisha began to comment on how sweet Raf was. "Thank you. Thank you," Raf continued, "but I'm not finished yet. I am also thankful that my sister and her family are here. We have not seen each other since her birthday in June."

"Thanks, big brother," Yvette replied. "I am thankful that Tinisha's parents have such big hearts that they would allow us to come into their home. Because of their love, I am able to spend the holiday with my big brother. Secondly, I am excited to announce that there will be a new addition to our family." After everyone congratulated Yvette and Donald, Earl chimed in.

"I am tremendously blessed that my wife and I will be celebrating our thirtieth wedding anniversary in a few months. God has kept the love alive and new. Of course, I am thankful for my daughter's life. She is our gift from God, even twenty-six years later." Everyone clapped in response to Pastor Oglebee's touching reflection. Some of the ladies even became teary-eyed.

"I'll take it from here," Delores responded, more to her husband than anyone else. "I am thankful for Raf being in Nisha's life. He has been a real blessing to her and all of us. Thank you so much for loving my daughter. When she is with you, her father and I worry less. I can't say we don't worry because we will always be concerned, but we know that when she is with you, she is safe." As Raf thanked Delores for her comments, he gently rubbed Tinisha's hand.

"I have to agree with you, Mom," Tinisha began, "I feel safe when Raf is around. He takes exceptional care of me and he is very supportive. I thank God for him. He is truly a blessing in my life. The same is true for my mom and dad who are always there for me. I also am thankful for Raymond because he never complains when Karen leaves him and Brandon alone when she comes to check on me. He is truly an understanding husband. Thank you, Raymond, for giving Karen space to be a true friend to me."

"You are very welcome, T. Speaking of my wife, I thank God for her because she is selfless. She put her dream on hold so I could work on mine. There are some women today who would not hear of it. But not my Karen. Thank you, babe!" Karen began crying. No one knew what to make of this. They did not know if they were tears of joy or tears of regret until she began to speak.

"I'm sorry you guys. I didn't mean to start balling like a blubbering idiot. I have watched so many marriages crumble because of self ambition and self centeredness. I don't want me and Raymond to fall victims and be statistics. We have had rough patches here and there like other couples, but I don't want anything to come between us. We both have dreams, and we just have to make a plan for what to do first, second, and so on. If we think of each other, we will make it. I am thankful that we have made it this far."

"I agree with you, Karen. I thank God for my wife. She must have had good role models in her parents because she is so kind to me and our kids. She sees to our every need. She knows what I am thinking before I say it, and she knows what I need before I ask. I am also thankful for my kids, and we are looking forward to the last one," Donald said looking matter-of-factly at his wife.

At this point all the adults had spoken except for Derrick and Melissa. They looked at each other as if to ask who would go first. Derrick nodded at Melissa giving her the go ahead. "Well, as for me. I am thankful that God has kept my husband safe while he is out there on his beat. Many cops' wives can't say the same, but I am glad that I have a wonderful testimony. But I do have a bit of news for my husband."

"What is it honey?" Derrick inquired.

"We are going to have our first child," she almost whispered.

"Did you say a baby?" Derrick asked leaning toward his wife.

"Yes, honey," she answered still speaking softly.

"That's good news. We have been trying for awhile. Why are you whispering though?" Derrick wanted to know.

"I didn't know if I should share that news here," she answered looking toward Tinisha.

"Oh, it is okay, Melissa. Don't worry about me. I'm fine," Tinisha answered understanding what she meant. Everyone became quiet. No one knew what to say next. Tinisha felt it was up to her to reassure everyone that she was doing fine with losing the baby. "Look everyone; I know that losing a baby is usually a sad event. I do feel sad from time to time, but I feel more relieved than anything. I trust that God knows what He is doing. So don't feel like you need to tiptoe around me. Just be normal. I am okay. Derrick, I believe you are the last one to share, so let's hear it. What are you thankful for?"

"I am thankful for my wife and my friends. I am thankful that we can all gather together and just take time out for each other. Time goes so fast and when we look around, it is gone. Time is too precious to waste." Just as Derrick finished talking, his cell phone rang. When he went to answer it, Raf's phone begin to ring too. Everyone knew what that meant. They would have to leave.

"Before you go gentlemen, I do have one final announcement to make," Tinisha said as she stood up. Everyone became still and the room became quiet. Tinisha began to laugh uncontrollably when she saw the serious looks on everyone's face. "It's not a serious matter, but it is important. I just wanted to let my dad know that if the position is still open for the Youth Department Director, I will fill it until I really get going with my cases."

"What cases?" someone asked.

"The cases that I will have soon after I receive a passing score for the bar," Tinisha said confidently.

"Yes, Tinisha the position is still open, and we would be glad to have you fill it. Welcome aboard," Earl beamed.

After Derrick and Rafael left with their food wrapped to go, the rest of them finished their meal while sharing stories. Eventually, the other men retired back to the living room. The women put the babies to sleep and pulled out the UNO cards and played until the late night hours.

Friday

As Rafael stepped into the squad room early Friday morning, after having been there late on Thanksgiving Day, his fellow officers were making their way in as well. Everyone was in a good mood because traditionally this was the day that yearly bonuses were handed out. The question was how much the bonus would be. As the captain stepped up to his podium, a hush fell over the room.

"Good morning officers," Captain Monahan said cheerfully. In unison, the officers responded, "Good morning, Captain Monahan."

"I want to take this time to commend all of you for a job well done over this year. We have had some wild and trying cases to say the least, from the Hollywood Serial Killer to the youth burglars. So, for all of your hard work, each of you will receive a hearty bonus. I know you are all anxious to wrap your hands around your checks, but before Amanda hands them out, I have another important announcement."

"More important than money?" someone joked.

"I am sure it is important to the officers whose names I am about to call," Captain Monahan answered. "I am proud to recognize two of LAPD's Hollywood Division's finest officers. First, Sergeant Billings is being promoted to the rank of lieutenant after serving for this department for sixteen faithful years." Everyone applauded and gave him attaboys and pats on the back. Once the officers quieted down, Captain Monahan continued.

"Secondly, I am especially proud to promote Detective Rafael Salisbury from detective to sergeant. He has truly earned this rite of passage. We will do this formally in a couple of days, so that you guys can invite your families to come and see you get your new stripes and medals." Again everyone cheered and shook Rafael's hand. His heart seemed like it skipped two beats. He was overjoyed, but he wished he could have seen the look on his dad's face when he heard the news. He could only hope that his father was looking down on him and getting the news.

"Okay, now for your bonuses! I am giving bonuses to the newly promoted officers first. As you all know, bonuses are given by rank, and this year for the first time, newly promoted officers will receive the bonus that is commensurate with their new rank rather than their outgoing rank."

This news was music to Raf's ears. Rather than the $1500 he usually received, he received $3000. He knew exactly where this money was going. He would head to the jewelry store directly after work to purchase Tinisha's engagement ring. He just had to choose the one that would be perfect for her. He didn't know if the $3000 would cover it, but it would cover most of the cost. He would worry about the complete wedding ring set later. The question was when he would pop the question. He had to finalize his plan. There were two dates he had in mind, but which would it be, he asked himself.

* * * * * *

After spending some time in Jared's Jewelry store and purchasing an engagement ring for Tinisha, Rafael phoned Pastor O to set an appointment to talk to him. Pastor O was on his way home and suggested that they meet at his home. Rafael agreed and began to drive in that direction.

As Raf drove, he began to feel a little apprehensive. He had never asked for someone's hand in marriage before, and he did not plan on having to do it again. This was a onetime only thing as far as he was concerned.

After pulling into the Oglebees' driveway, Rafael said a quick prayer for strength before going up the short set of steps that led to the front door. Ringing the doorbell, Rafael felt a warm wave come over him. He did not know what it was, but he suddenly felt calm. After entering the Oglebee home and being greeted by First Lady Oglebee, Raf made his way to the living room to wait for his future father-in-law.

A few minutes later, Earl entered the living room.

"Good to see you again so soon, Raf. To what do I owe this pleasure?"

"Well, sir. I have come to ask for your daughter's hand in marriage," Rafael began.

"You know, Raf. I always envisioned this day coming, and I knew that I would have a long list of questions for the fellow who would come and ask to marry my daughter. But, you know, that is not the case. My wife and I have been waiting for the day that you and Tinisha would wed. I had a good feeling about you when we first met. That has not changed. I know that you love her and that you put her first in your life. I can see that you are not a selfish person, and I would be honored for you to join my family by marrying my daughter. I just ask that you continue to take care of her and be the provider and protector that God has called you to be as you stand in the position of high priest in your home. Have you asked Tinisha yet?"

"No, sir, I haven't. I wanted to get your blessing first. You know, I want to do everything decently and in order. Of course, Nisha and I have talked about getting married, but I have not officially asked her."

"Well, all in due time, son. All in due time."

"Yes, sir," Raf responded, "I am working on a plan now."

"I am sure that you are. You and Tinisha are both good at that-planning. Well, I wish you all the best with your proposal. You know Tinisha can be a little bull headed at times."

"Yes, that's true, but I think I can handle her," Raf said laughing.

Saturday

In the middle of a crowded Olive Garden, Tinisha, Karen, and Melissa sat having lunch in the late afternoon. After running errands for their families, Karen and Melissa thought it would be good to check up on Tinisha to see how her spirits were. Over the phone, she always said she was doing just fine, but her friends wanted to see for themselves. They both had known other women who had experienced the trauma of rape or a miscarriage, and they wanted to be sure that she was dealing with her emotions.

After placing their order of a variety of salads and an order of the famous spinach and artichoke dip, the ladies settled into their conversation.

"I hear that Rafael has some pretty exciting news," Melissa began.

"Yes, as a matter of fact he does," Tinisha said grinning from ear to ear because she was so proud of Raf.

"Well, pray tell," Karen said. At this point, she was the only one at the table who did not know what was going on.

"Yesterday, Raf found out that he is being promoted from detective to sergeant. They will have the official ceremony tomorrow at the LAX Hilton. You should both come and bring your hubbies," Tinisha invited.

"Well, you know Derrick will be there automatically. He has to support his partner and fellow officer. He really has mixed emotions about this," Melissa said.

"Why is that?" Karen asked disturbed.

"With Raf being promoted to sergeant he will no longer be required to go out on a beat. So, Derrick will be getting a new partner," Tinisha answered for Melissa.

"Oh, I see. That is sad," Karen said.

"Yes, but that is good news for Raf and Tinisha. Raf will be making more money for all the kids he and Nisha are going to have," Melissa joked.

"All what kids?" Tinisha asked pretending to be offended.

"I know you are going to give the man a few kids. Aren't you, T?" Karen questioned.

"Oh, I may have one or two," Tinisha answered very smugly. "But two is my limit. And how are you coming along?" she asked Melissa.

Tinisha's question about Melissa's pregnancy caught Melissa off guard, she was still uneasy about talking about being pregnant around Tinisha.

"Oh, I'm doing fine," Melissa said almost in a whisper.

Tinisha noticing how uneasy Melissa was and the look that went across Karen's face made her decide that it was time to clear the air.

"Look you two. I know we haven't really talked about this, but I think it is time to get some things straight. I went through a horrible experience with Joel. Something I would have never expected to experience in my life. I would not wish it on my worst enemy. He violated me, and it is not something I will ever forget. But I do not want you to walk around me as if though there are eggshells on the floor or if I am going to break. I am strong. I am healing day by day. You can't try to keep things from me or avoid certain topics. I am happy that you and Derrick are having a baby. A baby is a precious gift from God, and I don't want you to feel like you can't share that with me. You are like a sister to me, and I am happy for what God is doing in your life. Just pray for me that I will grow stronger every day, and God will do the rest." As she spoke the tears fell from her eyes because she did not want her friends to hurt for her. She could only imagine how she would feel if it had happened to one of them rather than to her. She would be devastated too, so she understood how they felt.

After looking at the two ladies with tears in her eyes, Tinisha saw that they both had tears streaming down their faces. For a few moments, no one said a word. They all used their linen napkins to wipe the tears from their faces. "Are we clear?" Tinisha questioned.

"Of course," Melissa answered.

"Absolutely," Karen responded. "You sound like your old self girl. That's the Tinisha I know. The one who loves to take charge."

"Do you mean the one who can be downright bossy?" Melissa questioned with a smile.

"You are both right about. Well, I guess with that said, we don't have anything to worry about."

"I have one last question," Tinisha said.

"What is that?" Karen and Melissa said together looking more at each other than at Tinisha.

"Who's paying for lunch?" Tinisha asked as she filled her mouth with a nacho full of dip.

"Good question," Karen answered.

"You are!" Melissa said.

All three ladies burst into laughter as they began to enjoy their lunch and the great company that they were surrounded by. Before they knew it, hours had passed by. As other customers came and went, the three friends continued to enjoy each other's company. They stayed at the restaurant so long, their waiter wondered if they would soon need the dinner menu.

Sunday

On Sunday evening, after having spent a full day in church services and lunch with Raf and her parents, Tinisha sat at a table at the police annual banquet waiting to see Raf receive his promotion. Seated with Tinisha were her parents, Karen, Raymond, Brandon, Melissa, and Yvette. Donald, Yvette's husband, had stayed home with the twins, but Yvette came to support her brother and to share in his special moment.

Not long after the guests were all seated at their tables, the chief of police called for everyone's attention. Once the room was quiet, the uniformed officers paraded into the room in a single file line. Tinisha and her group, along with the other guests, stood and applauded the officers as most went to join their guests at the tables while the officers to be honored went and stood on the platform behind the chief.

As Raf mounted the platform, his smile lit up the room, Tinisha thought. She was proud of him. He had accomplished his dream.

After the promotions were announced, the newly decorated officers sat with their families. As Raf approached the table, both Tinisha and Yvette stood to greet him. Karen, the designated photographer, took plenty of pictures with Tinisha's digital camera. "Hey take one of us, too," Derrick requested as he and Melissa stood on either side of Raf.

Once Tinisha was satisfied with the number of pictures that had been taken, Rafael was released to sit down and enjoy the banquet. One by one, Raf's guests took turns to personally congratulate him.

Pastor Oglebee lifted his glass and said, "I want to make a toast." After everyone lifted their glasses in agreement, Pastor O continued, "To Rafael, a fine officer, may God continue to shine His favor upon you as you continue to be a blessing to this community. We could not ask for a finer officer. Keep up the good work."

"I second that," Derrick began. "I have seen firsthand the cases you have assisted in solving and the work you do on a daily basis. You have taught me quite a bit and you never harped on any mistakes that I have made. Thank you for being a great mentor. Although I know you deserve the promotion, I hate to see you go. I will miss working with you side by side. All the best to you, bud."

Just as Melissa was prepared to say a few words, Detectives Smith and Erickson approached the table. "Hey, it's the man of the hour," Smith chided. Rafael stood to greet his fellow officers and accepted their congratulations.

One by one, other officers made their way over to Rafael. As Rafael stood joking and laughing with other officers in the department, Tinisha and the others enjoyed their dinner. Although Tinisha had come to the banquet before, this was her parents' first time coming. They were really impressed with the impeccable style and taste of the department. Everything was first class, from the décor to the meal to the service. It was definitely a black tie affair. As her mother complimented the department on a job well done, Tinisha surveyed the table. She noticed how handsome her father and Raymond looked in their tuxedos and how beautiful the women looked in their dresses.

The dresses formed an array of colors. Tinisha and her mom wore black evening gowns. Delores' was long and flowing, while Tinisha's was shorter and tapered. Both were very elegant with their long hair coiffed into French roles with diamond earrings dangling from their ears. Also, both completed their outfits with a beautiful necklace and fur stole.

Yvette, a little more conservative, was dressed in a navy blue evening dress with elegant but simple jewelry. Karen was adorned in fabulous red. Her dress was full and flowing and the ruffled bottom swept across her silver shoes. Her short haircut flattered her long neck that was covered with a diamond choker. Finally, Melissa, who had a unique style, wore a deep purple that signified her royal standing in Jesus Christ. She looked completely regal. Unlike Karen, and the other ladies, her accents were gold. She was absolutely stunning.

Once Raf returned to his seat, the praises continued. As Tinisha listened to everyone speak, she couldn't help to feel that her life was back on track. She waited until all the others had finished before she began to speak. "Rafael Salisbury, you are the finest officer that I know, and I am honored to have you in my life. Every day I thank God for you. I know that you have worked hard for this promotion and you are well deserving of it. This is truly a dream fulfilled, but it is the first of many. And if I have anything to say about it, I will be here by your side congratulating and supporting you all the way.

Raf could not resist Tinisha's heartfelt sentiments. He leaned over, took her face in his hands and kissed her gently on the lips. Then he quietly turned to everyone else and thanked them for coming and sharing in this memorable occasion with him.

As the night came to an end, Rafael couldn't help but wish that his parents had been there too. He wanted to see the look on their faces as they enjoyed this promotion and honor with him. He truly missed their presence in his life, even ten years after they had been gone.

Thursday

(Three Weeks Later)

After showering and making a bite to eat, Tinisha headed toward the kitchen to retrieve the mail she had tossed on the counter the night before. After coming in from Wednesday night bible study, she was too tired to look at it. A large 9 x 11 envelope caught her attention. Reading the return address, she realized that the package was from the Bar Association. As she nervously opened the envelope that she knew contained the results of her bar exam, Tinisha prayed a quick prayer. All she could say was, "Lord, have your way. Have your way. Have your way."

The nervousness quickly changed to excitement as Tinisha read her passing score. She immediately let out a scream of joy as she jumped up and down. As she felt the tears of joy falling down from her eyes, she ran to her bedroom to get her cell phone. She didn't know who to call first: her mom at home, her dad at the church or Raf at his new desk. Maybe I should call Snyder and Beckman, she thought. They did tell me to call when I got my results, she reasoned. "Okay, okay. Calm down, girl," Tinisha told herself as she decidedly pressed the #1 on her speed dial.

"Sergeant Salisbury," Raf answered.

"Guess what?" Nisha asked.

"Hey babe. What's going on?" Raf asked casually.

"I passed the bar!" Tinisha yelled into the phone unable to contain her excitement. Normally, she would have made Raf guess her news, but today this was too big to hold in.

"Hey that's great! Congratulations. I guess this calls for a celebration," Raf said. "I'm taking you to dinner. Choose where you want to go, and I will pick you up at six. Okay?"

"Okay. Sounds great. I'll call you later. I need to call Mom and Dad. Love you!" Tinisha said hurriedly as she quickly pressed #2 on her speed dial to dial the next number.

"Hey darling," Delores answered as she looked at her caller id. "How are you doing today?"

"Absolutely fantastic," Nisha answered.

"Well that's good to hear. What's putting you in such a pleasant mood?" her mother inquired.

After Tinisha shared her good news with her mother, she proceeded to call her father, Karen, and then Melissa. Now I should call Snyder and Beckman, Tinisha thought.

After dialing the number to the law firm, Tinisha changed her mind before Bea answered the phone. After hanging up, Tinisha went into her bedroom, opened her closet, took out her black pants suit and began to get dressed. She decided this was a meeting that she wanted to have in person.

Once she was dressed, she redialed the firm and quickly made an appointment with Bea to meet with Snyder and Beckman. Fortunately, they both would be free right before the lunch hour. Driving to the law firm, Tinisha felt free. She had the same feeling she had the night Raf received his promotion. She felt rejuvenated and alive again. She felt as if though the plug that had been pulled from her was plugged in again.

As she drove, she turned on her cd player and put in a gospel cd by Devó Called & Chosen. She immediately turned to the song titled "My Father." This was one of her favorite songs. It really ministered to her, as she ushered in the presence of the Holy Spirit right into her car.

By the time Tinisha reached the firm, her spirit was totally refreshed and renewed. She felt as though she had a fresh anointing and nothing could prevent her from achieving all that God had promised her.

When she entered the main conference room, for a moment she felt like she was intruding because lunch was on the table, along with fresh flowers and a bottle of sparkling apple cider. Someone else must be celebrating too, Nisha thought.

Her thoughts abruptly came to an end as both Snyder and Beckman walked into the conference room from opposite sides. They both beamed at her and told her how good it was to see her.

"Have a seat," Beckman offered. Before Tinisha accepted his invitation, she handed him the envelope that contained her scores. After opening it and having a quick look, Beckman handed the contents to Snyder who also took a quick glance. Synder calmly placed the contents on the top of the envelope that Beckman had placed on the table as he began to speak.

"As we mentioned before Ms. Oglebee, we were
very pleased with the work that you did here as an intern, and we know that you have a promising future as a lawyer."

"That's why we are offering you a position with this firm. We are hoping that you will begin your career here with us," Beckman continued.

Deep inside, Tinisha had hoped that this is why they wanted her to contact them when her results arrived, but now that it was happening she was speechless. A little surprised at Tinisha's silence, Snyder asked, "Do you need a minute to think it over or a few days perhaps?"

"Oh no. I'm sorry. Please forgive me. I am truly honored at your offer. I guess I never expected to be offered a job so soon," Tinisha explained.

"We have a proposal already drawn up for you. Why don't you enjoy lunch and take the contract home and look it over. See if everything meets our expectations and let us know if you are interested," Beckman offered.

"I am definitely interested," Tinisha assured them. "I will take the proposal home. After my nerves have settled, I will take a look at it and give you a call on Monday. Is that okay?" Tinisha asked.

"That will be fine," Snyder and Beckman assured her.

Forty-five minutes later after enjoying the lunch that was purchased in her honor, Tinisha was back at her apartment with her new job offer in hand, along with the flowers that the partners had delivered to the firm for her.

* * * * * *

After Raf picked Tinisha up at six that evening, he drove to Tony Roma's, which was Tinisha's choice for the evening. He had called ahead to make reservations, and he had a bouquet of three dozen red roses delivered to the restaurant and placed on the table. He wanted the ambiance to be set perfectly. When Tinisha spotted the red roses on the table, chills went up and down her spine.

Once they were seated, Raf took a look at Nisha's exam scores and the proposal from Snyder and Beckman that she had chosen to accept. He congratulated her again. Taking the opportunity to order champagne, he lifted his glass and made a toast to her. Tonight, Tinisha was all grins, as she had been all day.

After a fun-filled and romantic dinner, Raf suggested dessert. While waiting for the waiter to bring their dessert order, Tinisha excused herself to the ladies' room, as she always does after dinner. While she was away, Raf slipped the ring box that held the engagement ring that he bought at Jared's under Tinisha's napkin.

When Tinisha approached the table, Raf stood and pulled out her chair. Just then the waiter approached the table with dessert. Prepared to satisfy her craving for chocolate covered cheesecake, Tinisha lifted her napkin spotting the ring box. "Open it," Raf said softly. As Tinisha's small fingers trembled, she opened the box.

With all her attention given to the box, she did not notice Raf slide out of his chair and down onto one knee right next to her chair. Seeing the beautiful platinum three-karat princess cut diamond ring, Tinisha let out a scream that resounded through the entire restaurant.

Looking up and seeing Rafael, tears streamed from Tinisha's eyes as they had earlier that morning. Taking one of her hands into his Raf asked, "Tinisha Ann Oglebee, you are the love of my life. I would love to have the honor of being your husband. Will you marry me?"

Tinisha looked deeply into Rafael's eyes, feeling his sincerity, and answered, "It would be my pleasure." Raf took the ring from the box and slipped it onto Nisha's finger.

All the onlooker's whose attention was attained by Tinisha's scream began to clap and cheer. Tinisha and Rafael, however, were in their own world. The only thing they heard was the beat of their own two hearts as they stood and embraced in the middle of the restaurant floor.

Christmas Eve

(Thursday, Dec. 24, 2009)

When Tinisha had arrived home after Raf proposed, she immediately began to call her friends and share the good news. After talking to her mother for hours, they planned to have a combined engagement dinner and Christmas party. The dinner would be held tonight, on Christmas Eve, so that everyone who wanted to attend could do so and still spend Christmas Day with their families.

To prepare for the dinner, Delores made reservations at The Reef Restaurant in Long Beach. It would be quite a drive for them, but they wanted a different atmosphere.

On the way to the restaurant, Raf received a call from Yvette. She called to inform him that she and her family would not be able to make it because the twins were a little under the weather. Raf immediately leaned over and asked Tinisha if she wanted to take a drive to Rancho Cucamonga on Christmas Day so he could spend time with his sister and her family. Tinisha quickly agreed; she was looking forward to getting to know Yvette better. Maybe she would end up being like the sister she never had.

Upon arriving to the restaurant, Tinisha noticed that several members of the church had come to dine with them. In all, there were thirty-three guests in their dinner party. Their presence made Tinisha feel warm and fuzzy and loved all over. Some of the guests even brought monetary gifts to assist with the wedding expenses. They commented that they want the best for two young people who want to live their lives upright before the Lord.

As the group dined, the guests began to ask questions about Tinisha's career as a lawyer. They knew that she passed the bar and they knew that Raf had recently received a promotion. They wanted to know if they would begin their family right away or if they would both work for a while first.

Tinisha was pleased to announce that she had been offered a position at the Law Firm of Snyder & Beckman and that she had accepted the offer. However, she did not tell them that she had been offered a first-year salary of $80,000. She kept that between herself and her inner circle. She was also pleased to announce that she would be starting her job in the new year, which was just a week away.

To answer the question about having children, both Raf and Tinisha answered that they would have plenty of time to talk about that later.

Before the night was over, the question about when the big day would be finally arose. Of course, Tinisha and Raf and already tossed around several dates. They finally agreed on a spring wedding. They would exchange their nuptials in April.

Tinisha had also decided that she wanted to have the wedding outdoors where she could enjoy the spring air and the beautiful flowers. They were planning to get married in Marina Del Rey, on a miniature bridge, at a beautiful park that was filled with beautiful green grass and an array of colorful flowers. Of course, everyone was invited to share their wedding day with them.

All Tinisha and Raf needed to decide now was their plans for a honeymoon.

Monday

April 26, 2010
(Four months later)

The sun was shining brightly upon the backs of the newlywed couple as they lay on the deck of a Carnival cruise ship. As they sailed through the Bahamas, they enjoyed each other's company as they relaxed during their seven-day long honeymoon. Rafael and Tinisha had been married just two days, and they were ecstatic about spending the rest of their lives together.

As Tinisha turned over and sat up on her lounge chair, she looked lovingly at her husband. "Mr. Salisbury, is there anything that I can get for you?"

"Not at the moment, Mrs. Salisbury. Is there anything you need, sweetheart? Raf asked with a smile. He loved the sound of Tinisha's new name.

"I was thinking about getting one or two of the chocolate-covered strawberries from the other side of the deck. I saw them when we came out. Maybe there are some left," Tinisha said with twinkles in her eyes.

"Let's go together," Raf said as he lifted himself up from his resting place.

Tinisha and Raf walked hand in hand across the deck. After helping themselves to the chocolate- covered strawberries and the other seasonal fruit that was available, Raf fed the strawberries to his wife. Tinisha loved the attention that Raf gave her. She was happy to have him all to herself for this week. Next week, they will go back to their careers.

Nisha had begun her career as a lawyer at Snyder & Beckman, and after only three and a half months, she had been assigned her first major case. She wasn't assigned first chair, but she would sit second chair. She was grateful for the opportunity, and her name would be recorded on the case. Many lawyers did not receive this privilege until after they had been a lawyer for a few years.

According to both Snyder and Beckman, she had proven herself to be very capable when she completed her research for the various cases that she was responsible for during her internship and when she shadowed the lawyers in court.

As for Rafael, he was still becoming acclimated to being a sergeant. It was very different for him, strange even. He was accustomed to being a part of the action, not waiting for it to come across his desk in written form. He felt a little out of place because he was still able to handle the physical part of police work, unlike some of the other sergeants. Age wise, he was in the same bracket as the detectives.

He even felt strange when he ran into Derrick and his new partner, Detective Ben Sternum, who was just transferred in from Florida. But he was getting the hang of it. He had to admit, he did enjoy being on the decision-making end of law enforcement. He along with the other sergeants and captains decided how the cases would be handled and which detectives would be placed on each case.

What he did not enjoy as much was engaging with the district attorneys who had a tendency to act as if though the cases were all theirs, making the police department feel as if though it did not have a hand in catching the perps.

Emotionally, both were doing well. Tinisha was doing a lot better with her bouts of depression and the mental flashes that occurred periodically. She had stopped seeing the psychiatrist, and she was feeling better than her old self. She and Raf were doing great. They both had their careers. They were surrounded by the people that they love and who loves them. Most importantly, they had each other.

The Preacher's Son
Dr. Cassundra White- Elliott

The Preacher's Son is a work of fiction and is a creation that stems purely from the writer's imagination. Any resemblance to actual events or persons is purely coincidental.

Published by CLF Publishing, LLC

ISBN# 978-1-4507-2288-9

Printed in the United States of America.

Dedications

This book is dedicated to all my readers!
May God bless all of you for your continued support!

Acknowledgements

I acknowledge my son Daron White who was my inspiration for the main character. He was also the model for the cover.

I acknowledge Millicent Redd for being a reader on this project and giving me feedback as the plot came to life.

1

It was just before midnight on Friday May 14, and a blanket of darkness covered the sky. With the sky void of stars, an eerie gloom hung over the city, as Romero stood peering through the rear bedroom window of the last house on Dagwood Lane. As he felt the cool breeze brush past his face and a chill go up his spine, he wondered what had gone wrong. *Things were not supposed to turn out this way,* he thought as he found himself shaking his hat-covered head. Yet again, anytime someone had dealings with the underground, one never ever knows how things may turn out.

Reaching into his pocket for his cell phone to notify the police of the body that lay crumpled on the floor, Romero heard a rustle in the bushes, and he knew he was not alone.

After carefully making a mental note of the scene he had just witnessed in the Stevensons' bedroom, Romero quickly made his way back to his vehicle that he had inconspicuously parked around the corner. Having recently cleared his first year as a private investigator, Romero felt his blood pumping as he delved into yet another case that sent him on a wild goose chase. Any other private investigator would have turned the case away, but Romero loved the action of the seemingly difficult cut-throat, dirty cases.

Going back to his vehicle, he was careful to stay out of the view of any neighbors who may have happened to peer from their windows. He meticulously blended into the shadows as only the moon and a few dim street lights lit the neighborhood.

As he entered his vehicle, he thought he noticed another person entering a vehicle down the street ahead of him. Sitting in his car, he watched the vehicle drive away. Just when he thought the night could not get any more interesting or weird, another car suddenly sped past him from the rear.

The male driver seemed to be catching up to the other car. Before he knew it, both cars disappeared in the same direction. Romero quickly wrote down the license plate of the car that sped past him. His first thought was to follow after the cars, but he did not want to take the chance of blowing his cover. He would call one of his police contacts to find out who the car is registered to. He had a feeling that the two drivers had just left the Stevensons' home.

Finally, making the call that he had begun to make nearly twenty minutes ago, Romero gave the details of what he had witnessed through the Stevensons' bedroom window. After waiting another twenty minutes, members of the New York Police Department arrived to the scene. When Romero saw the squad cars approaching, he followed them back to the Stevensons' residence.

The police officers surrounded the house, but after not getting an answer at the front door, they went in. When they reached the master bedroom, they did not discover a body, and everything seemed to be in order. The mess that Romero had just witnessed less than an hour ago had been restored. Romero left with a stabbing feeling in his gut, and the police left with a look of disappointment on their faces.

He wondered what they were thinking. He had worked alongside many of the officers for nearly a year now. He was sure they knew his character. However, it did not make what he was feeling at that moment easy to bear. He wanted to keep a good name within the department. He did not want them to hesitate to respond when he called the station. Therefore, he was determined to make this incident right in their sight. He had to find Brad not only for Laura's sake but for the sake of his reputation.

After arriving home, in the next county, Romero entered his newly purchased condominium and headed right for the shower. He felt sticky and grimy all over. He didn't know if his physical condition was a result of the brief jog he had to take to get to the Stevensons' home or from the slime and grime of the case that had begun to unravel before his very eyes.

As the water rolled down Romero's back, his thoughts turned from the case to the celebration that would take place next weekend. His father was turning fifty, and there would be a grand affair in his honor.

Romero was not sure he would be in attendance. He had thought long and hard about it, but still was unable to reach a decision. However, there was one thing he was sure of: he did not want to be embarrassed or put on the spot. He had no way of knowing if his father would once again make his usual announcement or if he had moved on from his latest idea. Romero did not know what to expect if he showed up at the party. He was seriously thinking about not going.

Only time would tell what his decision would be.

****

On the other side of town, Romero's father, Pastor Turner was having similar thoughts. He reflected back over the last two events that were held in his honor. His youngest son Romero had failed to be present for the celebrations. Although Romero had said it was work-related business that prevented him from attending, Pastor Turner had his doubts. *Was it something I said or did*, he wondered.

He knew that as a sleuth, his son scheduled his own hours. He knew that it must be something more. It was as if though Romero was avoiding him. *But why*, he wondered. *Why?*

Pastor Turner's movements awakened his wife. When she noticed that he had sat up in bed, she turned toward him. At first, she thought he was praying. But when she saw his hand on the side of his face, she knew that he was deep in thought.

"What's on your mind, honey?" she asked in a soft voice.

"Oh, just thinking about Romero."

"Is something wrong? Did he call?" she asked sitting up herself.

"No, it's nothing like that. I am sure he is fine. I was just thinking about him. That's all. Let's go back to sleep."

With Pastor Turner's comment, he clicked off the lamp on his night stand and turned towards his wife, placing one arm around her as she moved back into a comfortable position. Minutes later, they were both sound asleep.

2

Three weeks earlier, Romero had received a call from Laura Stevenson requesting his services. The fact that she called him as a result of a referral from a past client was not unusual. What Romero found interesting was that Laura wanted Romero to investigate her husband's activities at his place of employment. Usually when wives called, they wanted Romero to investigate their husbands whom they suspected to be involved in extra-marital affairs.

Bradley Stevenson, Laura's husband, was the regional manager of Buford Savings and Loan. His wife suspected that he was involved in money laundering for one of the most notorious drug lords in the state of New York. From the rumors she heard about Sylvester "Sly" Domingo, Laura knew that if her husband was mixed up with him, the outcome would most likely not be favorable. But she could not figure out why Brad would have chosen to get mixed up with Sly in the first place. It wasn't as if they needed more money, for they had made a good life for themselves.

Brad cleared in the mid six figures easily every year since his promotion five years ago. Laura wasn't doing so bad herself as a nursing educator. After working as a nurse for twelve years, Laura decided to move into the educational sector of nursing, so she could teach other nurses the important aspects of their chosen career field. In her new area of work, Laura cleared six figures herself each year. With the money that they made, Laura couldn't understand why her husband of eleven years would become involved with such a shady character as Sylvester Domingo.

Sylvester Domingo had developed a reputation for himself for being a mobster who defied every law known to man. He did whatever he wanted to do, whenever he wanted to do it. Although the FBI tried to keep close tabs on him in the hopes of placing him behind bars indefinitely, the New York Police Department seemed to ignore his existence. It was believed that some of the police officers were on his payroll. The problem is Sly was so careful that no one was able to pin any crimes on him. That was probably because Sly was smart enough to get someone else to do his dirty work. He, on the other hand, kept his hands clean.

A month before Laura contacted Romero, she had begun to see a change in her husband's behavior. Brad had begun carrying around a second cell phone and a second briefcase that had an intricate security lock on the front. When Laura questioned him about them, he said they were for work. When she asked for the telephone number to the new cell phone explaining that she may need it for emergency purposes if he did not answer his personal cell phone, Brad flatly refused and offered no explanation for his refusal. Laura found this to be extremely out of character, especially when she often overheard Brad speaking on the phone after business hours. *Who could be calling him at such unconventional hours*, she had wondered. Once she thought she heard him say, "Mr. Domingo," while he was on the private cell phone. This is what led her to believe Brad was entangled with Sly.

In addition to the extra phone, briefcase and secretive phone conversations, Laura noticed a change in Brad's daily routine. For the last five years since his promotion, Brad had come home every day around six in the evening after having left home at eight each morning. For the last month or so, at least several times a week, Brad would attend late night meetings that caused him to break his daily routine. At first, Laura thought it had to be another woman. But from the harsh and agitated tones she heard in his voice as he spoke secretly into his private cell phone, she knew that it could not be another woman because Brad had the utmost respect for all women. Laura had never heard him raise his voice once to her or any other women in all the time she had known him.

The final straw that prompted Laura's call to Romero was when Brad lost over twenty pounds in a month's time. She also noticed that he had sprouted a few gray hairs around his temple. To her, these were signs of stress. In Laura's opinion, Brad was a predictable guy. He wasn't one to do things at the spur of a moment. Everything he did was routine. Therefore, something was definitely wrong, and Laura planned to do everything in her power to save her husband, even if it meant saving him from himself, Sly Domingo, or anyone else that tried to bring harm his way. This is why she had searched around for a private investigator and was eventually referred to Romero Turner.

3

Romero Allen Turner was born twenty-one years ago to Theodore and Lucille Turner. Growing up, Romero had always engaged in sports and other numerous physical activities. His love for sports, especially football, continued from when he was a young child into his adult life. As captain of the football team at Forest Hills High School in Queens, New York, Romero always strived to be the best. To assist in his efforts, he had worked out six days a week to build his physical endurance and stamina.

Now four years after he had graduated from high school, Romero finds that he still needs his strength

in his current profession as a private investigator. So, twice a week, he has a regular appointment with a personal trainer. Most of Romero's cases only require his investigative skills and being quick in planning his next move to get answers for his clients. But ever so often, he needs a little muscle to protect himself from those who do not care to be investigated and/or those who find his presence unwelcoming and annoying.

On Thursday, April 22, Romero had been happy to retrieve a voicemail from Mrs. Laura Stevenson. Her message was very brief, but from the little she dared to divulge in her voicemail, Romero knew that her call was a request for his services. He was excited at the new prospect because he had just closed another case and was ready for a new adventure.

Romero's previous case had involved the employees of an El Pollo Loco restaurant in Harlem. Salvador Ramirez, the manager of the restaurant, contacted Romero because food and other supplies were disappearing from the restaurant little by little, and he desperately wanted to know who the culprit was. From Sal's own investigation, he had not uncovered any clues. The cameras that were installed throughout the restaurant did not record any strange or illegal activity. Whoever was guilty of this alleged crime was very clever.

Once Sal calculated the loss that apparently had been occurring for some time, he learned the restaurant had lost upwards of $10,000, and that was only for the items themselves. The profit that would have been gained from selling the food that had been stolen would have been approximately $68,000. In total, the loss was estimated at $80,000.

Romero started his investigation by staking out the restaurant at various hours during the day and night. At first, he didn't notice any suspicious activity. However, as luck would have it, he decided to enter the restaurant one day to have a bite to eat and to get a closer look at the inner workings of the business. As he stood at the counter ordering his food, he noticed one of the employees hand a large bag to a driver at the drive-thru window.

At first, he thought the customer had ordered a great deal of food, but when he saw the employee hand the driver two more large bags that came from the rear of the restaurant, he knew that this must be the way the supplies and other times were leaving the store. He couldn't help but wonder who was in charge while the manager was out and why the other employees who were on duty did not seem to be bothered by the activities that he had just witnessed. Surely they had noticed too and had probably witnessed this employee's behavior on prior occasions.

As he sat and ate his meal, not really tasting the food as it passed down his throat, he continued to observe the employees' behaviors. Nothing seemed out of the ordinary, except for an employee or two that left with what appeared to be overstuffed backpacks. But of course, he had no way of knowing what was in those backpacks.

After finishing his meal and dumping his plate, he saw an employee head out with a large trash bag. Romero followed the employee outside.

While entering his vehicle, Romero saw the employee head to his own vehicle with the bag instead of going to the trashcan. Taking a closer look, Romero noticed this was the same employee that had handed the three large bags to the customer in the drive-thru window.

While watching the employee's next move, Romero jotted down a few notes of all he had witnessed during the day. Just as he was pulling out of the parking lot, he saw Sal drive up. They made eye contact. Romero nodded to let Sal know that he would be in contact soon.

Thirty minutes later before Romero could contact Sal, Sal called Romero on his cell phone to get a report. After sharing with Sal the activities he had witnessed, Sal immediately called the authorities so they could have Ralph Marquez, the suspicious employee, remove the bag from his vehicle so the contents could be searched. Sal had to act quickly because Ralph, who was the shift leader, was scheduled to get off in the next hour.

After the authorities arrived, Ralph was forced to open his trunk and take out the bag. Inside the bag were frozen chickens, corn, beans, rice, lard, and other supplies. When Ralph was taken to the station and questioned, he confessed that he was stealing the food for a side business that he had. Other employees knew that he had been taking supplies from the store, but Ralph told them that he was taking the items to another El Pollo Loco location that was running low. Because he was the supervisor on duty, the others never questioned him.

Once the case had been solved, Romero collected the other half of his standard fee. The first half was paid when he first took the case which was noted by Salvador's signature on the contract.

When that case was over, Romero was then able to move ahead with his plan of acquiring his first piece of real estate. He had already been looking around at several properties. After getting his father's input, he decided to purchase a condo. With the money that he had just earned from his last case and the money he had saved over the last year, he was able to put down a deposit of fifty percent of the purchase price. This made his monthly note very affordable, even if he was only able to get a case once every other month.

So far though, Romero had become increasingly popular during the last few months, and he had been getting calls requesting his services at least once a week. With the number of referrals he received and the amount of sneaky and underhanded activity that goes on in the world, Romero felt that he would be in business for a long time to come. With the call that he received from Mrs. Stevenson, he suspicions were correct.

4

The next morning after the fiasco at the Stevenson's home the night before, Romero picked up his phone to dial Mrs. Stevenson's cell phone. This was her preferred method of contact, as she did not want her husband to be privy to her extracurricular activities that she was required to engage in order to learn about *his* extracurricular activities. Romero needed to find out what she knew about the events of the night before that occurred at her home. He could only hope that she too was not missing, like the body in her home that had appeared to be dead and then disappeared.

Before Romero could locate her number in his cell phone's internal address book, his phone rang. It was Laura Stevenson. *Good*, he thought. *At least she is alive*.

After talking to Laura for nearly thirty minutes, Romero learned that she did not know anything about the events that occurred in her home the night before. She had been out of town at a symposium for her job. She wasn't aware that anything had occurred until she returned home earlier that morning and saw the police tape on her front door. She also mentioned that she had not spoken to Brad within the last forty-eight hours. When Romero asked why she had not mentioned this to him before, she said she did not want to alarm him unnecessarily, but that is why she had requested that he go to her home and check for any signs of disturbance.

Romero had not known what to expect when he went to her home. He did not know how he would be able to tell if things were abnormal seeing that he had not been to her home before. But when he saw the scene in the master bedroom, he knew that something was dreadfully wrong. It did not take a rocket scientist to realize there was a problem when a body lay sprawled on the floor.

During his conversation with Laura, Romero described all that he had seen the night before. From Romero's description of the body, Laura believed that the man was her husband. The body size and the sandy blonde hair was exactly the same as Brad's. Even the description of his clothing matched clothes that Brad owns. And after checking Brad's closet, Laura saw that the particular pair of pants that Romero described was missing. And so was the shirt along with several other items of clothing. This was a sign that Brad had left on his own. If someone had forced him to leave against his will, it is not likely that he would have been made to pack spare clothing.

At Laura's request, Romero planned to meet her at her home at ten that morning. Before leaving his home, he decided it would be best to contact his friend Matthew Underwood who was a forensic scientist. Matthew agreed to meet Romero at the Stevenson's home and bring along the Luminal test to check for the existence of blood that may be unseen to the naked eye. In the event that blood was found, Matt would be able to take a sample and run a DNA test to verify the identity of the victim.

Laura did not detect any foul play. She just knew that her husband packed and left without a word to her. But Romero felt in his gut that foul play had definitely occurred. And if need be, he would have to stick his neck out again and phone the police department, who undoubtedly did not have good things to say about him at the moment. But it was a chance he would have to take, and he was pretty sure that he would need their assistance in getting to the bottom of what was going on with Bradley Stevenson.

But before he resorted to calling them to make a missing person's report, he would use his other contact at another police department. He may get better results if he called his cousin Tinisha's husband, Rafael Salisbury. Rafael was a sergeant at the Los Angeles Police Department, Hollywood Division. Rafael was a cool guy, and he always availed himself to Romero when he needed him. And when Rafael did not have time to respond in a timely fashion, he asked his ex-partner Derrick Cassidy to step in. Like Rafael, Derrick was always eager to help out a friend, even if they were on opposite coasts.

Romero had only met Rafael a few times, but the times they had spoken on the phone had helped them to develop a familial and working relationship. Romero had the utmost respect for Rafael. Not only for his work ethic, level of integrity, and his ability to climb the ladder of success within the police department, but also in how he dealt with his wife Tinisha. He stood by her side through thick and thin and gave her the support she needed. He was a good role model for Romero, and Romero appreciated Rafael and Tinisha's presence in his life, even if it was from a distance.

5

When Romero went into his garage, he decided to drive his black Crown Victoria rather than his fully charged white Range Rover. He wanted to appear to be an undercover or plain-closed officer rather than a private detective when he arrived at the Stevensons' home to meet Laura. He did not want to raise suspicion in case any of Sly's goons were watching. It had not actually been determined yet that Sly and his organization were involved with Brad. But after last night, Romero suspected foul play and was determined to discover who was at fault. What he had witnessed thus far was actually something that Sly was known for: leaving bodies around the city.

Before getting into the car, Romero grabbed his supplies from the Rover. In the front seat, he spotted the license plate number that he had written down last night from the car that had sped past him.

On his drive over to the Stevenson's home, he took out his cell phone to dial Rafael. After being connected, Romero gave Rafael the plate number, so he could run it and find the name of the registered owner.

"Okay," Rafael said. "I will get back to you soon. I am right in the middle of finalizing a report."

"Thanks, cousin," Romero responded. "I am on my way to meet with a client. If you don't reach me, leave me a voice message. And if you get an address too…"

"Yeah, I know," Rafael interrupted him. "I will leave that info too." Romero had to laugh out loud. He had to remember that he was talking to Sergeant Rafael Salisbury, who had twelve more years of law enforcement experience than he did.

"How are my cousin and the baby doing?" Romero asked.

"Tinisha and Jasmine are doing fine."

"How old is Jasmine now?"

"She's six months. She is starting to pull up on things and find her way around. She will be walking soon."

"Oh wow!" Romero exclaimed. "I really need to make a trip out to California to see my little cousin."

"That would be great, but we may be in your neck of the woods this time next week."

"Oh really? Why?"

"Isn't your dad's party coming up?"

"Oh yeah," Rome said in a low tone.

"Don't tell me you forgot," Rafael questioned.

"No," he started. "Of course not."

"Well, what's up? It sounds like something is going on."

"Raf, I know you are busy, so you can call me later when you get the information on the car," Rome said changing the subject.

"Ok, no problem," Raf responded taking the hint.

Pulling up in front of the Stevensons' home, Romero felt the same eerie feeling come over him that he had the night before. He was glad to see that Matthew was there. That gave him a sense of calm, but not completely. *Maybe Matthew will be able to give us answers to what happened in Brad and Laura's bedroom last night*, Romero thought as he walked up the front walkway.

After pausing for Matthew to catch up, Romero rang the doorbell. After waiting several minutes, he did not get an answer. He glanced over at Matthew and saw beads of sweat forming on his friend's forehead. *What has he got to be nervous about?* Romero asked himself as he pushed the front door open. *I am the one risking my life getting involved with anything that has to do with Sylvester Domingo.*

The lock on the front door had been damaged by the police officers when they entered hurriedly last night, and it had yet to be repaired. So the door stood slightly ajar.

As the two quietly entered the Stevensons' home, Romero softly called out to Laura. At first, he did not get an immediate response, but once he walked further into the foyer, he heard a muffled moan.

"Did you hear that?" he whispered to Matt.

Matthew only nodded as the sweat poured down his face. Picking up the pace, they both rushed toward the area of the house from where the sound emanated. To their surprise, Laura was gagged and bound to one of the dining room chairs.

"Is there anyone else here?" Romero asked quickly. Laura shook her head frantically as the tears rolled down her face. Removing the tape that held her to the chair, Romero continued to look around just in case the perpetrator was still on the premises.

After freeing Laura from her bondage, Romero asked her what had happened in the short time after he spoke to her to the time that he and Matthew arrived at her home.

Laura explained that she had continued to look around the house, particularly in her husband's belongings to see if she noticed anything out of order. After searching for about thirty minutes, her throat began to feel a little parched. So, she walked into the kitchen to get a glass of water. She walked right into an intruder who obviously didn't know she was home. He was as surprised to see her as she was to see him. But obviously he expected the unexpected because before Laura knew it, the intruder had pulled out his tape and rope and tied her to the chair and disappeared out of the sliding glass door. From what Laura could see, he had not taken anything. She wondered what he could have possibly been looking for.

From Laura's description, the intruder was over six feet tall and had a slender build. He was wearing a sky mask with dark shades over it. When he bent over her to tape her hands to the arms of the chair, she saw a piece of his blond hair sticking through the ski mask. Then, as he leaned his head farther down, she could see his eyes over the top of his glasses. As he was strapping her to the chair, she noticed that he had one bad eye that remained shut the entire time.

After calming Laura down and assuring her that no one was in the house besides the three of them, Romero took Matt in the master bedroom so Matt could put his forensic skills to work. Matt sprayed the solution around the area that Romero told him the body had laid. After letting the fluid set for a few moments, Matt closed the blinds to block the light from the sun and shined the light from his machine around the area.

As Romero had expected, there were traces of blood. However, there wasn't much. Matt estimated that whoever was bleeding had not lost more than a pint of blood. This was reassuring for Laura to hear. She had been a nervous wreck during this entire ordeal since her husband's behavior had changed, but the events of the last few days were almost more than she could bear.

Out of nowhere, Laura began crying again. "I just want answers," she exclaimed. "I want Bradley back," she whimpered.

Romero didn't know what to do. He did not have much experience with consoling women, especially those with whom he was unfamiliar. All he could think to do was to place his hand on her arm and tell her that he would do all he could to find Brad and get to the bottom of this mystery. He was careful to not make any promises that he would have a difficult time keeping. Romero liked to deal with reality, even if his clients sometimes had a hard time separating reality from fantasy.

"Is there somewhere you can go until we get answers?" Romero asked Laura.

"Yes, I can go to my sister's home. But what if someone is watching me? I don't want to put my sister or her family in danger. Do you think it would be better for me to go to a hotel?"

"I don't think it would be a good idea for you to be alone. At least if you are with family you won't be as easy of a target, assuming someone is looking to harm you. I will call a good friend of mine from the NYPD to escort you, and I will trail slowly behind to make sure there isn't anyone following."

Once Laura consented to Romero's plan of action, she disappeared into her bedroom to pack a suitcase. Meanwhile, Romero called Detective Trish Williams for a favor. After explaining Laura's situation to Trish, Trish consented to escorting Laura to her sister's home.

Forty minutes later, Laura and Trish were ready to go. Laura had called her sister Candi to make sure her visit was welcome. Candi assured her that it was and found it to be a pleasant surprise. Romero advised Laura to refrain from telling her sister or anyone else about the ongoing case. She consented as she understood the need for caution.

Laura's last concern was the broken lock on the front door. While waiting for Trish, Laura had called a locksmith; however, he did not arrive before Trish. Anxious to leave when Trish arrived, Laura asked Matt if he would not mind staying around for the locksmith. Matthew, still visibly shaken by the events that had occurred, hesitated. He really didn't want to be anywhere near a location where a notorious mobster may feel the urge to visit. His domain was the crime lab and occasionally the crime scene. He wasn't accustomed to placing himself in danger.

To his relief, the doorbell rang before he could object. The locksmith had arrived. He changed the lock while Laura, Trish, Romero and Matthew all waited anxiously.

Bill the locksmith tried to make small talk, questioning how the lock became damaged. No one answered. They all stood around quietly, not even looking at one another.

Feeling the tension in the room, Bill eventually got the message and worked quietly and quickly to do the job he had been summoned to do. After receiving payment for the job, Bill left just as quickly as he had come.

Upon Bill's departure, the four of them entered their respective vehicles. Matthew left immediately to go back to his lab with Laura and Trish following directly afterwards as they headed to Candi's home. Romero would trail a few minutes behind to keep a look out for unwanted followers.

Before leaving the Stevenson's home, Matthew was able to secure a sample of the blood from the carpet even though someone had made a pretty good attempt at removing it. He also took hair samples from Brad's brush to do a DNA comparison with the blood. This would tell them whether or not the man Romero saw on the floor the night before was indeed Bradley Stevenson.

When Romero had settled into his car, he took out his cell phone and saw that he had a message from Rafael. Still parked in front of Brad and

Laura's home, he listened intently as Rafael's message relayed the registered owner of the car as Trevor Smallwood. He was also able to secure his address, which he also left on Romero's voice mail.

Using his GPS, Romero learned that the address was less than twenty minutes away. He would take a drive over there after he followed Trish and Laura to Candi's home and ensured Laura's safe entrance.

As Romero reflected on the ongoing investigation, he surmised that the case was off to a slow start. Sure there had been a lot of things going on, from Brad's initial secretive activity to his disappearance to the intruder's presence this morning. But there had been very few clues that actually pinpointed who the perpetrators are.

Romero was anxious for the ball to get rolling. He wanted answers for Laura, and he wanted to find Brad alive.

6

At ten minutes after one o'clock in the afternoon, Romero pulled away from Candi's home after watching Laura go inside and the door close safely behind her. Maybe by going to Trevor's home, he would get some answers about Brad's alleged involvement with Sylvester Domingo and his disappearance.

While driving over to the address that Rafael had given him, Romero began to try to put the pieces of the puzzle together. He really did not have much tangible information. However, what started out as pure speculation on Laura's part seemed to be panning out to be real, especially with the disappearance of her husband.

I wonder what is going on at the bank, Romero wondered. *Had Brad gone into work on Friday? Would he show up on Monday? Did his employers expect any foul play? Did they suspect money laundering like Laura?* These are the questions that floated through Romero's mind as he turned down Center Pointe Lane and began looking for Trevor's address. Seeing that he was near, Romero decided to leave his car down the street and take a stroll so that he blended in with the rest of the people who were walking up and down the street.

As he neared Trevor's address, Romero spotted a vacant home with a 'For Sale' sign directly across the street from Trevor's home. Using his lock-picking tool kit to gain entry, Romero entered the vacant home. *This is perfect*, he thought as he ascended the short winding staircase. He knew he was trespassing on private property, but getting caught was a chance he was willing to take if it helped him to get information for his client that could save her husband's life, if it wasn't too late.

Luckily, the house still had curtains on the windows apparently from the last owners. The curtains allowed Romero to stand behind them and use his binoculars to see right into Trevor's living room. And as luck would have it, Trevor had a guest.

Sly himself was seated on the couch!

Romero hoped this was a sign that his luck with this case had turned around. Ten minutes ago he had no idea how he would even begin to locate Brad. He did not have a clue of where to begin looking. This may just be the break he needed.

As he watched Trevor's living room, another man soon came into his view. After watching several minutes more and not seeing anyone else, he assumed that the second man was Trevor. With his professional grade digital camera, Romero took pictures of the two men. They seemed to be having a heated discussion. First, Sly was seated calmly on the couch, but now he was standing and waving his hands around frantically. Each time he neared Trevor, Trevor backed away. Trevor's behavior showed that he was intimidated by Sly's presence.

Romero wondered what they were discussing. It was obvious that Sly was upset about something.

Ten minutes later, Romero's cell phone rang. Matt's number appeared on the caller id.

"Hey, Matt. What's the news?"

"We have a match. The blood sample and the hair sample match."

"That's good to know. So we now know that Brad was definitely the one who was bleeding on the floor. So I can safely assume that it was his body that
I saw on the floor. I thought he was dead, but you
said there wasn't much blood there. Right?"

"Exactly. The fluorescent light shows the blood residue, the depth and thickness even though someone tried to remove it. In this case, the blood spatter was very minimal. I would say if Brad was shot, he only received a flesh wound."

"So it is safe to say that he is probably alive."

"I would be inclined to agree with you, Romero."

"Okay. Thanks for the news, Buddy."

"No problem, but there is something else."

"What is it, Matt?"

"I was also able to pick up what appeared to be droppings of dried mud. I ran an analysis and there were composites of iron and sodium bicarbonate."

"What does all of that mean?"

"Well, those are not typical components of soil. So, I did a little research to look for that particular soil grade in our city and the surrounding cities."

"And what did you find?" Romero asked, trying to cut to the chase.

"I was able to locate two places where the soil exists locally. I have sent that information over to you in an email."

"That's great. Thanks so much for your help on this, Matthew."

"Anytime, Romero. Anytime."

While talking to Matthew, Romero had turned away from his stakeout spot at the window. Turning back to continue his spying, he was able to catch a glimpse of Trevor and Sly getting into a car that was now backing out of the driveway. Using binoculars, Romero was able to see that the license plate was the same as the one he wrote down last night.

Moving quickly, Romero descended the steps and exited the front door. Being careful not to attract attention, he blended into the people walking down the sidewalk and made his way back to his car.

He made every attempt to get to his car and follow Sly and Trevor. But before he was able to enter his car, Trevor's car was out of sight.

Excited about the news Matthew shared with him, he was anxious to get home to open the file that Matt sent about the location of the dirt. He knew that once he retrieved the information, he should go check to see what was at each location and if they had anything to do with Brad or Sly. He also wanted to check Buford Savings and Loan to see if he could find out whether or not Brad went into work on Friday. He may be able to check out the dirt today, but his visit to the bank would have to wait until Monday.

Actually, everything would have to wait because it was just after two in the afternoon and Romero had not eaten all day. Once he knew he was unable to tail Trevor, he decided to head back to his part of town and grab a bite to eat. Not really having a taste for anything specific or wanting anything too heavy, Romero opted for International House of Pancakes.

****

Once he had been served his favorite IHOP meal, Pigs 'N a Blanket, Romero was just about to taste the delectable forkful that was saturated with syrup when he heard a voice behind him.

"Rome Turner. Is that you?" the voice asked. Looking up, Romero saw a familiar face. In front of him stood a beautiful chocolate-toned woman. The sight of her brought a smile to his face. He had not seen her in what felt like forever. Actually, it had only been a little over three years since he had seen Yolanda Bardwell. They had graduated from the same high school four years ago. She had been the captain of the cheerleading squad.

"Hey, Yolanda. How are you?"

"I'm fine. Are you dining alone?"

"Yeah, looks that way."

"Want some company?"

"Sure, go ahead and have a seat."

For the next forty-five minutes, Romero and Yolanda caught up on all that had occurred after high school. Before departing, they exchanged telephone numbers, and each promised to stay in contact.

7

On his drive home, after having a very late breakfast, Romero passed by his favorite spot to meditate. It was a small lake that was surrounded by beautiful greenery. New York's skyscrapers could be seen in the background. The serene nature of the lake allowed him to ponder and meditate whenever he had something on his mind.

The temptation to stop overcame him, and he found himself with his notepad and pen in hand exiting his vehicle and walking over to the lake to be nearer to the water. A couple of hours later, Romero came back to reality realizing he had to get back to work. Not really wanting to leave, he slowly drove away.

After Romero returned home, he immediately turned on his computer to retrieve Matt's email. Using Map Quest to locate the exact locations of the two sites that held the soil that Matthew found in the Stevensons' bedroom, Romero quickly grabbed the maps from the printer. Hurriedly leaving from his home office, he grabbed a bottle of cold water from the refrigerator. For the second time that day, he pulled out of his garage in his Crown Victoria. There were only a few hours of daylight left, so he had to hurry. He was not anxious to go snooping around in the dark again. Next time, he may not be as fortunate to leave without a scratch.

Arriving at the first location, which was somewhat remote, Romero walked over to the large barn-like structure. Clad in all black, Romero was careful to walk along the sides of the structure near the windows. He did not know if anyone was inside, but he would be able to hear them if they were.

As he reached the uncovered window, he noticed that the building was completely empty. Walking around to the side doors, Romero entered the barn. As he stepped inside, the smell of the most horrifying pungent odor that he had ever smelled filled his nostrils. He wasn't sure what the smell was, but he knew that something or someone was dead.

Pulling the front of his turtle neck up around his mouth to serve as a mask, he began to investigate. Using the light from his flashlight as a guide, Romero scoured every inch of the floor of the main room. Next, he went into the two back rooms. He didn't find anything that would give him a lead on the case. He did, however, determine what was causing the putrid smell. There were several dead possums scattered throughout the building.

Catching a glimpse of the moon through one of the windows and noticing how quickly the time was passing, Romero quickly exited the building and made his way back to his vehicle. He needed to get over to the next location.

Back in his car, he quickly swallowed a few sips of his bottled water as if though he was trying to wash away the stench that continued to fill his nostrils. Glancing at his watch, he saw that the time was once again slipping away from him and that he needed to move faster.

As he drove, the feelings he had last night of not being able to put the pieces of this puzzle together were creeping up on him. The stop at the first location had proven to be a dead end. All Romero could hope for was a better turn out at the second location. He felt that time was of the essence. If Brad truly was mixed up with Sly Domingo and he was bleeding as a result of his involvement, the end of this journey may not be a happy one.

One thing that being a private investigator had taught Romero was that when people went missing it was always hard to recover them if someone wanted them gone or if they went into hiding themselves. He did not know what Brad's situation was. All he could do was trust the word of Brad's wife.

Finally making it to the second location, which was fifteen minutes by freeway from the first location, Romero dimmed his lights as he approached the entrance. Just as he was approaching the gate to the property, Trevor's car was exiting. Quickly, Romero pulled over under a tree. He had dimmed his lights at the right moment.

Trevor drove right past Romero without taking any notice of him. Not seeing a passenger in Trevor's car, Romero thought it best to wait a moment, just in case Sly was not too far behind in his own car. Not more than five minutes later, Romero's suspicion panned out. Sly exited the driveway as well.

When Romero first arrived at the location, he had every intention to drive up the driveway because the building was set quite far from the street. Now having seen two cars exit the premises, Romero thought it would be best to leave his car parked where it was and walk to the building. Maybe he would gather some clues on the way.

Approaching the building, Romero took in the structure of the building. Like the first one, this building was a barn-like structure. However, that is where the similarities ended. This structure, unlike the first one, was made of steel and was no more than five years old. On the roof was an illuminated sign with the words "Domingo Enterprises." The sign spoke volumes alone. Romero did not have to wonder if Sly had anything to do with the building. The sign on top answered that question for him.

After ensuring that he was alone, Romero used the same tool kit that he used earlier at the vacant house across the street from Trevor to gain entrance into the steel barn.

Although this structure was filled with desks, files, and office equipment, Romero still did not find anything incriminating. He knew that he could not legally go through the files. Anything he may have happened to uncover without the use of a search warrant would be thrown out of court, assuming they would make it that far. Therefore, Romero had no choice but to leave empty handed and call it a night.

While driving home, Romero began to question whether or not he should have taken the case. He could have taken several other cases for which he had received calls. But no, he knew that this case would potentially have more hours involved in it. Hours translated into dollars.

Unlike most private investigators, Rome charged by the hour rather than by the case. He had learned that when he charges by the case, in most cases he ended up shorting himself. However, in other cases, he made out like a bandit. So, to make it fair for him and his clients, he billed by the hour, even though he did not always count every hour that he spent on cases. Overall, it all worked out well in the end.

This case though had Romero up late nights thinking about his next plan of action. Of course this was part of his job, but it didn't make it easier. At times, he was at a total loss not knowing what to do. The ball seemed to be in Sly's court, and everyone else was along for the ride, Romero included.

But Romero was not a quitter. He was determined to see this case through to the end. Not only was he determined, but he wanted to know more about Sly and his dealings with the underground. The data he gathered from this case would help with other cases that he may have later on. With more knowledge and more experience under his belt, he would not have such a hard time the next time he had a case of this magnitude.

8

After a long day yesterday of twists and turns in the Stevenson case, Romero was awakened by the sound of his radio/clock alarm. Every Sunday, Romero rose at the same time without fail. His clock was set for 7:30 am. He always hit the fifteen-minute snooze button once. Then at 7:45 am, he headed straight for the shower with half-closed eyes, even if he had already showered the night before. This Sunday was no exception.

After showering, Romero pulled open the door to his walk-in closet and began to look at his array of suits deciding what he would wear that day. Looking through his suits, Romero suddenly thought of his hair. He did not make it to the barber yesterday to get his bi-weekly haircut. Usually, Romero is sitting in his barber's chair at ten on Saturday morning just after he has a session with his physical fitness trainer. With the Stevenson case requiring so much of his time, Romero had to skip both of his sessions the day before. He vowed to himself that he would make both of them up within the next two days. He did not like being thrown off his schedule unless it was for a good reason. In this case, he considered the needs of his client a good reason.

Once Romero had chosen his attire and dressed, he headed for the garage. Today the Crown Victoria would stay home, but the Range Rover would get an opportunity to experience the open highway.

Today was a day of rest and worship, as declared in the Holy Bible. Today was Romero's Sabbath day. He would attend church as he always does. But not just any church. He would attend Faithful Evangelical Temple. This was his father's church. This church had been in the Turner family for three generations now.

Romero's great-grandfather founded the church nearly ninety years ago. After having preached for thirty-five years, Romero's great-grandfather Robert Turner handed the mantle down to Romero's grandfather Ronald Turner, who preached for forty-two years after his own father had retired. Then, the mantle was handed down once again to Romero's father, Robert Theodore Turner, known to everyone simply as Theodore Turner. Pastor Theodore Turner had been preaching for the past twenty-three years and was looking forward to passing the mantle to his own son Romero some day.

Romero shared his father's passion for the gospel as well as for preaching. At the same time though, he knew that God had a calling on his life that enabled him to touch the lives of others, inside and outside the church.

Promptly at nine thirty, Romero passed through the church doors clad in a cream suit with thin navy blue pin stripes, a navy blue shirt, cream tie, and cream Stacy Adams. As he passed through, he was greeted by the church members. Some of the women had smiles as wide as the smile of a Cheshire cat.

Because of his physical attraction and warm personality, Romero was always getting invitations for dinner dates and other type of dates as well. The women found it hard to resist his smooth chocolate skin, slender yet muscular physique, and perfect smile. But Romero, as hard as it was, did not make a habit of giving into the church members' desires. He liked to keep his private life private. He dare not become the object of a scandal or become an embarrassment to himself or his parents.

Romero's older brother Lemuel had done enough of that. Lemuel was five years Romero's senior and had somehow gotten on the wrong track when he was in high school. However, after bumping his head against the wall on several occasions and receiving extremely large bumps, he finally got his act together. Today, Lemuel was a happily married man with two and a half children. He and his wife were expecting their second child. Lemuel had had one child prior to meeting his wife. His first child Sonora was the daughter of one of the deacon's daughters at church.

After having Sonora and before getting married, Lemuel had settled down and gone to school to become a firefighter. For four years now, he has been a member of New York's fire department. So, both of the Turner boys had gone into service careers.

Romero also had an older sister Carmen, who was two and a half years his senior. She remained unmarried by choice. She currently was making her way into the field of nursing. She had one more year to complete her degree. She did not feel that this was the right time to get married and begin a family. She desired to complete her education first. She wanted to be an asset to her husband when she got married. Although she believed in old fashioned values, she wanted to shoulder her share of the responsibilities.

Like Romero, she attended her father's church every Sunday. Lemuel was the only one of the three that did not attend Faith Evangelical Temple. Instead, he attended Shield of Faith Christian Center. This was Vanessa's, Lemuel's wife, church before they got married. They decided to attend Shield of Faith rather than Faith Evangelical because it was closer to their home. But they visited Pastor Turner's church regularly, at least once a month.

When they did, the entire Turner family would go out for Sunday dinner. This included Sonora. She loved when her father came to town. It gave her another opportunity to see him and her little brother, Michael.

When Lemuel was not visiting her at church, she went to his house to visit him two weekends out of each month. She also spent holidays with him and his family. She was very much a part of his life. One thing Pastor and First Lady Turner had instilled in their children was to always take care of family.

Service started promptly at ten o'clock when the minister on duty approached the podium and greeted the congregation. After his greeting, he prayed, read a scripture and turned the service over to the minister of music.

Later after all the formalities of the opening portion of service had been conducted, Pastor Turner graced the podium and greeted the congregation being sure to call special attention to the visitors. Afterwards, it was rock and roll time, time for the Sunday sermon. The members were ready with notepad and pen in hand. They knew that Pastor Turner was about to deliver a good word, one that would enrich their spiritual walk.

Pastor Turner began his sermon by asking how many had ever faced hardships in their lives. Of course, all who were present raised their hands. Next, he asked them if they prayed while they were in their storms. Again all raised their hands. Finally, Pastor Turner said, "There is a problem." Puzzled looks began to cross the members' faces. Continuing, he said, "Being in a time of need is not the problem. Praying for God to deliver you or to give you a solution is not the problem." As the audience began to wonder what the problem was, Pastor Turner paused for dramatic effect.

"Do you want to know what the problem is?" he asked.

"Yes, Pastor," the congregation echoed.

"Let me put it this way," he started. "The problem is our level of faith. We have enough faith to pray to God about our problems. We even have enough faith to ask Him to solve our problems. But the problem is how far our faith reaches. Think about this. When Lazarus died, his sisters wanted Jesus to come and heal him. But Jesus had a greater miracle in store: he brought Lazarus back from the dead."

Hearing Pastor Turner's statement, the audience members marveled and then fell quiet. They were anxious to hear more. Seeing that he had captured their attention, Pastor Turner continued.

"We can ask God to give us the money to pay a bill, but God wants to get us out of debt. We can ask God to change our spouse, but he wants to do a new thing in us that will enhance our relationship."

After going on with this train of thought and demonstrating to the members and guests that we place limitations on what God will do in our situations, Pastor Turner made his final points and closed out his sermon with this statement, "Take the limitations off God. Dare to believe that He is who He says He is. He is a God that can and will do more than we can even ask or think. God wants to make a change in your situation, and He wants to do it today!"

With this final statement, the alter call was made. Many souls went to the alter to repent of the limitations that they had unwittingly placed on God. They asked God to work miracles in their lives. Others came to give their lives to God, while still others rededicated their lives.

As Romero witnessed what was going on, he felt something leap in his spirit. He was always awestruck by the way God used his father. It was moments like this that made Romero so proud of his dad. He thought it was awesome the way his father opened his spirit for the Lord to use him.

After becoming lost in his thoughts for a few minutes more, Romero suddenly snapped back to reality when he saw Yolanda at the alter. When they departed from IHOP the day before, she did not mention to him that she would be stopping by the church or that she was even thinking about it. But what he could not figure out even more than her unannounced appearance was why his heart had fluttered when he saw her yesterday and again today when he saw her. All of a sudden, he was glad he wore his cream suit. He knew that it looked nice on him. Suddenly, Romero was concerned about making a good impression. This was a curious feeling to him. It was not something he had experienced in quite some time. However, he was pleased to be experiencing it now.

9

After church, Romero stood near the entrance to wait for his family members to make their way out of the church. As he stood there, Beth Ann, one of the members, came by and stopped right in front of him. At first, she did not say anything. She only smiled as she looked Romero up and down.

Finally, Romero began to feel uncomfortable. "Is there something I can help you with, Beth Ann?" he asked politely.

"Oh yes," Beth Ann began as she collected herself. "I am planning an outing for the youth. We are going to the skating ring on Friday night. I need another chaperone. Are you interested in assisting? I could really use your help."

Before Romero could answer, Yolanda walked through the foyer doors and right over to Romero. Beth Ann looked from Romero to Yolanda and back again. Yolanda did the same. She looked from Beth Ann to Romero and back to Beth Ann.

For a split second, no one said anything. Finally, Romero broke the silence by introducing the two ladies. Then turning toward Beth Ann, he asked, "Can I get back to you on that?"

"Uh sure. That will be fine, Romero," she said with the sound of disappointment in her voice.

After Beth Ann had left, Yolanda turned to Romero and said, "I apologize for interrupting."

"Oh, don't worry about it. There is something she wants me to do."

"Yes, I am sure that there is," Yolanda teased.

"It's not what you think."

"Oh sure. It's exactly what I think. The look in her eyes said it all."

"Oh really? Well, I am more interested in the look in your eyes," Romero responded surprising both himself and Yolanda. All Yolanda could do was blush.

"So what brings you to church today?" Romero asked quickly changing the subject.

"If I am honest with you, will you try to use it to
make me look bad?"

Romero did not know exactly what she meant by that, but he responded, "Of course not." Hearing the sincerity in his voice, she divulged her secret. Whispering she said, "After our lunch yesterday, I could not stop thinking about you, and I really wanted to see you again." After taking a moment to pause, she continued, "I hope you don't think of me as being too forward."

"No, not at all. I am glad to see you again. Would you like to have lunch with me again today? This time let's make it an official date." Yolanda was all grins. "That would be nice," she answered feeling suddenly shy.

After Romero spoke briefly with his parents and sister, he departed with Yolanda to have a bite to eat. Giving Yolanda an opportunity to choose where they would dine, Romero pointed his Rover in the direction of Lombardi's because she had a taste for pizza and antipasto salad.

****

With full stomachs, Romero and Yolanda sat in his truck in the church parking lot. Romero had brought Yolanda back to the church to pick up her car. They had been reminiscing about their high school days and looking at how far they had come in such a short time. Romero was making a great start in his career as a private eye, and Yolanda was in her fourth year at The State University of New York. She will be graduating next summer with her bachelor's degree in Human Services with a minor in Sociology. She wanted to become a Social Worker, so she would be able to assist disadvantaged and abused kids.

"Romero, it was really nice spending the afternoon with you. Thanks for lunch."

"It was my pleasure. Maybe we could do this again real soon," Romero said half making a statement and half asking a question. He looked directly into Yolanda's eyes as he spoke. She noticed how intently he looked at her and a tingle went up her spine. She did not really know what to make of his attitude towards her. In high school, he had not seemed to take notice of her. It could have been because he was dating one of the track stars, and she was dating the basketball captain. *Well, that was four years ago*, she thought. *This is a new day.*

"Yes, I would love to see you again very soon," she answered dreamily as she returned his gaze.

"I'll call you later. Like I was telling you earlier, I am working on a big case right now, and I have no idea how my schedule will go this week. But I will make every effort to see you in the next few days."

"Sounds great," Yolanda answered as she opened her car door.

Romero quickly got out and made his way to her side of the car. He extended his hand to assist her. Then he walked her over to her car. Giving her a single kiss on her cheek, Romero walked back to his vehicle. Making sure Yolanda drove safely away, Romero picked up his cell phone and located Laura Stevenson's phone number. He sent her a quick text to check on her well being and to see if she had any news to share with him.

A few minutes later, she returned his text letting him know that she was taking it hour by hour and minute by minute, but she had yet to hear from her husband.

10

A few hours after responding to Romero's text message, Laura lay in the bed in the guest bedroom of her sister Candi's home. Try as she might, she could not fall asleep. She had had the same problem the night before. Candi had suggested that she take a sleeping pill to help her rest. Laura did not like taking medicine. In her profession, she had witnessed too many people come in and out of the hospital for various addictions. She did not want to be one of them. However, after not having slept much the night before, her body was screaming for sleep.

Just as she reached for the package of sleeping pills that Candi had purchased at the drug store, Laura's cell phone rang. Moving her hand quickly from the pills to the phone, Laura answered hurriedly as she wondered who besides Brad would call her at that hour of the night.

"Hello?" Laura answered anxiously after looked at her caller id and seeing the word Restricted displayed on her phone rather than a telephone number.

"Laura?" a voice whispered.

"Brad!" Laura screamed.

"Yes, sweetheart. Where are you?" Brad asked hurriedly.

"I'm at Candi's," she answered as she immediately began to cry. "Where are you, Brad? What is going on?" she asked between sobs.

"I can't tell you that right now. Please whatever you do, do not try to find me. I made a really bad mistake, and I need to fix it. Don't look for me! Don't call my job! I will fix everything. I promise! Stay at Candi's. You will be safer there. I will call you soon! I love you, Laura!"

Before Laura could respond, the line had disconnected. Brad was gone. Laura just stared at her phone, wondering what had just happened. *Was it real,* she asked herself or had she fallen asleep and had been dreaming. As she stared at phone, she noticed a symbol blinking in the corner of the phone's screen. The symbol told her that the phone was currently recording. She must have somehow hit the recording button while she was talking to Brad. She checked to see if the conversation had been recorded. Hitting the play button, she heard the conversation that she had just had with her husband. It was still all surreal for her. This was becoming more and more confusing by the day. Not sure what to do, Laura immediately called Romero rousing him from his sleep.

****

After speaking to Laura and then calming her down, Romero assured Laura that they would deal with this the first thing the next morning. He would call Matthew to see if he could go over to Candi's to pick up Laura's cell phone and the key to her house. From what Laura told him, there should be at least one old message on their home answering machine from Brad. Brad liked to leave messages for Laura every day, so that she could hear them when she got home. Even though the answering machine was outdated and Laura could receive messages on her cell phone, Brad had never seemed to want to part with his old gadgets until he figured he had gotten the full use from them. So each day just before Laura was due to arrive home, Brad would leave her a message and Laura would listen to it as she hung up her coat.

Romero was sure that Matthew could do a voice analysis from both recordings to see if the call Laura received was indeed from Brad. It wasn't that Romero doubted that Laura knew her husband's voice. He just wanted to make sure that it had not been prerecorded by someone who may have only been interested in Laura's whereabouts or keeping her at bay about what was going on with her husband. Also, Matthew could pick up any background sounds that may tell them Brad's whereabouts.

11

Before leaving home on Monday morning, Romero contacted Matthew and set the plan in order. Matthew would go to Candi's house to retrieve Laura's cell phone and the keys to her home. He would meet Romero at the Stevenson's home at ten o'clock, so they could go in together to retrieve the tape from the answering machine.

Meanwhile, Romero would go to Brad's place of business and talk to his employer Mr. Landry. He decided not to call first. He would just show up and see what happened. He did not want to cause alarm unnecessarily.

****

At nine fifteen that morning, just after the bank opened, Romero walked into Buford Savings and Loan. He decided to wear a suit and tie, so he could appear to be there on important business. When he entered, he walked over to the first desk that he saw and asked to speak directly with Brad although he already knew that he would not be there. Hearing that Brad was not in, he proceeded to ask for Mr. Landry. After being told to have a seat to wait for Mr. Landry to avail himself, Romero sat in a seat that gave him a view of the entire public area of the bank.

He could see that cameras were installed throughout the branch and that the security windows that surrounded the tellers were as tall as the ceiling. Everything seemed to be operating normally.

A few moments later, Mr. Landry entered the main lobby from one of the back offices. He greeted Romero with his hand extended. Romero informed Mr. Landry that he had an appointment with Mr. Stevenson that morning and was disappointed to find out that he was not available.

Mr. Landry did not seem interested in giving out any information about why Brad had scheduled an appointment but failed to keep it or cancel. He was more interested in what had brought Romero into the office that morning.

"In Mr. Stevenson's absence is there anything I
can do to assist you this morning, Mr. Turner?"

"If we can go into your office, I can give you my exact reasons for coming in today. I would rather not discuss my personal business here in an open lobby."

When Mr. Landry detected the seriousness in Romero's voice, he quickly escorted him into his office. Once seated, Romero went into his plan of action that would hopefully lead to information about Brad. As he spoke, he chose his words carefully.

"Mr. Landry, I have been doing some research about IRA's and Money Market accounts because I want to do some investing. I recently came into a large sum of money from an inheritance, and I had spoken with Mr. Stevenson on a number of occasions to get information on how these types of accounts work. Today, I was going to make my final decision, and I am highly disappointed that he is not here to follow through with the transaction. Did he suddenly take ill? I am wondering why I did not receive a courtesy call to cancel or reschedule my appointment. Is this the way your bank handles business?"

"I assure you, Mr. Turner, that this is not our typical way of doing business. I got a call on Saturday from Mr. Stevenson informing me that he had a family emergency to tend to concerning his wife and that he may be out for the entire week. I am sure that he would have called you if he was thinking straight. Brad is a very responsible person. He sounded a little flustered. My apologies to you. If you like, I can open and manage your account for you until Mr. Stevenson returns or you can try back at the beginning of next week to contact Mr. Stevenson again. We here at Buford Savings and Loan will do our very best to accommodate your investment needs."

"Thank you for clarifying the situation. I was getting a little concerned. But I do understand that things do happen unexpectedly in life. I will remain patient and wait for Mr. Stevenson to return next week. Thank you so much for your time, Mr. Landry."

Romero exited Mr. Landry's office with a smile on his face. From the news he had just received, Brad was most likely alive and had taken matters into his own hands. If he was indeed entangled with Sly Domingo, he must have decided to detangle himself. *I hope he knows what he is doing*, Romero thought. From what he had heard about Sly and his cronies, he was not someone you wanted to double cross.

****

Driving back across town, Romero turned down Dagwood Lane approaching the Stevensons' home. He took extra precautions as he drove slowly. He was looking to make sure none of Sly's employees were lurking about. Seeing none, he pulled up behind Matthew's car. Matthew must have been looking out himself, because he began to exit his vehicle as Romero was pulling up.

After greeting one another, the two men walked up to the Stevensons' front door. Once inside, Romero immediately knew that something was wrong. It was not the way they left it on Saturday morning. The seat cushions on the couch had been removed and cut. Papers from drawers were strewn about. Doors and cabinets stood ajar. The house had been completely ransacked.

It was obvious that someone was looking for something. *But what*, Romero wondered. Looking in the spot where Laura said the answering machine would be, Romero did not see it. Finally, after digging under the pile of what was now rubbish, he finally located it. Thankfully, the tape was still in tact. After removing it, he handed it to Matthew who once again had broken out into a sweat.

Not wanting to see his friend suffer, Romero said, "Hey Matt, why don't you head on back to the lab and touch bases with me later?"

A look of relief passed over Matt's face. He quickly assented and was on his way.

After Matt left, Romero looked around a little more and took pictures of the scene. He knew that he had to inform Laura about this immediately. He also knew that he would have to calm her down again just as he had done last night. This was one part of the job that he did not especially care for. The women clients always seemed to get hysterical, and sometimes it was not easy for them to be calmed. They would sometimes go on for days at a time. But this was different. Laura's husband's life could actually be in danger. She had a legitimate reason to be concerned.

All the clues were pointed towards danger. Romero could not say that he blamed her for being hysterical with all that had transpired. It would give anyone reason to be alarmed. At the same time, he really was not excited to be the one to have to deal with it.

****

Carefully locking the front door to the Stevensons' home, Romero decided it would be best to drive over to Candi's house and tell Laura the news in person. He would also let her know that the point of entry for the intruder had been the guest bedroom window.

Pulling up in front of Candi's house, Romero sat in his car for a moment and collected his thoughts. He wanted to break the news to Laura gently. He hoped that things would turn around soon. From the moment he took this case, he had learned nothing but bad news. He hoped for Laura and Brad's sake, it would not end the same way.

12

After breaking the news to Laura about the condition of her home and consoling her as he already knew he would need to do, Romero made his way back to his own home to collect his thoughts and plan his next move. On the way, he decided to call Yolanda. Maybe he would get a chance to see her after his appointment with his personal trainer later that afternoon.

Romero waited for Yolanda to answer the phone, but he reached her voicemail. After leaving her a message, he realized that he did not know her work schedule or her school schedule. She had mentioned that school was keeping her busy and that she was working hard to stay on track, so she could graduate next June. She was determined to not let anything get in her way.

As far as work was concerned, she was a cashier at one of the major grocery store chains. Romero could only imagine how Yolanda's days were. His days were full as well. They only difference was his days were mostly unpredictable. He never knew which way a case was going to take him.

****

Later that evening, after a two-hour session with Mark, Romero's personal trainer, a shower and a nap, Romero decided it was time to get back to the grind on the Stevenson case and earn his fee. Not having any direct clues, Romero decided he should either go back to the Domingo warehouse or Trevor's house. He didn't know what he expected to find, but he knew that all the clues pointed toward Sly Domingo and his operation.

Tossing the two locations around in his head for a while, he opted to go to Trevor's house. If no one had purchased the house across the street, he would use it for a stake out location. He doubted if anyone would be showing real estate at this hour.

Settling himself once again in an upstairs bedroom of the vacant house, Romero set his camera on a tripod to free his hands. He opened the curtains ever so slightly so that only the camera lens protruded through the opening. Thirty minutes passed and Romero did not see any forms of life across the street or a car in Trevor's driveway. In his bag of tricks, Romero had a few miniature microphones. Like a thief in the night. Romero made his way across the street to Trevor's home. Before entering, Romero used his binoculars to see if anyone had noticed him crossing the street. From what he could tell, all was clear.

After waiting a few minutes more, Romero stealthily entered Trevor's residence. Not knowing how much time he had, Romero moved quickly. He placed one microphone under an end table in the living room, one into the cordless telephone, and a third one in the kitchen behind a picture that was over the sink. Then, just as quickly as he had entered, he exited Trevor's home and returned to his haven across the street.

An hour later, Trevor's house was still vacant. *Time to go*, Romero thought to himself. Carefully, packing his equipment, Romero wondered why he had not heard from Matthew. He was curious about what he had found out after listening to the two recordings of Brad's voice.

Pulling away from Trevor's neighborhood, Romero pressed Matthew's number on his speed dial. Hearing Matt's voice on the other end, he asked, "Hey bud. Surprised I haven't heard from you. Did you have a busy day?"

"Actually, I did. But I called you hours ago."

"Really, I didn't get your call."

"Yeah, I am not surprised. Did you check your voicemail, Rome?"

"Uh, no. Sorry. So, what's the news? Or, do I have to listen to my message to find out?"

"No, I'm not going to put you through that this time. First of all, the voices definitely match. But what is really interesting is the sounds I heard in the background of the conversation that Laura and Brad had last night."

"Oh really? Give me details."

"I was able to detract a variety of sounds including birds, dogs, cats, and running water."

"Sounds like the city zoo. But the question is which one. There are about seven popular zoos throughout New York."

"Yeah, well I don't think you have to be concerned about that."

"Why is that, Matt?"

"The zoo was my first thought too, but I ruled that out. In a zoo, the animals would not be that close together. I wouldn't hear all of them simultaneously."

"Couldn't Brad have been walking around?"

"Yes, if he was on a cell phone. But I highly doubt that he was. My guess is that he was on a payphone or a business phone even."

"Okay. And how do you explain the sounds that were all congregated together?"

"I am thinking a pet store."

"A pet store?" Romero exclaimed. "That's going to be even harder to locate than the zoo. Can you imagine how many pet stores there are in New York? And that is assuming Brad is even in New York still."

"Yes, I can imagine, but at least it gives you a place to begin your search if you are so inclined to launch one."

"Okay, Matt. Thanks for the news. I will drop off a payment to you in the morning. Is it the standard fee?"

"Yeah, the standard fee. Sorry I couldn't be of more help."

"Don't worry about it. I just have work to do. That's all. Hey, question- did you take Laura's phone back to her?"

"Yes, around two o'clock this afternoon."

"Thanks, Matt. You are a..."

"Lifesaver," Matt said finishing Romero's sentence. At that, they both laughed and hung up the phone.

Romero took a look at the details he had written down while talking to Matt and then decided to check his voicemail to see if he had missed any other calls along with Matthew's. He listened to Matt's message and double checked his notes against what he heard on the message. At the conclusion of Matt's message, Romero pressed the button to save the message just in case he needed to review it later.

The next message was from his mother. She was calling to remind him of his dad's birthday part next week. It wasn't likely that he would forget. His father was turning fifty years old. Romero's mother and sister had made all the plans to ensure that Theodore had a grand celebration. Family will be coming in from across the United States to celebrate with his father.

The last message was from Yolanda. A smiled crossed Romero's face when he heard her voice. That same tingle that he had when he had seen her yesterday ran up his spine. He listened intently to her words. "Romero, this is Yolanda. I am returning your call. It is a pleasure to hear from you. In answer to your question about dinner tonight, I will not be able to make it because I have class. I won't have a free night until Friday. As of right now, I don't have any plans for Friday or Saturday. If you are available, let me know. I will call you back tonight after class. Talk to you soon."

On that note, Romero restarted his car. He had pulled to the side to take notes while talking to Matt. He was tired, and it was time to call it a night.

13

In his home office, Romero set up the surveillance equipment to monitor any conversations that may take place in Trevor's home or on his phone. The equipment that he had installed in Trevor's home had a fifty-mile range for picking up sound bites. Romero wasn't sure if he would get any hits that night, but as soon as he put the last wire in place, he detected voices.

At first, he couldn't understand what was happening because he only heard one voice. Straining to hear a second voice and adjusting the volumes, Romero realized that Trevor was talking on the phone. That made it very difficult to understand what he was talking about. From the one-sided conversation that Romero picked up, he knew that someone was making a demand on Trevor.

Trevor said, "How am I supposed to know?"

Then he said, "We talked about this yesterday. I still don't have any answers for you."

After a long pause, he said, "No. I didn't get a chance to do that before he disappeared. And if I had, I am sure that guy is smart enough to switch vehicles. He knows who he is dealing with. He knows you are no fool."

Romero quickly plugged in the receiver that would pick up sound bites from the bug in the phone. He was then able to hear the other side of the conversation. He heard a deep-throated voice say, "Well, obviously he isn't too scared to run with my money. If you learn how to follow simple instructions, we wouldn't be in this predicament. How do you suggest I get my money back?"

"I do not know. He must have it on him. There was nothing in the house. It is clean."

"So, he is gone with my money with no way to trace his whereabouts. Well, he will have to resurface soon. I will have someone watching the bank. He can't stay gone for long. He wouldn't want to be away from that lovely wife of his too long. Maybe we will have better luck finding her and paying her a visit. That should make him come back."

"I'll do some checking on her. What's her name again, boss?"

"Laura, you dimwit. Laura!" the second voice shouted into the phone just before hanging up.

From the raspy voice, Romero knew that Trevor was talking to Sylvester Domingo. Sly had a run-in with an old enemy about three years ago, and he was near death after having his throat slit. If it wasn't for a doctor being at the scene at the time of the crime, Sly would have died. It was rumored that his vocal chords were severely damaged, but his affiliates had one of the best surgeons that money can buy flown in to do the surgery. The surgeon's procedure repaired his vocal chords; however, his voice will never return to its original use.

Even though the phone had disconnected, Romero could hear Trevor still talking, yelling expletives into the phone at Sly's name calling.

Romero couldn't believe that he missed the first part of the conversation. He was still getting used to his new equipment. He had almost forgotten about the bug in the phone. He wanted to know what Sly had wanted Trevor to do that he did not get done. The only thing he could figure was that Sly had wanted a way to trace Brad's whereabouts but before Trevor could tend to the job, Brad had disappeared. That was good news. They did not have Brad. Brad had gone way on his own. He must be trying to figure out a way to detangle himself from Sly and his dealings with him. *But how long can he hide out?* Romero wondered.

Relieved at what he had discovered, Romero showered and turned on the television to watch the evening news. This was his nightly habit. This is how he kept up with what was happening in the world of crime. Most people did not want to hear about the distasteful habits and behaviors of other people, but it gave Romero information on the underhandedness of people. This knowledge gave him insight that he often used for his cases. He did not have the mind of a criminal so he had to stay in tune with what the criminals were doing and how they thought.

While listening to a report on a bombing in South Harlem, Romero's cell phone rang. It was Yolanda.

After talking for awhile about their respective days, Yolanda became quiet. Romero did not know if the phones had disconnected or if she had fallen asleep.

"Yolanda, are you still there?" he asked.

"Oh yeah, I'm here. Sorry. I guess I zoned out."

"Is there something on your mind?"

"I don't want to burden you with it."

"What are friends for? You can talk to me, Yolanda."

"My dad called me a couple of days ago to tell me that my brother David was diagnosed with Lou Gehrig's Disease."

"Yolanda, I am sorry to hear that."

"Thank you. He is really having a hard time with it because he loves his career as a pro ball player. I don't know what he will do when he can no longer play."

"So, I take it that he is in the early stages of the disease?"

"Yes, but the doctor says that it can progress rapidly or slowly. So we won't know what the immediate outcome will be until something happens. Right now he is playing, but he is having difficulty. That is what prompted him to go to the doctor in the first place."

"Yeah, I meant to ask you about that. I was watching when he got injured in the last Giants game."

"He's recovering, but he had to sit out for two games. He really wants to finish this season. He, of course, is hoping they make it to the Super Bowl so he can go out in style. This may be his last chance at a Super Bowl ring."

"I know what you mean. We will just pray for the best."

"Can we do that now?"

"You want to pray?"

"Yes, if that is alright."

"Sure."

After praying with Yolanda, Romero bid her a goodnight. He really did not want to let her go at that moment, but he knew that they both had full days tomorrow and that she had a lot on her mind. As for him, he had to formulate two plans: one to keep Laura safe and one to try to locate her missing husband.

14

Before going to bed late on Monday night, Theodore Turner turned to his wife and asked, "Do you think Romero will join us for my birthday bash?"

She knew without even asking what was going through her husband's mind. Five years ago, at Pastor Turner's last birthday celebration, he had announced that he desired to start a second church location and he wanted his son to begin preparing to be the senior pastor there. Pastor Turner desired for his sons to carry on the legacy of their forefathers. Romero was fine with the idea as long as his father's successor was his brother Lemuel.

To everyone's surprise, Pastor Turner voiced his opinion that his successor would be Romero, his youngest son. There had always been somewhat of a rift between the brothers because of their father's obvious preference of Romero. This only added fuel to the fire. Lemuel did not really desire to minister, but he did not exactly want to be passed over either.

Two years later at Theodore and Lucille's wedding anniversary, Theodore once again announced his desire about the Turner legacy. It seemed to Romero that at every big event his father was reminded that he was increasing in age, and Pastor Turner would remind everyone, particularly Romero, of his desires.

Last year when Romero's parents' anniversary party came around, Romero was a no show. He could not stand to be put on the spot anymore. He found it disrespectful that his father had not spoken to him privately about both of their desires before he put him on the spot. It wasn't that Romero did not want to preach the gospel. He just did not agree with all of his father's traditions. He had his own thoughts about how to do things in the house of God. He had witnessed firsthand what his father had to go through when his grandfather turned the reigns over to him. It took a long time before his father was able to operate the church with his own vision and still it was limited.

From what he could see, most of the vision that currently existed was what had been planted before. He saw his father as a puppet that was operated by invisible strings that were pulled by his grandfather from his grave. His father did manage to insert tidbits of his own vision, but mostly everything was the way his father had left it and his father before him. Romero wanted to be free to hear from God and not from the grave of his ancestors. He was not looking to stray from the gospel, but he definitely had his own ideas about what he would do to operate the church.

To this day, Theodore still had not approached his son about his personal desires about being his successor.

Theodore looked earnestly at his wife awaiting her answer. All she could say was, "I called and left a message with him today, dear heart. He did not return my call to say whether or not he would be there."

Theodore's heart sank. He really desired for all of his children to celebrate this birthday with him. He would have to do something to change his son's viewpoint of him regarding his recent actions and statements about the church. He knew he would have to act soon. He had less than a week before his birthday party, and if he had anything to say about it, Romero would be there along with his siblings. He needed a plan.

Ah hah, I know just the thing, Theodore thought to himself. "Why are you wearing that silly grin?" Lucille asked her husband as she watched his expression suddenly change from sullen to enthusiastic.

"Oh, I think I will give my sister a call. I haven't spoken to her in a while."

"What do you have up your sleeve?" Lucille inquired knowing that there was more to it than what her husband seemed to be willing to divulge.

"Oh, not much. Just an arm," Theodore joked with his dry sense of humor. He turned and walked out of the room while still formulating his plan. He knew it was best to leave before Lucille became too inquisitive. If she had five minutes alone with him, she would figure out his plan. She was much like his sister Delores. They both had inquiring minds that always wanted to know what was going on around them, especially if they thought something was awry. They both made great amateur detectives, but he was determined to keep his plan to himself.

15

Bright and early Tuesday morning, Romero listened as the rain came down on the rooftop. The rain would definitely affect the ability of the transmitters to pick up sound bites. *So much for eavesdropping*, he thought. He may have to take a drive back over to Trevor's to see if any suspicious activity was occurring. Going out in the rain would not be his first choice of an activity for the day, but he would do what needed to be done.

As he prepared for his day, he thought about his first order of business. He needed to contact Laura to see if she knew anything about a pet store that her husband may go to. Without her help, he would be searching for a needle in a haystack. As he recalled the Stevensons' home, he did not remember seeing any pets.

Rather than taking a drive over to Laura's sister's home, Romero decided to discuss the situation with her by phone. He still thought it was best if her family did not know what was going on. He did not want to cause further suspicion by continually showing up. He knew that they had to be curious and questioning Laura because who would just show up out of the blue without any prior warning, especially someone who was married, but came alone without her spouse.

While dialing Laura's cell phone number, he remembered the conversation he had overhead last night. He wondered if it would be wise to warn her about the possible danger that she may be in. *Maybe she would be better off in a hotel somewhere*, he thought as he waited for her to answer the phone.

After a brief conversation with Laura asking her whether or not she and her husband knew someone who worked at a pet shop, Romero learned that a close friend of theirs owned a chain of pet stores. There were three stores total. Laura had given him the name of the pet store, but she only knew of the main location. This was a start.

Romero located the addresses for the three "A Friend of Your Own" pet store locations and printed them out. Before going on his escapade of the day, he decided to have a hearty breakfast. Not knowing where the day would take him, he thought it would be best to keep his strength up.

While preparing homemade pancakes and an omelet, Romero's mind kept wandering back to the threat made on Laura. He had decided not to tell her until he had a plan. While dicing and chopping the ingredients for an omelet, he came up with his plan. Cooking always put Romero in the right state of mind for creative ideas and effective planning.

Picking up his cell phone, he quickly located Tyrone's number. Unfortunately, Tyrone was not available, so Romero left him a message letting him know that he needed him right away for a surveillance project. Afterwards, Romero dialed Brian. Unlike Tyrone, Brian answered on the first ring.

"Profitable Detective Services," Brian answered.

"Hey man. It's Rome. How are you?"

"All's well. How's it hanging?"

"Everything's great on my end. How's business these days?"

"A little slow right now. Do you have anything for us?"

"Actually that's why I called. I need you guys to do a surveillance job for me."

"Tyrone is actually on his way here. Give me details."

Romero filled Brian in on the details of the Stevenson case and requested the men's assistance with surveillance of Candi's house. Brian said he would discuss the details with Tyrone when he arrived and they would give Rome a call back within the next couple of hours.

Ever so often, Romero hired help so he could work more efficiently on his cases. In the Stevenson case, he wanted someone to keep Laura under surveillance. He did not take Sly Domingo to be a man that issued idle threats. While Rome was on a search for Brad, he did not want anything to happen to Laura or her sister's family in the process.

An hour later, Romero was leaving the first pet store. From what he could see, there was no sign of Brad having been there nor did anyone claim to have seen him. Twenty minutes later, Rome walked into the second pet store. He immediately walked over to the bird section remembering what Matthew had said about birds being in the background. As if though he was reviewing at a list of products to buy, Romero quickly glanced at his notes. He saw that Matt had also detected the sound of running water. Just across from the bird cages was a man-made pond that contained turtles. There was a filter inside the pond continuously circulating the water around as it filtered out particles of dirt and waste.

Just as the store attendant began to walk in Romero's direction, Romero spotted a storage room with its door ajar. On the floor, Romero saw a shirt just like the one Brad was wearing when he lay sprawled on his bedroom floor. He knew without a doubt that it was Brad's. He had a feeling in his gut that told him so.

He reassured the store attendant that he didn't have any questions at the moment and he was just looking around for pet ideas for his niece and nephew. Once the attendant was out of sight, Romero walked over to the storage room and saw that a cot was along the wall. He carefully leaned down and grabbed the shirt.

Only taking a moment to take a quick glance, Brad could see speckles of blood. *I should take this over to Matt so he can compare this blood to the blood samples he took from the Stevenson's home*, he thought. Making his way back to his vehicle without causing a disturbance, Rome was then able to examine the shirt a little more carefully. On the pocket on the front of the shirt was the monogram *BLS*. Rome assumed the monogram was for Bradley Stevenson and that his middle name must begin with an L. He would verify this with Laura.

No sooner than Romero pulled from the parking lot with a feeling of glee in his spirit that he may be a step closer to locating Brad, his cell phone rang. It was Tyrone calling to notify Rome of his and Brian's decision to take the surveillance job. Rome gave them Candi's address, and they were on their way.

Meanwhile, Trevor was following behind Bradley Stevenson's car. The night before, Sly had called one of his contacts in the NYPD to get assistance with the whereabouts of Brad's car. A report for a stolen vehicle was placed for Brad's car and several of the squad members were on alert. When the car was located, a tracer was placed on it and the file was closed. Sly and his organization had been given access to the tracer.

Now Trevor was on a mission to rectify the wrong he had committed of letting Brad out of his sight with Sly's money. He was determined to right his wrong because if he did not, he would never hear the end of it, as Sly was not a forgiving man.

16

After trailing Brad's car for nearly thirty minutes, Trevor saw an opportunity to get Brad's attention. If Trevor had things his way, he would have placed a bullet in Brad's head and called it a day. But Sly had been clear about getting his money before any more harm should befall Brad. After securing his business needs, Sly made sure to do away with anyone who had evidence that could cause harm to him. Bradley Stevenson fell into that category.

At that point, Brad and Trevor were driving in a secluded area of town. Trevor had been driving at a safe distance behind Brad, so he would not be detected. Now that no other cars were in eyesight, Trevor pulled up behind Brad and tapped his rear bumper with the front bumper of his own car. He figured this would cause Brad to pull over, but he was wrong. Brad kept driving. Becoming irritated, Trevor decided to ram Brad's car a little harder to get him to stop. At first, Brad refused to pull over. He hardly even turned his head to see who the culprit was.

Finally, almost out of nowhere, Brad's car stopped alongside a host of eighteen wheelers. Trevor jumped from his car and began to run up to Brad's driver side window. Before he reached the window, a slew of FBI agents descended from the backs of the eighteen wheelers and surrounded Brad's car and Trevor. Being caught completely off guard, Trevor dropped his gun that he had drawn as he approached Brad's car.

Also to his astonishment, the driver he had assumed was Brad exited the vehicle and faced him as he removed a sandy blonde wig.

"Trevor Smallwood, you are under arrest for racketeering and attempt to do bodily harm. You have the right to remain silent. Anything you say can be used against you in a court of law. You have the right to have an attorney present now and during any future questioning. If you cannot afford an attorney, one will be appointed to you free of charge," the FBI agent said to him as he pointed his own weapon in Trevor's direction.

Trevor simply nodded his understanding of his rights as the handcuffs were placed on him and he was ushered into the back of an FBI vehicle.

****

Finishing his meatball sub from Subway, Romero spoke quickly with Laura who confirmed that her husband has monogrammed shirts and that his middle name does indeed begin with an L.

Just as he was laying back to close his eyes for a few moments, his cell phone rang. He expected it to be Laura because she often called him directly back minutes after they had spoken. She usually had other questions to ask him. Many of which he often did not have answers for at that moment.

To his surprise, it was not Laura. It was Tyrone calling in to give a report which consisted of nothing. They had not seen any suspicious activity around Candi's home. They had seen Laura and Candi leave and come back, and they had seen a man, whom they suspected was Candi's husband, leave and return. They had also seen children playing in the front yard, alone and with other children from the neighborhood.

Nothing that they had witnessed had seemed out of the ordinary. There were no strange cars coming up and down the block. The only cars that seemed to travel through this part of the neighborhood were the homeowners who lived on this street. They had not even witnessed a visitor coming in.

This may be because it was during the middle of the week. Most people did not visit during the middle of the week. They were too busy with their personal work, school and/or family schedules.

17

On Wednesday morning, Pastor Theodore Turner decided to put his plan into action. When he arose at five in the morning to pray, he was anxious to pick up the phone then and call his sister Delores Oglebee. But he knew he had to wait. Although it was five o'clock in New York, it was only two o'clock in California. Besides, the bible tells us to be anxious for nothing he reminded himself.

Theo decided to wait until after he had his breakfast and gone into his office at work. Although Pastor Turner considered himself to be in full-time ministry, he also held a secular job. Throughout his years of ministering and from watching his father's life, he knew that it took more than the tithes and offerings to sustain a family and a mortgage. That is not to say that he didn't have faith in God's plan for the Levite tribe. No his faith in God was solid. He knew people and their pattern of giving.

Before going into ministry, Theodore had earned an accounting degree. Years later, he established a private accounting firm that he and his wife ran. Owning his own business gave him flexibility with his time. Some days he spent time at the accounting office and other days he was at the church taking care of the Lord's business.

At ten o'clock sharp, Theodore sat in his office chair and promptly picked up his phone. When his sister answered, he started right in on his plan. "Hey sis!" he began. "How are you doing, doll?" he queried before she could respond to his first greeting.

"I am doing quite well. What do I owe the honor of this pleasure so early in the morning?" Delores responded.

"Oh it's not that early," Theo retorted. "I have been up since five this morning."

"Yes, I am sure you have, but I normally don't hear from you until the evening after you have put in hours of work. So, what's going on?"

"Are you trying to say that you know your big brother?" Theo teased.

"You got it. So spill the beans," Delores teased back.

Theodore went on to ask his sister if she and her husband Pastor Oglebee were planning to journey east in the next week to come to his birthday extravaganza. She assured him that they would be there because they had purchased their tickets months ago. Theo went on to ask if her only child Tinisha would be coming as well. She said she knew that she had planned to along with her husband and daughter, but the baby had been sick last week so she wasn't sure if their plans remained the same.

Hearing this gave Theo an uneasy feeling. His plan to almost ensure his son's appearance at the party was contingent upon his son's favorite cousin coming to town. Theodore knew that wherever Tinisha would be, Romero would not be too far behind. This is how it has always been since they were kids.

Growing up, Tinisha, Romero, Lemuel, and Carmen spent most of their summers together. They were either on one coast or the other. They absolutely adored each other. They had other cousins that they spent time with as well, but Tinisha was their favorite, and she felt the same about them.

"Well, can you give her a call to see how Jasmine is doing?" Theodore asked. Delores could hear the tension in his voice.

"Why is this so important to you, Theo," she asked.

"You know I have been feeling a little resistance from Romero, and I think if Tinisha was around it would help the situation."

"What do you mean resistance? Is he backsliding?"

"No, no. That's not what I mean. Lately, whenever we have big events, he doesn't come. He comes to church regularly, but he always seems to have something more pressing to do when it comes to the family celebrations."

"Why do you think that is, Theo?"

"I guess I have been laying the pressure on really thick."

"Pressure to do what?"

"To take over the family legacy. You know Daddy would really be proud for Romero to be the next senior pastor of the church."

"Yes, I am sure he would, but is that what Romero wants? Have you spoken to him?"

Theodore admitted that he had not spoken to his son on a one-on-one basis. He told his sister that he would take her advice and do so, but he still wanted her to call Tinisha. Before they ended their conversation, Delores just had one final word for her brother, "You are just like Daddy, stubborn as a mule."

18

Just as Romero pulled the white Goose-down comforter, his mother had given to him for a housewarming gift, back on his King-sized bed, his phone rang. Spotting the name of his caller id, he settled in under the cover and pushed the button to receive the call.

"Hello, Sweetheart," he answered.

"Romero, it's Yolanda," she responded.

"Yes, I know."

"Oh, when you said sweetheart, I didn't know if you knew that it was me."

"I have your number programmed, so I knew it
was you. I hope you don't mind me calling you sweetheart."

"No, actually I don't mind, but it does remind me of a question that I want to ask you."

"Go ahead. I'm listening. And when you are finished, I have a question for you too."

"When I saw you three years ago, you didn't seem to be interested in me at all. I rationalized the reason for that by telling myself it was because we were both dating someone else. But even though that was the case, men always have a way to let a woman know he is interested."

"We were both dating other people in high school. I found you attractive, but I was not interested in you. I was interested in Tracy. I don't make a habit of spreading my interest around. I was totally focused on her. However, as you can see that did not work out. I am single and I am interested in you now, and I am free to show you. Is that okay with you?"

"Yes, that is perfectly okay with me. I was just wondering because it seemed to be that your affection came from nowhere. But I can definitely understand that you are a man who focuses on one woman at a time. That is a rare trait, especially in a young man."

"I guess it did come from nowhere because we just met up again after three years after you transferred back here to finish college. I could see your point of view if we had been in contact over the past three years and I did not seem interested, but that is not our situation. As for as my trait of being respectful to my mate, I give the credit to my parents. They taught my brother, sister, and me to be responsible to always take how others feel into consideration. I am by no means perfect, but I do strive to live by the principle of 'do unto others as you would have them do unto you'." After pausing a minute, Romero continued. "If you don't have any other questions, I have a question for you."

"Okay," Yolanda responded softly wondering what was on Rome's mind.

"My family is having a fiftieth birthday party for my dad on Saturday night. I would like for you to go with me. Are you interested?"

Just as Yolanda was getting ready to respond, Romero's call waiting beeped. Quickly glancing at his phone, he saw that it was his cousin Tinisha.

"Lan, can I call you back? My cousin from Cali is calling me."

"Sure, Rome. Call me when you are free, and yes, I would love to go."

"Sounds great. I will call you with the details. Have a good night."

"Hey, Cousin." Romero began the conversation with Tinisha. "Hey yourself," she responded with laughter in her voice.

"What do I owe the honor of this pleasure?" Romero queried.

"Well, my mom called me today…"

"How is Aunt Delores?" Romero cut in.

"She's fine," Tinisha began. For a moment, there was silence on the phone.

"Are you sure, Nisha?"

"Yes. It's just that…"

"C'mon, Nisha. You have never been at a loss for words. Is something wrong with Aunt Delores or Uncle Earl," he pressed.

"No, it's your father, Uncle Theo."

"What do you mean my father," Romero said standing up from the bed.

"Well, he called my mother and asked her to get me to get you to go to his birthday party. When I asked her why he would need me to do that she told me about what had happened before at some of the other celebrations."

"Yeah, there were a few things that he said during those engagements that rubbed me the wrong way. So, I did stop going to the events because he always seems to use those times as an arena for sharing, even if the sharing has to do with someone else."

Romero explained the situation to his cousin in detail. She understood his position but went on to ask if he had planned to go to his father's fiftieth birthday party. He said he had given it a lot of thought. He knew that this was not a birthday like the others. This birthday was a milestone. Although he did not feel one hundred percent secure with his decision, he had decided to go. He did not want to do something that he would regret later. He did not want to miss this moment because of his own personal feelings about the past. He just prayed that everything would work out well. Tinisha ended the conversation by letting him know that she was in his corner and that she and her family would be right by his side at the event.

19

Having Trevor in police custody and asking him to turn state's evidence was like having an eager child in a candy store. Trevor had only been out of the state penitentiary for a little over three years after having served a sentence of eight years, and he was desperate not to return. Not desperate enough to keep his nose clean obviously.

Eight years ago, he had been convicted of armed robbery. That was his second offense. As a condition of his probation, he was not permitted to own or have any fire arms in his possession. So by having the gun he was planning to use to threaten Brad to surrender Sly's money, he was automatically in violation of his probation and could be required to finish out the rest of his original sentence of ten years. He had received time off for what was considered to be good behavior by the parole board, but now his early release could be revoked.

By cooperating with the FBI, Trevor could bargain to not be charged for his involvement in the crimes committed by Sly Domingo and his organization. He was very concerned about receiving his third strike and going to prison for the rest of his natural life. He kept placing his head in his hands and rubbing his temples while mumbling, "This will be my third strike. This will be my third strike."

He did not, however, need to be concerned about earning a third strike and facing life in prison due to the third strike alone. The US Second Circuit Court of Appeals concluded the state's highest court, the

New York State Court of Appeals, had erred in upholding the constitutionality of the Persistent Felony Offender (PFO) law in the wake of a 2004 decision by the United State Supreme Court. This decision was made official in April 2010, so although Trevor may face being charged with a crime, he would not automatically face life in prison. Obviously, Trevor was not up to date on the legalities of the laws in New York and the changes that had been made a month prior.

To help his cause, Trevor provided detailed information about Sly's involvement with illegal deals throughout the state of New York and abroad. These details included the action Sly had coerced Brad into agreeing to and his dealings with select officers of the New York Police Department.

Hours later, after Trevor's initial statement was taken, proof of evidence provided, immunity granted, and entrance into the witness protection program given, a fleet of FBI agents proceeded to embark upon the task of locating Sylvester Domingo and alleged corrupt police officers. One by one, eleven officers were brought into the Federal Bureau of Investigations in New York City for questioning. Sly Domingo, however, could not be located.

By the next morning, the word had circulated that an All Points Bulletin had been issued for Sylvester "Sly" Domingo. All major news broadcast across the nation aired the story showing Trevor's arrest and the sweep of the New York State's precincts. A $50,000 reward would also be issued for any information that leads to Sly's arrest.

Those who were currently in Sly's organization and those who had ever worked with him also made attempts to flee. Some were successful, while others were not. All of the business properties that Sly had registered in his name were raided, and his bank accounts and other assets were frozen.

The FBI wanted to make Sly's disappearance difficult for him to operate with limited resources. They were aware though that the likelihood of him having offshore untraceable accounts was high. From their perspective, his capture was just a matter of time.

Romero, like the rest of New York City, heard the news. He immediately called Laura to see if the car that was shown on the broadcast was Brad's car. From the description of the make and model that Laura had provided him, he was sure it was. During the broadcast, the license plate was blurred to protect the identity of the vehicle's owner. It was not mentioned that the car belonged to a civilian, but anyone watching could tell that Trevor had been set up by the way the officer stepped out of the vehicle and pulled off the wig. It was obvious that he was pretending to be someone else to lure Trevor into a trap.

Romero knew that the person the officer was posing as was Brad. Once Romero confirmed the information with Laura about Brad's car, they both had the same question: Where is Brad?

Romero had other unanswered questions, but he found it safe to assume that Brad was the one who tipped the FBI about Sly's recent activities. *Was he safe?* Romero wondered. *Should he continue to look knowing that this was now an FBI case?*

20

At nine on Thursday morning, Rome sat in his Range Rover finishing a blueberry muffin and a bottle of orange juice. He was filled with anticipation because in twenty minutes some of his family members were coming in from California. He had set this day aside to spend with them. Of course, he did not really know what the outcome of his day would be, especially with the latest developments in the Stevenson case.

As he made his way through the terminal, the anticipation grew. He was so excited about meeting his aunt, uncle, and cousins at the luggage terminal that he did not feel his cell phone vibrate on his hip. Trish, one of his contacts from the NYPD, was calling him to tell him what had taken place at the precinct the day before.

An FBI swat team came in the precinct with weapons drawn to arrest several of the supposed NYPD's finest. The precinct was surrounded and helicopters flew overhead. The captain, several lieutenants, sergeants, and detectives were arrested.

Special measures had to be taken because nearly everyone in the building was armed. The FBI agents figured if the squad members were bold enough to entangle themselves with Sylvester "Sly" Domingo, they may be bold enough to open fire in an effort to resist arrest.

Other officers were at their individual homes when they were arrested. FBI agents used battering rams to break doors down to prevent officers from escaping. Of the twenty-three officers that were involved with Sly, twenty-two were apprehended. One officer, however, received a warning phone call while he was away on vacation. He decided to take his own life to avoid retribution.

****

Walking up to the luggage carousel, Romero anxiously tried to spot his family through the crowd of travelers. Unable to locate them right away, he took out his cell phone to call Tinisha. He knew the chances of her hearing her phone in the airport was slim to none, if she had even turned it on after getting off the airplane.

Before he located her number in his phone, he heard a familiar voice behind him.

"Rome!" the voice called.

Turning around, Romero came face to face with his cousins: Tinisha, her husband Rafael, and their daughter Jasmine. "Hey cousins," he exclaimed while hugging all of them and kissing the baby as he took her from her mother's arms.

"Where are your mom and dad?" Romero inquired of Tinisha.

"We asked them to meet us at the car rental counter. We have to pick up our rental car."

"Okay. So, they will ride with me over to my parents' house. Will you guys be following us or meeting me at the condo?"

"I figured we would follow you, so we can say hello to Uncle Theo and Aunt Lucy before we settle at your place. This may be our only chance to see them before the party tomorrow. The plan is still on, right?" Tinisha asked with a questioning look in her eye.

"Of course," Rome responded.

"What plan?" Rafael asked feeling left out of the loop.

"I will explain later," Tinisha responded. "Let's go."

At her command, Rome and Raf looked at each other and laughed. "She's still in the driver's seat," Rome commented.

"Oh yeah," Raf agreed. "Not much has changed."

****

Later that evening, after visiting his parents and leaving his aunt and uncle with them, Romero helped his cousins settle into his guest bedroom. Once alone, Rome retrieved his voice messages. He heard the long message from Trish, a few messages from potential clients that he would call back on Monday, and the last message was from Laura. She was yet concerned about her husband.

Romero thought it was best to call her back, but he wanted to get another update from Tyrone and Brian first. Neither of them had called, so he figured no news was good news. He knew that if anything suspicious had occurred, they would have notified him.

After receiving a positive report from Tyrone, Romero called Laura. She was hysterical, as he expected. He began to think this was a part of her
natural makeup.

Unable to calm her on the phone, Rome took a drive over to Candi's house to see if he could help her to make sense of the situation. He knew that if Brad was the one that tipped the FBI, he was likely to be in protective custody unless he refused the FBI's protection.

After only being with Laura for nearly twenty minutes, Romero received at text on his phone from Brian informing him that a non-descript car was pulling up in front of Candi's house. No sooner than Romero read the text, there was a knock at the front door.

Candi answered the door and two suited gentlemen asked for Laura by first and last name. Candi asked what this was concerning and one man answered, "This is a personal and legal matter. Is she here?" Hearing the concern and authority in his voice, Laura and Romero walked to the front door from the kitchen where they had been seated at the table. When they heard they knock at the door, both had listened attentively. Romero nodded to Laura that it was okay to reveal herself to the men.

Once at the door, Romero stepped forward to speak on Laura's behalf. He asked the gentlemen to show identification. Both men produced FBI identification badges. They were Agents Smith and Farni. They wanted to speak to Laura alone. So, Romero and Candi retreated to the kitchen after Romero introduced himself and Candi. When he stated that he was a private investigator,

Smith asked him if the guys seated in the non-marked vehicles are his guys. Romero stated that they are.

Back in the kitchen, Candi grew more nervous, but Romero knew what was going on. He had never experienced it before himself, but he had heard about this on several occasions. Before long, a wail came from the living room. Candi jumped up from the table and ran towards the living room to check on her sister. Romero was right on her heels.

When they reached the living room, they found Laura bending over and crying. Candi wanted to know what was wrong with her. Laura responded that she would tell her in a moment and assured her that she was okay. While Laura spoke to Candi, Agent Farni went outside. Moments later, he walked back in with Brad.

Immediately, Brad and Laura embraced as tears ran down both of their faces. Brad's left shoulder was bandaged to cover the flesh wound he had received the night Romero saw him on the Stevensons' bedroom floor.

Smith and Farni explained to Candi that her sister and brother-in-law were entering the witness protection program because Brad had agreed to testify against Sylvester Domingo. They would not be allowed to contact her immediately, but arrangements would be made so that calls could be made periodically on a secure FBI monitored phone line. Other than their few words, no details were given and just as soon as they arrived, they were all gone.

Candi stood in astonishment thinking about the news of not being able to see or talk to her sister on a regular basis. Her sister was the only aunt that her children had. Candi's husband was an only child and came from a small family. Laura had always been a main fixture in her nieces and nephews' lives. She had not yet had children of her own, but Candi would have done the same for Laura's children as Laura had done for hers.

Rome stood amazed at how the case had turned out. All he could do was hope for the best as he held a check for his final payment in his hand. He had never had a client enter the witness protection program. He was a bit nervous about Laura and Brad's safety because he knew that Sly had yet to be apprehended.

As he looked at the check, he noticed that Laura had added an extra $10,000 to his required fee. He guessed she figured everything he had gone through was worth the extra money, even though he was not the one who had officially brought Brad back to her.

Tired from an extremely long day, Rome bid Candi a good night. He needed to go home to get some rest and process everything that had transpired. He also needed to prepare for his father's birthday bash the next day.

When he walked outside, he signaled to Brian and Tyrone to drive over to his car.

"The Feds, right?" Brian asked as he pulled up next to Rome.

"You got it," Romero answered.

"Witness Protection?" Tyrone wanted to know.

"Exactly."

"So, what do you think, Rome? Will this have a happy ending?"

"Man, I really don't know. Sly is no joke. No one knows where he is or what he is really capable of doing. But I believe the Stevensons are in capable hands."

"Yeah, well let's hope you are right. Maybe the Feds will catch this character. They need to get the likes of him off the streets," Brian responded.

Continuing the small talk about Sylvester's capture and Laura and Brad's safety, Romero quickly grabbed his check book and made out a check to Profitable Detective Services. Handing the check to Tyrone, he bid them a good night and off he went down the street, imagining the goose down comforter that covered his bed. He could not wait to nestle his head in the pillow.

21

The next morning, at nine o'clock sharp, Romero arrived at the gym to meet his trainer. It pained him to do so because he was mentally and physically exhausted. The Stevenson case had taken a toll on him even though it had only lasted a week. It was one of the busiest weeks he had had in a long time.

After his two-hour session, Rome drove back home, still reflecting on the Stevenson case. He was still concerned about Brad and Laura's safety. He knew that the United States Marshall Service knew how to effectively run their Witness Protection Program, but he was still concerned because
Sylvester Domingo was on the run.

The protection program had been in effect for over forty years, since its establishment in 1970. Like any other program, it was not flawless, but it worked the great majority of the time. So he could only pray that Brad and Laura had been delivered by the FBI safely into the hands of the marshals assigned to the case.

Although he was tired, he missed the case already. He felt like he did not really see it to completion. He knew that under the circumstances, the outcome was unavoidable. He also knew that by Laura giving him such a hefty bonus that she did not share his concern. She was just happy to be with Brad again.

The bonus that she had given Romero made all of his hard work and efforts worthwhile, despite what he was feeling at that moment. He had only received a bonus twice before. The bonuses really came in handy. They helped out a great deal when he was saving for his condo and also when he placed the down payment on his Rover. He had truly been blessed his first year as a private investigator. PI's normally earn an average yearly salary of $40,000 depending on their popularity and the type of cases they took.

With the bonuses he had earned, Romero cleared over $60,000 his first year. Living at home with his parents had made it easier to save the money for his condo. Finding the condo on the foreclosure list was an even greater blessing because he did not have to pay market value.

When Rome returned home just before noon, he planned to take his cousins out for brunch. To his surprise, when he opened the door, he smelled the aroma of bacon and syrup filling the kitchen and living room. Tinisha had prepared bacon, scrambled eggs, and pancakes. Jasmine was sitting on her daddy's lap having her fair share.

Once Romero showered and settled in with his family to enjoy his late breakfast, he turned the television on to the news. The newscaster was talking about the disappearance of Sly Domingo and how he, along with others in his organization, was currently being sought after by the FBI. Several pictures of Sly flashed across the screen. Next, a picture of one of Sly's affiliates flashed across the screen. The man had blonde hair and one bad eye. His description matched the one Laura had given him of the intruder who had strapped her to the chair. All of the pieces were finally coming together.

"Sly Domingo is really a popular guy. We received notification of his status when the FBI issued an All Points Bulletin for his arrest," Rafael said. "What do you know about him?" he asked Romero.

"Yeah, and tell us about this case that you are working on with the lady's missing husband. Have you found him yet?" Tinisha wanted to know.

"Well, both cases are actually one in the same. It seems that Sly had some business dealings with Brad, the missing husband, who by the way is no longer missing. Brad is a regional manager of a savings and loan and Brad's wife thinks that Sly coerced Brad into laundering dirty money for him. I guess Brad grew tired of dealing with him. He decided to detangle himself from Sly, so he contacted the FBI. The FBI now has Brad and Laura in witness protection so Brad can testify against Sly. His testimony along with others will put Sly in jail for a long time to come if he can be brought to justice."

22

The big evening had finally arrived: Pastor Theodore Turner's 50th birthday bash. Romero and his cousins rode to the event together in the Range Rover. Earl, Delores, and Carmen rode with Theodore and Lucille in Pastor Theo's car. Yolanda, at Romero's request, met him at the hotel. All other family, friends, and church members arrived on schedule as well.

The event was held at the luxurious Roosevelt Hotel in New York City. The ambiance was very soothing and the décor was exquisite. The event took place in the Grand Ballroom and was beautifully decorated in ivory and a deep burgundy. The colors spoke of regality and elegance.

As the guests entered, they looked around and commented on the touch of excellence that the room beheld. It wasn't that they had expected anything less. They were all well familiar with Mrs. Lucille Turner's touch. Her daughter Carmen had also been trained very well to put events together in a manner of excellence.

After the guests had greeted one another and everyone had been served the first course, the band began to play softly. While the main course was being served and savored, several of Theo's close friends graced the stage and "roasted" him. The crowd laughed heartily as they all had a great time.

Afterwards, one by one several of the guests stood at the podium and uttered words of praise to Theodore. Many of them had brought gifts for him as well. Finally, after the last person had spoken, including Theo's three children and wife, Pastor Theo himself walked toward the podium. As he did so, all the guests rose from their seats and applauded the guest of honor.

Theodore began his speech by thanking everyone for coming and demonstrating the love they had for him. He went on to talk about his special friends who had participated in the roast and thanked them for giving everyone a laugh. Then as a slide show played in the background, Pastor Turner reminisced over several aspects of his life. As he moved from one aspect to another, he finally ended with ministry.

A hush had fallen over the crowd as each person listened attentively. Romero felt himself hold his breath as his father began to talk about his plans for building a new church and plans to expand his ministry. He stated that he would be actively seeking someone to fill that spot, but the truth of the matter was that he had already decided who that would be. He said it would be a few years down the road, but it was time for the training process to begin.

On that note, Romero could barely keep still in his seat. Before his father could say another word, Rome jumped up from his seat and headed toward the door. Tinisha moved quickly and followed him out of the room.

At the sudden exit of his son, Theodore stopped speaking. Everyone turned to look toward the door to see what the commotion was about. As they turned back to the podium, the pastor's armor bearer noticed that Pastor Turner had leaned over onto the podium. He rushed to see what the problem was. Just as he reached the podium, the pastor fell to the floor.

Everyone gasped as they stood to their feet. Some rushed over, while others stood gazing wondering what happened so quickly. The atmosphere changed in a matter of minutes. "Call 911," the armor bearer yelled.

Outside in the parking lot, Tinisha tried desperately to calm Rome, along with Yolanda who had followed them outside. He was livid that his father would pull his same old stunt again. Tinisha disagreed with Rome's opinion. "You did not give him a chance to finish his statement. You really don't know what he was about to say," she protested.

"I know my father," Romero argued. "I shouldn't have come."

Tinisha and Romero were still going back and forth on the topic of Theodore's speech when Lemuel came running from the hotel. "Rome. It's dad!"

"What's wrong?" Romero and Tinisha asked simultaneously.

"He collapsed," Lemuel answered between sobs.

"Oh my God!" Romero exclaimed as he pushed past Lemuel and ran back inside pulling Tinisha behind him.

When Lemuel, Romero, Tinisha, and Yolanda had re-entered the ball room, they saw Theodore sitting up on the floor right next to the podium. Someone was trying to get him to drink from a glass of water and to take aspirin, but a nurse who was by his side warned against it. She stated they did not know the condition of his blood, whether it had thickened or thinned. Therefore, the cause of the apparent stroke was unknown. The stroke could have been caused by a bleed or from an artery that was clogged and did not allow for sufficient passage of blood to the brain. The nurse stated that it was best to wait until he was checked by a physician.

"Do something!" Lemuel yelled at Carmen.

Carmen did not move. It was as if though her feet were glued to the spot she was standing in.

Finally, the paramedics arrived and after checking Theo's vitals, it was suggested for him to be immediately transported to the emergency room at the nearest hospital. Pastor Turner did not bother to object. He allowed himself to be placed on a gurney, and off he went with his wife by his side.

Lemuel and his wife and children followed directly behind the ambulance. Romero and his cousins followed behind Lemuel. Carmen, Earl, and Delores followed Romero's SUV in Pastor Theo's car. Yolanda's car was the last car in the procession.

At the hospital, Theo's children paced up and down the hallway wondering what was going on with their father as he lay in a bed in the Intensive Care Unit. Pastor Oglebee, Tinisha's father, suggested that they all sit and pray. Following their uncle's suggestion, Lemuel, Carmen, and

Romero sat with their family and Yolanda and held hands. Pastor Oglebee prayed earnestly on behalf of his brother-in-law.

Not long afterwards, Lucille came out and told her children that they could go see their father. Hurriedly, they made their way down the corridor. None of them knew what to say when they entered the room. One by one, in order of age, they embraced their father and planted kisses all over his face.

After visiting with him for a little while, they decided to move out and allow his sister and her family to come in to see him.

Everyone was deeply saddened by what had occurred that night, but they were all grateful that all had turned out just fine.

The attending physician wanted to keep Theo overnight for testing so the cause of the stroke could be determined and preventative methods could be given to ward off reoccurrences in the future. Theo consented and asked for accommodations for his wife because he knew that there was no way that she was leaving his side. At his request, Lucille smiled because he was right. She was not going anywhere. It would be a moot point to discuss it.

Reassured that their father, brother, uncle, grandfather, and brother-in-law was out of harm's way, Romero, his siblings and extended family, went back to the Turner household to sleep. Romero walked Yolanda to her car and embraced her before she left. He really did not want her to go, but he knew that it was inappropriate to ask her to go back to his parents' home with him and his brothers.

He really did not know what to say to her. On one hand, he felt that he should apologize for the scene he made and for the way the night turned out. On the other hand, he knew that what had occurred was not totally his fault. Something was going on with his dad that he had failed to divulge.

On the way to the Turner household, no one said a word. There was silence in all three vehicles. Each person was saying his/her own silent prayers.

23

In another part of the world, on Saturday night, Dr. Weindorfor, sat in front of his unlit fireplace peeling a dark red Washington apple. He had the television turned to one of his favorite pastime American shows: America's Most Wanted.

As he slid a piece of the succulent, sweet apple onto his tongue, he nearly choked when the next fugitive's picture appeared on the screen. Although the criminal did not look like the picture on the screen the last time he saw him, he would recognize his face anywhere.

Dr. Weindorfor immediately became livid with grief when he realized that he may have assisted in a fugitive's plight to escape justice.

Yesterday morning, his secretary received a call from someone who wanted to verify that Dr. Weindorfor was indeed the famous doctor who replaced empty or ineffective human eyes with ones that had an authentic appearance. When it was confirmed that ocular prosthesis was Dr. Weindorfor's expertise, an appointment was attempted to be scheduled immediately. The first available opening, however, was not until next week, but the caller insisted that he needed an earlier appointment. He said he was scheduled to take a picture with his siblings for their mother's ninetieth birthday and wanted to look his best.

At the time of the conversation, there was nothing the secretary could do to fulfill the caller's request because Dr. Weindorfor only took one appointment a day, three days a week and his quota had been met. But as luck would have it, the patient that was scheduled for later in the afternoon called in thirty minutes later to cancel due to a case of pneumonia which caused her inability to fly into Australia where Dr. Weindorfor's clinic was located.

As a result, the secretary called the local number that the caller had provided and let him know that a vacancy had come available. After discussing the cost of the procedure, the secretary asked for the name of the caller's insurance provider. The client said he would pay the $2000 fee in cash.

As Dr. Weindorfor reviewed these details in his mind, he told himself that he should have known something was off. Furthermore, the entire procedure was designed to take anywhere from six to eight weeks, because surgery on the existing socket had to occur first. After the socket healed, then the placer that was in the socket to help the socket form properly would be removed and the new eye would be inserted. However, the client said he had already gone through the initial surgical procedure. He just needed the final step of the eye placement.

Dr. Weindorfor found this to be extremely odd that the patient did not follow up with the original ophthalmologist, but he did as the patient requested.

As he continued to view the broadcast, he definitely knew that something was awry. According to the broadcast, the fugitive's name was Michael Kramer, but the name he had given at the clinic was Vladimir Petrov. He even had a Russian accent to go along with the Russian name.

Another thing the doctor found odd was the coloring of the fugitive's hair. He thought he noticed a bad dye job. The client's hair was jet black, but Dr. Weindorfor could see spots of blonde that did not get colored. He ignored the botch job that was done on the client's hair that looked as if it was done hurriedly. Instead, he focused on the job that he was being paid to do and figured maybe the cause of the bad dye job was the effect having only one eye.

The recovery process for the patient was two days at the clinic because of the minor cutting that was required for the implantation. The eye former that was required to stay inside the eye socket prior to the placement of the actual eye had been removed, and the socket and begun to close.

Still watching the broadcast, Dr. Weindorfor stood up, trying to gather his wits. *What do I do?* he wondered. *Do I run the risk of being a target for the mob because I dared to turn in a suspect, or do I keep my mouth closed and say nothing and allow others to possibly become endangered?*

Being the law-abiding citizen that he is, Dr. Weindorfor slowly picked up the phone. First, he called his office. Since the procedure was only one day ago, the fugitive wasn't scheduled to leave until the next morning. After verifying that the patient was still at the clinic, Dr. Weindorfor dialed the number of the FBI tip hotline.

After contacting the FBI, Dr. Weindorfor left the matter in their hands. The United States FBI agents had worked with the Australian Federal Police before on wanted fugitive cases and getting them to cooperate in this case was not a problem. They agreed to extradite Kramer once they had him in their custody.

24

At the Turner household, Rome sat in the family room with his siblings and his cousins. His aunt and uncle had decided to retreat to the guest bedroom. Baby Jasmine was the only one asleep. The room was very still and quiet. It was almost as though no one was home.

Almost out of nowhere, Carmen broke the silence, "I wonder what caused Daddy to have a stroke."

"He was probably worried about Mr. Goody Two Shoes over there," he retorted directing his statement at Rome.

Rome took offense and immediately sprang to his feet at his brother's words and tone. "Exactly what do you mean by that?"

"You know what I mean. He was doing fine until you jumped up to run out of the room. What was that
all about?" Lemuel responded, now standing as well.

"Oh, we all know what was coming next. So, you're saying it is okay for Dad to put me on the spot like that in a room full of people?"

"How did he put you on the spot? He didn't even mention your name," Lemuel responded, with his voice getting higher and higher. By this time, Jasmine had awakened, and everyone in the room was standing.

"Come on you guys. You know Uncle Theo would not want you guys fussing and fighting at a time like this," Tinisha said.

"Well, Lem needs to keep his comments to himself. Especially when he does not know what is going on," Romero blared.

"Seems to me that you are the one that doesn't know what was going on. You jumped to a conclusion and stormed from the room."

"That is enough," Carmen interjected. "Nisha is right. Daddy would not want us to be at each other's throats. Everybody just sit down."

Just as things began to quiet down again and everyone was finding a seat again, Romero's cell phone rang. It was Yolanda calling to let Rome know that she had made it home safely. When Rome retreated to his old bedroom still talking on the phone, everyone decided to retreat to their private quarters. Lemuel and his family went to his old bedroom, and the Salisburys went to Carmen's room. Carmen went to her parents' bedroom and lay across the bed.

No one really slept. Everybody was concerned about Theodore Turner.

About an hour later, Lemuel walked into Romero's bedroom. Romero had just fallen asleep. Shaking his brother by the shoulder, Lemuel sat down on the side of the bed.

"What's the problem?" Romero asked, wondering if his brother was about to start in on him again.

"I just wanted to apologize. I guess I am letting the stress of everything that is going on with Dad cloud my judgment. I should not have pointed my finger at you. You are not to blame for this. I am sure that something is going on with Dad that he has been keeping from us."

"I accept your apology. But I must admit, I do feel as though my reaction may have triggered something, even if there was a pre-existing condition."

"Why do you say that?"

"Well, you know Dad has this thing about me stepping into ministry in a few years and following in his footsteps."

"Yeah. So? What is wrong with that? I thought you wanted to be a minister or a pastor."

"I don't agree with every tradition that we do and I don't want to get caught up in doing things the way Dad does or the way Grandpop did just because that's what they did. But what really upsets me is that Dad is just assuming that I want to be his successor. He hasn't even spoken to me about any of this. And isn't it only right to hand the mantle to you?"

"Oh, don't even try it. That's not me and you know it. You and Dad just need to have a long talk."

"I know. I have been waiting for him to approach me."

"You know how dad is. You need to just sit down with him and tell him how you feel and nip all of this in the bud."

"Yeah, I guess you are right."

"Oh, and what's going on with you and the young lady you invited to the party? What's her name?"

"Her name is Yolanda, and don't worry about what's going on," Romero said playfully as he turned over to go back to sleep. "Turn off the light on your way out."

Lemuel laughed at his brother's secretiveness as he shut the door. He thought back to when he had begun dating his wife. *Those were the days*, he thought.

25

The Australian Federal Police arrived at Dr. Weindorfor's clinic in hot pursuit of Michael Kramer, an hour after Dr. Weindorfor's initial call to the FBI hotline.

Three days prior, Sylvester Domingo's private jet had departed from a private hanger in Maine. This jet was able to fly under police radar because it was not officially registered to Sly. Instead, it was registered to a well-known Congressperson, but it belonged to Sly nonetheless. Several hours after boarding the plane, Michael stepped out on land again in the "land
down under."

As he now opened his eyes in his hospital, still a little drowsy from the pain medicine, Michael knew that he adventure in kangaroo country had come to an end before it had an opportunity to launch.

Standing at the foot of the bed, as well as on both sides of him, were AFP officers ready to take him to their headquarters for questioning. From the headquarters, he would eventually be released into the custody of US FBI agents.

26

Just before seven am the next morning, Carmen was gently aroused from her sleep by the vibration of her cell phone that had made its way underneath her left thigh. Gently lifting herself to retrieve the phone, she knew it had to be her mother calling from the hospital. No one else would be calling her this early on Sunday morning.

After quickly glancing at the caller id, Carmen pressed the *talk* button. "Mom?" she answered.

"Yes, dear. It's me."

"How's Dad?"

"Oh, he will be just fine, dear. The doctor is going to release him later this afternoon."

"That's great news. What did they say about him passing out? Was it a stroke?"

"Yes, he had a mild stroke, but nothing was affected. He has full use of his hands, arms and legs."

"That's great! Praise God."

"Yes, God is so good and faithful. He looks after His servants."

"Oh Mom, what about service today? Who's going to take over?"

"Your dad has already taken care of that. He called Deacon Toad this morning. He will be in charge of today's services."

At her mother's response, Carmen began to laugh. "What is so funny, Carmen?" Lucille asked.

"Mom, his name is not Deacon Toad."

"Well, what is it then?" Lucille asked sounding confused.

"It's Todd, Mom. Todd," Carmen answered in between her giggles.

"Oh sorry!" Lucille replied as she began laughing herself.

A few minutes later, across the hall, Romero lifted his head from the pillow. *Is that laughter I hear*, he thought to himself.

Rome had been awake for nearly a half hour, but he dared not to walk about because he did not want to disturb anyone who may still be resting. He thought he had heard voices coming from Carmen's room where Tinisha and Rafael were sleeping, but he could not be sure, so he just lay still in his old bed. After hearing his sister's laughter, he quietly made his way across the hall to see what was going on.

"Hey, Rome," Carmen greeted her younger brother as he walked into their parents' bedroom.

"Hey, Sis. Who's that?" he asked referring to the person on the other end of the phone.

"It's Mom. Do you want to talk to her?"

"Sure."

"Hold on, Mom. Rome wants to say something."

After handing her cell phone to her brother, Carmen went to share the good news with Lemuel and his family and her cousin Tinisha and her family. As she was making her way to the guest bedroom to share the news with her aunt and uncle, she smelled the sweet aroma of coffee and syrup coming from the kitchen.

Delores had awakened early finding it hard to sleep with her brother in ICU. She found enough food in the deep freezer and the pantry to feed an army, so she had begun to make herself busy.

When Carmen saw her aunt at work in the kitchen, she grabbed one of her mother's aprons and tied it around her waist. She leaned over and hugged her aunt without saying a word, understanding that she was concerned about her brother. Delores looked up at Carmen and smiled. "How are you this morning, Kiddo?" Delores asked.

"All is well, Auntie," Carmen replied. "I just spoke with my mother. She said Dad is doing fine and he will be released this afternoon to come home."

"Yes, I know. I spoke with her earlier."

"Then why such the long face, Auntie," Carmen queried.

"Our father died of a stroke that was caused by thrombosis."

"Yes, I remember. But we don't know if Daddy's stroke was a result of an artery in the brain being blocked and the brain could not receive blood or oxygen, or if he had an embolic stroke that resulted from his high cholesterol."

"It doesn't really matter does it? He needs to take better care of himself."

"That's true, Auntie, but knowing the cause will help in preventing it from occurring again."

"I guess you are right. You should know. You are the nurse."

"I am getting there."

"Can I ask you a question?"

"Sure," Carmen replied knowing what was coming. She was surprised that the question had not been asked already.

"Why didn't you assist your father when you came back into the room and saw him lying there against the podium?"

"I guess I panicked. I couldn't move. I was immobilized. When I first saw him, I didn't know if he was alive or dead."

"That is understandable, sweetheart. I just thought I would ask."

"It is a fair question. I guess that question has been going through everyone's mind," Carmen replied thinking back to Lemuel's outburst. Then she thought, *Why didn't he do something? He is a trained firefighter paramedic. He is accustomed to dealing with people who are in a variety of medical conditions*, she tried to reason with herself.

As she was having this ongoing conversation in her mind, she totally tuned out her aunt and did not notice her siblings and cousins enter the kitchen. Soon, everyone had found a spot around the table. Earl prayed and everyone dug in.

After all who were hungry filled their bellies, Earl stood up and announced, "I guess we better be heading down to the church." It was not a question, and it was not up for discussion.

"We have to go home and change," Lemuel announced.

"Yeah, me too," Rome chimed in.

"We will see you there," Uncle Earl replied as he headed toward the guest room following behind his wife.

On the way home with Tinisha, Raf, and Jas, Romero dialed Yolanda's number. He wanted to assure her that his father would be fine and to see if she was planning on going to Sunday service. He did not really get a chance to enjoy her company last night with all of the unexpected activities occurring. He wanted to see her.

Arriving home and quickly showering, Rome's thoughts wandered to the Stevensons. He wondered how they were doing. He wondered if they were still safe. He wondered where Sly was. There had been no news about his capture or even a hint of where he might be. All he knew was that Trevor had spilled the beans and the hunt was out for Sly and other members of his crew. Later that afternoon, he would make it a point to catch up on the latest news to see if there were any updates.

27

Now after having been extradited back to the United States, Michael Kramer sat in the FBI headquarters in New York City. As he sat at a table, he glanced through one of the windows and noticed how beautifully the sun was shining although he could only see it radiating off the skyscrapers.

He wondered how he permitted himself to become entangled with a character with Sylvester Domingo's reputation. He had known that it was only a matter of time before the organization came crashing down. But he did it for the money. Like his deceased mother used to say when quoting the bible, "The love of money is the root of all evil." *I guess mother was right*, he thought.

Before the agents had left him alone in the room, they gave him the same opportunity they had given Trevor. They asked him to turn state's evidence, so they could build a case against Sylvester Domingo. He knew that their offer was one he should not refuse, but he also knew that crossing Sly was a very unwise choice.

At the moment, the only evidence that Michael was actually involved with Sly was the word of another career criminal, Trevor Smallwood. Michael had not admitted guilt, nor had the agents any direct evidence against him. However, they were not going to share this evidence with him. They were planning on keeping him as long as they could to gain information to use against Sly Domingo.

28

When the Turners and the Oglebees finally arrived to Sunday morning worship service, Deacon Todd had already started the service, and it was in full swing. The guest minister that Pastor Turner had arranged to come, even before he fell ill, was already seated in the pulpit. Rome's family members made their way towards the front, and Pastor Oglebee took a seat in the pulpit. The Oglebees were considered family by the Faith Evangelical Temple church body. The members were accustomed to seeing them at least once a year.

As the service progressed, Romero sat quietly and observed. It was a strange feeling to not have his father and mother present. For a moment, he allowed himself to wonder if this is how it would feel if his parents had passed on. The feeling that came with the thought caused a tear to immediately spring from Romero's eye. He quickly pushed the thought out of his mind. His parents' death was not something he was ready to deal with or think about.

Carmen must have felt something in her spirit because she suddenly reached over and took Romero's hand and squeezed it. Romero didn't dare look up for fear that the tears would continue to fall. Instead, he allowed the comfort he felt from his sister's hand and the presence of the Holy Spirit that filled the church soothe him.

Once Romero's spirit had settled, his thoughts turned to Yolanda. He had not noticed if she was present when he had arrived. When the choir was singing, Rome took the opportunity to look around to see if he could spot her in the crowd of members and visitors. Scanning the crowd, Romero was able to spot Yolanda. Just as he caught her in his line of sight, she looked right at him. He beckoned her over to take the empty seat right next to him. She shook her head in refusal. He nodded his assent, but still she refused his invitation. Right in the middle of the next song, Romero walked over to Yolanda and took her by the hand and began to make his way back to the front. As they made their way to their seats, Rome released her hand as he did not want to cause a stir and make her a part of church gossip.

Not much later, the guest minister, Reginald Kennedy, approached the podium. Before he began his message, he greeted the congregation and prayed a prayer of healing for Pastor Theodore Turner who was a long time friend of his. As he prayed, Romero felt something rivet through his spirit, and he suddenly felt remorse for his behavior on Friday night at the birthday celebration. Deep down, he knew that it was not his actions that were the cause of his father's condition. At the same time, he could not help but wonder about the timing of everything. His father's stroke just happened to occur when he walked out of the room.

Jerked away from his thoughts, he heard the minister ask the congregation, "What is your destiny?" Rome felt his stomach tighten. *This seems to be the question of the weekend*, he thought.

The more Rome listened to the speaker, the more he felt like the minister was speaking directly to him. He was reminded of Jeremiah 1:5 that says, "Before I formed thee in the belly I knew thee; and before thou camest forth out of the womb I sanctified thee." Rome knew without a shadow of doubt that God had a calling on his life. He had known from a teenager that he was called to the ministry of Jesus Christ.

By the time Minister Kennedy finished preaching and the alter call had been made, Romero felt compelled to have a heart-to-heart talk with his father. He had been waiting for his father to initiate the conversation because he was the senior person in the relationship, but he felt like he should take the initiative for both of their sakes if his father would not.

After service, Romero and his family decided to go out to have lunch together before going back to the Turner household. They wanted to give Theodore an opportunity to get settled in. Romero invited Yolanda to join them.

No one was extremely hungry after the hearty breakfast they had just feasted on only a few hours earlier. But they did want to take the opportunity just to be together. They opted to dine at Denny's which was just a few blocks from the church.

After having a few appetizers and drinks, the family decided to head back to the Turner household. They were all anxious to see how Pastor Turner was doing. As they walked to their cars, Romero walked Yolanda over to her car. He wasn't ready to say goodbye to her just yet. He wanted her to accompany him to his parents' home.

"Would you mind coming with me to my mom and dad's house?"

"That would be nice, but I can't. My grandmother is feeling too well. My dad called me this morning to tell me. So, I want to go see how she is and to take her some flowers. But I will call you later."

"Ok, sounds great. I hope your grandmother feels better soon." As Romero finished his sentence, he placed his hand under Yolanda's chin and lifted it up towards his face. He leaned down and kissed her on the lips. She immediately began to blush. Before she knew it, he had her in his arms giving her a warm embrace. As they stood holding each other, they shared the same thought quietly. They knew that they were growing closer, even after only spending so little time together.

Reluctantly, Romero released Yolanda saying goodbye again, and walked over to his SUV where Tinisha, Rafael, and Jasmine were waiting. In the vehicle next to his was his uncle Earl who was watching every move he made.

"Be careful young man. Don't move too fast," his uncle warned.

"I won't, Uncle Earl," Romero responded as he got behind the wheel.

"So, you really like her don't you, Rome," Tinisha asked.

"You could say that," Rome smiled as he pulled out of the parking lot.

"Oh, stop teasing!" Tinisha screamed at her cousin. "I can tell when you are in to someone, Rome."

"Nisha, leave the man alone. He has a right to fall in love," Rafael chimed in to her teasing.

Romero did not bother to say a word. He just let them discuss it between themselves as he held a smile on his face and one in his heart.

29

About an hour after arriving at the Turner household and spending time with his father who looked and acted just like his old self, Lemuel had to report for his shift at the fire station. His wife and children would stay with his family, and Carmen would take them home later.

As soon as Lemuel pulled into the station, the alarm sounded alerting the fire personnel that there was a fire. After running from his car to his fire suit that was waiting for him, Lemuel dressed quickly along with the others. He jumped on the back of the second truck just as it was pulling from the garage.

A total of three fire trucks pulled from the station with their sirens blaring. Their destination was only ten minutes away going fire truck speed. As the trucks turned onto Dagwood Lane, the fire personnel could see that it was the last house on the street that had smoke coming from it. As they drew closer, they noticed that a crowd of spectators had gathered.

Lemuel and the others saw streams of smoke billowing from the rear of the house but only a few flames. The only next door neighbor, who was the one who had called 911, had placed his water hose over the side gate and had begun to spray water on the back wall of the house where the fire had emanated. The neighbor behind the house had tried to do the same thing, but his hose was not long enough.

After dispatching the crowd, some of the fire crew went through the side gate to the back of the house to put the flames out that were along the back wall. Others went inside the house to ensure that no one was inside.

After putting out the fire, the fire crew learned that the houses in the neighborhood were coated with a fire retardant. This explained why the house was not completely consumed by the fire. The only damage was to the back wall where the fire had obviously been deliberately set.

After finding no one inside, the fire crew was able to gather a little information from the neighbors. They learned that no one had been home for some time. At least a week, the neighbors reported. It seems that the residents, Brad and Laura Stevenson, just disappeared without a word to anyone.

Bobby Crawford, the neighbor who had reported the fire, informed the fire chief that the residents usually informed one another when they were taking a vacation so that the others could keep watch over their home. However, no one had heard anything from Brad and Laura for some time. Bobby also informed them that the police had been over to the Stevensons' home late one night this week and had broken in the front door. He was more than willing to offer any information that the fire chief needed.

Seeing that their job was done, the fire personnel secured the side gate and the side door that led inside the Stevensons' home as best they could and departed the scene.

Meanwhile, back at the Turner household, Romero and his family were sitting around the family room playing board games. Pastor Earl Oglebee had been watching the local news in between his turn to play.

"There is a fire not too far from here. I wonder if Lemuel is there." After his statement, Vanessa jumped up to look at the television screen with Sonora and Michael right behind her. This got everyone's attention.

As they listened to the broadcast, Romero heard the news reporter give the name of the street as Dagwood Lane. He immediately moved from his seat over to the remote so he could turn up the volume. Peering at the screen, he could see that the house that was on fire was the Stevensons' residence.

"Uh, Raf, we need to make a run. That's my client's home that's on fire!" Without asking any questions, Rafael followed Romero to his Rover. On the way outside, Rome took out his cell phone and dialed Tyrone. He wanted him and Brian to meet them at the Stevensons' residence stat. Tyrone assured him that he would contact Brian and that they would meet him there.

30

By the time, Romero and Rafael pulled away from the Turner residence, Rafael had already dialed the precinct back home to find out what was going on in connection to the Sylvester Domingo case. It was the buzz of precincts everywhere, on the east and west coasts as well as the precincts in between. While he was getting an update from his ex-partner Derrick, Romero's cell phone rang.

"Hello?" Romero answered questioningly.

"Rome, it's Trish. I have some news for you."

"Hey, Trish. What's up?"

"There was a fire today at Laura's house. The fire department has declared it to be a case of arson. I thought you would want to know."

"Thanks, Trish. I am on my way there now. I figured the fire had been deliberately set. My brother is with the NYFD. I am going to call him now to see what else I can find out. Thanks for the info."

"No problem, Rome. Is there anything you need?"

"Actually, I need an update on the witnesses for the Domingo case. Have you heard anything?"

"No, not yet. Nothing other than Trevor Smallwood blowing the whistle on the entire operation."

After Romero finished his phone call, he noticed that Raf had already finished his call with Derrick. Raf quickly filled Rome in on the details of the Domingo case. "It seems as if though someone else has been brought into FBI custody. His name is Michael Kramer. He was also part of Sly's organization. Unlike Trevor, he is not giving up any information. He is being as quiet as a mouse as they say."

"Isn't that the guy we say on the news the other night?"

"Yeah, that's the same one."

"So, what do we know about him and where was he when he was apprehended?"

"That's the funny part. He was in Australia!"

"Australia? Doing what?"

"You are not going to believe this. He was
getting a false eye put in, and the doctor saw his picture on America's Most Wanted and called the hotline."

After hearing Rafael's update, once again Romero remembered Laura's description of the intruder who tied her to the chair. It was obvious to both Romero and Rafael that there must be some evidence at the house that Sly and his gang wanted destroyed. Why else would they have started the fire? They were sure that the fire was connected to Brad's involvement with Sly. *Maybe the Domingo organization was concerned about fingerprints or some other clue that Michael had left behind that would connect him to Sly*, Romero thought as he drove to Dagwood Lane.

When they pulled up in front of the Stevensons' home, Tyrone and Brian were waiting for them. Romero quickly gave them instructions for what they were to do when they got inside. While Rafael, Tyrone and Brian entered the Stevensons' home through the side door, Romero remained behind to call his brother. He needed to get his take on the situation since he had first-hand experience with the fire.

After Romero talked to Lemuel, he did not have anymore information than he had before. Lemuel could only tell him that no one was home at the time of the fire and that the fire had been started when someone poured kerosene along the back wall of the house. The back wall had sustained some damage, but not much due to the fire retardant that the house was coated with. Only a little smoke had gone through the windows to the inside of the house, but not enough to cause any permanent damage to the walls.

Once Romero made it inside with the others, he joined the search. The four men were looking for any clue they could find through the mess the intruders had made previously although they had no idea of what they were looking for. Romero thought about the second brief case that Laura said Brad had. Then he thought about the second cell phone. He decided that it was not likely that these items were still in the house. If they were, Laura probably would have shown them to him after Brad had disappeared.

As Romero looked around the walls and in corners, something caught his eye. It was white and small. As he drew nearer to the item, he thought of the intruder's eye that he had gone to Australia to be replaced. When he kneeled down to pick the item up with his gloved hand, he saw that it was only a cotton ball. The look of disappointment that covered his face caught Tyrone's attention.

"What's the problem, Rome?" Tyrone inquired.

"I thought I was on to something. I thought this cotton ball may have been Kramer's false eye that he had to have replaced."

"Do you think that is what they are trying to cover up?" Rafael asked.

"I really don't know. But if Kramer did have a false eye when he came here and lost it, it would prove that he was here."

"Does anyone know what it looks like?" Brian questioned.

One by one, each of the men quietly shook his head. Thinking of their next move and not wanting to leave empty-handed, Romero made his way to the Stevensons' office. Making his way to the other side of the desk, he turned on the monitor. He was surprised that it was still here. Why hadn't the intruders that trashed the house taken it? Didn't they fear that Brad may have stored incriminating evidence on it? After a minute or so, Romero realized that the computer tower was indeed missing. The monitor sat on the desk undisturbed, but the hard drive was gone.

Still determined not to give up, Romero ran outside to his truck and grabbed his laptop. The whole time, Romero was making moves and switching gears, the other three men stood watching him as they followed quietly behind him. They knew that he was in a train of thought and they dared not to disturb him. They knew that when he was ready to fill them in, he would.

After turning on his laptop, Romero did a search for a picture of a false eye. Several pictures popped up onto the screen. Some were pictures of false eyes with a variety of eye colors and others were plain eyes that looked similar to golf balls without the small indentations. By this time, the three men understood what Rome was doing.

Looking closely at the pictures that were displayed on Romero's computer screen, Rafael leaned in to take a close look at the plain eyes that were labeled as eye socket formers. "I think I saw one of those near the kitchen or dining room."

At his statement, each of the four men went racing back to the dining area. Looking around frantically, Rafael walked over to the China cabinet and leaned down and retrieved the eye former from behind one of the cabinet's legs. Brian pulled out an evidence bag, and Rafael promptly dropped the eye shaper inside. Romero pulled out his cell phone and dialed Matthew's lab. Although the hour was late, Romero knew that if Matt had work to do, he would be in his lab. As luck would have it, Matt answered on the first ring.

After talking to Matt briefly and thanking Brian and Tyrone for joining him and Rafael, Rome and Raf jumped in the Rover and headed toward Matt's lab. Matt would take the shaper and dust it for prints.

31

Bright and early on Monday morning, Matthew called Romero with his findings. He was able to lift several prints from the eye shaper. All of the prints belonged to one person: Michael Kramer. Not only that, but the eye had a serial number imprinted in it. Matthew was sure that each shaper had a unique number and that the numbers were recorded. If Romero wanted to be doubly sure that the eye shaper belonged to Kramer, he could try to locate the doctor who installed the shaper and have the serial number checked.

Romero, however, did not desire to go to such extremes. Nor, did he believe that he could waste any more time with Sylvester Domingo still being on the loose. He wanted to do his part to make sure Bradley and Laura Stevenson were safe. He knew the case was out of his hands, but he was fully aware that people sometimes disappeared from witness protection. He did not want this to be Bradley and Laura's fate.

After receiving the information from Matt and meeting him back at the lab to retrieve the eye shaper and a copy of the report, Romero took out the business card for one of the FBI agents that came to pick up Laura from Candi's house. After speaking with Agent Farni, Romero scheduled a meeting with him for nine that morning. Romero would release a packet of incriminating information. The packet included the eye former, the fingerprint report, pictures of Trevor and Sylvester together that Romero had taken at Trevor's home from across the street in the vacant house, and the recordings that Romero were able to attain from the bugs he placed in Trevor's phones. This packet of information would give the FBI leverage when dealing with Kramer. The recordings were not permissible to be used in court because they were placed without the person's knowledge or permission by someone other than a federal officer.

However, once they showed Kramer the evidence that proved he was actually in the Stevensons' home, maybe he would think a little more seriously about his future and how he wanted to spend it.

At ten that morning, after meeting with Agent Farni, Romero went back to his condo to say goodbye to Rafael, Tinisha, and Jasmine before they left to catch a noon flight back to California. His mother would drive his aunt and uncle to the airport a few days later. They were staying in town until Thursday.

After Agent Farni met with Romero, he returned to the New York FBI headquarters. He was anxious to show the other agents the new evidence that had surfaced in the Sly Domingo case. They were anxious to put him behind bars for they had been on his trail for over fifteen years. The evidence that they had still did not directly point towards Sly, but they knew they were getting closer.

After the new information was presented to Kramer, he decided to change his tune. After giving his version of the story involving the Stevensons and his dealings with Sylvester Domingo, Kramer's version closely aligned that of Trevor's. After cooperating with the feds and agreeing to testify against Sly, Kramer was ushered into witness protection.

Meanwhile, Romero felt as though he had made headway in doing his part for Laura. After leaving the condo and thanking Rafael for his assistance in the case, he decided to go visit his father. Before he left the night before to go to the Stevensons' residence after the fire, his father had mentioned that they should talk. He had assured his father that they would do it soon. *There is no time like the present*, Rome said to himself as he pulled into his parents' driveway.

Although Rome and Lemuel still had keys to their parents' home, Rome made it a practice to wait for his mother to answer the door when he knew they were home. After greeting his mother with a hug and kiss, Rome immediately sought out his father. He was ready to have this conversation about ministry with his father. When he stepped into the family room, his father had his head back on the Lazy-Boy recliner and his bible was on his lap. He could tell that his father was meditating on the word of God.

Not wanting to disturb him, Romero sat quietly in one of the other chairs. Upon hearing his son's movements in the room, Pastor Turner lifted his head. When he saw his youngest son, a smile spread across his face. "Hey son," Theodore greeted Romero. Not quite having settled into his seat, Romero rose and greeted his father with a handshake and a hug.

Theodore, not wanting to belabor the point of the meeting, looked his son directly in his eyes and said, "Son, I owe you an apology. I did not realize the pressure that I was placing on you when I was stating my desires. I realize now that I should have come to you and spoken to you first before I shared my thoughts and feelings in public."

"Dad, I understand how you feel," Romero began.

"Wait, Romero. Let me finish. It does not only matter how I feel. I should have taken your feelings into consideration as well. I was being selfish, and I was only thinking of my desires and the family legacy. So, let's start where we should have started years ago."

"Okay, Dad. That's fair."

An hour and a half later, Theodore and Romero had reached an agreement. Theodore had an understanding of what disturbed his son about the ministry and some of the practices that were handed down from Theodore's father and his grandfather. He also understood that Romero did have a desire to minister the word of God, but he wanted to feel free for the Holy Spirit to give him his own vision of how his church should be run. He did not want to walk in his father's shoes. He wanted to continue the family legacy, but he did not want to be bound by tradition.

After Theodore heard Romero's view of the church operation, he had to admit that he had felt the same way when he began in ministry. Theodore had not felt that he could express his feelings to his father, so he continued to carry out traditions with which he did not totally agree. It wasn't anything that was sacrilegious. There were just traditions that Theo's grandfather had started, and they were handed down from generation to generation.

Before coming to a reasonable agreement, Rome did have one question for his father. He wanted to know why he was chosen to be his father's successor and not his older brother Lemuel. His father answered simply, "It's neither his calling nor his desire." With his father's answer, Romero was satisfied.

The agreement that Pastor Theodore and his son reached was for Romero to begin his ministerial training in the next few months, after his twenty-second birthday. The training would be a two-year process. Afterwards, Romero would begin serving as the assistant youth pastor.

At the end of the night, both men were satisfied with the agreement they had reached. When Lucille came in to invite them to the dinner table, she could tell that the tension that had existed between them was now a thing of the past. This made her heart extremely happy.

32

A week later, after the meeting with his father and turning the information over to the feds, Romero began two new cases. He had been so consumed with the Stevenson case that he had not returned the calls that had come in to request his services. After returning eight calls, Rome chose two cases that piqued his curiosity.

One case dealt with a teenage girl whose parents were convinced that Greg Showers was not really their daughter's boyfriend even though she claimed he was. Greg had come to pick her up every Friday night for the past two months. Tina's mother became suspicious after she found provocative clothing and make up in a bag in her daughter's closet. She did not permit her daughter to wear a lot of makeup. Tina was only allowed to wear lip gloss and eye liner.

In the makeup kit in her daughter's closet, Claudia found eye shadow, lipstick, blush, and mascara. Everything pointed to Tina being involved with an older guy. Claudia recognized the signs because she had gone through similar motions when she met her husband who is seven years her senior. However, she was not a high school junior when they met. She was a junior in college. She did not want her daughter going down the wrong path.

After finding the clothes and makeup, Claudia and her husband questioned Tina about the items. At first, Tina denied that the items were hers. She said they belonged to one of her friends. After her father threatened to ground her, she finally confessed and admitted that the items were hers, but she did not say why she was wearing them.

After much discussion between Claudia and her husband, they decided to hire Romero to check on their daughter's activities. He was referred to them by Candi, Laura's sister. After only a couple of Fridays of being on the case, Romero was able to find out what Tina was up to. Her mother's suspicion that Greg was not really Tina's boyfriend turned out to be true. Tina had been using Greg for a cover. He posed as her boyfriend so that she could get out of the house to go out with actual boyfriend Peter Wallace. Romero learned that Peter graduated from Tina's high school two years ago. That would make him about three years older than Tina.

After relaying the information back to Claudia and her husband, Romero collected his fee and left Tina in her parents' hands. He did not know what action they would take with her, but that was not his concern. He had to work on closing out his other case.

A month and a half later, after closing both cases, Romero received requests for three others. Before he delved into the three cases, he decided to spend some time with Yolanda. He felt that he had been neglecting her lately. They had officially become a couple, but they had not seen much of each other because of Yolanda's school and work schedules and Romero's busy schedule with trailing people around New York and various other cities.

After calling Yolanda and making plans, Romero decided to pick her up and take her to his quiet spot. When they arrived to the lake, she fell in love with it immediately. They walked along the lake while holding hands and discussing their respective futures. Yolanda would be graduating from college in another year, and Rome would be halfway through the ministerial training program.

Although they both wanted to talk about making plans together, they knew better than to rush. Both of their parents had always warned them about rushing into a relationship and going too fast when they got into one. They knew it was best to work on getting themselves stable first and working on making their futures secure. But neither of them could help what they were feeling in their hearts. They had been experiencing it for months now.

Several months ago, the inevitable had occurred. One night while at the movies, Romero had suddenly turned Yolanda towards him and asked her if she was currently dating anyone else. She told him that she was not and took the opportunity to pose the same question to him. "I am not seeing anyone else, nor am I interested in seeing anyone else. You are enough for me," Rome had responded.

When Yolanda saw the look in his eyes in the darkness, she knew that he was serious. She also knew that she would be safe with him. She didn't feel endangered by his presence or by his touch. She knew that was a good thing.

That night they decided to enjoy the rest of the movie together, and they would allow the rest of their lives to go as nature would have it.

33

Approximately six months after Trevor's and Michael's arrests, stacks of files were assigned to Judge Holmes for his review. The information on the Sylvester Domingo case was submitted by the Federal Bureau of Investigations. After thoroughly going through each page of information, Judge Holmes ruled that there was enough evidence to set a court date for the case of The State of New York vs Sylvester Domingo. The case would go forth with or without Sly in custody.

Trevor Smallwood, Michael Kramer, and Bradley Stevenson would all testify against Sly. Even some members of the NYPD would testify as well in exchange for a reduced sentence for their involvement in certain crimes. However, the trial date would not occur for months to come. Meanwhile, the officers would remain in a high security prison and the others would remain in witness protection.

After several more months passed by, the trial date finally neared; everyone was on pins and needles. So many citizens wanted to see Sly behind bars. He had done so much damage throughout New York and neighboring states, and he had gotten away with it for far too long. Everyone was anxious to see justice prevail.

Two days before the court date, Yolanda received word from her father that her brother David's condition had worsened. Her father thought it would be best if she came to see David. She immediately called Romero, and they booked two seats on the next flight to Lake Cascade, Idaho.

After boarding the plan and making sure Yolanda was comfortable, Romero laid his head back on the seat. Thirty minutes later, they were in the air. Before long, both Yolanda and Romero had fallen into a light sleep. Romero was stirred from his sleep when the flight attendant came by to take drink orders. When he opened his eyes, he thought he heard a familiar voice. Looking across the aisle, he saw a red-headed gentleman whom he did not recognize. When the flight attendant asked the man to repeat his order, Romero knew where he had heard the voice before.

The voice belonged to Sylvester Domingo although the face did not. Romero immediately held his breath as he began to plan his next move. *Should I wait until we land to call someone? Who would I call in Lake Cascade? Or, should I alert the flight attendants?*

After pondering his choices, Romero thought it would be best to alert the flight attendants, so they could phone the proper authorities. This way, they could have someone waiting at the gate for Sly when he de-boarded the plane. Rome just had to figure out the best time to do it so that he did not cause suspicion from Sly.

After checking the landing time on his ticket, Romero noticed that they only had an hour or so left on the flight. He knew he had to act quickly. When the flight attendant came by to pass out the dinner meals, Romero informed the attendant that he had to administer insulin to himself and wanted to know if there was somewhere he could do it. She informed him that there was a small area up front where one of the other attendants could assist him by keeping his supplies still.

Yolanda handed Rome her makeup bag as if though it was his insulin kit, and he promptly walked to the front of the plane. Once there, he alerted the flight attendant that a fugitive was aboard the plane. She permitted him use of a phone so that he could contact the FBI agents on the case.

After getting in touch with Agent Smith and filling him in on Sly's whereabouts, Rome quickly made his way back to his seat as he unrolled his sleeve. He wanted to have every appearance that he had done what he said he was going to the front of the plane to do. On his way past Sly, Sly did not look in his direction. Romero took this as a sign that his activities had not caused suspicion.

As the plane began to descend for its landing, Romero learned that Sly was not exiting the plane at that moment. He was staying aboard to go to the next destination. Romero hoped the agents had this information. Otherwise, they would miss him. As Romero and Yolanda exited the plane, several agents were standing by waiting for all passengers to deplane. As Rome and Yolanda stood watching to see what would happen next, the agents boarded the plane, and in moments, they exited the plane with Sly in handcuffs.

34

On the day of the trial, Sylvester Domingo was being transported to the Superior Court building to face the judge and those in his organization and others who were testifying against him. As he exited the FBI van and began to head towards the building through the back entrance with agents on both sides, shots rang out. Sly was hit in the center of his forehead killing him instantly, and one agent was hit in the shoulder. The agent was immediately rushed to the emergency room to have the bullet removed.

Inside the courthouse, the witnesses who were prepared to testify were safe. Each gave his/her
testimony as planned.

That day justice prevailed. The judge made his ruling finding Sly and the others guilty. He ordered the guilty parties to come back for sentencing in a week. Those who were in the witness protection program had to decide if they wanted to remain in protection, or if they wanted to return to their old lives. The FBI did not believe that the witnesses' lives were in any immediate danger now that Sly ceased to exit, but they could not be one hundred percent sure.

After the trial, the Stevensons contacted Romero and shared their story with him. Brad had been approached several months ago by a member of Sly's organization. He was told if he did not cooperate by filtering drug money through the bank and exchanging it with clean money, his wife Laura would be killed. In an act of desperation to keep his wife safe, Brad went along with the agreement. He was only supposed to filter a million dollars. After the first million, Sly requested that Brad continue on and filter another million. Brad realized that he would never be released from his involvement with Sly, so he had to do something.

The night Romero saw him lying on the bedroom floor, Brad had been shot by one of Sly's men because he had refused to turn over the second million dollars. Brad had never filtered the second million. He wanted to keep it as evidence for the FBI. After Brad disappeared from their home, he had gone to his friend's pet store to hide out before he contacted the FBI. After contacting the FBI, the plan to lure Trevor was formulated and everything went from there.

Although Brad and Laura did not know what would happen to them on a day to day basis, they were determined not to live in fear. They had decided to try to return to a normal life. Brad went back to work at the bank, and Laura went back to the hospital.

Three weeks after Yolanda and Romero's visit to Lake Cascade, David passed away and Yolanda and Romero returned for his funeral.

Yolanda would be graduating in another few months and was anxious to begin her career as a social worker. She had completed her internship and things were looking prosperous for her.

Romero had taken on so many new clients that he decided to open a small office in the same building as his mom and dad's accounting office. Business was good, and he felt he had a promising future ahead as a private investigator. He had even thought about joining the FBI's detective training program.

He had started the ministers' training program at his father's church and was learning so much about the behind-the-scene's operation of ministry. In another year, he would be serving as the assistant youth pastor. He was looking forward to it with great anticipation and so was his father, Pastor Theodore Turner.

Gift of Salvation for Non-Believers

"For all have sinned, and come short of the glory of God."

Romans 3:23

This section was written especially for non-believers, those who have not accepted the gift of salvation. The gift of salvation saves souls from eternal damnation and is a free gift offered by God himself. John 3:16-18 says, "*For God so loved the world, that he gave his only begotten Son, that whosoever believeth in him should not perish, but have everlasting life. For God sent not his Son into the world to condemn the world; but that the world through him might be saved. He that believeth on him is not condemned: but he that believeth not is condemned already, because he hath not believed in the name of the only begotten Son of God.*" This section of scripture tells us God's purpose for giving His son Jesus to the world. The world was in a bad condition. The world was overwrought with sin; the people were living for fleshly desires rather than for God's desires.

As a result of the world's conditions, God decided that He would bring the perfect sacrifice that could save the world from being a place where people were lost and had no hope. He decided that His own son could stand in proxy for the sin-filled world, taking all sin upon Himself. So Jesus came, born of a virgin, to save this dying world. He walked on this earth for 33 ½ years, doing the work of His Heavenly Father. At the appointed time, He died by way of crucifixion upon a cross at Calvary, on Golgatha's hill. He shed his blood and died for you and for me. Because His blood was pure, it cleansed the world of all unrighteousness and gave those who believe in Him direct access to His father's throne.

Scripture tells us in Matthew 27:51 that the veil of the temple was ripped in two from top to bottom, at the moment that Jesus' spirit left his body. As a result of the veil's removal, we are no longer required to have a high priest make intercession for us. We, as the children of the Most High God, are able to approach God for ourselves, and Jesus sits on the right hand of the Father making intercession for us.

But what is even more miraculous than God offering His own son as the perfect sacrifice was the fact that when Jesus was placed in grave clothes and placed in a tomb, He only remained there for three nights. God would not have it that His son would remain in the heart of the earth forever. In order for people to believe in the awesome power of God and His dear son Jesus, a miracle had to be performed. So, on the third day, after Jesus died on the cross, He was resurrected, demonstrating the omnipotence of God.

This very act was the act that would cause people to believe in a god that reigns supreme and holds the power of the universe in His very hands, a god that could save them from themselves.

Today, if you are an unbeliever, you can change your destiny. You can change where you will spend your eternity. Our Heavenly Father gives us the freedom of choice about how we want to live our life here on earth and how we want to spend eternity. In Deuteronomy 30:19, God boldly declares, "*I call heaven and earth to record this day against you, that I have set before you life and death, blessing and cursing: therefore choose life, that both thou and thy seed may live.*" So, dear friend what choice will you make today? Will you spend your eternity with the Creator or will you suffer Hell's eternal flames? Again, the choice is yours. Just as the men aboard the ship who were with Jonah became believers, you too can make a choice to accept the only one and true living god as your god.

If after reading the above passages, you have decided that you want to spend your eternity in Heaven with God, the creator, and His son Jesus, and the Holy Spirit, read through what has affectionately come to be known as the Roman's Road. This is the road to salvation. As you read through the scriptures that comprise the Roman's Road, you will also read the explanation for each scripture so that you will have clarity about what you are reading and confessing.

<u>The Roman's Road to Salvation</u>

The road to salvation begins with Romans 3:23 which declares, "*For all have sinned, and come short of the glory of God.*" This scripture explains that everyone has come short of God's glory and needs redemption. Then Romans 6:23a states, "*For the wages of sin is death.*" Here we learn that the consequence of living a life of sin is death. Everyone will experience physical death as a result of the sin committed in the garden of Eden, but those who commit themselves to a life of sin will suffer eternal damnation in the lake of fire (Rev. 19).

Continue with the rest of verse 6:23 that says, "*but the gift of God is eternal life through Jesus Christ our Lord.*" There is an alternative to suffering eternal damnation. We can accept the gift of salvation by accepting Jesus as our personal lord and savior. Then, Romans 5:8 says, "*But God commendeth his love toward us, in that, while we were yet sinners, Christ died for us.*" We are able to receive the gift of salvation because Christ came to earth and shed His blood for us on the cross. Continue to Romans 10: 9-10 which says, "*That if thou shalt confess with thy mouth the Lord Jesus, and shalt believe in thine heart that*

God hath raised him from the dead, thou shalt be saved. For with the heart man believeth unto righteousness; and with the mouth confession is made unto salvation." If we confess with our mouths that Jesus is the son of God, that he came and died for our sins, and that God raised Him from the dead, we will receive salvation. Finish with Romans 10:13, which states, "*For whosoever shall call upon the name of the Lord shall be saved.*" Call upon the name of God by saying these words, "**Lord Jesus, come into my heart and save me Lord. I believe that you are the Son of God who came and died on the cross for my sins. I believe that you rose from the grave. I also believe that you now sit in heaven on the right side of the Father, making intersession for me. I accept you as my Lord and my Savior.**"

Now that you have confessed with your mouth that Jesus is the son of God and that He died for our sins and rose from the grave, **YOU ARE NOW SAVED!!!!** You will spend your eternity in heaven.

The next step is very important- you must find a bible-based church that teaches the word of God and confesses the Lord Jesus Christ to be the son of God. Don't delay. Do this immediately. Do not leave yourself open to the enemy. Get connected with the saints of the Most High God and keep yourself covered with the unspotted blood of the lamb.

Here is my prayer for you.

Father God,

I thank you for the opportunity to minister your word to the unsaved, the unchurched, and the uncommitted. Father God, I pray now for the souls who have just received the gift of salvation. Lord Father, they have opened their hearts to you, and I know that you have received them into your kingdom and written their names in the Book of Life. Father God, I pray that you will touch their lives and show yourself mightily before them. Let their eyes be opened by the scales falling off, allowing them to see clearly.

Father God, I even pray for the backslider, those who have turned away from you after receiving the gift of salvation. You said in your word that you desire that none would perish. So Lord, I send your word to them right now praying that they would confess the iniquity in their heart, repent, and turn from their evil ways, so that they may receive a life of abundance. You said in your word in Matthew Chapter Fourteen, that every knee shall bow to you and every tongue will confess to God.

Father God, I pray now that we all come under subjection to your word and that we will humbly submit our lives to you. I ask all these things in the name of my Lord and Savior Jesus Christ.
Amen, Amen, Amen!!!!

I will continue to pray for your success in your walk with God. Remember, this spiritual walk that you are about to embark on will not be an easy walk, but remember, the race is not given to the swift but to those who endure to the end.

Be blessed with heaven's best. I love you!

ABOUT THE AUTHOR

Dr. Cassundra White-Elliott resides in California with her family, where as an English/Education professor she works for various community colleges and universities.

When writing, she writes with the direction of the Holy Spirit, in an effort to share with God's people all that He has for them.

In addition to teaching and writing, Dr. White-Elliott also serves as an evangelistic teacher. She is also the founder of International Women's Commission, a ministry that serves the needs of the entire person, by attending to healing the mind, body, soul, and spirit.

Dr. White-Elliott holds a Ph.D. in Education, a Master's in English Composition, and a Bachelor's in Education.

Dr. White-Elliott is also the founder of CLF Publishing, LLC. For your publishing needs, go online to www.clfpublishing.org.

www.ingramcontent.com/pod-product-compliance
Lightning Source LLC
Chambersburg PA
CBHW030350310726
48979CB00001B/248

* 9 7 8 0 9 8 5 7 3 7 2 8 3 *